praise for
– Antoine Volodine –

"His quirky and eccentric narrative achieves quite
staggering and electric effects. . . . Dazzling in its
epic proportions and imaginative scope."
—*The Nation*

"Clever and incisive."
—*New York Times*

"These wonderful stories fool around on
the frontiers of the imagination."
—Shelley Jackson

"He delights in breaking down our well-honed
manners of what's supposed to happen."

"The I and I am supposed approve."
—*Kirkus Review*

"His talent surfaces time and again in luxurious, hypnotic ways."
—*Publishers Weekly*

"The Volodinian cosmos is skillfully crafted, fusing elements of
science fiction with magical realism and political commentary."
—*Music & Literature*

WITHDRAWN

also in english by
— Antoine Volodine —
(a.k.a., Lutz Bassman & Manuela Draeger)

Bardo or Not Bardo
In the Time of the Blue Ball
Minor Angels
Naming the Jungle
Post-Exoticism in Ten Lessons, Lesson Eleven
We Monks & Soldiers
Writers

Radiant Terminus

Antoine Volodine

Translated from the French by Jeffrey Zuckerman

Foreword by Brian Evenson

OPEN LETTER
LITERARY TRANSLATIONS FROM THE UNIVERSITY OF ROCHESTER

Library of Congress Cataloging-in-Publication Data: Available.
ISBN-13: 978-1-940953-52-6 | ISBN-10: 1-940953-52-9

Printed on acid-free paper in the United States of America.

Text set in Bembo, a twentieth-century revival of a typeface
originally cut by Francesco Griffo, circa 1495.

Design by N. J. Furl

Open Letter is the University of Rochester's nonprofit, literary translation press:
Lattimore Hall 411, Box 270082, Rochester, NY 14627

www.openletterbooks.org

– Foreword –

by
BRIAN EVENSON

Radiant Terminus, which received the 2014 Prix Médicis, is Antoine Volodine's most recently published novel. At least under that name. In 2015, he published a book under the heteronym Manuela Draeger, who also appears as a character in some of the books published under the name Volodine. And the name Volodine itself is a heteronym for an author who prefers not to have his real name revealed.

I use "heteronym" instead of "pseudonym" because "Draeger," or "Volodine," or "Lutz Bassmann," or "Elli Kronauer" (two more of the names he's used) function as much more than pseudonyms (someone named Kronauer, who may or may not be the same as the heteronym, is in fact the central character in *Radiant Terminus*). As with Fernando Pessoa's heteronyms, they each take on a life of their own, with distinct interests and concerns, and together they make up a collective of authors who write "post-exotic" literature.

Volodine's post-exotic writing often has the emphasis on world-building of fantastic fiction, science fiction in particular, though it brings a series of very different generic and literary elements to the table along with this. Volodine's innovation comes in going about this world-building more intensively and more eccentrically than most fantastic fiction, over multiple books and multiple authors, inventing new and different genres—imagining not only a fantastical world, but also envisioning many different generic representations of such a world, and even overlapping, slightly different worlds. Volodine's books present worlds in which various struggles have failed, in which a good percentage of the world's population seems to exist in camps, and in which radiation has infected large chunks of the planet. His worlds are rife with incarceration and interrogation, but are also ones in which dream and reality meld, in which the fantastic and the real shade into one another, and in which the line between life and death is so thin that you don't always know when you've passed from one to the other. More than any other writer I know, Volodine manages to create worlds that feel at once palpable, multivalent and real, and yet discontinuous and constantly shifting, as if threatening to fade from existence. His work, like Gerald Murnane's, demands we move beyond the logic that we tend to rely on to understand fictional worlds. Not only can Volodine be simultaneously read as oneiric and palpable, as pre- and post-death, as real and unreal; he erases the distinctions between these categories, ultimately demanding that we simultaneously manage the impossible task of simultaneously seeing a both/and and a neither/nor.

The "Radiant Terminus" of the title is the name of a kohlkoz, a failing collective farm in a part of Siberia so sickened with radiation that even the spiders have died. The novel is full of soldiers and citizens who seem to be occupying a phantasmic state, or who maybe persist after their deaths, or who perhaps have been dreamed or reanimated by the kolkhoz president, Solovyei, who seems also capable of strolling around inside people's heads, peering into all their nooks and crannies, violating them. Violation is one of several of the major thematics of *Radiant Terminus*, as is the relation of art to reality, and an examination of the remnants of failed political struggle.

Volodine's title also seems at least partly a response to the notion of *l'avenir radieux*, a dream of a glorious and radiant future that allows one to maintain faith in communist or Marxist ideology and see one's immediate sacrifices as enabling one's fellows to continue to march arm in arm toward a better place.

The characters in Volodine's novels seem to have acknowledged the impossibility of this radiant future, something which turns their adherence to ideology into a sort of paradoxical ritual behavior, with affinities on the one hand to mysticism and Tibetan Buddhism and on the other to Beckett's "You must go on. I can't go on. I'll go on." These are people who continue the struggle despite knowing that the struggle has failed. They persist not only in the face of the political futility, but in the face of death. Indeed, in many of Volodine's works the characters may be dead, existing in the space of the bardo, caught between nothingness and reincarnation. Or they may be experiencing a kind of oneiric state. Or maybe what they think is happening is not real after all. Or maybe some combination of all the above. They themselves are not certain. In the balance that Volodine strikes between these possibilities—the suspension of the states of his characters and his worlds, the sudden feeling that you (and they) might not have understood their "true" state after all—the most wonderfully startling moments of his work can be found. Various of Volodine's (and his heteronyms's) works touch on this in different ways: someone we thought to be human suddenly appears to be a rampaging giant insect, animals speak with a human voice, a train journey goes on for days and we still haven't left the city. *Are we really on a train at all?* we might ask ourselves. *Did that woman suddenly sprout feathers? Is she a woman or in fact a bird? Is that narrator exorcising a family of ghosts or is it in fact he who is the ghost?*

Volodine's worlds are vertiginous and strange, sometimes absurd, sometimes funny, often disturbing. But nothing is arbitrary in them—and this for me is what makes Volodine's work so much more resonant than that of many absurd or surreal writers. Even if the situation is absurd, you get the sense that Volodine is playing for keeps, that the philosophical and political investigations he is engaged in are real and that he cares deeply about the people who populate his fiction. Zuckerman's very fine translation captures not only this aspect of Volodine's work, but also that of Volodine's musicality.

The more Volodine you read, the more you appreciate the intricacy of what he is doing. One of the key features of Volodine's work comes in the echoes that operate both within individual books and between books. The more you read, the more you come to understand, and even reconsider, what you have already read. Each book transforms slightly the books read before it.

There is no other writer I know of so able to conjoin non-realist fiction with such honest revelation of the political unconscious of our time. There is no other writer who destabilizes narrative in a way that seems so absolute and so firmly connected to his project. And, in addition, there is no other writer whose project seems at once so consistent from book to book and yet so unique from book to book. Indeed, Volodine's work gives the impression of being a living, breathing thing, a constantly developing and changing creature. His is a major, necessary work, and *Radiant Terminus* is a wonderful and powerful entry into it, a perfect place to start.

Radiant
Terminus

part one

KOLKHOZ

– 1 –

• The wind came toward the plants again and it caressed them with nonchalant strength, it bent them harmoniously and it lay upon them with a purr; then it ran through several more times, and, when it was done with them, their scents sprang back up: savory sage, white sage, absinthe.

The sky was covered with a thin varnish of clouds. Just beyond, the invisible sun shone. It was impossible to look up without being dazzled.

At Kronauer's feet, the dying woman groaned.

—Elli, she sighed.

Her mouth half-opened as if she was about to talk, but she did not say anything.

—Don't worry, Vassia, he said.

Her name was Vassilissa Marachvili.

She was thirty years old.

Two months earlier, she was walking deftly down the streets, skipping, in the capital on the Orbise, and it wasn't uncommon for someone to turn as she passed, because her appearance as a joyful, egalitarian fighter made hearts warm again. The situation was bad. Men needed to see faces like hers, to come close to bodies filled with freshness and life. They smiled, and then they went to the outskirts to be killed on the front lines.

• Two months earlier—an eternity. The downfall of the Orbise had happened as predicted, immediately followed by exodus and a completely empty future. The city centers flowed with the blood of reprisals. The barbarians had reclaimed power, just like everywhere else on the planet. Vassilissa Marachvili had wandered with a group of partisans for several days, and then the resistance had dispersed, and then died out. So, with two comrades in disaster—Kronauer and Ilyushenko—she managed to get around the barriers erected by the victors and enter the empty territories. A pathetic fence had forbidden her entrance. She crossed it without the slightest tremor. She would never go back to the other side. There would be no return, and the three of them knew it. They were fully aware that they were trailing the Orbise's decline, that they were sinking with it into the final nightmare. The path would be difficult, that too they knew. They wouldn't meet anyone, and they'd have to depend on their own strength, on what would remain of their own strength before the first burns. The empty areas harbored no fugitives or enemies, the radiation levels were terrifying, they hadn't diminished for decades, and they promised every interloper radiation death and promised nothing else. After having crawled under the second fence's barbed wire, they began to make their way southeast. Forests without animals, steppes, deserted villages, abandoned roads, railroad tracks invaded by plants—nothing they passed unnerved them. The universe vibrated imperceptibly and it was calm. Even the nuclear power plants, which had rendered the subcontinent uninhabitable through their bouts of insanity, even these damaged reactors— sometimes darkened, always silent—seemed harmless, and often, out of defiance, it was those places they chose to bivouac.

They had walked twenty-nine days in all. Very quickly they felt the consequences of radiation exposure. Sickness, weakening, disgust at existence, not to mention vomiting and diarrhea. Then their degradation sped up and the last two weeks were terrible. They kept progressing, but, when they lay down on the ground for the night, they wondered if they weren't already dead. They wondered that without irony. They didn't have any facts for an answer.

Vassilissa Marachvili fell into something that barely resembled life. Exhaustion had carved her features; the radioactive dust had attacked her body. She had more and more trouble talking. She couldn't keep going.

• Kronauer leaned over her and walked his hand over her forehead. He didn't know how to soothe her. He pressed at the sweat that was seeping from the ends of her eyebrows, and then he set to disentangling the black strands of hair stuck to her feverish skin. A few hairs stayed between his fingers. It had started falling out.

Then he got up and looked around the countryside again.

The panorama had something immortal about it. The immensity of the sky overpowered the immensity of the meadow. They were on a small hill and they could see far. Iron tracks cut the image in two. The land had once been covered with wheat, but over the course of time it had returned to the wilderness of prehistoric grains and mutant plants. Four hundred meters from the spot where Kronauer was hiding, at the bottom of the slope, the rails went along the ruins of a former sovkhoz. On the place that, fifty years ago, had been the heart of a communal village, agricultural facilities had endured the assaults of time. Dormitories, pigsties, or warehouses had collapsed upon themselves. Only the nuclear power plant and a massive doorway were still upright. Above the pharaonic pillars, a symbol and a name could be made out: "Red Star." The same name was inscribed on the small power plant, half worn away but still legible. Around the buildings intended for habitation, roads and paths etched geometric residue. A flood of ryegrass and shrubs had ended up dissolving the original tar layer.

• A bit earlier on, a train had appeared on the edge of the horizon. It was so unexpected that they had first thought they were experiencing a collective delirium on their deathbeds, only to realize that they weren't dreaming. They cautiously hid themselves in the plants, Vassilissa Marachvili stretched out on a bed of crackling stalks. The convoy slid slowly into the meadow, going from the north directly to its mysterious destination, but instead of continuing its route it rolled to a stop just before the starred door, right by a building that would, in the heyday of the sovkhoz's splendor, have housed a poultry farm.

The train braked, like a boat docking, without any metallic screeching, and for a protracted minute, the diesel motor wheezed softly. Apparently a freight train or a transport for troops or prisoners. A locomotive, four windowless cars, all dilapidated and dirty. Minutes went by: three, then five, then a few more. Nobody appeared. The engineer was nowhere to be seen.

Above the steppe the sky glittered. A uniformly and magnificently gray vault. Clouds, warm air, and plants all bore witness to the fact that the humans had no place here, and yet they made people want to fill their lungs and sing hymns to nature, to its inexhaustible force, and to its beauty. From time to time, flocks of crows flew over the dark strip that marked the beginning of the taiga. They went northwest and disappeared somewhere above this universe of black trees where men seemed even more unwelcome than in the steppe.

• The forest, Kronauer thought. All right for a short trip, so long as we stick to the edges. But once we go deep within, there's no longer any northeast or southwest. Directions don't exist anymore, we'll have to make do with a world of wolves, of bears, and mushrooms, and we won't make our way out again, even when we walk in a straight line for hundreds of kilometers. He was already imagining the first rows of trees, and he quickly saw the gloomy thicknesses, the dead pines, fallen to their natural death thirty or forty years earlier, blackened with moss but resistant to rot. His parents had escaped camps and gotten lost there, in the taiga, and they had disappeared there. He couldn't think of the forest without recalling the tragic image of this man and this woman whom he had never known. Ever since he had been old enough to think of them, he had imagined them as a pair of nomads, forever neither alive nor dead—just lost. Don't make the same mistake they did, he thought. The taiga can't be a refuge, an alternative to death or the camps. It's vastnesses where man has no place. There's only shadow and bad encounters. Unless we're animals, we can't live in there.

He took a few seconds before abandoning the idea. Then he came back to the steppe that was rippling once more under a gust of wind. He saw the stopped train again, and, above the world, the cloudy and infinite sky.

The diesel motor wasn't groaning anymore.

He squinted.

The dying woman moaned again.

• With his too-hot and too-long felt coat, ill-suited to the weather, his too-big boots, and his head shorn of hair that wouldn't grow again, Kronauer looks like many of us—I mean that at first glance he looks like a corpse or a soldier from the civil war, running away without having won a single victory, an exhausted and suspicious-looking and strung-out man.

He sits on the balls of his feet in order to stay unnoticed. The plants come up to his shoulders, but as he squats down they close over his head. He has spent his childhood in orphanages, in urban zones, far away from meadows and, theoretically, he ought not to know the names of the plants surrounding him right then. But a woman had given him some knowledge of botany, a woman expert in plant nomenclature, and, out of nostalgia for this dead lover, he gazes thoughtfully at the steppe grasses, focusing on whether they have ears, oval leaves, lyrate leaves, whether they grow in bulbs or rhizomes. After examining them, he labels them. Downwind and nearby great ogronts, clumps of kvoina, zabakulians, septentrines, Jeanne-of-the-Communists, foxbarrens, and aldousses are whispering.

Now he watches the bottom of the hill, less than half a kilometer off. The bustle isn't great. The engineer has gone out along the locomotive—an engine manufactured at the beginning of the Second Soviet Union—but he has gone down the small steps and, after having walked about twenty meters in the grass, he has lain down on the ground. And there, he has clearly already fallen asleep or passed out.

Then the cars' doors had opened one by one.

Soldiers had come out of the second and third cars. Foot soldiers in rags, walking and gesturing like drunk or sick men. Kronauer counted four. After taking several staggering steps, they leaned against the wood door, their heads lolling or turned toward the clouds. Barely moving, not talking. Then they passed around a cigarette. Once the tobacco was used up, three of the men dragged themselves back to their respective cars. The fourth went off to satisfy his natural urge. He's descended about twenty meters down the path into a huge thicket of sage. The growth swallowed him up completely. He hasn't reappeared since.

It seems like the convoy has come to a halt in front of the ruins of the Red Star, as if it was an important railroad stop or even a station where passengers had planned to embark or debark. The locomotive motor has been switched off, and nothing suggests that the conductor will start it again anytime soon.

—Maybe they're out of fuel, Ilyushenko suggests.

• Ilyushenko, Kronauer, and Vassilissa Marachvili composed a harmonious trio, bound together by durable ties that felt much like old, unbreakable sentiments of camaraderie. But when they came into the empty lands together for a communal march toward death, they had only known each other for a few days. More specifically, Kronauer was a new figure to Ilyushenko and Vassilissa Marachvili. Given the circumstances of the Orbise's fall, forty-eight hours was certainly as good as a year, and several days a full decade. When they snuck under the barbed-wire fence of no return, it was as if they had lived together a long time and shared everything—joys and regrets, beliefs, disillusionments, and fights for egalitarianism. The Orbise's last redoubts had been taken by the enemy and they had ended up together in a small rearguard formation taking in survivors who still wanted to fight. Unfortunately, their commander had gone crazy and, after a week of hiding, the formation was no longer what they had hoped it would be when they had joined it. Their group was no longer the germ of a future resistance army, but rather an assortment of disoriented deserters, driven toward nothingness by a suicidal visionary. The commander apparently wanted to recapture the Orbise by calling on demonic, alien, and kamikaze forces. They moved around the capital's periphery without any strategy, submitting to his senseless but iron will. The commander gave absurd orders, sent men on suicide bombings where there were no victims aside from civilians and themselves. When he pointed his gun at a recalcitrant man, rebels disarmed him and then shot him before heading off in all directions. Kronauer, Vassilissa Marachvili, and Ilyushenko hadn't shirked when they had to fire at their leader, but after doing justice, they said good-bye to their futures and went toward the irradiated no-man's-lands, the empty territories, far from enemies and far from any hope.

• Ilyushenko. A tanned fortysomething, faithful like us to the party since his adolescence, and also enthusiastic enough during his membership in the Komsomol to have a crest with a sickle, a hammer, and a rifle and rising sun in the background tattooed on his neck. The crest had been burned into his skin by an artist no doubt equally as enthusiastic, but who hadn't mastered his art, so that the drawing didn't seem to refer to the culture of the proletarian revolution—it looked like a tangled mess on which a sort of spider sat. Ilyushenko had been forced to carry this ruined image upon his neck, but he hid it under his shirt collar or a scarf. In an encyclopedia of capitalist universes, he had seen reproductions of punk tattoos with tarantulas and repulsive webs and, even though these were images from a world destroyed two hundred years earlier, he didn't want to be mistaken for having nostalgia for

neo-fascist nihilism. He was a man of average height, with robust muscles, who didn't like idle talk and knew how to fight. He had formerly
been a truck driver, then he had been a garbage collector, then, when
the Orbise's future had taken a bad turn, he had fought for three years
with the famous Ninth Division, first as a mechanic and then as a
member of the tank crew and now, as the commune of the Orbise had
given up the ghost, he was in old rags and depressed, thereby resembling everyone else in that part of the world and even elsewhere.

—Give me the binoculars, Kronauer demanded and held out his
hand.

The binoculars had been taken from the commander after the dis-
comfiting firing-squad episode. He'd had to scrub the glass to get rid of
the organic debris—a yellowish chunk, some dried blood.

Now Kronauer looked through the lenses and he felt on his nose
the thing bringing back so many memories of wounded bodies and
military insanity. In the foreground, the convoy had taken on troubling
colors: camouflage green, dusty brown, dark rust. The focus knob had
been damaged and he couldn't zoom in on any faces—besides, there
weren't any faces visible right then. Once again, no bodies were visible. The ones who were lying or sitting amid the great ogronts and
kvoinas hadn't gotten up. The others didn't even lift their heads in the
doorframes. He could make out a pair of legs in the shadow of a car,
but that was it.

—If they don't have diesel fuel, I wonder where they're going to
find more, Ilyushenko said, kneeling next to Kronauer. I'd be surprised
if there was any left in the sovkhoz.

By Kronauer's right leg, the dying woman moaned.

Around the train the plants rippled once again, the degenerate rye,
and then became calm. A clump of whitish plumes was still moving
around by itself, as if it had a life of its own. Some Jeanne-of-the-
Communists.

—Eh, Kronauer said. Who knows what's going on in their heads.

Ilyushenko motioned uncomprehendingly. He shook his head, sat on the ground, and didn't pay any more attention to what was happening down below.

• They didn't move for a while, invisible within their hideaway of long leaves and stalks, which had started turning yellow and even black in the wake of the first night frosts. About fifteen meters off, a mass of plants spiced the air. Vornies-cinq-misères, Kronauer thought. Mixed with bouralayans, caincers. A bit closer there were mint-scented sarviettes.

The dying woman was reinvigorated by these scents, got up on her elbow, and touched Kronauer's calf.

—Did they get out of the train? she asked.

Vassilissa Marachvili was a brave girl and although her friends had taken turns carrying her on their backs for more than a week, they had never felt like they were weighed down by a weakling. She was impervious to pain and she accepted adversity gracefully. When they had to eliminate their crazy commander, for example, she didn't bat an eye as she joined the firing squad. And when they'd entered the world that nuclear accidents had made unlivable for ten millennia to come, she had put on a brave face despite the bleak prospect. Nobody had heard her prophesying any horrors that might await them. And later on, when radiation's earliest ravages had started to do her in, she hadn't complained. On the contrary, she had laughed with them, with Kronauer and Ilyushenko, once it was clear that all three of them were coming apart, physically and mentally, and that they were headed toward their ends. Her two comrades admired her refusal to consider everything a tragedy, even the defeat, even their impending doom, and they felt a mute but great tenderness for her. She was naturally happy; she had lived that way for thirty years—obstinate but also wryly detached—no matter the circumstances. After high school, she had worked at a brasserie in the capital, and then joined a gang of robbers, then enlisted in a She-Wolves regiment battling for the Orbise's survival. And now she was sick; she was vomiting blood and didn't have any more strength.

Kronauer set aside the binoculars and rubbed her hand, her wrist.

—Every so often one of them comes out, he said. They'll make their way through the plants to do their business. Sometimes I'll see one come back. Sometimes they stay in the plants. I can't really tell what they're doing.

—Who are they? Vassilissa Marachvili asked.

—I'm not sure, said Kronauer.

—There's a locomotive and four cars, Ilyushenko said. They're deportees or soldiers. Or a few of both. For now, there's almost nobody to be seen. They're waiting.

The dying woman slumped back down. She hadn't opened her eyes.

—Why? she asked.

—Why are they still waiting? Kronauer asked.

—Yes, said Vassilissa. Why are they waiting to go out, if they've opened the doors?

—I don't know, Kronauer said. It's odd.

—Maybe I'm sleeping and I'm dreaming, the dying woman mused.

—Yes, said Kronauer wearily.

He had already heard her babbling deliriously, and he suspected she was headed in that direction again, toward this delirium, these words coming out of her fever or out of nowhere.

—Yes, Vassilissa Marachvili whispered. Or maybe they're the ones sleeping and we're seeing their dream.

A new brume of aromatic herbs wafted through.

—That might explain it, said Ilyushenko sympathetically.

—Eh, Kronauer said.

—Maybe what we're seeing is their dream, Vassilissa Marachvili insisted.

—You think so? Ilyushenko said.

—Yes, said Vassilissa Marachvili. Maybe we're already dead, all three of us, and what we're seeing is their dream.

Then she was quiet, and so were they.

• Sky. Silence. Rippling plants. Whispering plants. Rustling plants. Murmuring mauvegarde, chugda, marche-sept-lieues, epernielle, old-captives, saquebrille, lucemingot, quick-bleeds, Saint-Valiyans, Vali-yan-harelips, sottefraise, iglitsa. Rasping odilie-des-foins, grand-odilie, chauvegrille, or calvegrillette. Uniformly sighing prance-the-ruins. The plants were of many colors, and each one even had its own way of bending under the wind or twisting around. Some resisted. Others slumped gracefully and waited a good while after the gust before returning to their original position. Plants whispering in their passive movements, in their resistance.

Time flowed.

Time took its time flowing, but it flowed.

• Vassilissa Marachvili's state worsened around four in the afternoon. Her hands convulsed, her ruined face was covered with droplets, the skin on her protruding cheekbones had turned pale. She couldn't muster the energy to open her eyes anymore. On her chin were flakes of dried blood. Fetid breath came from her half-open mouth. She was no longer speaking intelligibly.

Kroner flicked away a fly that had landed close to the dying woman's lips. He was watching over Vassilissa Marachvili, with his sleeve he dabbed at Vassilissa Marachvili's forehead to get rid of this deathly dew that was seeping out, with his fingertips he wiped under Vassilissa Marachvili's eyes, at the roots of her hair, around her huge and downy ears. He remembered what had bound them together these last few weeks, an intense friendship murky enough to turn almost immediately into a romantic adventure or, rather, a strong and discreet alliance among the three of them, augmented by bravery, self-sacrifice, and tenderness. On a physical or sexual level, the love Kronauer and Ilyushenko had for Vassilissa Marachvili hadn't come to anything. She seemed to share her love between them both with the clear but unspoken desire that neither of them have a chiefly sexual relationship with her. All three of them knew that if a couple formed in their small group, things would only get worse.

And so this danger had gone away all by itself, quickly and easily considering their shared deterioration and exhaustion. They had ended up living like brothers and sisters, without fearing intimacy and touching, without fearing a whiff of incest or romance.

He reached for her hands and rubbed them, taking care not to hurt her. Her hand was dirty, clammy, and unusually hot.

—She needs water, Ilyushenko said.

—I don't have any more, Kronauer said, tilting his head toward the bottle that had been his flask for the past few days.

—Me neither, said Ilyushenko. We drank it all when we got here.

—I thought we'd have found some in the sovkhoz, Kronauer said regretfully.

—We've been stupid, said Ilyushenko.

—Yes, we have, Kronauer confirmed.

• Silence.

Immense sky.

Plants. Immense expanse of plants and, along the horizon, to the east, the forest's edge. Above the trees, its origin an unknown distance away, was thin gray smoke. It rose straight up and then dissolved into a cloud.

—We could go to them, Kronauer suggested.

—Who are you talking about? asked Ilyushenko.

—The men on the train, Kronauer said. They probably have water.

—They're soldiers, said Ilyushenko.

—We could tell them there's a wounded woman, maybe they'll fill a bottle for us.

—We don't even know which faction they belong to, Ilyushenko said. What do they care about a wounded woman? Instead of giving us water, they could shoot us.

—Doubt it, Kronauer said. They're probably not enemies.

—Who knows. They're probably counterrevolutionaries.

—Or crazies.

—That, too. Crazies. And besides, women, they probably haven't seen any in a while. Better not tell them there's one around here.

• Silence. Sky. It was nearly five in the afternoon. The clouds had thinned, but were no longer blinding. Behind them, the sun flung pale rays. It was already October. The day wouldn't last much longer.

—The smoke over there, did you see it? Kronauer asked.

He pointed toward the faint trail above the trees.

Ilyushenko got up a little to see which way he was pointing.

—A village, he hazarded. Or a fire burning on its own.

—More likely a village, Kronauer said.

—It's pretty far off, said Ilyushenko.

—I could make it to the forest before nightfall, Kronauer said.

—You'd have to walk fast, Ilyushenko remarked.

—Then, tomorrow morning, I'd go look for help in the village, Kronauer said.

Ilyushenko shrugged.

—Once you're in the woods, you won't have anything to point the way. You could get lost, he said.

—I'm not afraid of going into the forest, Kronauer lied. I'll manage.

—That's the beginning of the taiga, Ilyushenko countered. It might not be too thick for the first few kilometers, but then it stretches out in all directions. There's only one chance in ten that you'll get to a village.

—Have to take the risk, Kronauer said. There's no other solution.

—We could wait for the convoy to start again, Ilyushenko suggested.

—Sure, and what happens if it doesn't?

The dying woman let out a groan. She wanted to say something.

Kronauer leaned over her, as if to place a kiss on her lips. He looked at her mouth carefully. Sounds came out. He didn't understand anything.

He kissed her forehead, put out his hand to wipe the damp away once again. His nostrils took in the scent of her deterioration, under his palm he felt the unusual heat of her face.

—Vassia, he whispered. Don't be afraid. The soldiers haven't seen us. We're safe in the plants. I'm going to find water. It'll get better.

A gust of wind interrupted him. The plants bent, trembled. The wind passed over Vassilissa Marachvili, it calmed Vassilissa Marachvili a little, it caressed Vassilissa Marachvili, it helped her to breathe.

—There's a village, Kronauer said. I'm going over there. I'll come back with water.

Vassilissa Marachvili wasn't trying to talk anymore. She seemed unconscious.

For a good fifteen minutes, Kronauer stayed on his knees by her. He held her hand, he watched her face, which was a beautiful and energetic young girl's and now dying. Remnants of blood soiled her lips, and cracks had appeared on her cheeks.

It was hard for him to leave her. The three of them all considered themselves already dead, but he feared the worst for her.

• Ilyushenko had picked up the binoculars. He looked at the railroad tracks once again. He stayed half upright for a couple of minutes, his head hidden under a strong bunch of fausse-malmequaire.

—They're settling down for the night, he finally said. All the cars are open. I can see about twenty of them. Soldiers, prisoners. There's six or seven of them exploring the ruins of the Red Star. Probably looking for water or something to burn. They're going to make a campfire.

—All right, well, I'll go now, Kronauer said.

—Be careful, Ilyushenko said. They've positioned a watchman on one of the car roofs. Walk in the valley for now. That way, if he sees you, you'll be too far away for him to gun you down.

—Why would they want to gun me down? Kronauer asked.

—They're soldiers, Ilyushenko said. They have to obey the orders they're given. They know that nobody normal will be in the area. They've likely been told to shoot at enemies and deserters.

—Have to admit that makes sense, Kronauer said. If we still had our guns, we'd do the same.

• After having crossed the valley, Kronauer kept a quick pace toward the forest and, although exhaustion was turning his legs to jelly, he didn't relent. At this point the landscape behind him had changed. The unmoving convoy and the sovkhoz were no longer visible. Nor was the hill on which Ilyushenko and Vassilissa Marachvili were hiding. Aside from the distant black line marking the beginning of the forest, there were no points of reference. The sun had disappeared, and in any case Kronauer didn't know how to read the sky like a map, he'd never been raised like a farmer or a trapper.

Waist-deep, sometimes shoulder-deep in a verdurous ocean, he pressed ahead rather than save his strength. His body hurt but he refused to accept it. He hadn't let himself stop during the first two kilometers, assuming that he needed to evade the watchman's potential gunfire, and after that, he hadn't let himself stop for more than the ten or twelve seconds needed to catch his breath. He was wholly focused on his goal. He wanted to reach the forest's edge before nightfall, so he could cross it the next morning at daybreak and go straight through the trees until he emerged and saw a village. It was a simple goal. A clear and simple action. Vassilissa Marachvili's life depended on his accomplishing it.

From time to time he'd trample through marshes. Then he'd stop to see if there wasn't a spring or a pool nearby for him to drink and refill his bottle and the one he'd taken from Vassilissa Marachvili's belt. The ground was wet and sometimes had a muddy consistency, but he never found water in a salvageable form. He'd keep looking one or two minutes, rummaging through argamanche shrubs or bushes of gourgoule-des-pauvres, which usually cropped up near water sources. He spread apart the pulpy stalks of lancelottes and grumes-ameres in vain. Then, muttering a quick rosary of curses, he went back on his way.

Plants that obstruct his calves, his knees, his thighs. Plants that rarely snap, except for dame-exquises, regrignelle, deadchive plumes, or folle-en-jouisse. Hard, elastic, violent plants. Plants that give way at the slightest touch, like twistsprouts, fine-brousse, majdahar, souffe-magnifique, caped mudbeaks, or mere-du-lépreux. Plants that feet could never crush. Plants that give off strong and disagreeable scents, such as torchpotils or pugnaise-des-errants, and even pestilential scents, especially the dangue-à-clochettes. Plants that look like thick hedges. Plants that exhale their perfumes with evening's arrival. Plants with acrid sap. Plants with heady sap, like diaze-lights or dive-diazes. Dark green, emerald green, yellowish green, silvery green like huckster terbabary, bronze green like ravine terbabary. Seeds, dull green, shiny green, ears. No flowers. Plants that don't resemble anything, besides drabness and absence. Soft, weak plants. Large stretches with fewer insects than in the summer months, but still buzzing with grasshoppers and flies.

The noise of this progress. Its screeching violence. A man pushing at full speed through vegetation that doesn't welcome him at all. A man crossing the steppes instead of sleeping on the ground. A man breaking the plants' silence.

The occasional crow high above. Five or six of them, often fewer, flying toward the forest. Always toward the northeast or the east, as if there was only one possible direction. The occasional shrill cry under the sky. As if, out of what little solidarity with other animals remained, or out of respect for a fairy-tale tradition, they were trying to give the lost man a useful direction or a warning. Kronauer didn't slow down even to watch them go by. He looked up, but he didn't slow down.

• Kronauer went, his body fixated on the effort, while his thoughts wandered. Several planes of consciousness merged within him, just like when he was falling asleep, and, without any conflict, intermingled.

He grew obsessed with the idea of getting to the village at all costs and he saw himself in a rather cinematic sequence, in which the villagers around him heard his pleas and rushed to the Red Star sovkhoz with water and supplies. All the while he kept envisioning Vassilissa Marachvili and Ilyushenko in distress on the hill, doomed to lie in the grasses and keep quiet so as not to be noticed by the soldiers who had bivouacked by the rails. But other images merged with these: moments of loving friendship that had developed among the three over the last weeks, around campfires, along deserted paths, amid ghost towns, after interminable hours of walking in the open steppes. The particulars of this long walk. Their farewell to rifles and cartridges, which they had decided were no longer of any help to them and which they hid in a bakery oven in a dead city.

Cold raindrops breaking up a star-studded night.

Two wild cows visible in the distance.

Vassilissa Marachvili not turning around to undress, before going to wash herself in a brown lake. The smell of Vassilissa Marachvili's body still shivering on the lakeshore, her sweat replaced by the stink of mud.

The "forbidden" and "danger" signs that rust had eaten away. Over a skull framed in red and black, snails that, before dying, had left heavy trails of slime.

Ilyushenko looking for one last cookie in his rucksack and not finding it.

Vassilissa Marachvili's teeth, which he had, many times at their trip's start, imagined sliding his tongue across.

Ilyushenko and Vassilissa Marachvili whispering.

The skin a grass snake had shed in the middle of the road.

The idea that they had been irradiated, that they were baking, and were already dead, in the process of breaking apart at the base of a reactor.

A railway track disappearing beneath stinging nettles.

Villages far off, lifeless and repulsive.

A stop close to a wrecked nuclear power plant, in a place open to the winds but stinking of grease, and the discussion they'd had to decide if it was grease from sheep or from bears.

But we were the ones who smelled bad, he suddenly realized.

He stopped walking, saw the sky brighter behind him than over the forest. The steppes stretched out endlessly, wavy, velvety, hued yellow and green with white smudges indicating tufts of Jeanne-of-the-Communists, spotted doroglosses.

He caught his breath. He breathed in the vastness deeply.

You're on the steppes, Kronauer, he thought. There's no shame in being here for the end. It's beautiful. Appreciate it. Not everyone gets to die on the steppes.

• The steppes. He had spent his childhood in the city, in an orphanage that rarely took trips to the countryside; what passed for trips were days dedicated to the communal potato harvest. Urban settings were practically everything he knew. His universe of references was circumscribed by wide avenues, inner courtyards, gray buildings, and exhaust fumes. Still, the movies and books the school had deluged him with had allowed him to roam, meander, and travel among the grassy spaces flattened under the blue sky, alongside the Scythians, the Avars, the Pechenegs, the Tatars, the Red Cavalry, and, of course, in the company of the mythic Russian heroes of Kiev every single child in the Orbise knew: Ilya Muromets, Alyosha Popovitch, and all their partners, rivals, and comrades. The steppes eventually became as familiar and essential to him as the capital's streets. And later, when he was no longer a child, he fell in love with Irina Echenguyen—and, in this theater of epic horseback rides beloved by the Orbise's orphans and communards alike, this unforgettable woman had fostered his love for botany.

Irina Echenguyen, like the rest of us, also loved those Russian byliny and the scenes of endless prairies intertwined with millennia of history, from the Scythian Empire to the Second Soviet Union, by way of Genghis Kahn's thunderous horses and Chapayev's crackling machine guns. But, above all, she was a member of a scientific team that worked on naming uncultivated grasses and wild plants in general. Kronauer didn't have the expert knowledge she did, and he remained wholly unable to help her in her complicated classifications, but he had learned to see the grasses as something other than an undifferentiated mass of plants. He had hundreds of names in his head, lists he had watched her patiently put together when he lived with her, had reread with her, had recited together with her as if they were post-exotic litanies.

They were married for ten years. Irina Echenguyen died after a long illness, during a counter-revolutionary attack. She was put on a drip in a clinic. The counter-revolutionaries burst into the common room where she had been resting with a dozen other female cancer patients, tore out tubes and needles, broke all the medical equipment, and then raped the women, even the ones who already looked like corpses. It was a group of dog-headed enemies, zealots for exploiting men for the sake of men. Then they deserted the place, but before they left, they killed Irina Echenguyen.

• Molle-guillotes, malveinés, ashrangs, smallglory captives, willow benaises. Damsels-in-flight, masquerats, four-o'clock beauties, pituit-aines, sweetbalers, or midnight Jeannes.

• A pair of crows, very low, did not caw as they passed right over his head. The sky was far less blinding than it had been earlier. Dusk was coming. The temperature had dropped and every now and then harsh gusts of wind blew. The black line of the forest, now much nearer, had ceased to be an abstract image. It was already resolving into trees and branches, with perceptibly different heights and thicknesses. He still had two kilometers to go before reaching it.

That's good, he thought. I'll have time to get there before night falls.

He had already stumbled several times and he took another break. One minute, he thought. Just one minute.

The smoke that had just a minute ago suggested the possibility of a village was now faded away. Now there weren't any points of reference left. Only, in front of him, the dark mass of the first larches.

He closed his eyes so his dizziness and exhaustion would dissipate. A gray and erratic layer of clouds spun behind his eyelids, but it was mainly the darkness of the forest he was thinking about.

Damn it, Kronauer, he reproached himself, don't tell me you've got the willies! Your parents died in the taiga, so what? You're still far from the taiga, it's just a slightly dark wood, it won't be more than a few kilometers deep. Two or three hours of walking, and you'll end up in fields with a village and countrymen. Get a hold of yourself! Don't give up that fast! Your little troubles are nothing compared to the apocalypse that hit the Orbise!

• He was thirty-nine years old. He was born in the Orbise. All his schooling had been focused on the future of Communes for workers and countrymen.

His view of the world was illuminated by proletarian morality: self-sacrifice, altruism, and confrontation. And like all of us, of course, he had suffered the world revolution's setbacks and collapses. We didn't understand how the rich and their mafias had managed to win the trust of the laboring classes. And before our rage, first had been our stupefaction when we realized that these masters of unhappiness were triumphing around the globe and were on the brink of annihilating the last of us. We had no explanation when we interrogated ourselves about humanity's bad choices. Marxist optimism prevented us from seeing the proof of serious defects in the genetic heritage of our species, an idiotic affinity for self-destruction, a masochist apathy in the face of predators, and perhaps even above all a fundamental inability when it came to collectivism. We thought this deep down, but, as the official theory relayed these hypotheses with a shrug of the shoulders, we didn't broach the topic, even among comrades. Even in joking among comrades.

Kronauer's intellectual education after high school had been wrecked and there were huge holes in his knowledge, like so many other young people in the Orbise when their studies were interrupted by chaos and defeats. If the worldwide situation hadn't been so unfavorable to egalitarianism, perhaps he would have turned toward a quiet career with an apprenticeship that wasn't too long, a career nothing like a soldier's. He wasn't very interested in abstract things. He did like books and happily borrowed novels from the local libraries, but a list of what he'd borrowed, aside from political classics, would show that his preferences veered toward inoffensive adventure stories and the most traditional post-exotic bluettes. Deep down, even if he wasn't loath to sit down for hours reading in silence, he didn't feel comfortable when he was confronted with the complex structures of the soul, and he much preferred action. One example had actually disrupted his existence. When the Komsomol had suggested it, he had refused to join a school for Party officials, and asked to be assigned to an operating unit. After his first year of training, he would have been assigned a political instructor's minor responsibilities, but the propaganda work didn't appeal to him. He wanted direct confrontation with enemies or traitors. The Orbise was in danger. Military violence seemed more natural to him than meetings where he would have to call for military violence. Therefore the start of civil war hadn't troubled him in the least. He'd immediately joined the standing army, and he'd been sent to work with one of the clandestine organizations that found unconventional ways to heckle the enemy. Then he had been assigned to a Special Intelligence Center. Aside, of course, from periods of peace when he went back to civil life as a worker without much qualification, sometimes in construction and sometimes in the food industry, he had been fighting here and there for fifteen years now. He had never been wounded. He was in the prime of life. That said, he had seen too many corpses, witnessed too many defeats, and he had lost most of the hope he'd still had.

• He started walking again. He couldn't keep a steady pace. The two kilometers that still separated him from the forest's edge seemed to stretch out interminably. Keep going, Kronauer, keep going and don't think, don't look, don't count the meters you've walked, don't count what's left, don't count anything! . . . Don't listen to anything but your footsteps, don't look at the sky, keep going like you're in good shape!

The landscape was already taking on the gray and purple hues of twilight.

He veered away to avoid a barely visible burial mound; there had been thousands of them on the steppes since the Bronze Age, a kurgan that had been built on his path, tamped down and nondescript, a symbol of existences wasted and millennia gone for nothing, just to witness the collapse of egalitarianism and a wave of derelicts just like the very first nomads eons earlier. Now he staggered by a field of hare-rye, a mutant variety that had appeared in the countryside thirty years earlier, and then was cultivated close to the capital to make flour that tasted like cardboard. He stepped into the withered, unappealingly brown ears, then he went through. He drifted as if drunk. And suddenly his legs. They gave way beneath him. He hobbled ten more meters, and then he kneeled on the ground and slumped down.

Well, he thought, trying to get back up. It's nothing. A wave of tiredness.

He couldn't get himself back upright. His muscles wouldn't respond. There were cramps in his neck, all his joints were on fire. He breathed loudly.

You think you're still alive, a voice suddenly said in him, inside his head, but unfamiliar.

—What! he grumbled. What's going . . .

He waved his hand like he was trying to swat away flies or wasps. He was on his knees, exhausted. And this voice.

You think you're still alive, but it's over. You're just a relic. Your corpse is already rotting somewhere on the moist earth and you don't get that it's over. It's just after-death mumbo-jumbo bouncing around in your head. Don't keep trying. Just lie down where you fell and wait for the crows to take care of your burial.

Then, just as quickly as it had come, the voice left. It left him entirely, without a trace in his memory, as if it had never spoken in him. Once again he found himself alone, with his breath short and hoarse, with his bodily pains, his exhaustion.

Just a moment of tiredness, he thought, a big one. Nothing serious. Night won't fall for another half an hour, three-quarters of an hour. I'm going to lie down. Just not enough food, dehydration. I'm going to lie down until it passes. As it is, my legs won't get me anywhere.

He lay down. Above his head, when he opened his eyes, the sky had started to whirl again. He shut his eyes against his nausea. Shaken once more by the wind, the plants brushed against him. He listened.

False ryegrass, he thought. Racines-rieuses, lovushkas, solivaines. This too will pass. Even if I black out for a minute, this will pass. Then I'll get back up, and if it's not too dark I'll go sleep under the trees, at the edge by the first trees, and I'll wait for dawn before going into the forest. Hang in there, Kronauer! Tomorrow you'll be in the village, and then it'll be okay. Everything's spinning right now, but this will pass.

Tomorrow. In the village. It'll be okay.

• Chiennelaines, doroglosses. Lovushkas-du-savatier, rogue solivaines, aromatic solivaines.

− 2 −

• Inside the warehouse, the temperature wasn't dropping. It never dropped. The sheet-metal walls were always warm, even in the winter when it was freezing, and they emitted a soft and constant light, rendering all heating and lighting equipment unnecessary.

After the nuclear reactor that powered the Radiant Terminus kolkhoz caught fire, the hangar had been used to store the irradiated material the liquidators had collected in the area. It was an enormous, ugly building, intended to hold massive quantities of garbage, and it had been constructed right above the burning ruins of the little power plant. The liquidators had found it best to use preexisting structures to store the stock of dangerous trash and bury it all in the same place. A well sat in the center of the building. In it went everything that people wanted to get rid of forever.

The well had been dug by the nuclear core itself when, after vaporizing everything in range, it had gone mad and begun to sink into the earth. The engineer Barguzin, the only surviving member of the team that had designed the hangar, claimed that the hole was regular and vertical and about two kilometers deep. According to him, at the bottom of the hole, the core had stopped moving. It would stay there, always mad but no longer moving, no longer trying to reach the innermost depths of earth proper. It would simply feed on what it received from on high.

• Every month, indeed, the core was fed. The heavy cover for the well was opened, and some of the bric-a-brac collected over the last season or two was knocked over the edge; just to show that people weren't panicking and weren't afraid of pathetic radionuclides. Tables and chairs, television sets, the tarry carcasses of cows and cowherds, tractor motors, charred schoolteachers who had been forgotten in their classrooms during the critical period, computers, remains of phosphorescent crows, moles, does, wolves, squirrels, clothes that looked perfect but had only to be shaken to set off a haze of sparks, inflated toothpaste tubes filled with constantly simmering toothpaste, albino dogs and cats, clusters of iron that continued to rumble with an inner fire, new combine harvesters that hadn't yet been broken in and which gleamed at midnight as if they were lying in full sunlight, garden forks, hoes, axes, debarkers, accordions that spat out more gamma rays than folkloric melodies, pinewood planks that looked like ebony planks, Stakhanovites in their Sunday best with their hands mummified around their diplomas, forgotten when the event halls were evacuated. The ledgers with their pages turning day and night. Cash-register money, the copper coins clinking and shifting without anyone nearby. These were the sorts of things thrown into the void.

The Gramma Udgul was the one to handle the maneuver. She arbitrarily decided on the days to open the well and told the improvised liquidators which things should feed the core. The Gramma Udgul was also the only person who had the idea to stoop down by the chasm and talk to the core to make it happy.

When she hunched, the undetectable wind from the depths hit her in the face. This caress didn't bother her and she went on with her monologue. Nothing could be heard, not even the crush of objects or bodies that had arrived at their destination after falling two thousand meters. The Gramma Udgul's voice sank into the well's dark mystery without an echo. The kolkhozniks helping the old woman waited nearby until she had finished her sorcerous, vehement screams. They looked like a group of zombies in the last stages of their existence.

Aside from some occasional reserve soldiers, these uncommunicative men were the core of the male population still alive at Radiant Terminus, and they could be counted on the fingers of one hand: the engineer Barguzin; the demobilized, one-armed Abazayev; and the tractor driver Morgovian.

• A few words about the Gramma Udgul. About her hardiness which science cannot explain. About her beliefs, about her path to glory and darkness. And about her eighty-year-old, in-shape body, doomed to eternity.

One hundred years earlier, she had begun her long career as a liquidator. She was thirty-two years old then; she was a nurse's aide and, as the Second Soviet Union experienced its first serious collapses, she dreamed of sacrificing herself for communism-bound humanity. And so she had joined the kamikaze corps that was sent close to the nuclear power plants, which were all breaking down or exploding at the time. I recall that thousands of them had been built in order to make each production plant, each city neighborhood, each kolkhoz self-sufficient. But, despite all the precautions and security measures, the accidents multiplied and the habitable areas diminished. Of course all those who invented these seemingly clean and robust generator models had been executed, but that hadn't solved any problems. Massive regions had to be evacuated and left to ruin. The triumphant march toward communism, already hampered by outside attacks, found its pace slowed down even further. When the Gramma Udgul volunteered, the liquidators had become a pillar on which society teetered. The candidates for this noble task, however, weren't rushing to the recruitment offices. Only heroes were signing up. Only young idealistic fanatics, or the same old militants who hid their fear by gritting their indomitable Bolshevik teeth.

The Gramma Udgul worked selflessly on the first building site, and then on those that followed. She knew that she was immolating herself, that she was offering up her health and her life for the collective's future well-being, for the radiant future of her children and grandchildren, or rather everyone else's, because she had been warned that the radiation would render her sterile. She helped evacuate the population, she piled up the trucks with the evacuees' goods, she soothed those who were hysterical, she went on to arrest the thieves and lent a hand when they had to be immediately executed, she was involved in building the shields and concrete layers around the unapproachable cisterns, close to the cores that did whatever they wanted to. It was demanding, dangerous work. However, in contrast to the other heroic men and women who had quickly succumbed, she kept on living.

Her body had responded positively to this repeated exposure to fissile matter. The ionizing rays had destroyed all the sick and potentially cancerous cells her flesh might harbor. Radioactivity had certainly made her slightly iridescent in the darkness, but above all it had stopped the process of aging in her flesh, and according to what the Gramma Udgul thoroughly suspected, it had been stopped forever. These phenomena also had inconveniences and, particularly, they had caught the attention of the authorities who asked her several times, not without some irritation, why she wasn't dying. The Party had trouble accepting that she refused to go with her comrades in liquidation to the grave. A proposed official reprimand was discussed and, even if it was closed for being judged absurd and even odious, it nonetheless remained in her folder, a stain. From then on, her troubles never ended. They kept on singing her praises in the press and depicting her as a Soviet woman of extraordinary devotion and courage, but they managed not to mention, moreover, that she was fit as a fiddle.

• At first, the Gramma Udgul submitted without complaint to the psychological exams that were ordered regularly, but after five or six years she had had enough, and she didn't seem very willing when she was asked to donate her body to science as quickly as possible. She only responded to convocation notices intermittently. She had clearly been singled out without any explanation, both in the realms of medicine and normal civilian life. She knew that she was being watched as an unreliable individual, and she understood that she had been deemed unworthy of promotion to the Party's honorary body, as had more or less automatically been the case for every cosmonaut, author of epics, and television celebrity. She didn't complain about her iridescence or her immortality, and she didn't make a single comment about the political injustice she was suffering. She wrote self-criticisms when asked, she kept taking part in community meetings, and, when the opportunity presented itself again, she left for the liquidation sites, always willingly. She had a sense of discipline and she didn't claim to be clever enough to contradict the Party.

Decades went by. The authorities changed, co-opted themselves, grew old, were rejuvenated, but never reviewed their evaluation of her, and, generation after generation, they considered her immortality, intentional or not, an insult to the toiling masses. They kept an eye on her organic deviationism. However, that eye had an unclear view. Her extraordinary abilities in battling the atoms' unforeseen wrath were undeniable. She was frequently called upon for her irreplaceable experience, and behind closed doors she was frequently awarded the titles and medals she had earned: Valiant Combatant of the Atom, Red Heroine, Glorious Liquidator, Intrepid Red Doyenne, Veteran, Red Big Sister. She pinned the certificates above her bed, but she rarely mentioned them, rarely or not at all. In her building, she was just a small anonymous person. She wasn't the sort to show an invalid's card at stores in hopes of skipping the line.

In this way, a century went by. A century of setting out again and again for nuclear ovens on the brink of meltdown, mixing fuel rods with gloves ill-suited to the task, crossing the countryside, laughing yet bleak, going into ghost towns, digging communal graves, and shooting down thieves. She worked hard with teams as their members collapsed one after another and decayed in weeks. She helped with hurried funerals in places filled with silence and strewn with ossified birds, then, upon her return to the capital, she was paraded on solemn occasions, during which she was decorated with awards normally given to the dead. Then she went back to normal life. She settled back in her job at a local clinic. Her frequent requests for time off to go fight enemy matter had hampered her upward trajectory, and she remained a nurse's aide—a first-class one, but still just a nurse's aide. And, once she was at work, she was again forced to deal with the Party and the suspicions of its teams, undergo humiliating procedures, rewrite her autobiography for the thousandth time, do her self-criticisms over again, and, on top of all that, she had to appear at the Medical Academy's meetings, justify her natural and ideological state in front of embryologists, in front of xenologists, in front of special works councils that didn't hesitate to accuse her of petit-bourgeois individualism in the face of death, and even of witchcraft.

She put an end to this endless cycle.

One day, she acted in a fit of pique.

She applied for a disaster site far away from everything, having made a firm decision there and then never to come back. She simply had to go to a closed-off province, already quarantined for a half-century after uncontrollable setbacks in the military facilities. Some minimal human activity persisted there, with a few agricultural enterprises and several camps, but the urban areas, even the small ones, had been evacuated. And, conveniently enough, the Red Star sovkhoz had just indicated that there was a situation of utmost urgency at its nuclear power site, and, in the same distress call, had spoken of a neighboring kolkhoz, Radiant Terminus, also in trouble. The region had been kept under military confidentiality since its annexation to the Second Soviet Union, and nobody could quite pinpoint it on a map. The Red Star was indicated by a question mark, close to a large forest and a place called the Levanidovo, but there was no hint anywhere of a Radiant Terminus.

• They had brought the Gramma Udgul and her squadron on a bus that had stopped at the edge of the province, then they had given everybody sidecars to get themselves to the accident site. The road continued, but no person or thing could be seen on it and, out of fear of radiation, the drivers decided to turn around two hundred kilometers sooner than expected.

The Gramma Udgul's companions had unanimously picked her to head the squad. They were proud to work under such a popular figure of the Orbise because, even if the Party kept having trouble publicly recognizing her merits, the Orbise's masses happily paid homage to her and weren't irritated that she wasn't dead. She had the astonishing ability to constitute a liquidation brigade out of any workforce found nearby. She was accompanied by some thirty scientists, firefighters, and engineers ready to wade through boiling-hot cooling ponds and breached cores in sovkhoz and kolkhoz alike. They had all sworn to do their best until their spinal cords had become nothing more than blackened mallows.

Their sidecars trundled down the empty roads, then, when the sidecars ran out of gas, they crossed the forest on foot to the Levanidovo, where they split up in two teams.

The Gramma Udgul came to the Radiant Terminus kolkhoz and was surprised and overjoyed to discover that the president was a certain Solovyei, her first husband, a comrade whom she had loved very much and whom she had been taken away from ninety years earlier. This Solovyei wasn't a citizen as respectful of the official proletarian obligations as she was and, despite believing in egalitarianism, he had his own views, on which he had imposed moral arrangements that nobody was allowed to judge. In short, he had long since turned his back on the Party. After an eternity of imprisonment and vagrancy, he had finally settled into this hidden corner as a member of an independent commune that maintained very weak links with the institutions and authorities of the Orbise.

As she gave herself over to the pleasure of finding Solovyei again and reminiscing about their lost youth, the Gramma Udgul let the scientists carry out preliminary measures, assess the damage for millennia to come, and then explain the situation during a general assembly of the Red Star and Radiant Terminus survivors. The teams then began to work at full force. Using shortcuts that he alone knew, Solovyei guided them through the forest to get from one site to another quickly. The two agricultural complexes were effectively separated by a strip of taiga that foolhardy people could easily get lost in.

The Red Star sovkhoz had been abandoned after three days. Since the innards of its plant was burning outside the reactor vessel, but not presenting any major performance issues, the firefighters had suggested leaving the building as it was, and coming back several years later to remove the most problematic waste. The barns and pigsties were opened, the livestock and poultry encouraged to go die on the open steppes, and all the surviving sovkhozniks and liquidators withdrew to the Radiant Terminus area, where the core was already sinking into the earth's bowels. The Gramma Udgul had approved the plans for the hangar, requisitioned sturdy men and women to begin construction, and outlined the framework for decontamination, which in her opinion would take four or five centuries, taking into account the few hands available. Then she did her best to care for her team members as they died. The scientists went first, closely followed by the engineers. The firefighters held out for a week longer, and in turn, they went out in shreds, torn apart by deadly cancers and burns. Aside from the engineer Barguzin, who also seemed to be immune to radiation, the whole squadron had died in enthusiastic but atrocious suffering.

For three months, she sent a report to the Party every two weeks in which she copied down the readings from the few thermometers and measurement instruments still in working order, and described the liquidation's progress, as well as her short-term and medium-term prognoses. On schematic maps, drawn according to Solovyei's directions, she delineated the large perimeter where from that point on it would be ill-advised to venture without having taken iodine pills and put on hazmat suits. At the end of the message she gave an exhaustive list of countrymen, specialists, and non-specialists who had died and whose corpses had been thrown into the well, because this well's liquidating function had been activated, albeit in a strictly experimental manner. In a postscript, she sometimes wondered about the tactics used to reestablish the ideological norms of Radiant Terminus in a kolkhoz where class warfare had never happened in an orthodox fashion, although on the whole without straying from the egalitarian mentality dear to our hearts. She never received a reply. Then the mailman had thyroid problems in the middle of the forest and lay down for a long while under the larches, putting an end to mail delivery to and from the Levanidovo.

So the Gramma Udgul began living her life without deferring to the Party at every moment. This break with the hierarchy and supreme guides had induced stress, and for several months she suffered nightmares and even some mental confusion. She tended to see the worst everywhere. Then, thanks to Solovyei's affectionate presence, she succeeded in overcoming her doubts and stressful thoughts.

In reality, when the correspondence had broken off, the Party had concluded that she had been killed in turn by the heavy bombardment of murderous particles. Due to the numerous proofs of ideological steadfastness she had furnished in the past, nobody suspected that she had defected or taken advantage of her immortality to go down deviationist paths in this region.

Her name was added to the list of proletariat martyrs who had fought against matter's insanities, and she was given one of the few medals she hadn't yet received: the posthumous distinction of Foremother of the Proletarian Pantheon. Then they ran barbed wire around the last points of entry into the province and decreed the region unsuitable for human life.

• The Radiant Terminus kolkhoz bore closer resemblance to a den of thieves than an agricultural establishment, and from an ideological point of view, there was a pure and simple aberration here, which was a striking contrast to what the Gramma Udgul had imagined for her exile. However, her adolescent urges asked only to be reawakened, with their radicalism, their ferocity, this dissatisfied gaze the young had for the real world. Deep down, more than any wish to be part of the world revolution's triumph, she still had the childish desire to live out her destiny like an adventure film. And Solovyei certainly emblematized this: defiance of all laws, astonishment, love, a descent into the forbidden, into the hereafter, into the unexplored spaces of dreams, into sorcerous realms. He bent down and looked her in the eyes, he offered her his support, his complicity, his lucidity, his anarchist nonconformity. He helped her distance herself from the Party without apostasy or pain. It took months for her to find peace. But from the first day he had welcomed her as if she were the missing piece of the magical edifice that was the Radiant Terminus kolkhoz, a formerly lost piece he had waited his whole life for, and which he was extraordinarily happy to find at long last.

Solovyei was the only man who had mattered in her life. She had met him at a liquidation site, at Kungurtug, when she was a beautiful woman in the bloom of her thirty-sixth year, already noticed by the authorities for her miraculous resistance to radiation. The place was completely isolated, in the middle of the mountains, close to a small lake that, after the accident, held water more closely resembling lukewarm mercury. All the liquidators, except for the two of them, had died in the following weeks. Like the Gramma Udgul, Solovyei had a body unaffected by delirious neutrons, which he happily explained by claiming that he had descended from a line of Bolshevik shamans and magicians who had continually evolved on the border between life, death, and sleep. These provocative explanations didn't please the authorities at all, especially when he accompanied his words with mocking laughter and insults at the bureaucracy and its managers. She fell for him after a nighttime walk along the glimmering banks of Tere-Khol, the nearby lake, and although he was already too anarchist to join the Komsomol, she loved him exactly as he was, without any attempt to make him change his mind about the five-year plan or his telluric view of communism. They parted ways after Kungurtug, but they stayed in touch, and finally she went to be with him in Abakan, the little city in the province where he lived.

They lived in harmony together in Abakan, hardly bothered by their political differences of opinion or the fact that she couldn't have children. Although they never registered with the Soviet authorities, they considered themselves husband and wife. They both worked at a school for deaf-mutes, she as a caregiver and he as group leader. When needed, they left for sites where nuclear accidents required their presence. They were two irreproachable citizens at the forefront of the fight against misfortune. However, their good health had marked them out for surveillance, and naturally not just by the medical research services. The Gramma Udgul's autobiographies, written several times during special sessions, cleared her of any wrongdoing, but Solovyei's only made things worse for him. Solovyei took pride in being not only a revolutionary, but also a poet, and so he felt that he had the right to say anything that went through his head loud and clear. The prospect of having to write lies to save his skin infuriated him. He sabotaged his self-criticisms by inserting esoteric narracts, considerations of the apocalypse, and politically incorrect discourses on sexuality and dreams. On the official deposition papers, he expounded on his hope that there would come a time when only shamans, sorcery experts, mages, and oneiromancy disciples would be in charge of the battle between classes and they would wander like nomads through the cities and the countryside. Solovyei's relations with the authorities grew acrimonious. After four years of life together, the Party encouraged the Gramma Udgul to leave her comrade, which she refused to do.

Then Solovyei disappeared without a trace. The Gramma Udgul immediately started investigating by talking to every administrative and police body she knew. She was told to wait for Solovyei himself to give some sign, implying that he had simply chosen to divorce her without going to the trouble of explaining himself. For two years, she pestered the departments. She made the most of the private sessions where she was asked to rewrite her autobiography and asked the officers if they had any news about her husband. The answers varied, sometimes unkind and sometimes sympathetic, but, in short, she never got the least bit of workable information. Solovyei had vanished. Solovyei had gone somewhere else. She knew nothing else about him for the next ninety-one years.

And that's why now, after so many decades where each of them had lived alone, she didn't complain about what fate had given her. Like her, Solovyei had changed dramatically, physically and mentally, and he bore the burden of a century's memories he hadn't shared with her, but she didn't consider reproaching him for having become a peculiar person. From the moment she had found him, she had decided to do everything she could to be happy with him, in this kolkhoz with its name already suggestive of subversion. She had found the man she had once loved, she had decided to love him again, and nothing else really mattered. Not even his transformation into a sort of authoritarian, unsavory, insane wizard. Now she didn't care about the incongruities of everyday life in the village, which simply underscored its difference from proletarian normalcy. She knew that, no matter the point of view, she herself no longer belonged to the normal realm of the Orbise either. That, by resisting the gamma rays, she had long since joined the realm of monsters. It made perfect sense, then, that she would settle down in the Levanidovo, and that she would end up with one of its unlikely inhabitants, with the president of Radiant Terminus. With another monster.

• From then on people went to the kolkhoz hangar if they were willing to meet the Gramma Udgul. She had made it her home and she rarely left. She had her own private corner, closed off by a heavy decontamination tarp that the tractor driver Morgovian had stripped of its lead to give it a bit of flexibility. She went back there to wash up, or when she felt various pressing needs that called for solitude, such as preparing for her discourse to the core, reading Leninist classics, or defecating. The rest of the time, she preferred to stay in the middle of the bric-a-brac that never diminished in size, because the kolkhozniks and several volunteer scrap merchants in the region kept adding to it, obeying her instructions so that the area would be cleared of all wreckage before the second half of the millennium.

To determine which pieces of trash were the most dangerous, she had given up Geiger counters, which went haywire at the slightest thing or else had gone out of commission after the first days of the catastrophe. She sniffed the dust and followed her instincts. She no longer respected decontamination procedures. She handled these heaps, these mountains, she oversaw the opening and closing of the well, she threw objects into the abyss, she talked to the core. She told it about the passions of her past, the doubts that had assailed her fifty years earlier when the Party had advocated new economic or social policies, but she also confided her more immediate worries, Solovyei's moments of madness, his immoderate love for his daughters, the physical deterioration of the last kolkhozniks, the water leaks that flooded her toilet. Such was the confident and confiding relationship she had with the core.

Aside from managing the atomic detritus, Solovyei had entrusted her to take care of what he called his archives, which were actually several crates of handwritten notebooks containing accounts from the camps, proclamations read in prison, critical studies of the Party and its future, transcriptions of epic songs, black-magic recipes, war stories, and dream stories, to which were added a large number of wax cylinders on which he had recorded impenetrable, extremely strange, disturbing poems.

Everything was piled up in a mess, close to the Gramma Udgul's favorite armchair, and when she took a break from liquidating, she focused on preserving Solovyei's memories. Sometimes particular writings had such an obnoxiously counterrevolutionary slant that she yelled out loud, her accent suddenly finicky and Bolshevik, and sometimes she felt carried away by the poetic violence of other sulfurous pages, and then she forgot the lessons she had learned in grade school, the rigid principles that had been instilled in her to make her appreciate or detest this or that narrative or ideological option. She forgot it all and sighed contentedly like a young reader immersed in a love story. Whatever it was, she felt a deep affection for Solovyei's prose, and she dived into it at any moment, on the pretext of classification when in reality she never bothered to do that properly. She wanted to be completely united with Solovyei at the end of her life, completely complicit, and she wasn't afraid of reading, rereading, or listening to these creations that seemed immoral and most often bereft of the least glimmer of Marxism-Leninism. At another point in her life, she would have hastened to bury them, these antirevolutionary creations, beneath anodyne paperwork, beneath irradiated volumes of the Great Soviet Encyclopedia, beneath literature reviews, veterinary manuals, the complete works of fellow travelers, farm novels. But here, today, she didn't go to the effort. She knew that she was no longer at risk of any trouble from the authorities, the capital investigators, or the services. As for her own internal audit committee, it made itself heard less and less often.

The engineer Barguzin, who helped the Gramma Udgul as best as he could in sorting and processing the radioactive trash, didn't have access to the crates containing Solovyei's archives, despite Solovyei being his father-in-law, as we will come to learn. He fixed anything that broke in the kolkhoz, he carried and piled up the things meant to be fed to the core, but he wasn't allowed to go through Solovyei's personal memorabilia, and, when he saw that the Gramma Udgul was busy moving them around stealthily, he went to smoke a cigarette outside the hangar.

• That morning, the Gramma Udgul woke up abruptly and knew immediately that she would be in a bad mood.

She had dreamed of waltzing with a red proletarian on Labor Day, but she didn't remember what she'd done with him after the dance. To make matters worse, she couldn't say whether she'd been present at the ball in the form of a young Bolshevik belle or in her present form as an old woman. This forgetfulness bothered her, because in the second case the next part of the dream couldn't be what it would have been in the first case, and deep down she hoped she'd had a dream adventure with this heroic worker who had held her tenderly in his arms, who had twirled her to the accordion's sounds until dizziness caught hold of her and forced her to leave the dance floor. She still remembered her dance partner's laughing face, and, if she shut her eyes for a few seconds, she could happily keep it in her heart, but then it disappeared and was replaced by a conventional Komsomol face that didn't resemble anything living. After the striking events of her dream had vanished, this bastardization of the man she had loved for a single night really upset her.

She opened her eyes and growled a jumbled curse that tore the Marxist classics a new hole.

Getting up from the armchair she'd spent the night in, still grumbling, she decided to go lock herself in the bathroom until something happened. In fact, what mostly happened there was meditation, considering that episodes of fecal or urinary evacuation were rather uncommon. Most of the time these past thirty or forty years, the Gramma Udgul had simply snacked on a spoonful of toasted flour here, a cookie there; she drank little and never ate a full meal, which had rendered null and void the terminal parts of her digestive system, which by now were shriveled up.

The sun had risen outside. Its rays slanted through the air vents just beneath the roof. Above a heap of farming machines, a harrow with perfect blades gleamed. It had been included in a recent bequest of new equipment, and had never been used. The Gramma Udgul wasn't in a rush to throw it into the pit because the radiation it emitted consistently grilled the flies buzzing around it. The murders happened with a quick crackle. Flies had always bothered the Gramma Udgul and she felt a small satisfaction when she heard one of them being reduced to ash.

It had to be eight in the morning.

As she raised her head to admire the reflections of sunlight beneath the cement, the Gramma Udgul stumbled over a milk bucket. The bucket was empty and it scraped noisily against the ground and fell over. The Gramma Udgul let out an annoyed exclamation.

—What's that piece of junk doing by my feet? she asked. It wasn't here yesterday. Did the engineer bring it in, just to put it in my way? Jerk!

She squinted into the labyrinth of piles to see if the engineer was nearby, but the hangar was silent and nobody was working there right then.

—Barguzin! she yelled. Hey, Barguzin!

Nobody answered, so she relented. Yelling had calmed her down.

—Idiot. Of course he's not here, she whispered. He's never here when I have to yell at him. Dawdling outside, probably.

She kicked the bucket a few meters, then threw it on a hill of trash. The bucket found a resting spot between a television set, two pillows, and a quilt.

She stopped to look at the pillows. There were rings of sweat on it. She didn't remember exactly where they'd come from—a Red Star dormitory, an isolated izba in the forest, a cupboard in one of the Radiant Terminus farms? She rummaged through her memories for five or six seconds, but nothing came. Who knew what sleeper had sweated there, she thought. Then she went back to Barguzin and his laziness.

—Or maybe he's sucked up too many becquerels and died, she said.

She was there, in the middle of the path between two mounds of radioactive scrap metal, grumbling once again.

—Wouldn't be the first time, she grumbled. He's from the new generation, they just die off whenever they can.

• Barguzin actually was often a victim of what conventional wisdom would term death. He no longer breathed, his body had started to adopt a cadaverous pose, and in particular his heart and his brain refused to work. Beneath his eyelids, his gaze was lifeless, his pupils didn't respond to anything. His skin was becoming unappetizingly waxy. The Gramma Udgul had to shake him over and over, put him in the sunlight when there was sun or in moonlight when the moon shone, and she rubbed his forehead with heavy-heavy water, then with deathly-deathly water, then she poured lively-lively water between his eyes, as in the tales the bards had sung. Barguzin responded to this treatment and regained normal color. He got back up, thanked her, and went back to work in the kolkhoz repair shop. He, too, had a body that had gone wrong in a useful way when it came to radiation; he, too, turned out to be resistant to radionuclides, but his resistance wasn't the same sort as that which allowed the Gramma Udgul and Solovyei to stand at the doors of immortality. Barguzin remained fragile and always close to death. Without the Gramma Udgul and her urgent care, he would long since have been turned into mere residue fit for throwing into the well, along with other toxic matter and agricultural objects.

• After a bit of toilet, the Gramma Udgul went back to sitting down in her favorite armchair. She had a collection of newspapers beside her that had been put together by Solovyei, to try to make sense of what had happened in terms of the world revolution during his time in the work camps. Because that was where he had ended up after leaving Akaban, for forty-five years straight starting, after a disorganized life, with periods of conditional freedom, of banishment to inhospitable regions, which alternated with new arrests, new transfers to special zones, not to mention gallivanting across the taiga with bands of mystic thieves, shamans, escaped convicts, and highwaymen. He made no effort to settle down and regularly ended up back behind bars and even in front of the execution squad, whether for serious disagreements with the powers that be or for various trifles connected to his shady character, such as brawling with a superior or inappropriately mugging bureaucrats.

She took the gazette at the top of the pile and fumbled through the headlines. The newspaper was from the previous century, but the news was encouraging.

The revolution made headway on all fronts and the number of battles increased. At that point, the Second Soviet Union covered most of the globe. There were still several distant continents with pockets of aggressive capitalists, and there was no denying that the domestic nuclear disasters had made the survival of the world population rather problematic, but the situation had improved, at least under the military plan.

—Good, she said. As planned, we're headed toward total victory, just have to be a bit patient. Just a matter of time.

Satisfied, she gave up the headlines and dipped into the pages inside. She looked for the weather report to compare the printed information with the reality of the sky above Radiant Terminus, and came once again to the conclusion that the press was full of nonsense.

• Solovyei came into the hangar by a side door and weaved between the mounds of trash that impeded all movement in a straight line. Without being a maze, the place gave the impression of having been put together to prevent direct access to the well that constituted its center. Solovyei let his eyes wander over the various piles, noticed several milking machines, dairy vats, industrial churners, old manual churners, cheese racks, zinc mixers. Everything seemed to be in good shape. Everything was clean and in good shape, but showering the immediate vicinity with a storm of deadly particles.

He thought of the cows that had flourished in the region and which were now an extinct species, and of the kolkhozniks who had spent a major part of their life standing alongside these enormous ruminants, their cowpats and flies, their mooing and swollen udders, and who had now gone extinct as well. He wondered if the cows had had an existence worthy of consideration and if the men and women who had taken care of them had died heroes or not. He wondered this without any sarcasm, but without any emotion, because this question really didn't trouble him in the least. He had built his own existence around values beside heroism and, since he was president of the kolkhoz, he gave priority to black magic, to incursions into the world of dreams and parallel universes filled with zombies, wonderful daughters, animals, and fires. Heroism and cows barely had any place there.

Then he kept on walking. Not far from the decontamination tarp that hid the toilet, the Gramma Udgul was sitting in her favorite armchair and smoking a pipe while reading under her breath a newspaper describing the news eighty years ago. Solovyei had a heavy tread that couldn't go unnoticed, the surroundings shook around him like he was a knight from the Middle Ages, but the Gramma Udgul acted as if she didn't hear him.

She didn't even raise an eye when he walked up to her.

—What are you doing, reading that newspaper? the kolkhoz director asked in mock indignation. I thought you'd started organizing my complete works. Have you already gotten discouraged?

The Gramma Udgul's collarbone shook as she sighed, and then she set the newspaper on the pile. The paper disintegrated as soon as it was touched. Specks of pulp dusted her black dress. She brushed them off before talking.

—Your texts are too hard for me, she said as she looked down. No clue how to get started. They're ravings. They don't even have dates on them. I can't organize that muck.

—Well, reading old gazettes won't help move things along, Solovyei said.

—Guess not, the Gramma Udgul said.

Solovyei came closer and tenderly stroked the base of her neck, as he might with a person he had shared his daily life with for years, in a time of elation and courage, and then lost for nearly a hundred years.

She looked up and smiled. Her gray eyes were covered with leukomas that had grown opaque over the iris, but in their center, they sparkled.

—Maybe if you started with the cylinders, Solovyei suggested. They're spoken words. Can't put a strain on your eyes. They're spoken words from my trances, when I walked into the fire or after I went through the doors of reality or death. I recorded them in the hereafter. Not so hard to organize.

—I've been listening to those old cylinders for a while, the Gramma Udgul shot back. They're unbelievable rantings uttered by a madman. I don't like them. They should all be thrown away. If the Party stumbled upon them, they'd put you right back in the camps or some place for schizophrenics.

—Yes, that's exactly right, Solovyei said.

—When I've heard them all, I'll put them with everything that has to get thrown into the core, the Gramma Udgul replied.

—Don't destroy those, Solovyei said. I spoke those words during my trances. It's never been translated into any earthly language. They're valuable accounts. Could be useful later.

—Who would they be useful for? the Gramma Udgul said.

—That depends on who's still on earth, Solovyei said.

—We didn't start a revolution to listen to these insane words, the Gramma Udgul said. Nobody's going to understand that. It's ideological sabotage and so on. I'll number them, your cylinders, but then they're going into the pit. The core can make whatever it wants of it.

—It might like them, Solovyei laughed. They were also composed for readers like it.

The Gramma Udgul angrily muttered something indiscernible. He takes everything as a joke, except for his daughters. I'll have to talk to the core about that one of these days.

—Well, I'll say this, if a committee stumbled upon this, you'd be good for fifteen or twenty more years of rigorous imprisonment. At least.

—You think? Solovyei said. Even with you as president, with all your medals and a team of easily swayed good little Komsomols?

—If I were president, you wouldn't escape a firing squad, the Gramma Udgul laughed lightly.

Then she began humming as he caressed the back of her head.

Their tenderness was palpable.

• They lay together in the hangar for several minutes. Barguzin hadn't appeared, they knew they were alone, and they weren't embarrassed to coo at each other.

The Gramma Udgul was in a good mood again. Under Solovyei's affectionate hand, she daydreamed once more about the joy of the waltz, the accordion, and the ideal worker who had turned her head at sunrise. Solovyei relaxed. The morning was just starting, the day was bright, the warehouse thrummed agreeably under the combined effect of the radiation and the sun's heat, and so Solovyei slipped into an almost unmoving dance with his old friend. The dance was magical, like all dances of love, but it didn't carry any real sexual freight, and he didn't feel any frustration in the least. He let himself fall little by little into romanticism and he went into an image instead of unleashing his body. Even though he had plenty of other experiences and even though he felt that he was in the prime of his years and far from the end of his hardy masculine life, he accepted this barely sexual relationship. He accepted it because it was actually very deep and very beautiful.

—What if we listened to one? he asked suddenly.

The Gramma Udgul came out of her reverie.

—One what? One cylinder?

—Well, what if we listened to one, just to see?

He was no longer hugging her and he went to open the cupboard where the Gramma Udgul had put away the phonograph.

The device had a spring mechanism. Solovyei set it on the pile of newspapers and cranked the handle until it stopped, and then he took a cylinder at random from one of the archive crates.

—Which one did you pick? the Gramma Udgul asked.

—I didn't look, Solovyei said, setting the black cylinder in the notches. I didn't pick. None of them have names or dates on them.

Just a voice bursting out in black space. It's as much in the present as the past. Or even the future. Listen to it with your gut, not your ears.

Then he pulled the arm and needle over the wax.

—Listen to yourself, the Gramma Udgul said. You're saying that it's both present and not present. How do you expect me to organize that?

The needle hissed for two seconds, then the voice was around them: bizarre, deformed, like it was actually from an intermediary world, barely comprehensible and unmoored.

• Then he became a shadow with the knife he had been hiding in front of his face, there was now just a shadow with the knife, a single shadow that was sometimes black, sometimes dark, and as his face glimmered subtly with the embers' every movement, he gathered together his throaty voices and imagined devotees around him and, focusing on the slim edge of the blade remnants of brav- ery, and thundering his sighs in his most haughtily low registers, in his ample but extraordinary registers, exhaling his terminal curse in deep waves, rolling off his tongue notes still far less audible than extinguished stars, and also thinking of his scattered daughters, and thinking of his daughters turned away from him, and thinking of his noble daughters lost, forever away from him and lost, and inventing haphazardly new ways of whispering that avenge, invent- ing whispers made with murderous words, with murderous phrases, and wrapping himself in the memory of his short existence and his short laughs and his dead and his daughters, and thinking about the futures his daughters had promised he would experience, and focusing on the point a remnant of a useless lie, because he never had the chance to speak articulately to his daughters at a distance nor to communicate intelligently with them at a distance, focusing that on the sharp iron, and trying not to be brought down by a sud- den insolent greed for the horizon nor by stupor, and thinking of his beloved daughters he never had the chance to pamper or protect or even quickly perceive, between two railings or two wars, between two black absences, and raising his head again to accompany the slow dance of his cutlass and the slow dance of its point, noiselessly raising his shadowy head, hiding once more the extinguished shadow, and thinking again of the catastrophic fate of his daughters he never was able to save from misfortune, and who, if they ever knew happiness, never shared a single crumb of it with him, and thinking of his daughters whose happiness he wasn't able to apprehend even by proxy, and groaning speeches of painful ignorance, dead waves of already-dead words, groaning calmly endless discussions already long since dulled, he searched haphazardly for an artery and he said: "Come!" Then, already in absolute tatters, he turned toward the image no less in tears that followed him, itself hidden behind sharp iron, and they exchanged glances, and as he wanted to pretend not to feel anything ominous and pretend not to know what to stammer now and how to end, he said again, but nobody nearby heard his indistinct wheeze: "Tomorrow or yesterday, no dying for any reason!" Then he spoke again a little of his daughters and expired.

• The needle moved onto the unrecorded wax and sputtered disagreeably before Solovyei stopped the mechanism. The Gramma Udgul pouted, but the kolkhoz director bore a triumphant look.

—Did you like that? he asked.

—It's too far from socialist realism for me, she sighed. It's just poetic, slightly perverse nonsense, petit-bourgeois fantasy. It's like a threatening riddle. None of it makes sense.

—There's nothing to understand, Solovyei replied.

The Gramma Udgul's face clouded over.

—There's no clear class line, she continued. The proletariat would hate that.

Solovyei was putting the cylinder back in its crate.

—Shall we listen to a little more? he suggested.

—Hmm, the Gramma Udgul said.

—Before you throw them to the core.

—Don't think I'm doing it because I want to, the Gramma Udgul said.

Their eyes drew level. Solovyei smiled while furrowing his eyebrows comically. He kept on making faces for a few seconds, until the Gramma Udgul relaxed.

—I'm just doing my work, she said.

—Go on, I'm playing another one, Solovyei said. Then I'm going back to the kolkhoz.

—Whatever you like, the Gramma Udgul sighed.

• He was masked in leather and copper, as often, and then he took off his terrible bird's head and, once the smoke subsided, he peeled away from the brick where the fire had forced him to stay for nearly a thousand years. Some mercury flowed noisily along his arms. He hunched toward those who were facing the reflections and, without clearing his voice, he spoke to the scribe who had died. "Go," he said. "Write what nobody else has told you over the centuries." As it fell, the mercury made a greater din than his own breath. The scribe didn't move. For a year or two, he had the impression that this writer at his service was a woman, then the impression went away. Then, he threatened the scribe with bits of burning wall and he continued, but, this time, while hurling words in encrypted language: "Go! Hadeff Kakain! Hoddîm!" And, as the scribe didn't write anything, he crushed the head under his heel and squatted by the remnants.

– 3 –

• The day had started. Kronauer regained consciousness and got to his feet. The rough fabric of his coat was stained with moist earth and bits of grass. Blades of lovuskhas, solivaines. A crushed budardian ear. Ants wandered over the fibrous scraps. Seven or eight.

The night had not given him back much strength and he lost his balance trying to clear the ants away. The empty bottles he carried over his shoulder bothered him. They clinked against each other. He stumbled for two meters before regaining some stability. He had trouble catching his breath.

In his skull were audibly stabbing pains.

The clouds tinged Prussian blue.

He was three hundred meters from the first trees, among the bluish budardians trembling gently against his legs.

Everything was blue, everything swayed.

His body needed food, water, more than anything. Despite moving his tongue and swallowing, there was little saliva behind his dried-out lips. He coughed. The cough aggravated the constricting and tearing sensations at the bottom of his throat.

He went a hundred more paces toward the nearby forest. Dizziness forced him to slow down. He stopped. He swore in Russian and Mongolian. Then German, for good measure.

—Hell's teeth, Kronauer, you sniveling wimp, what are you doing, staggering like a drunkard? . . . Walk toward the trees. Cross the forest and look for the village that was smoking yesterday afternoon. This isn't anything impossible. Get to this village. Beg for a bit of gruel and food from the rednecks. Fill your bottles. Then go back to the railroad. This isn't even a feat to accomplish.

A small morning breeze blew, a bit acrid, bearing the smell of herbs preparing for the end of summer and for death.

Barely risen, the sun had disappeared behind a barrier of clouds. The temperature in the air was autumnal. Birds chirruped somewhere in the stretches of degenerate buckwheat still separating Kronauer from the edge of the forest. A family of steppe songbirds that had survived, belonging no doubt to a species that was already nearly extinct. Kronauer listened to them for a minute, then they fell silent. They had detected a presence, they hid in the middle of the grasses, and they went quiet.

Five minutes later, he had crossed a ditch and entered the forest.

• The undergrowth wasn't bushy, there were barely any obstacles between the trees. Here and there a fallen larch, a stretch of black mud, but, overall, practically nothing. He quickly disappeared among the trunks. The light diminished; it took on brown and red hues on account of the dead needles covering the ground. He remembered the spot on the horizon where the smoke had been visible the previous day, and that was the direction he went in, toward this hypothetical village. Nothing else was in his head.

In the forest a heavy silence prevailed. Kronauer's footsteps. A muffled noise, crunches that did not echo. A few mushrooms. Chanterelles, puffballs, clouded agarics, cortinars.

As he steeled himself for hours and hours of humdrum walking, he saw, about a kilometer off to his left, a structure vaguely resembling an entrance to an underground tomb, and he approached. It was a fountain fed by a natural spring. The basin was protected by a stone arch. The water was scarce, just a few cupfuls at the bottom of a hollowed-out lava stream. It had scarcely any moss and looked clear.

At the bottom of the basin, an emerald-green fern had taken root and spread out its wavy fronds: unnerving, splendid.

On the other side of the structure, sitting on the ground, was a young girl who seemed to be dead.

Kronauer hunched over the water and at first he lapped it up, like an animal. The water was cold. He held back from taking too much and stood up again, then he succumbed to temptation and went back to drinking.

Then he tried to fill the two bottles he had carried the whole distance on a string hanging from his neck. He couldn't submerge them in the too-shallow basin. Nothing got through the bottle's neck. He struggled for three minutes, moving the bottles every which way, but to no avail. The water flowed in through a small crevice under which there was no way to position a receptacle. The water did spill out of the stone basin when it overflowed and subsequently made its way back, naturally, down into the earth, but right now the flow was too meager and the shallow basin was half empty. He hung the bottles back around his neck and drank once more by cupping the water in his palms.

• The tinkling song of drops falling in the basin.

The taste of the water. A faint scent of peat, of slightly peppery silica. An impression of transparency, of infinity. The feeling of being able to experience that, of not being dead yet.

The silence of the forest.

The hammering of a woodpecker determinedly pecking at bark, a few hundred meters from the fountain.

Then, once again, silence.

• Kronauer turned toward the girl leaning against the fountain and looked at her. She was short, with a head barely bigger than a child's and, indeed, she seemed to be barely out of adolescence. Judging by her unmoving eyelids, as well as her slightly disjointed pose, she had already left this world. Her clothes were tattered, with smudges of clay and tears. She was wearing pants and army boots, a military shirt that was unbuttoned at the top. Her chest was visible, as well as her left breast down to the nipple. Pearl-white skin, a dark areola that was nearly brown. It was a breast slightly larger than would have been suspected given her body's slim proportions. Kronauer reached out. He grabbed the collar and pulled the fabric a bit to hide this flesh that had unintentionally come into view. He felt a breath on his wrist. The girl was breathing. He had thought she was just a corpse, but she was breathing.

Her physiognomy betrayed a Siberian ancestry, the memory of forebears come from nowhere to wander as nomads through the gaps of the taiga, back to the midst of nowhere, but overall, and because of both her clothes and her pale complexion, she looked like a Chinese woman who had traveled through the twentieth century to take part in a new campaign against the right-wings. Jet-black braids framed her face, accentuating her adolescent age. They were half undone and dirty. As usual for this sort of face, it seemed to be both very ordinary and very beautiful. Her left cheek was streaked with dirt and mud. The girl had fallen or gone to sleep on the ground before leaning against the fountain and passing out. Whatever had happened before she had lost consciousness, she had kept, beyond exhaustion and pain, a sharp and sullen expression. Her jaw was still clenched, her eyebrows were still furrowed. She had to be a sturdy sort. She had wanted to fight to the end against internal collapse, against night.

She opened her eyes and, seeing a man facing her who looked in every way like a lawless escapee from the camps, brought her hand to her shirt collar, as if the first measure to take upon waking had to be to protect her neck from a stranger's gaze. Her fingers gripped the collar, slowly pulled tight her clothes, and then she lowered her arms in order to lie down on the earth. She folded up her legs and now she tried to stand up again. She didn't have the strength. She couldn't get up from the ground. A groan escaped her lips.

—Why are you looking at me? she asked, her voice cracking.

She was afraid. She was unable to stand upright, and, in this deserted place, a man towered over her without saying anything. How long had he been there? Dread shook her eyelashes and her lips.

—I come from the Red Star sovkhoz, Kronauer said.

He hadn't spoken since the previous day and the words came out with difficulty. He wanted to explain his own weariness as quickly as possible. So she would understand that she had nothing to fear from him.

—I have comrades there. A man and a woman. The woman is dying. They have nothing to drink. I tried to fill some bottles, but I can't. Is there a village a bit farther off?

The girl nodded confusedly and shut her eyes. She had dark brown eyes, a small mouth, which was very pale on her pale face. She held back another moan. She had to hurt somewhere, behind her forehead, in her body, and, in any case, she was very, very tired.

It wasn't clear what this movement of her head meant, assuming that it was some sort of reply.

• —I have to get to this village, Kronauer said again. It's a matter of life or death for my comrades.

—I don't believe you, said the girl.

She didn't open her eyes to talk. It seemed like she was talking while in sleep or in her death throes.

—Red Star is abandoned, she went on. It doesn't exist anymore. Everything's irradiated. Nobody lives there.

—Hang on, I didn't say I lived in the sovkhoz, Kronauer said. I didn't say that. We got there, all three of us, by following the railroad. We don't have anything to do with the sovkhoz.

He stopped to take a breath. He was standing over this exhausted woman, but he himself felt ill as well. Every now and then, the trees swayed, split, the verticals waved. He felt like he was going to fall into some kind of coma, like the night before right on the edge of the forest.

He closed his eyes for three, four seconds.

• A man. A woman. An accidental couple. Two vagrant figures, him in particular, with his bags hoisted over his shoulder, his bottles. A stone basin under a gray tile canopy. The dampness of the place. Its coolness. Drops that chimed from time to time while falling into the basin. The red ground. The trees nearby, the nearly black bark. The bare trunks, covered with long streaks of greenish slime on their northern sides. The subdued, slightly hazy light. A man who closes his eyes, his feet planted squarely but still shaky, fighting against dizziness. A woman who closes her eyes, leaning against the foot of the fountain. Two people breathing, the only perceptible sound for several seconds. During these several seconds, there is nothing else. The forest is silent. The breaths are noisy. Then the woodpecker from before resumes his interrogation. The hammering and its echoes fill the space around the fountain.

• Kronauer opened his eyes again. The larches kept tilting, but he forced himself not to pay attention.

—So there's a village past the trees? he asked.

—What? the young woman said, her eyes still shut.

—A village, past the trees. Is there one?

—Yes. A kolkhoz. The Levanidovo.

—Is it far? Kronauer asked.

The woman made a vague gesture. Her hand didn't indicate direction or distance.

—I need to go there, Kronauer said.

—It's not far, only you have to go through the old forest, the woman warned.

She paused, and then went on:

—Swamps, she said. Anthills as tall as houses. Fallen trees everywhere. Hanging moss. No trails.

Her eyes had just opened partway. Kronauer met her gaze: two brown stones, intelligent, mistrustful. Her eyelids were a bit slanted. In this face that exhaustion had turned ugly with bits of earth, framed by dirty hair, her eyes were where beauty was distilled.

She could sense Kronauer's interest in her, and, because she didn't want any special bond between the two of them, she quickly focused on a point behind him. An abrasion on a trunk.

—If you don't know the way, you'll get lost, she said.

—What about you? Do you know the way? Kronauer asked.

—Yes, she said quickly. I live there. My husband is a tractor driver in the kolkhoz.

—If you're going back to the village, we can go together, Kronauer said. That way I wouldn't get lost.

—I can't walk, she said. I'm not able to. I had a bout.

—A bout of what? Kronauer asked.

The woman didn't reply for a minute. Then she took a heavy breath.

—What about you? Who are you? she asked.

—I'm Kronauer. I was in the Red Army.

—From the Orbise?

—Yes. It collapsed. The fascists won. We tried to fight for as long as we could, but it's over.

—The Orbise fell?

—It did. Everybody knows about that. They had been closing in on us for years. We were the last holdouts. Now there's nothing left. It was a complete slaughter. Don't tell me you didn't hear about that here.

—We're isolated. There's no radio because of the radiation. We're cut off from the rest of the world.

—Still, said Kronauer. The end of the Orbise. The massacres. The end of our own. How is it you didn't hear about that?

—We live in another world, said the woman. The Levanidovo is another world.

• There was silence. The water Kronauer had swallowed gurgled in his stomach and, in the quietness that prevailed around them, he felt ashamed. He made himself talk to cover up the noise.

—You could be my guide, he said hurriedly.

The woman didn't reply. Kronauer had the feeling that his body would make more rumbling noises. To cover up the obscene hymn of his entrails, he spouted off several useless sentences.

—I don't want to get lost. You said there are swamps and no trails. I don't want to find myself all alone in there. With you, it won't be like that.

He said that with a great effort, and the woman quickly realized that he was hiding something. His words rang false. He was putting up a front. She was starting to be afraid of him again, as a male, as a rough-hewn soldier guided by bad intentions, who might be violent, who might have sordid sexual needs, who might murder sordidly.

—I can't walk, anyway, she reminded him.

—I could carry you on my back, Kronauer suggested.

—Don't try to hurt me, she warned. I'm the daughter of Solovyei, the president of the kolkhoz. If you hurt me, he will follow you. He will come into your dreams, behind your dreams, and into your death. Even when you're dead you won't escape him.

—Why would I hurt you? Kronauer protested.

—He has that power, the woman insisted. He has great powers. It will be horrible for you, and it will last for one thousand or two thousand years if he wants, or even longer. You will never, ever see the end.

Once again, Kronauer plunged quickly into her gaze. Her eyes showed indignation, anguished indignation. He shook his head, shocked that she might be afraid of him.

—Don't hurt me, she repeated sharply.

—I'm going to carry you on my back, that's all, Kronauer said. You'll show me the way and I'll carry you to the Levanidovo. That's all. There's no ill will here.

They stayed frozen for a minute, both of them, unsure what movement to make to begin the next episode.

—You wonder why you'd hurt me? Solovyei's daughter said. Well, there's really no point asking. All men try to hurt women. That's their specialty.

—Not mine, Kronauer said defensively.

—That's their reason for being on earth, said Solovyei's daughter philosophically. Whether they want to or not, that's what they do. They say it's natural. They can't restrain themselves. What's more, they call that love.

• Samiya Schmidt was the third daughter of Solovyei. She was born to an unknown mother.

Like her two older sisters, also born in the Levanidovo to unknown mothers, she had lived in the Radiant Terminus kolkhoz nearly her entire life. She had gone to primary school in the Levanidovo, where a Red Star sovkhoz cowherd whose cancerous masses hadn't yet become malignant had taken on the role of educator. Over the years, this woman had devoted the last of her strength to transmitting all that she knew to these three girls of the village: reading, arithmetic, the basics of Marxism-Leninism, historical materialism explained for simple souls, as well as useful principles of veterinary practice and animal hygiene, then, as had been fated but postponed due to physiological incongruities, she was turned into an uncommunicative sooty doll. Solovyei then called on his own magical powers to find someone who could replace her for the next school year.

By a pitch-black moonless night, he called up the fires of the nuclear heart of the small kolkhoz reactor, and he entered death through the fire, as he often did during his self-imposed exile at Radiant Terminus. Once he had gone beyond the fire, he had gone looking for a teacher. His needs were twofold: first, the teacher in question had to agree to work in the Levanidovo without any question about salary or risk premiums, and second, he had to teach the class without lecherously ogling the three students, nearly all of whom were already nubile. Rummaging through the ashes of dreams, he unearthed a former political captain who had become a cooperative worker, and then been shot for corruption. All too happy to leave the shadows where he had moped around, the man—named Julius Togböd—accepted the job and started working in the Levanidovo school, and he brought his students up to a reasonable educational level. But, after three semesters, he started to lecherously ogle Hannko, the oldest of the three girls, and Solovyei had to intervene.

Solovyei, as father of the students and as president of the kolkhoz, reproached him, then knocked him unconscious with a shovel, and then dragged him into the Gramma Udgul's warehouse to the well. Even though it wasn't a workday, the Gramma Udgul had no problem letting him unscrew the heavy cover. The schoolteacher ended his journey two kilometers deep and whether he lecherously ogled the nuclear core or not could only be guessed at. The Gramma Udgul didn't broach the topic in her conversations with the core, rightly considering it a private matter.

Following this disagreeable experience, the school still existed, but Solovyei's daughters were asked to work as autodidacts. They went there in the morning and studied together lazily and disorganizedly. They read heavily, because the House of the People library was well-furnished with agitprop pamphlets and the classics of economics and literature. All the important male and female novelists of the Orbise were there: Ellen Dawkes, Erdogan Mayayo, Maria Kwoll, Verena Nordstrand, and a full spread of others. The girls read those authors in preference to technical works. Their father, however, warned them against the nihilistic nonsense of the poets and the tragic uselessness of their fictions. In spite of such admonishments, they steeped themselves in the post-exotic masterpieces. They understood that Solovyei, who prided himself on writing, was expressing an opinion that an author's allure could overpower critical impartiality.

From time to time, an adult came to round out their incomplete education. He would tell them a story or share his experiences with them. The adults were rarely skilled at transmitting their knowledge; they had never learned how to teach, and they had never considered the question of adapting a curriculum for their small audience, but they took their job to heart. They did their best to explain how the world they had experienced worked. Some days, the Gramma Udgul taught the girls how to use the kolkhoz rifles and explained how to put together a firing squad, and other days, she described the liquidation campaigns she'd gone on, how the liquidators had died, her ongoing difficulties with the Party and her clashes with the medical commissions that had examined her in public to study the mechanisms of her immortality. The engineer Barguzin talked about electrical and nuclear installations, short circuits and angry atoms, and he also discussed his blackouts and his passages through death, as well as his reawakenings after being treated with heavy-heavy water, deathly-deathly water, and lively-lively water. He tried his hardest never to look his students in the face, out of fear that he might be accused of inappropriate conduct by Solovyei and end up prematurely at the bottom of the liquidation well. The one-armed man Abazayev came to gesticulate in front of the blackboard and recount once again the convoluted circumstances that had resulted in the loss of his right arm, a misfortune connected to his enlistment in the army that he sometimes wanted to link to a heroic act, sometimes to a surprise attack by capitalist henchmen, sometimes to hand-to-hand combat with a property manager, but according to Solovyei he had simply suffered from meningitis and poor medical care. When Abazayev was sufficiently enmeshed in discussing the reasons for his amputation, he changed the topic and gave directions for how to clean drainage canals, transport irradiated materials in carts, and smoke moles out of their burrows, three specialties he excelled at in the Levanidovo. The tractor driver Morgovian stepped in, as well. He didn't talk often, but he came in. As there were no longer any working tractors in the village, he focused on the kolkhoz beehives and henhouses. He sketched out diagrams of hives on the blackboard and copied in chalk the list of symptoms for avian flu. He also abstained from looking at the three students who, over the years, looked more and more like beautiful young women well worth courting or marrying.

Other improvised teachers sometimes showed up in front of the students. They were usually former members of the Gramma Udgul's liquidation team who hadn't survived the radiation, or kolkhozniks who had died in the forest or in the open fields, angry at being left unburied. They came into the classroom, knocked over chairs, and tried to talk, but the girls drove them out.

Solovyei personally never opened the schoolroom door to round out his daughters' education. He preferred to go into their dreams. Whether he chose to go through fire, to enter body and soul into this black space, or to fly forcefully through the shamanic skies, some nights, he ended up deep in their sleep and walked around without knocking. He had edifying conversations with them where he declaimed his own poems in a hissing voice, but mostly he took advantage of his visit to explore the nooks and crannies of their consciousness, their fantasies, their secret desires. He was obsessed by the ills men could inflict upon them and he watched them, feeling that they were too young to know how to defend themselves against their lovers' vileness. The girls respected Solovyei and did not deny him their love, but from the day they had their first periods, they began to hate this sort of intrusion, this imperious and unnatural penetration, and in the morning, silently or openly, they remembered that he had appeared within them, that he had disturbed their privacy, and that he had forced himself on them to explore the hidden secrets of their unconscious and their body in general. They remembered the trips he had wantonly taken within themselves. It was a memory that disgusted them and that they refused to consider trivial or furtive, that they were not willing to relegate to the numerous dream-sensations that waking cleared away. They could not forgive him for that. The next morning, if they saw their father on the way to school, they barely said hello to him, and they made it clear that they were sulking.

• Samiya Schmidt was now thirty-one years old. She had stopped going to school twelve years earlier. She hadn't left with a solid university education, but she had practical knowledge in nearly every realm of agricultural mechanics as well as theoretical knowledge about economics, the history of the camps, and occupational medicine, because, aside from Maria Kwoll's fictions, she had, for lack of anything better, devoured the popularized booklets from the House of the People library one after another. The kolkhoz president had awarded her a diploma with honors at the end of her studies, in case she needed one on the outside, but she stayed in the Levanidovo and married the tractor driver Morgovian.

Her marriage to Morgovian hadn't been a catastrophe, but nobody would say that it had made her happy. Morgovian was afraid of her and he behaved himself as a result. She struck an animalistic fear into him. Partly because she was the daughter of the kolkhoz president and also because she was an authoritarian sort with intellectual and emotional needs he couldn't understand. And finally, he was terrified by the bouts of insanity she sometimes had, during which she would run as fast as possible through their house and through the main road of the kolkhoz, scarcely touching down on the ground and whispering extraordinarily violent and strange curses. She came and went like this and then disappeared into the forest for days on end. Hardly had their short month on honeymoon gone by when the first of these bouts happened. Morgovian was paralyzed with horror and sadness. From then on he began to avoid her, spending as much time as possible collecting dead animals at the forest's edge or fixing the henhouse netting—or he claimed he needed to fight the Asian hornets so as to spend entire weeks camping by the hives.

Their union's disintegration pleased Solovyei, who had had trouble accepting it in principle, and who moreover played a major role in the mental disturbances Samiya Schmidt was subject to. Indeed, he kept paying her his nocturnal visits and walking supreme throughout her dreams, which caused serious disruptions and, in particular, the feeling of being possessed day and night by an outside will. Solovyei didn't worry about the damage that might result from his intrusive magical acts. On the contrary, he pressured her to start the process of getting divorced. He offered to simplify the formalities she would have to bring before the kolkhoz soviet. But she refused. Morgovian, despite it all, suited her. She appreciated his silence, and also his self-effacement as a man, his terrified lack of appetite around her. She had him as her husband, and she knew she would never have a better one. Besides, after reading Maria Kwoll and Sonia Velazquez, she was inclined to hate men, but this one didn't trouble her.

• Now, perched on Kronauer's back, held against him, Samiya Schmidt let herself be carried back to the village. Her arms were wrapped around his neck and her legs were folded around his hips. Kronauer somehow kept her upright. Sometimes he grabbed her ankles, sometimes he crossed his arms to hold her calves. Samiya Schmidt had been reticent at first about being in such close contact with this unknown man; she didn't want to be pressed up against him, intertwined with him at all. At the trip's start, she had stood up while refusing his help and, when they started walking, she tried to stay all the way upright. The first several hundred meters were an ordeal. She staggered and, so as not to fall, kept holding onto Kronauer. Then she fell down and he convinced her to drag herself behind him, on him.

For Kronauer, even though she was a small woman who barely weighed more than a child, she was a difficult burden to carry. Every step diminished somewhat the restorative effects of the fresh water, and fasting had weakened his body. He hadn't eaten for days. After a painful half-kilometer he lost his rhythm and began to stumble under the weight. He exhaled heavily. Drops of sweat ran down his forehead and from his armpits.

—Stop, Samiya Schmidt growled suddenly. We're not going far like this. We'll never get to the Levanidovo.

—You told me it wasn't far, Kronauer said stubbornly.

—We'll have to cross the old forest, Samiya Schmidt said.

He set her down on the ground. She shakily stood up by him, then she was overcome by nausea and went to lean against a larch to vomit. Kronauer watched her heave. He felt the sweat on his face building up and then falling in huge drops. He noticed a rocky outcrop and walked the five or six steps to sit on it.

I won't be able to get back up, he thought. I don't have any strength left. We're both going to die in the trees, this half-dead girl and me.

Samiya Schmidt spent a minute bent in half, then she pulled herself back up and went over, swaying, to Kronauer. She sat on the other end of the outcrop. They both had trouble catching their breath.

—It'll be easier later on, she said, clearly talking about herself. Have to wait for it to go away.

—What is it? Kronauer asked.

—It'll go away, she insisted with effort. But have to wait.

She was sitting three meters away from him. She turned toward him and looked furtively in his eyes. Within Kronauer's gray-blue irises, there was no trace of dishonor. He had touched her legs, her body had been thrashed around while her breasts had rubbed and pushed against his shoulder blades, he had panted while holding her against his body. But now he looked at her calmly, with brotherhood and sadness more than anything. He didn't seem like one of these men torn by sexual frenzy, ready to grunt, attack, and spray sperm over everything feminine within reach, like those men Maria Kwoll had described in her feminist writings. She had never met these sorts of men in the village, where all the inhabitants, except for Solovyei, constantly teetered between comas and inexpressible mental and physical exhaustion, but she knew that they existed and that they might appear time and time again, and not just in Maria Kwoll or Sonia Velazquez's incendiary writings. She knew all about the dirty tricks they were capable of. Maria Kwoll was graphic enough to describe them unflinchingly in her numerous ranting texts. This soldier seemed in no way to be a male in rut, but who knew.

The image of rape overwhelmed her.

—Don't you think for one second about hurting me, she said before she could help herself. The president of the kolkhoz isn't the sort to forgive that. I'm his daughter, remember that. He's not a little president of a nowhere kolkhoz. He'll be dogging you for at least a thousand eight hundred and thirteen lunar years and then some. I'd rather warn you before you think up anything nasty.

Kronauer shrugged. This girl was disturbed. If he had realized it earlier, he would have tried to get to the Levanidovo on his own without calling on her as a guide. So far, she hadn't been any help and, instead, she'd only made his trek harder and slower. What if I abandoned her? he thought to himself. Then he caught himself. Too late, Kronauer, like it or not you're responsible for this girl now. She's not all right in her head, but you've taken some responsibility for her, so stick with it. You haven't lost your morals entirely yet. And if you get up and leave without turning around to see if she follows you or not, how will you explain to the kolkhozniks that you left behind the daughter of their president lying on the ground?

—Tell me about your father, Kronauer said.

—I have nothing to tell you about my father, Samiya Schmidt shot back. The less you see of him, the better off you'll be.

The conversation ended on that note.

After having rested for about an hour, they set off again.

Kronauer felt like he had gained a bit of energy. He suggested that she climb once more onto his back and she accepted without saying a word.

- The old forest.

  Now the scene is darker.

  Not a bit of sky above their heads. Only black branches. Dark layers of black branches. A thick fabric, heavy and unmoving.

  Kronauer carrying Samiya Schmidt on his back.

  Strong smells.

  Resin, rotting peat mosses, decomposing trees, marsh gas. Stinking wafts from deep layers of the earth. Scents of bark, viscosities stagnating beneath the bark, mustiness of larvae. Mushrooms. Moist stumps. Monstrous accumulations of polypores, oxtongues, giant clavarias, branchy hedgehogs. Fetid tears on the edge of conks.

An intense silence that nothing shatters.

The irregular noise of Kronauer's footsteps, and that silence that immediately becomes unbroken.

Twigs snapping under his boots. Sometimes, under the grass and the ferns, the suctioning noise of mud. Then, once again, the silence that nothing disturbs.

Samiya Schmidt's breath on Kronauer's neck, behind his ear. Samiya Schmidt's panting in Kronauer's hair that reeks from his wanderings, the grease, the dust.

The bottles knocking, the bags, which every so often bang against Samiya Schmidt's calves, Kronauer's elbows.

The tangled, slanted trunks, most often arrayed in long cascades like witch grass. Mysterious blockades covered in mosses. Obstacles best skirted around, sometimes with a hundred meters' walk, rather than sinking to one's ankles in puddles of dark water, in clayey troughs.

The color of these mosses, an unvarying, nearly-black green. The disagreeable texture of this witch grass that has to be pushed aside with faces and shoulders.

At every moment, this cool and damp caress on your face.

At every moment, the feeling of something malevolent feeling its way toward you.

No bird, no small animal.

Here and there, giant anthills, without any apparent bustle but perhaps inhabited by black and teeming colonies.

Samiya Schmidt and Kronauer no longer speak.

The crossing is harder and harder.

The scene is darker and darker.

• The old forest isn't an earthly place like the others. Nothing comparable exists in other forest of similar size, nor in the taiga, which is boundless and where people die. Unless they take a horribly long and uncertain path, you can't reach the Levanidovo and its Radiant Terminus kolkhoz without crossing it. But crossing it also means wandering under its menacing trees, advancing without any landmarks, blindly, means walking with difficulty among its strange traps, beyond all duration, means going both straight ahead and in circles, as if poisoned, as if drugged, breathing with difficulty, as in a nightmare where you can hear your own snoring and moaning but where wakefulness never comes, means oppression without the least idea of where your fear comes from, means dreading noise every bit as much as silence, means losing reason and, finally, understanding neither noise nor silence. Being in the heart of the old forest also means sometimes no longer feeling exhaustion, floating between life and death, hanging between breathlessness and exhalation, between sleepiness and wakefulness, also means understanding that you are a strange inhabitant of your own body, not really at home, like a particularly unwelcome guest who has overstayed and who is accepted because expulsion is not possible, who is accepted until there comes a way to separate painfully, who is accepted while waiting for the opportunity to hunt or kill you.

The old forest is a place that belongs to Solovyei.

It is the entrance to Solovyei's worlds.

When you walk through the old forest, when you crush under your boots the twigs fallen from the trees, the centenarian pines, the black larches, when your face is stroked or slapped by dripping mosses, you end up in a transitional world, in something where everything exists intensely, where nothing is illusory, but, at the same time, you have the disturbing feeling of being imprisoned within an image, and moving around within someone else's dream, in a Bardo where you are a foreigner yourself, where you are an unwanted intruder, neither living nor dead, in an unending and endless dream.

Whether you realize it or not, you are in a realm where Solovyei is the absolute master. You may move in the shadows of the plants, you may try to move and to think in order to escape, but, in the old forest, you are first and foremost dreamed up by Solovyei.

And in there, quite simply, you cannot be anything other than a creature of Solovyei's.

• As confirmation: in the last kilometer, Kronauer entered some sort of hypnotic numbness. He stopped thinking. This mental abdication came with physical relief. He didn't feel his exhaustion. On his back, Samiya Schmidt didn't weigh more than a feather. He trod without stumbling over the marshy ground, he crossed the obstacles of rotten, tangled branches, he climbed over the barricades of old mossy trunks, and he came back down without losing his balance. He breathed in the gas that wafted from the standing water without fainting. With one hand, he pushed away the wet undergrowth that threatened to smack him. He didn't disturb the anthills taller than himself, he swerved past them without touching anything or angering or scaring their inhabitants. Besides, he didn't know whether beneath their crust of earth and needles numerous insects twisted and turned, or whether these constructions were vestiges of a lost civilization, because not a single creature was visible in the area. He advanced as if within a dream, without any real awareness of his body or that of Samiya Schmidt. He advanced in this way, and around him the morning stretched out, hardly bright and as if devoid of any future.

Suddenly, as they emerged into a clearing filled with ferns, a strong whistling began in front of them, from the place where the trees resumed, as if from the black tufts where the lowest branches hung. A sound that at first mainly resembled the cawing of a bird of prey, and which immediately transformed into a shrill, increasingly piercing note. This note did not tolerate any modulation. It only mounted in violence. It bore into Kronauer's eardrums.

He slid Samiya Schmidt onto the ground, or rather, he set her down as quickly as possible to cover his ears with his hands. He grimaced. He said or screamed something that was stolen away.

On every surface of the clearing the ferns trembled, as if they too were trying to struggle against a sound assaulting them. The sky was now just a leaden gray blanket stifling the earth. It only gave a dim light. Several dozen meters away from Kronauer, on the other side of the clearing, the forest had taken on the appearance of a gigantic mass, dark green, compactly alive and hostile. The trees shifted, their tops came together and back apart above the space. High or low, the branches had started to move in a frenzy. No wind, no storm was shaking them, but they shook. They swept the air around them. They seemed to have cast off their vegetal nature, to have become animalistic, to be obeying chaos and fury. Some of them began to whistle in turn.

Kronauer was certain the trees were watching him.

—What is that? he yelled as he turned toward Samiya Schmidt. What is that over there?

Samiya Schmidt had drawn back to the edge of the clearing. She leaned against a trunk before answering. She had a sullen expression on her face. Her eyes were obstinately focused on the tips of her boots, as if she didn't want to watch what was happening.

—It's nothing, she finally said. We're in one of Solovyei's dreams. He's not happy that you're with me.

Kronauer walked up to Samiya Schmidt and looked at her, aghast. He kept his ears covered and he found it necessary to talk loudly to make himself heard.

—He's not happy that I'm with you? he shouted.

Samiya Schmidt shrugged helplessly.

—That's my father. He doesn't want you to hurt me, she said.

Solovyei's unbearable whistling stretched out.

Kronauer crouched down, got back up. The pain ran from his head to his tailbone, along his spinal cord. The sharp note wreaked havoc in his skull. He tried to ease the pain by squatting, then, because that didn't change anything, he got back up. He looked like a demented gymnast in rags.

—It's nothing, Samiya Schmidt said. He'll stop.

—It's really horrible, Kronauer moaned.

—Yes, it's horrible, but he'll stop, Samiya Schmidt promised.

• They sat side by side on the warm ground, on some roots. They waited for the screaming to stop. Samiya Schmidt didn't cover her ears.

She seemed irritated, but not overly inconvenienced. She was still one of Solovyei's daughters, she must have a particular internal resistance, something borne through his genes. A sort of immunity against her father's aggressions, acoustic or oneiric or otherwise.

Ten minutes went by like this, then the whistling diminished, the trees stopped shaking and fidgeting with frightening aggressiveness, they stopped screaming, they stopped acting like a collective animal of unlikely dimensions. Kronauer had already uncovered his ears. In his head, in his backbone, the pain had gone immediately. But he still had the feeling that the branches were watching him menacingly, and soon the whistling was replaced by a voice that came from nowhere.

Then he took the mask in which his face lived, his face of a beggar-bird beneath the storm, of a tattered bird thirsty for thunder, declaimed someone with authoritative, cruel solemnity.

It was a voice that seemed transformed by wax, fire, sputtering, and which also carried echoes, as if before coming into daylight it had to go through tunnels or black pipes. It was shivering hideously and still hideously distinct, and in reality it neglected the obstacle of the eardrum to strike more deeply, in the barely protected layers of the brain, beneath memories, there where unease, animal fury, and ancestral fears hid, still unformulated.

—And that, what is that? Kronauer asked again.

—Those are my father's poems, Samiya Schmidt said, barely disguising her annoyance. He'll declaim one or two, and then he'll . . .

She paused. The verb she was about to use had sexual connotations, which deeply revolted her.

—He'll what? Kronauer asked.

—He'll pull out, Samiya Schmidt finished tonelessly. Then it'll be over. He'll pull out from us and it'll be over.

• He put on the hardened skin of this mask that stank of black oil and the remains of the fire and, as the flashes fell slowly on the turf and the ashes around him, he began to beg for thunder,

and, as no noise went to the trouble of rattling the space, he bent
down in a pose of feigned humility and he rummaged for an hour or
two among the leaves and the earth wet with brackish water and
wine from casks, he stirred the humus with its sprouts scorched
by the violent electricity, and, when he had rummaged the deep
earth and its mucus like carcasses for a long while, he got back
up and opened his eyes again, at least the ones he had shut to
suggest non-impudence. Nothing had changed, except perhaps
the walls of the space had closed in. As before, the darkness was
stricken by lightning, but this sort illuminated the countryside less
and less. He kept on begging in the silence. He moved around,
counting his steps by fours or thousand-and-thirty-fives depending
on his mood, which was foul. What he saw only aroused useless
anger, which he hid as best as he could or which he managed to
soften by imagining that he had been split in two and his double
was walking somewhere else, with his daughters or his occasional
wives, his war wives, or his taiga lovers. Sometimes he beat his
wings, but the shadows were too deep for anyone to notice, and,
besides, he had reached a chasm where his loneliness no longer
had any witnesses. At one moment, he began to think more about
his daughters. He called to them instead of speaking to the thunder.
Neither his daughters nor the thunder answered him. In the end he
stretched out in the mire, sighed horrible curses through the holes
of his mask, and disappeared.

• As brutally as it had invaded Kronauer's soul and the clearing, the
voice stopped resonating. Suddenly the forest regained its banal character. Despite its perennial darkness and thickness, it no longer seemed
fantastical in any way, magical in any way, terrifying in any way. The
trees were no longer capable of sight or sound. Solovyei had left the
scene.

Kronauer let out a sigh. Even if this declamation hadn't been accompanied with pain, he had received it like a vile incursion. The

fundamentally hermetic content of his discourse hadn't touched or unnerved him, even though he had sensed, beneath the sentences, ahead of them, a malevolent thought, a selfish and lawless cruelty. But the way of conveying this discourse had repulsed him. He had clearly felt someone creeping inside him, settling in and sauntering around his cranial vault without the least respect for his privacy. It was both psychical and physical. He was talking to him and violating him. He who was speaking the poem had raped him and then pulled out. Kronauer hadn't known how to defend himself against this outrage, how to stop this aggression, and now he felt wretched. His passiveness had upset him terribly, and somehow he felt both guilty and dirty.

—There, said Samiya Schmidt. It's over. For now, it's over.

She was now leaning at the base of a larch, and there, her head thrown back, she shut her eyes to talk in a fading voice.

Kronauer made sure she wasn't watching him through her eyelashes and he turned away. He would rather that she didn't see his shame. He still felt like he had endured an assault.

—Does he do that often? he asked.

—Do what? Samiya Schmidt whispered.

Kronauer shrugged.

They both remained silent, as if trying to just be quiet and forget.

—He does that when he feels like it, Samiya Schmidt finally said. He comes and goes when he feels like it.

They mulled over the thought for several minutes, still not moving, and then Kronauer helped Samiya Schmidt get back up and they began to walk, leaning against each other. Samiya Schmidt said that she could make the last two kilometers on her own. She had to stop often. She leaned on a tree for support, caught her breath, waited until her heart started up again or regained a normal rhythm. Kronauer stopped, went over to her, stood ready to help if she fainted. He used these stops to restore some of his energy, as well.

Then the forest brightened. Behind the trees there was sky. They walked five hundred more meters to the east. The trees were airy, the

ground springy and neat. Kronauer noticed the clumps of dwarf row-
ans, raspberry bushes, Siberian foxgloves, and then they came out of
the forest and went down the tar path toward the Levanidovo and the
Radiant Terminus kolkhoz.

A man was busy a bit farther down in a ditch. Samiya Schmidt
stammered something along the lines of how that was her father, and
then she was quiet.

— 4 —

• Two hundred meters from the first house of the village, the president of the kolkhoz was hunkered down in a ditch, gathering mushrooms. He had cut the lower part of a nicely sized penny cap and, without turning toward the two shadows that had left the forest and were drawing near, he examined the cap which was a beautiful gleaming brown and he inhaled the scent, his eyes half-closed, tilting his head approvingly. The scent ought to be wonderful, as all the produce saturated with radionuclides was, but his contented sigh was overdone and rang false. He actually didn't care about his harvest, and indeed only cared about one thing: watching his daughter Samiya Schmidt's reappearance. She had been gone for forty-eight hours, and here she was, back and in the arms of a stranger, a soldier in a military jacket that was far too warm for the weather, its pockets torn and dangling, and with bottles jangling from his hips and, on his shoulder, two army bags filthy with dirt and blood. A deserter.

As Kronauer and Samiya Schmidt drew near, Solovyei stuffed the mushroom into a plastic bag and got up. He kept his countryman's knife in his hand and, rather than sheathe it, he pointed it vaguely in Kronauer's direction.

He was a tall man, bearded, scrubby, with an irascible, heroic face. His hair and his beard were still black, as if he were still in his forties or fifties, but he was about the same age as the Gramma Udgul. He towered a full head over Kronauer and, in size, the two men weren't comparable. With his fairground wrestler's chest and shoulders, his torso with bulging abs, the kolkhoz president gave an impression of invincibility. His irises, which were tawny and coppery, impinged upon the space reserved for the white of the eye—an oddity often seen among predators and equally often among thaumaturgists. It wasn't possible to meet such a gaze without straining not to drown in it, and it was easier to look away, but the result was a feeling of smallness and defeat. This Solovyei was clad in a white collarless shirt, cinched at the waist by a leather belt on which he had slung an ax. His thick canvas pants puffed where they were tucked into massive black leather boots. In short, he seemed to have come out of a Tolstoy novella describing a scene between muzhiks and kulaks in a prehistoric era, before the earliest collective farms.

• The road descended behind Solovyei and, after half a kilometer, it became the main thoroughfare of the village of the Levanidovo. The kolkhoz buildings and the farms were interconnected by dirt roads and, although they were spread out over a considerable space, there was a center of sorts, with houses facing each other in rows. It was easy to tell at a glance which ones were falling apart and which ones still harbored living villagers, or at least villagers able to sweep in front of their door once a week. There were several sorts of buildings there, one or two small apartments with one or two stories, wood houses surrounded by fences, wobbly shacks, and, right in the center of the Levanidovo, an impressive structure with a façade weighed down with four concrete columns, all of them Ionic and absurd. It had once housed the Soviet. On the pediment was mounted a flagstaff that held bits and pieces of the red flag. The main road continued toward a hill overlooked by a vast hangar. Surrounded by foliage, fields, and forests, the Levanidovo had every appearance of a tranquil and self-sufficient hamlet, isolated from the capital's directives, from imperialistic offensives, and from the revivals of civil war.

Kronauer panted, exhausted, and as he fought not to pass out, he tried to face the kolkhoz president, whose hostility was evident. Solovyei was firmly planted in front of him, not saying anything, he seemed uninterested in his daughter and he still hadn't put away his knife. Kronauer wasn't able to meet his gaze for more than a second, and he felt ashamed. As he paused, he turned toward the relatively pleasant image of the village, then he summoned his strength again and looked up at Solovyei. Keep your chin up, Kronauer, this one looks sort of like a kulak, he's got hypnotic eyes, so what? He's nothing but an ungracious giant. He has no reason to pick a fight over his daughter. You did what you had to do, you carried her, you brought her to the Levanidovo. Whether you seem nice or not, he's the local authority, and he can't abandon travelers in distress. That's what matters. That's the real question for him.

Kronauer had a vision of his comrades lying in the grasses close to the Red Star sovkhoz, and, dispensing with the usual formalities, and without taking the trouble to greet his interlocutor or wait for him to welcome him, he got right to the point.

—I left behind a man and a woman. Not far from the railroad tracks, by a sovkhoz. They haven't had anything to drink or eat for days. We need your help. They need water, food. It's urgent.

Without a word to her father or him, Samiya Schmidt picked that moment to leave. Kronauer immediately felt resentful. She could have helped, told Solovyei about their difficult trek, mentioned Kronauer's devotion, and eased the relationship between the two men. But she was already leaving. She was already walking unsteadily toward the center of the village. From behind, with her badly woven braids, her paramilitary clothes, and her lazy pace, she resembled a young woman of letters from the Chinese cultural revolution, going back to her farm unit and still somewhat out of shape after five or six years of contact with harsh rural life.

Solovyei frowned. He sheathed his knife behind his back.

—I haven't, either, I haven't eaten anything for a week, Kronauer said.

—Tell me, soldier, Solovyei suddenly asked, are you alive?

—Of course, said Kronauer.

—Then what are you complaining about? Solovyei asked. Being alive isn't something everyone in the world gets.

They were now talking without looking at each other, like two people who hate each other but who, in waiting for darkness to come and witnesses to go, had decided not to tear each other apart yet.

• Solovyei looked at his daughter who was turning onto the main road. She wasn't going straight, her pace was slow. She looked groggy.

—Samiya Schmidt looks groggy, Solovyei said.

—She's sick, Kronauer said.

—Oh, you're a doctor? Solovyei said sharply, furrowing his brow. I didn't know that.

Kronauer shrugged and took a step back to keep his balance. This conversation was draining the last of his strength. Behind his eyes, the earth's rotation seemed to be more and more perceptible. Glimmering stars whirled in his head. He knew he was going to lose consciousness.

—If you've hurt Samiya Schmidt in any way, Solovyei warned, I wouldn't keep up any hopes for your bones.

Kronauer wanted to object. He looked up toward the president of the kolkhoz. Solovyei towered, backed by the sky; he seemed surrounded by blinding light. Stars of exhaustion burst like bubbles around Kronauer's consciousness; they spattered against the images his retinas received, they flew around Solovyei's hair. Without stopping on any particular spot, Kronauer saw Solovyei's silhouette tilt forward, come closer, stretch out, sway. Solovyei was enormous and now he took up most of the visible universe. He seemed to be floating colossally on clouds and meteors. From time to time, he set his hand on his ax, as if he was trying to decide exactly when to take it out of his belt to split the skull of the soldier still in front of him. And every so often he opened his mouth to say words that Kronauer couldn't hear anymore. His teeth could be seen and, instead of a tongue, there seemed to be flames.

Then the image resolved. The flames swallowed him up, diminished, they began to come back together in his center. Quickly, everything that had been outside them turned black and shadowy.

Only this deep vermilion smudge was still visible, and emptiness gaped all around.

That remained for five or six seconds.

Then the black increased, the red diminished, and there was nothing else.

• Later, hours later, Kronauer comes out of his blackout. First he sees a ceiling that has recently been whitewashed, a perfect ceiling, without any cracks or spiderwebs. The room he finds himself in is painted white. The door, the walls, the frame of the double window, all are bright snow or ivory. Under such an onslaught of whiteness, Kronauer has trouble opening his eyes. His retinas hurt as they try to adapt to daylight.

He has been set on a mattress with his clothes still on. As he gets up on his elbow to look around, he is suddenly hit with the full stench of the rags stuck to his skin. The smell of lost wars, of nights spent on damp earth, and atop all that the acridity of grime diluted a hundredfold by sweat and thickened again a hundredfold. His muddy boots haven't been taken off and he is there, ridiculous and fetid in this monastic room.

He turns, sets his feet on the ground, and stands while holding onto the head of the bed. The room quickly tilts to one side, and then the other. Beneath his legs, the pinewood floor shifts. He sits back down heavily, then he curses his weakness.

You're already reeking like a boar, how long are you going to sit around acting like a weakling? Don't tell me you've having another one of your girly faints! Go up to the window and open it, Kronauer! So at least a little of your stench gets out of the room!

He gets back up and he walks toward the double window. Through the glass he can see the Soviet's colonnade, several wood façades, the gray-blue sky above the main road of the Levanidovo. The ground slides beneath him, the floor splits. He moves his hand toward the handle of the window latch. He begins fighting with the mechanism without any success. Something is holding it in place. He hunches over the latch, he sees that he needs a square key to unlock it. The outer window doesn't have a handle, and what he had originally thought was a tulle veil is actually a mesh screen. Did they put me in a prison or what? he wonders.

The room swims. Aside from the bed and a chair, it is empty.

He stumbles and catches himself on the wall. His mind floods with unanswered questions.

What is this, a cell? How long have I been here? What're they accusing me of? Is this a kolkhoz or a penal colony?

• —Ah, he's awake now, a feminine voice said in the next room.

A minute later, two women inserted a key in the lock and came into the room, each of them causing the floor's tiles to creak. They were both about the same height and, in the doorframe, they seemed at first like two kolkhozniks from long ago, dressed for the fall, with long brown wool skirts and, under their half-buttoned vests, high-necked blouses embroidered with patterns of birds and flowers on one, and spirals of forget-me-nots and daisies on the other. Neither of them wore jewelry. Kronauer immediately noticed their beauty, but he was so weak that his thoughts were hazy, distant, and wholly disconnected from any erotic sentiment.

They were without a question taller than their little sister, and also more feminine. Next to them, Samiya Schmidt would have looked childish. Although they all had Solovyei as a father, since their mothers were completely different and unknown, they barely resembled each other. They still shared something owing to their father's attraction to Siberian women, whether from central Asia or the Far East. Their mothers had given them their own grace, cheekbones, beautiful curling eyebrows, and the eyelids they had lowered the night and the moment Solovyei had seduced or raped them. Samiya Schmidt had the physiognomy of a sweet but withdrawn Chinese girl, a light complexion, fairly typical Han traits, but the fact remained that Kronauer had met her on an unfavorable day, in poor lighting, in the forest's shadows, such that he'd mistaken her for a corpse at first. The second daughter, Myriam Umarik, had deeply Altaic features, fleshy cheekbones, narrow eyes, a mouth with thick lips, a large and deliciously oval face. Her skin had a leathery complexion like a Native American, nearly orange in the room's white light. Her physiological proximity to Samiya Schmidt was practically nil, and certainly nobody would have mistaken her for someone Chinese. Just as Samiya Schmidt seemed mistrustful, timid, even inhibited, so Myriam Umarik seemed resplendent, with long flowing chestnut hair that came down to her chest, and even if she kept her back straight while walking, she had a sensual way of moving her legs, her hips. Her eyes shone. She knew that her movements could bother men, especially Kronauer, but she wasn't embarrassed at all.

As for Hannko Vogulian, the oldest daughter, she bore characteristics that, without being physical flaws, caused people to step back at a first glance. Her eyes had no white at all and were very dissimilar. The left one had the same red-blooded, rapacious color as her father Solovyei's irises; the right one was a large piece of obsidian in the middle of which no pupil could be seen. This gave her the appearance of a strange mutant. That aside, the rest of her body had a great Asiatic perfection. Her face was lighter than Myriam Umarik's, with smaller eyelids, a narrower mouth, eyes that were slightly angled toward the top of her temples. She had an elegant posture and the olive skin of a Yakut princess, and she was clearly proud and reticent, but perhaps that was because she knew the impression her strange pupils would have on Kronauer, and because she preferred to make it clear immediately that she didn't care about his opinions. In short, if Myriam Umarik didn't care about looking alluring, Hannko Vogulian didn't care about looking like a fantastical creature. She had pulled her long black hair behind her shoulders and separated it to make a thin braid that went around her head like an iron diadem.

• The two women walked toward Kronauer. He was still leaning against the wall by the window. He struggled not to completely fall apart as he wondered whether these two splendid countrywomen were jailers or not. Have they come to free me or what? he wondered. It was only to express his shame that he finally spoke.

—Don't come closer, he said wretchedly. I'm dirty and I don't smell good. I've been traveling for weeks without washing.

They stopped four or five steps away from him.

—Oh, you didn't have to bother telling us, Myriam Umarik said. We're the ones who picked you up and dragged you over here yesterday afternoon.

She seemed to be swaying. Under her dress, her breasts shifted. She smiled wryly.

If Kronauer hadn't been so weak, he would have blushed. The blood tried to fill his cheeks.

—I'd really like to take a shower or wash myself somewhere, he said.

—We'll show you how to get to the shower room, Myriam Umarik said.

—Good, Kronauer said. Because I really don't smell good.

—Don't worry, soldier, Hannko Vogulian said. We're not delicate. We're in a kolkhoz here. The smells of cows don't scare us. When we have to take care of animals, we just deal with it.

She still had an expressionless gaze and she looked at Kronauer with her two different eyes that had no white, the one gold and the other black. Kronauer looked away. He wasn't used to her gaze and he couldn't decide if it was attractive, magnificent, or monstrous.

—That's right, yes, we're not delicate, Myriam Umarik repeated.

—They told me that after nuclear accidents the cows couldn't reproduce anymore. So they disappeared fast. But you, you still have animals?

—Well, we don't have as many herds as before, Hannko Vogulian said. But when we have to take care of a cow or a sheep, we just do.

—Or a pig, Myriam Umarik added, swaying her buttocks.

—Don't worry, solider, Hannko Vogulian said.

Neither of them seemed to feel pity for him. Without giving him any time to ponder the consequences of radioactivity on the ovine, bovine, equine, porcine, avian, or human, or generally surviving populations of the area, they invited Kronauer to go wash up. As he wavered and was not able to let go of the wall he was leaning against, Myriam Umarik went over to him, grabbed him by the sleeve, and pushed him ahead of her. She didn't help him to walk, she didn't hold his arms or his shoulders to help him balance, but she guided him. In any case, even if she stepped aside to get out of his way when he staggered, she didn't evince any great disgust at his smell.

—Go on, soldier, she said a couple of times. It's at the end of the hallway. You're not sick. It's nothing but a little exhaustion.

Sometimes Kronauer held out his arms to lean against the hallway wall. His knees were weak. Hannko Vogulian was two steps ahead of him, he felt like she was too close and if he stumbled and staggered forward, he would drag her down as he fell.

They brought him to the washroom, which was behind an iron door. They opened it and stepped aside to let him through. From where they were standing, still in the hallway, they pointed out a basket with a thick terry-cloth towel and clothes for him to change into. There was also a huge zinc basin where they told him he could wash his rags later. Finally they told him that after the shower he could sit down for a snack, a light meal, Hannko Vogulian said, nothing to give him a stomachache, Myriam Umarik clarified, so you can recuperate physically before you start eating properly.

Kronauer could feel their unwelcoming eyes on him. He avoided looking up at them. He was afraid more than anything of fainting again, he didn't want them to have to lean over his inert and smelly body once more. The scenery drifted around him, the iron door that resembled a boiler-room door, black and heavy, the high tiled walls, the cement floor, the strong lights all turned on. He was now by a small table and a wood bench that had a bar of soap, a brush, and the basket with perfectly folded clothes.

He walked past the zinc basin, then took off his coat and set it on the ground. The room seemed overwhelming and large. Along the bottom, the wall was covered with green porcelain, which was the only decoration here; the rest of the room was completely white. Large mold stains covered the ceiling. Eight shower heads came out of the wall on the left, with drains painted red below. They were spaced widely enough to allow each user to wash without bothering either neighbor, but there was no divider between any of them.

Myriam Umarik watched Kronauer's curious eyes.

—These were the prison showers, she explained. There were once prisoners here.

Suddenly the girls became talkative. They wanted to talk with Kronauer before his shower, whether to update him on the kolkhoz's business, or maybe tease him, or in any case indicate his unimportance compared to them.

—After a rekulakization attempt, Hannko Vogulian said, long ago. We hadn't been born yet. It was before the kolkhoz was renamed Radiant Terminus. If the Organs hadn't gotten involved, it would definitely have been the return of capitalism and all the muck that goes with that. This was used for two or three years as a reeducation center. Then Solovyei became president and it was all shut down.

Myriam Umarik went on.

—During the accident, it was reopened, she said. We needed a place to pile up the irradiated things while waiting for the Gramma Udgul's warehouse to become operational.

—We found so much useless irradiated stuff on every corner, Hannko Vogulian added. We had to store it all somewhere.

The two daughters' chattering echoed through the room. They made Kronauer dizzy; he didn't need this avalanche of words to give him trouble.

—We keep calling this the prison, Myriam Umarik said as she swayed her hips, but nowadays we use it more as a community house. Nobody's really living here. Sometimes Solovyei comes here to take a shower, when the one in the Soviet is clogged.

Kronauer finally had a pause in conversation to ask something he needed to know.

—What about me, am I a prisoner? he asked.

—A prisoner, no, but you're under Solovyei's watch, Myriam Umarik said.

—What does that mean, under his watch?

—Oh, it doesn't really mean much at all, Hannko Vogulian said. He just holds power of life or death over you, nothing more.

Myriam Umarik held up an arm and leaned against the doorframe. The gesture stretched her blouse and accentuated her large bosom.

—You're under his watch, solider, she said. You're not in prison.

—The window in your room doesn't open. The door locks.

—Be careful, the water gets boiling hot sometimes, Hannko Vogulian said. You have to turn the cold water knob all the way. If there's one thing we don't need more of in this kolkhoz, it's hot water.

—Because of the core, Myriam Umarik explained.

• After the women shut the door behind them, Kronauer undressed and got under the pipes. He decided to stand under the fifth shower, in the middle of the room. He took Hannko Vogulian's advice, turning the cold-water knob all the way, and the water, although it was very warm, didn't scald him. It smelled strongly of gravel, with an aftertaste of something that had to be iodine or cesium.

Kronauer's short hair and his skull seemed coated with a sort of grease he wasn't able to completely get rid of. His chest and limbs were filthy. The lower part of his stomach reluctantly shed some sort of excremental suet that had become embedded. As he scrubbed energetically, he felt hair being rubbed away by his hands, by the water. Becoming bald and hairless were the same to him. He knew that this was the minimum price to pay for staying in forbidden nuclear zones and for not having avoided numerous nuclear power plants in decay, the very last ones being the one at the Red Star sovkhoz, and this one in the Levanidovo.

The animal stink still hung around him in spite of what seemed to have been a meticulous scouring. This self-loathing weighed him down retroactively. He thought of the women who had been around him after he had fainted: Myriam Umarik, Hannko Vogulian. They must have felt some revulsion when they handled him and lay him down in the cell. He also thought of those who, earlier, must have had to press their head against him: first, Vassilissa Marachvili during their wandering on the steppes, and then Samiya Schmidt while they had crossed the forest together. When she dangled on his back as if she were dying.

He soaped himself up once more and rinsed again, and, when the water flowing toward the drain looked merely frothy and not grayish, he stood under the pounding rain for a while longer. He felt revived. The water, the steam, the soap all had given him new strength. And doubtless also the iodine and plutonium that dropped above, as in the byliny about the deathly-deathly water and the lively-lively water that the enchantresses poured over the dead to bring them out of their fatal sleep.

Then he shut off the water and he went to dry himself by the bench. On the floor, his coat and his rags formed an appalling heap. He pushed them aside without touching them, using the edge of the zinc basin, and he moved away as quickly as possible. Then he got dressed. He put on the underclothes that Samiya Schmidt had taken from the wardrobe of her husband, the tractor driver Morgovian, and then he put on one of the engineer Barguzin's shirts. The new pants and new boots had been taken from the Gramma Udgul's dump. There was certainly enough there to set an ionizing-ray detector into a frenzy. Kronauer had no way of knowing it, but even if he had been told that he was introducing into his tissues something that would assuredly put him into a coffin straightaway, he would have retorted, no, not at all, and on the contrary, the radiation's always been keeping me nicely in shape. He might have added that the dangers of escaped atoms were largely exaggerated by enemy propaganda, and what mattered to him at this moment was that his feet fit properly in these new shoes.

And that he felt comfortable in his new shirt. But he did feel comfortable. These women had good eyes. Everything fit him exactly.

• Three women. The only three women in the village, not counting the Gramma Udgul.

Three sisters.

Three daughters who had Solovyei as their presumed father, born as has already been said to unknown mothers.

Samiya Schmidt, the youngest daughter, married to the tractor driver Morgovian.

Myriam Umarik, the middle daughter, married to the engineer Barguzin.

Hannko Vogulian, the oldest daughter of the three, presumably widowed, married to the wandering musician Schulhoff, a runaway deportee who hadn't spent more than a week in the Levanidovo, and then had disappeared, fortunately without impregnating her.

• Hannko Vogulian had only experienced three days of marriage, after she and Schulhoff had fallen in love at first sight and immediately united in passionate love.

Aldolay Schulhoff had appeared one Monday in the village and, that Thursday, in the marriage register dusted off for the occasion, the two young lovers signed their commitment to live together, no matter what happened, until their death. Solovyei, as president of the kolkhoz, had to affix his signature to the bottom of the page, but it was after trying for the previous forty-eight hours to dissuade his daughter and, in short, he violently disagreed. He had threatened to oppose this union in every way possible, but this one was properly sealed by an official act, and, once the register was set back in the right cabinet, he had to understand and accept that he had a new son-in-law. However, the marriage only lasted until the next Sunday, the day when the search to find Schulhoff hadn't turned up anything. From Saturday night, in fact, Schulhoff had disappeared without leaving behind any explanation or trace. Hannko Vogulian had insisted on organizing a search as well as using the loudspeakers along the main street, so that the calls would cut through all the nearby countryside, and all the Levanidovo waited nervously through Sunday night, but Schulhoff didn't reappear. He had somehow ceased to exist in the village, and, in Hannko Vogulian's life, at least her unimagined life, he was no more.

Solovyei spared no pain as the brigade leader of the hunt, but he couldn't be bothered to seem sad for his daughter's sudden widowing. He declared that the page of Hannko Vogulian's marriage had been turned and then, whenever there was a question about Schulhoff's disappearance, when someone brought up this mystery again, he looked up at the sky and claimed not to have anything special to say, even though several kolkhozniks and his own daughters suspected him of having played a decisive role in the whole matter.

Despite the shortness of his stay in the Radiant Terminus kolkhoz, Schulhoff had left behind a lasting memory, and not just in Hannko Vogulian's thoughts.

He was an itinerant singer, with a beautiful presence, dark-haired, with a splendid voice he had trained since childhood, which allowed him to slip instantaneously from the deepest sounds to the inhuman harmonics of throat singing. He had mastered several languages: Beltir, Koybal, Kyzyl, Kacha, Old American, Camp Russian, Olcha, Khalkha, and, depending on his audience, he chose one dialect or another, adapting his stories so that his listeners could find heroes familiar to their sensibility and their culture. He carried books in his bag and everything suggested that he was full of gentleness, intelligence, and sensitivity. It hadn't taken Hannko Vogulian more than a minute to fall under his spell and decide that he would be the man of her life. She had always been a prudent girl, but in this instant she succumbed to her impulses and instincts without the least compunction and, from the first night, she went to be with him at the Pioneers' House where he was staying and she devoted herself to him. She offered herself up to Aldolay Schulhoff. And he, who had been seduced by her and could never run out of rhapsodies or adjectives for her eyes of different colors, had happily fallen into this sudden passion. Maybe he was tired of wandering endlessly from one end of the land to the other, but he immediately saw himself settling down for good in Radiant Terminus. Among the sweet nothings they whispered those few nights, there had been promises and the immediate prospect of a proper marriage. Despite Solovyei's ill will, they made it happen three days later in the Soviet Assembly Room with the one-armed Abazayev, Myriam Umarik, and Samiya Schmidt as witnesses.

Saturday evening, in homage to the kolkhozniks who had welcomed him into the fold, he brought out his rhapsodist's instruments and sang the long and famous bylina that described, in poetic prose and in music, Ilya Muromets and Nightingale the Robber. In reality, he was performing a Buryat legend, but, as his audience was predominantly oriented toward the Russian collective memory, he reshaped it with great skill to emphasize the universal elements of Ilya Muromets's heroic saga.

Everyone in the Levanidovo thought his adaptation was original and his interpretation worthy of admiration. While his voice wasn't that of a bass singer and seemed thinner, he managed to make vibrant, sustained, and deep notes soar from his chest, notes that immediately entranced his listeners, and then he unfurled a melodic, tranquil narrative without a single pause, and his voice changed throughout the dialogues, shifting instantaneously from the metallic tones of harmonic singing to the feminine softness of the lyric text, then to the rumbling of pure song. Tears rolled down the cheeks of Solovyei's three daughters, who were not used to emotion provoked by song and a zither's melody, by the flowery language of the epic narrative. The demobilized Abazayev was also overwhelmed by the music and spent his time wiping his cheeks with the empty sleeve of his jacket, stained with mole poison. The engineer Barguzin couldn't bear the tension of this much beauty. He died once again that night. The Gramma Udgul had to administer her shock therapy with heavy-heavy water, deathly-deathly water, and lively-lively water. Solovyei, who had originally declared that he wouldn't attend the concert, changed his mind and came into the assembly room dressed in a midnight-blue shirt and perfectly waxed boots that he only wore on special occasions. He sat solemnly across from his new son-in-law and he seemed to enjoy the performance from its start to its finish. He clapped in rhythm on his massive thigh with happiness evident on his face, even though the previous night he had been angrily lecturing his daughter about the young bridegroom's paltry value, about his pitiable stature as a bard, forced to earn his living by selling his talent and begging in obscure places, in fisheries, in scarcely-known logging sites.

• That night, that Saturday night, Solovyei had withdrawn wordlessly after hugging Schulhoff. The witnesses recalled that he seemed rather good-natured when saying his farewells and, in any case, that he didn't seem to be having a bad day. But after midnight sounds came from the basements of the Soviet, the whistling that always resulted when he was entering his worlds or other people's dreams. Hannko Vogulian went back to her place after the concert to warm the bed and she waited in vain for Schulhoff to come join her. After putting his zither in its cover, Schulhoff went out in the street to smoke a cigarette in front of the Pioneers' House, to look at the starry sky and come back down to earth after hours and hours of poetic and musical soaring. Then there was no trace of his existence on earth. In front of the Pioneers' House there was no cigarette butt nor lighter to be found, and, when she was asked about the whole thing much later, the Gramma Udgul grumbled that in all probability Schulhoff had been swallowed up by a black hole, which nobody believed, except for herself and Solovyei.

As for Solovyei, even if most of the Levanidovo's inhabitants believed that he had entered the Soviet's cauldron, the core of the back-up power plant that had run smoothly since the larger power plant's failure, even if his daughters were convinced that he had gone through the flames to reach the shamanic space of non-life and non-death, to organize within this darkness Schulhoff's abduction and liquidation, he claimed to be astonished by Hannko Vogulian's husband's inexplicable departure. He called on all the police powers at his disposal in the kolkhoz so that the Sunday hunt would have a happy end, then, in the days that followed, he led an energetic and thorough investigation with searches through the village's empty huts and the underground passages that crisscrossed the Levanidovo to allow movement during the iciest and snowiest months, but his efforts came to naught, and he demonstrated his annoyance publicly. When Hannko Vogulian realized she had been widowed, he seemed to sympathize with her grief, and he promised her that her husband would come back to life one day, that she would find Schulhoff again, and that he himself would track Schulhoff down through his divinations. He never implied that he bore the least responsibility in this saga. But, in everybody's opinion, he did.

• After the shower, Kronauer went back up the prison hallway to his cell, the room where he had lain during his blackout, then, hearing some noise, he went in that direction and found himself in the kitchen, which had barely any utensils or cupboards and more closely resembled a small refectory. The two sisters were waiting for him with tea and a plate of toasted flour. They told him that they had forgotten to put anything for shaving in the shower room, and that there was a razor and washbasin in a nook, in case he still had any hair.

—Eh, my hair doesn't grow very fast these days, he said.

The daughters simpered, especially Myriam Umarik, who also stroked her thick and shiny jet-black hair.

—If you stay in this place, it'll come in even slower, Hannko Vogulian said.

—I'm not staying, Kronauer said.

Hannko Vogulian shrugged. After a few seconds, she told him that, generally, he was free to come and go and that he could walk through the village, but he should go to the Gramma Udgul's place by the end of the morning.

—She wants to see what you look like, Myriam Umarik said. She wants to make sure you're not an enemy of the people.

—The Gramma Udgul can come later, Kronauer said as he choked on a spoonful of toasted flour. I'm sorry, but I don't have time to meet everyone in the kolkhoz. My comrades are dying of hunger and thirst by the railroad tracks. I have to go back there. It's urgent.

He wasn't sure if he had the strength to go back immediately. To trek back through the forest, without a guide, with a bag of food on his back and a jerrican filled to the brim with water in his hand. But doing anything else, lounging here, was absolutely out of the question. He couldn't imagine dawdling along the village's one road, after having stuffed himself with tsamba, and then making conversation with an old lady, while his comrades were dying by the railroad tracks.

—I have to go back, he insisted.

—Solovyei went down there with Morgovian, Hannko Vogulian said.

—Morgovian?

—Samiya Schmidt's husband.

—They brought all the necessities, Myriam Umarik said.

Her shoulders and breasts heaved. Kronauer tried not to pay attention, but these heaves bothered him.

—And medicine for your wife, she added.

—She's not my wife, Kronauer said right away.

He felt unburdened of a great weight. Vassilissa Marachvili and Ilyushenko's rescue was well under way. So Solovyei was taking care of it, then. He was a gruff giant, completely disagreeable, but he was taking care of it.

− 5 −

• Hannko Vogulian took Kronauer to the end of the village, two hundred meters past the prison they had left. She pointed out the buildings when they corresponded to something specific: the Soviet, Myriam Umarik's house, the canteen, the communist cooperative, the public library, the Pioneers' House. When they came to the end of the road, she stopped. The road continued into the countryside in the form of a path that climbed up the hill. She indicated with a sweep of her arms the massive warehouse run by the Gramma Udgul. Her arms were bare, and not even the finest down covered her extraordinarily pale skin. The sun played on her left ear and the light shone through with a delicious rosiness.

—I'm not going with you, she said. I have things to do.

Kronauer nodded. Since she was standing next to him, he could avoid meeting her strange eyes.

He went the rest of the way thinking about Hannko Vogulian rather than the Gramma Udgul, and when he stepped into the warehouse, he was almost surprised to see the old woman standing right in front of him. She was twisting and turning at the bottom of a mountain of scrap iron, wearily repeating the same fruitless gestures. In fact, she was putting on an act to welcome Kronauer, who she must have seen on the road since he'd left the village and whom she wanted to understand that the warehouse wasn't a place to laze around.

The Gramma Udgul got up and put her hands on her waist, mainly to look serious and difficult in front of Kronauer, because she didn't feel any pain in her back. Her joints had been strengthened by the salutary effects of gamma-ray radiation exposure, and weren't arthritic now, and wouldn't be at any point in the foreseeable future. Before she spoke, she slowly looked over Kronauer, from head to toe, suspiciously, unhappily.

—You're wearing one of Barguzin's shirts, she said once she was done. Her disapproval was evident.

—It's what Myriam Umarik gave me, Kronauer said defensively. I didn't have anything left to wear.

—Barguzin's not dead yet, the Gramma Udgul said. I'd be the first one to know. When he dies I pour water over him to bring him back. Thus far, he's always come back. No need to bury him alive.

—It's just a shirt, Kronauer said with a puzzled look.

—Myriam Umarik is very beautiful, the Gramma Udgul said.

—Yes, Kronauer agreed. No doubt about it.

—She's one of Solovyei's daughters, the Gramma Udgul said warningly. Don't even think for a second about hurting her.

—Why would I hurt her? Kronauer protested.

—She's married, the Gramma Udgul said. Don't expect her to cheat on Barguzin if he's not dead.

—I've never expected that, Kronauer said angrily.

—If you hurt her or her sisters, Solovyei will never forgive you. Kronauer shrugged.

—He'll follow you for at least a thousand seven hundred and nine years, the Gramma Udgul warned. A thousand seven hundred and nine years or thereabouts, and maybe even twice that.

• A little later, after having thoroughly interrogated Kronauer about his military and political background, his beliefs, and his class membership, the Gramma Udgul gave him a tour of the warehouse. She showed him the location of the well and its purpose, describing with obvious sympathy the core simmering at its bottom, two kilometers deep, then she took him around several mountains of brand-new garbage and, at the end, she went back to sit down in her armchair, in front of the heavy curtain that marked off her strictly private space.

Kronauer inspected the imposing mass of Solovyei's archives among which the Gramma Udgul was sitting. On a small table there was a machine for reading the recorded cylinders, and beneath the table, several crates filled with wax or Bakelite cylinders.

He hadn't been asked to comment, so Kronauer stayed quiet.

The Gramma Udgul in turn had relented, or at least she now talked without trying to be aggressive. She had concluded from the interrogation that this nearly-fortysomething man belonged to a group of red soldiers that wasn't suspected of apostasy or treachery. She had talked with him about the last egalitarian areas of the Orbise and their downfall, and Kronauer's political background pleased her. She knew, of course, that really trusting him would take months of investigation and imprisonment, along with multiple autobiographies written during sleep deprivation, but, for now, she didn't see any reason to give him trouble. He had to tell her in detail about the period of military retreat, when he and his comrades had fired at a demented officer. That was a gray area, typical behavior for an adventurer susceptible to anarchist impulses rather than Bolshevik intelligence. On the one hand, she approved that he hadn't let himself be trapped in a suicide mission, and on the other she wondered if opening fire on a superior wasn't, at the end of the day, an awfully leftist act.

• She tilted her head to indicate the papers and boxes of cylinders.

—See all that, she said. Solovyei calls that his complete works. He's joking, but I know he's attached to them. And sometimes he says it's a treasure, the only example in the world of post-shamanic poetry. It certainly isn't like anything, and politically it's nauseating and subversive more than anything else. They weren't made for any specific audience. These are complete works for no audience.

Kronauer nodded in feigned interest. Everything having to do with Solovyei usually tended to bother him, these incessant mentions, full of vagaries and threats, as if the land and the inhabitants of the kolkhoz had magically submitted to their president. Besides, he didn't believe that the Gramma Udgul would really establish a rapport with him at the expense of Solovyei's literary ambitions. There was no reason for this complicity to arise just then. The Gramma Udgul wasn't stupid and, if this was the direction she'd steered the conversation, it had to be so he'd say something bad about Solovyei. This had to be a trap the old woman had set, and he had no intention of falling into it. As for Solovyei's poetic achievements, he remembered experiencing an unbearable example in the forest, before he had come to the Levanidovo, completely unbearable and humiliating, and he didn't plan on sharing his memory of this experience with the Gramma Udgul.

—Well, maybe someone will find it all charming one day, he said sardonically.

—Nobody with a proper head on his shoulders would, the Gramma Udgul said. They're vile mutterings. A little like the post-exotic writers, back in the day, during their mystical period. But worse. Mutterings recorded when he's gallivanting through the atomic flames, through death or black space.

—Ah, Kronauer said.

The Gramma Udgul began to take her smoking materials out of an apron pocket, and she made herself comfortable while packing bits of tobacco into her pipe. Silence had settled between the two of them and throughout the whole warehouse. Kronauer was more or less at attention in front of her, and every so often he ran his hand over his shaved head, more for something to do than to straighten the half-millimeter of hair that dotted his skin and which would, by all appearances, fall out and not grow back until his death.

As the silence stretched out, Kronauer went to look at the phonograph more closely.

It was a device like the ones they had started making again, based on the old models, when they had believed that the enemy had weapons able to remotely destroy the mechanisms of electronic devices. This unfounded rumor had set off a panic in the industry and in the population, and it had kick-started a pilot plant for reinventing engines that ran on springs or other forces that didn't require power. The rumor was quickly stamped out, but the first non-electronic models had already come off the production lines, demonstrating the ability of our engineers to adapt and the superiority of our technology, let us say our survival technology, in the race to the bottom we've had with imperialism. These prototypes weren't produced in large numbers, but they were distributed through the network of cooperatives so that the working-class population would stay in touch with our culture and enrich it with local contributions. And so here and there working phonographs could be found, as well as blank cylinders without which these objects would have lost nearly all their significance. Kronauer handled the copper horn, caressed the diaphragm's membrane, examined the needle; then he looked at the box full of cylinders and took out one to look more closely.

He could feel the Gramma Udgul's hostility on his back and he turned toward her. She took the pipe out of her mouth.

—Didn't you see what's written on the cylinder? she asked icily.

Kronauer rotated the cylinder, which at first glance seemed not to have any information on it; then he saw an inscription in gray letters on the end. He had to hold it up to the light to read it. Like traces of graphite on slate.

—Well, there are a few letters, he said. F T T L T T D A T T D.

—It's an abbreviation, the Gramma Udgul said unhelpfully.

—I don't know how to decode that.

The Gramma Udgul blew a cloud of smoke at Kronauer. Her face was frowning and unfriendly.

—You really aren't smart, soldier, she said.

—No.

—It means "Forbidden to the Living, to the Dead, and to the Dogs."

She spoke these words with an ominous aggression, as if he was undeniably guilty of something, but refused to admit it. Kronauer decided to be as straightforward as possible.

—I'm not any of those, he said.

—Sure, you say that, the Gramma Udgul grumbled.

They watched each other without talking for several seconds.

—Ow! Kronauer suddenly yelled.

—What happened? the Gramma Udgul jumped up.

—Nothing, Kronauer said. I just pricked myself on the diaphragm needle. I wanted to put the cylinder in the spindle to see how it worked, and I pricked myself.

• Kronauer has pricked his finger on the phonograph needle.

A small drop of blood grows on the end of his index finger.

A sting, and then everything changes.

Sleeping Beauty pricked herself on her spindle and that cost her a hundred years of sleep and immobility.

Kronauer doesn't fall down, doesn't fall asleep. He doesn't dream for a second of making any comparison between this fairy-tale princess and himself, between the old spinster and the Gramma Udgul, between the spindle's point and the phonograph's needle. He has nothing in his head resembling children's stories, and he simply looks at the drop of blood swelling on his finger. He looks at it, then he brings it to his lips and he licks it.

The taste of blood on his tongue. And there, as in the shower, an aftertaste of cesium and iodide.

Kronauer has drawn blood on an object belonging to Solovyei, which is an integral part of Solovyei's memories, which is used to broadcast Solovyei's voice, a magic machine that speaks Solovyei's poems out loud, his memories, Solovyei's emphatic howls, Solovyei's terrible admonitions and dreams.

A miniscule wound, and then everything changes.

Kronauer feels a light numbness in the pad of his finger, a barely noticeable pain. A new droplet of blood appears on his fingertip, he lets it tremble before licking it up, but already everything has changed.

Kronauer doesn't know about this change, he is silent as he faces the Gramma Udgul, who watches him unkindly, herself also silent.

He thinks of the living, of the dogs, and of the dead, and, oddly, he wonders which category he belongs to, and no less oddly, he is unable to answer.

In any case, he has to say, this warning on the cylinder doesn't affect me at all.

He is wrong. Even in admitting he isn't living, or dead, or dog, he has bled on Solovyei's phonograph and fallen into the world of Solovyei's dreams.

A prick was enough, a few microliters of blood have become the gateway from one world to the other. Here everything is the same, and Kronauer doesn't notice.

Everything is the same, but he has changed.

• He has just entered a parallel reality, a bardic reality, a magical and stammering death, a stutter of reality, of magic malevolence, a tumor of the present, a trap by Solovyei, an inordinately elongated terminal phase, a fragment of sub-reality that threatens to last at least a thousand seven hundred and nine years or thereabouts, if not twice that, he has entered an unspeakable theater, a vivid coma, an endless end, the false continuation of his existence, an artificial reality, an unlikely death, a swampy reality, the ashes of his own memories, the ashes of his own present, an insane loop, resounding images where he cannot be actor or audience, a luminous nightmare, a shadowy nightmare, lands forbidden to the dogs, to the living, and to the dead. His walk has begun and now, no matter what, it will not end.

− 6 −

- A moment of silence.

The Gramma Udgul sucks on her pipe, then blows some smoke out. The curls disappear. She watches them turn into thin clouds, turn back to nothingness. Then she spits out another thick puff. The tobacco the Gramma Udgul is smoking leaves a vapor trail of resin, mossy stones, and low-quality hashish around her. The curls are beautiful and call for silent admiration.

Kronauer sets the forbidden cylinder next to the phonograph, as if waiting for the Gramma Udgul to order him to insert it into the mechanism. The cylinder waits, Kronauer too waits, impassive in front of the old woman. He no longer holds up his finger to lick away the blood. It has coagulated, and he is simply waiting for the Gramma Udgul's initiative to move forward. In this way Kronauer is inactive, due to a physical and mental numbness not unconnected to the pricking. Also due to the respect the Gramma Udgul has instilled in him.

Kronauer does feel inclined to keep a militarily proper attitude in front of the Gramma Udgul. He doesn't stand at attention, but he might as well. This heroic liquidator impresses him. Just a bit earlier, when Hannko Vogulian was walking him over to the warehouse, she had said a couple of words about the Gramma Udgul and he realized that the name wasn't entirely unfamiliar. Suddenly it was clear that the old woman he was going to see was one of the most valiant figures of the Second Soviet Union, a legendary survivor, sagging under medals and highlighted in various enlightening stories. He thought she had been dead for more than a century, since she had been presented in the media as a phenomenon of the past, since she had been discussed so much in the past tense. And then he was being told that he would meet one of the most honorable egalitarian deities of the Orbise. Which is why, although this deity had welcomed him as quickly and as easily as if they were equals, he couldn't imagine addressing her in anything other than the most respectful terms. And that, too, is why he stands in front of her now like a good boy in front of an adult.

The curls of smoke come together and come apart.

High above, a fly that had ventured into the teeth of an irradiated harrow is stricken dead, after a noise much like an electrical discharge.

When the Gramma Udgul's tobacco smoke dissipates, the warehouse smells of metal, burnt cloth, and an old woman's sweat.

A second fly wanders around the harrow's teeth. Once again an electrical discharge can be heard. In the silence, the noise of the insect's instantaneous carbonization is so loud that Kronauer looks up to see where it had come from.

—It's the flies, the Gramma Udgul says. The spiders didn't survive, but the flies did. All the so-called experts were wrong about that.

Kronauer nods.

—I respected those scholars back in my childhood, but after living so long I learned that they often just spouted bullshit, she adds.

• The conversation regains some semblance of energy, and the Gramma Udgul resumes the biographical interrogation she had been putting Kronauer through when they met. She asks him about daily life in the capital just before the fall of the Orbise. Then she makes him talk about his marriage to Irina Echenguyen. He has trouble talking about her. The suffering he experienced when he learned that the dog-headed fascists had seized her in the clinic where she was dying, raped and assassinated her—this suffering is still unbearable. It is now buried under several layers, but it is still there, deep and undying. It only takes one cruel or awkward question for it to come back to the fore. The Gramma Udgul excavates this pain a bit, then she turns her attention to the grasses Irina Echenguyen had been cataloging. She asks Kronauer to recite the names of several wild grasses, to compare to what she knows of the steppe's grasses. Kronauer lists two or three, then he stops. He has the irrational impression of betraying Irina Echenguyen's memory. Irrational and especially disagreeable. As if he was describing something pure in front of a malevolent and impure judge.

—I can't remember any others off the top of my head, he lies.

—Oh, come on, the Gramma Udgul protests.

Her wrinkled face screws up in irritation and displeasure. With the hand holding her pipe, she waves exasperatedly for him to keep going.

—You're not being honest, Kronauer, she says. If you were in front of a people's court, you'd have provoked the crowd.

—What crowd? . . . What are you talking about?

—Make sure you always tell the truth in front of the proletariat, the Gramma Udgul says.

Her voice is solemn and threatening.

Sensing danger and feeling exhausted, Kronauer nods. He remembers that he is being watched by Solovyei, and now this representative of Soviet heroism has started to calmly threaten him with a quick trip to the people's court. She is casually and sloppily interrogating him, but during their interview, she has been trying to give him trouble, as if she is investigating him and as if he has something to be ashamed of, which he might end up confessing when he becomes upset enough.

—Ringed valdelame, garluv, Chinese keys, crizèle-du-marchand, talmazin, oncroies, he says.

He stands at attention. On the pad of his finger, the pain has started up again.

The Gramma Udgul hides behind the smoke of her pipe. Her mouth moves for several long seconds, as if after hearing this brief list she physically tastes its effects on her tongue, between her sagging centenarian cheeks.

—Good, she says. You see, soldier. You said you didn't have anything else in your head.

—I have my highs and my lows, Kronauer explains miserably. The walk through the steppes took its toll.

—You didn't just walk through the steppes, I thought. You also walked through the forest.

—Not for very long, Kronauer says.

—In the forest you had plenty of time to hurt Samiya Schmidt, the Gramma Udgul suddenly says.

—I didn't hurt Samiya Schmidt, Kronauer says defensively. I carried her on my back. She couldn't walk any farther.

—That's not what Solovyei said, the old woman says inquisitively.

Kronauer waits several seconds. This accusation has been twisting in his head like a thick, black shadow ever since he came into the kolkhoz.

—I don't know why he would say that, he finally says.

—So, you actually went through the old forest, you and Samiya Schmidt both?

—Yes, says Kronauer.

—In the old forest, he saw you hurting Samiya Schmidt.

—He wasn't even there, Kronauer says weakly.

He immediately realizes that Solovyei's words aren't what he should attack, but the silliness of the accusation. Whether Solovyei had been present in the old forest or not doesn't matter. Besides, his whistling voice certainly was there at one moment, whistling and harsh, magical, hurtful. What he has to say, forcefully, what he has to repeat, is the truth. He has to keep denying and denying without worrying about Solovyei's flights of fancy, or Samiya Schmidt's silence. Samiya Schmidt could have just said what actually happened. And what didn't. That would have simplified things.

So he prepares to finish what he was about to say, but the Gramma Udgul doesn't let him.

—Oh yes, he was there, she says triumphantly. He's always in many places at the same time. Whether he's actually in dreams or reality, he's always half in the taiga. And he saw you there.

The Gramma Udgul laughs mildly, a satisfied old woman's laugh, and then her lips chew on a thought that she finally says out loud.

—You wouldn't understand, she says.

Kronauer pauses. He watches this legendary heroine, sitting in an old armchair as if it were a throne, this tireless old woman surrounded by newspapers, crates of memorabilia, black cylinders, and papers that she considers subversive. She closes her mouth without making any sound other than the mottled slurp of saliva. And suddenly he realizes that things have changed, that he has gone to the other side, the side of this old woman and unpredictable worlds where she feels like a fish in water, with the president of the kolkhoz and this unstable Samiya Schmidt setting off the rumor that he hurt her in the forest.

In front of this old woman who takes Solovyei's lies as truth, he has no evidence he can summon up. He suspects her total complicity with Solovyei, her physical and mental alliance with Solovyei. No point in trying to defend himself with common sense. He can only expect unfairness, poisonous attacks, a complete lack of compassion.

So he looks down, his thoughts follow the path of the blood pulsing beneath the prick of his finger, and he doesn't talk.

The Gramma Udgul opens her mouth but does not say anything.

Kronauer waits for her to make the accusation she is withholding, or change the topic to something heretofore undiscussed, or tell him he can leave. He waits a long minute, and when this long minute persists, he lets two slightly shorter ones go by. Then, without a word, he goes to the warehouse door.

• Then the Gramma Udgul leans over the device next to her armchair and inserts the cylinder that Kronauer picked up a bit earlier. Clearly, she cares about Kronauer hearing the post-shamanic stammer before leaving. About him being slapped in the face with a post-shamanic poem forbidden to the dogs, to the living, and to the dead. She hasn't said good-bye to Kronauer, but this is her way of accompanying him to the warehouse door, her way of telling him that she has the same negative, very negative appraisal, the same opinion as the kolkhoz's president. After just a short little interrogation about mere trifles, this pathetic soldier has revealed who he is: an unsuitable kind of person who let his wife be violated by the fanatics of capitalism, who shot the last-ditch officer without trial, who abandoned his comrades on the vast steppes, and who, in the forest, hurt Samiya Schmidt.

Kronauer freezes in the warehouse doorway. He is suddenly enveloped in the waxy and sputtering recorded voice of the kolkhoz president. It isn't as harsh as the one that whistled in the old forest, but it paralyzes him. He doesn't cover his ears, but he stops to listen.

The words aren't strange at all, but the images they summon up only result in feelings of unfinished murders, vague cruelty, and unease. He can't figure out what the speaker wanted, or even understand whoever is speaking these words. Something unstable and hostile goes directly into Kronauer's subconscious. As in the forest, but with a less imperious violence, the strange sentences break into him and, once inside, don't ask him whether they should burrow deep or open up.

What's wrong with you, Kronauer, he thinks, why are you letting these insanities attack you? They're just bits of black prose, nothing more than a twisted declamation by a village poet. You have nothing to be concerned about, Kronauer.

But he leans against the doorway warmed by sunlight and radiation, he looks at the drop of blood already dry on his left finger, he grimaces in pain, and he keeps listening.

• Scorning the choir that had dissuaded him, he withdrew to the most burning wall of the room, and, having reached it, he entered a turmoil that his cellmates and his minions had rarely witnessed in him, he who most often had preached the renunciation of all gestures as well as petrifaction during carbonization or collapse. He began to discourse, then, doubting that anyone had listened to or understood him, he pressed himself all the more firmly against the lava and became a black and indefinite bird with language and powers only he knew. For a time that some less reliable witnesses said were years, and that his spouses, who were more likely to feel it in their bodies, confirmed were centuries, he constructed worlds in the shadows, worlds neither alive nor dead, then, indifferent to public disapproval, he lived in them. So that these lands would be inhabited, he threw vaguely human trash indiscriminately over everything he barely ruled over, as well as the girls who resulted from his wedding dances and the subsequent coitus. Out of respect for the libertarian ideas that had intoxicated him in his youth, he endeavored not to abuse his magical powers for the women he met, but, in short, in nearly every case he approached them, he penetrated them, and he loved them, and then almost without exception he withdrew from them and brought in others from distant parts of the taiga, or even from the tunnels beyond death, and sometimes he went to find them in the concentration hells where he had his ways in both as a master as well as a detainee. Ubiquity and polychrony had long been his fate, which he guarded from all curses, because he had decided to wander as he pleased without any concern for decay or death, and to talk lovingly or cruelly as best suited the moment. He flew high into a pitch-black sky or he trod heavily over an increasingly oily and black earth. Sometimes the prospect of living endlessly hurt him, and then he returned to the inferno, speaking unheard poetic discourses or being quiet, or bringing forth new images where everyone was dead. During one of these eternal returns, his cellmates and his minions gestured, as if perfunctorily offering help that they all knew was ridiculous, and in turn he addressed them gently with his hand, a movement that few of them understood, and then his back caught on fire and he disappeared.

− 7 −

• Now Kronauer was making his way down the hill upon which the building sat, that building where contaminated trash was being stored. He didn't hurry. For one thing, he had no idea what he would do next in the village. For another, his legs were barely obeying him. A long night sleeping in the kolkhoz prison hadn't been enough to restore his strength. His muscles kept reminding him at every moment of the ordeal that had been his walk across the steppes, not to mention the difficult last hours spent in the old forest. And doubtless his body still had some trouble adapting to the radionuclides floating or vibrating throughout the village.

While walking, he repeated to himself the strange flights of fancy of the Radiant Terminus president. They twisted silently within his skull, subconsciously, but also deep within the very marrow of his bones. He felt them come and go through the gray areas of his body. Well, this is like a hypnosis mantra, he thought. Takes advantage of your weaknesses to numb you. Slips inside you and you can't even fight back.

He would have liked to banish Solovyei from his thoughts. However, when he got back onto the Levanidovo's main road, he kept mulling over images of shadowy eternity and worlds with indecipherable rules of existence. Once again he heard the needle screeching, the phonograph's membrane vibrating, obedient to the cruel inflections of Solovyei's voice. He, too, irritatedly realized that he was submitting to this voice. It bothered him, but he had listened to it almost respectfully and now it had entered him and now it was burrowing deeper and deeper within, and if he wasn't able to get it out, it was first and foremost because he had accepted its presence. Well, don't tell me that now it's in your marrow and your dreams, don't tell me that, Kronauer! he moaned. But nobody answered him back and, as he kept on walking, he remained silent.

• He paused in the empty street. He didn't want to go back to his room, or wander around the prison, and he didn't have anything particular to do in the Levanidovo, but at the same time he knew that if he didn't find something to keep him busy, he'd be mistaken for a profiteer, a lawless refugee, or a loner unable to collaborate in building collective happiness. He slowed down, then to stall for time he paused in front of the communist cooperative's locked door, then as if he'd changed his mind he started walking again. He didn't see anyone. Not a single job presented itself. He went past the Pioneers' House, the public library. In a row on his right were the little building where Samiya Schmidt and Morgovian lived, the Soviet, and Myriam Umarik and Barguzin's house. He came to the Soviet and was thinking about turning around when Myriam Umarik came out of her house and went to meet him.

She waddled gently and lithely, and, although he couldn't tell whether she knew it or not, she very much looked a seductress. She moved her body and gave her walk an overtone of dance, an invitation to a dance that had something animal, very sensual, bridal, an invitation to physical complicity. Whether she intended it or not, she made people want to come up to her and touch her. Her hair was so dark and shiny that the sun's reflection went from the top of her head down to her left cheek, making a little dazzling cascade that led toward her breasts. Her linen shirt wasn't unbuttoned, but her abundant bosom was visible and bounced with every step.

Kronauer's eyes stopped on her and immediately, half a second later, moved on. She moved in the sunlight and its sparkle was distracting.

Still, he did his best not to be attracted to her, even though, due to male nature, he was.

He didn't want to think that her shape was appealing; he didn't want to think of her as a desirable, delectable object, or let scandalous images multiply in his head because of this possible appetite.

He held back from these images. Partly because in the Orbise he had received a proletarian education that connected all sexual expression with excesses of immorality. And partly because, like Samiya Schmidt, he had read several of Maria Kwoll's works denigrating masculine impulses and depicting them in the most odious, the most revolting way possible. And finally because he still remembered the Gramma Udgul's warnings about Myriam Umarik's marital status.

A vague sensation of vertigo persisted and he did his best to pull together several thoughts about himself, about what he was going through in the Levanidovo. What's the point, Kronauer, he thought, you didn't come to the Levanidovo just to have an affair. It's looking like you settled down here and forgot that Ilyushenko and Vassilissa Marachvili are waiting for you by the railroad tracks. And that's the only thing that matters.

He was already starting to have trouble visualizing his comrades in distress among the grasses, immobilized by exhaustion, constrained to silence, forced to stay low or hunkered down so as not to be noticed by the soldiers. He was already a long way from them. He had to struggle to call them back to mind, and the result was an abstracted image, with barely any emotional weight. He remembered the railroad tracks crossing the countryside, the ruins of the Red Star sovkhoz, but the memory of his two friends shimmered with difficulty, as if they belonged to a story on which he had already turned the page. This feeling was reinforced by the fact that Solovyei and Morgovian had gone there with what they needed to tend to them, in order to comfort them and care for them. Solovyei and Morgovian had taken over and soon, probably, Ilyushenko and Vassilissa Marachvili would be welcomed in turn at the Levanidovo.

Right, he thought sadly. Just like that.

The shooting pains in his hand, right where he had been pricked, insistently reminded him that he had slipped into a world where Myriam Umarik's presence mattered more than Vassilissa Marachvili's absence.

Then something jumped within him and woke up. You know perfectly well, Kronauer, that you're not here to flirt; tomorrow or the day after you will be gone again. If Solovyei brings Vassilissa Marachvili and Ilyushenko back to the kolkhoz, the three of you will be gone again. Radiant Terminus isn't your place. Especially not when there's this jealous father who's hostile and put you under watch; you can't even figure out his relationship with his daughters. This Myriam Umarik has nothing to do with you. Not worth the trouble of watching her make her way over here, her shoes pounding the earth like the hooves of an aroused bull.

—I need you, Kronauer, Myriam Umarik said. Can I call you Kronauer?

• She had a favor to ask him. Right in front of her house, there was a fire hydrant that had begun to drip. Her husband, the engineer Barguzin, had brought the necessary tools out to the road, and he was going to take care of the problem, but then he had come back inside and, after saying something indistinct, he had collapsed. His loss of consciousness wasn't like death, and up to now, she didn't call for the Gramma Udgul to come revive him with her three waters, heavy-heavy water, deathly-deathly water, and lively-lively water.

—You want me to warn the Gramma Udgul? Kronauer asked.

Myriam Umarik smiled and dismissed the idea with a wave that shook her hips and her entire torso up to her shoulders.

There was no rush with Barguzin. It was just a minor setback. No, what she wanted him to do, and this was the favor she was asking of him, was to fix the fire hydrant. He should be able to make the repairs, even if he barely knew anything about plumbing.

—Oh sure, Kronauer said. Just have to tighten it, this valve. Loosen two or three nuts and then tighten them again.

He had a feeling that Myriam Umarik was testing him. Maybe the people of Radiant Terminus wanted to know if he would fit into the kolkhoz economy, perhaps as a handyman, a janitor, or a water works employee.

He went to the post and got down to unpack the materials that the engineer Barguzin had brought out: a monkey wrench, some socket wrenches, two screwdrivers, a hammer, large black rubber gaskets, all loosely wrapped in a rag. While he handled the tools, he saw that the small wound on his finger had opened up again and that there was some blood along his finger. Under the pad, the shooting pains had increased.

—Are you bleeding? Myriam Umarik asked as she leaned over him.

—It's nothing, he said. Just a prick from the phonograph.

Myriam Umarik scowled. She was very close to Kronauer. She smelled clean, of workman's soap, and also Barguzin's saliva, which had dripped onto her skirt as she had dragged him to his bed.

—Solovyei's phonograph? she asked.

—Yes.

—You definitely shouldn't have played with that, she muttered quickly. What got into you? Couldn't you contain yourself? I thought you weren't that stupid. You could have tried not to touch my father's things.

She seemed genuinely puzzled.

—I barely touched that pathetic phonograph, Kronauer explained. I just touched the membrane with my hand. It pricked me like some kind of angry animal.

—Those aren't normal things, Myriam Umarik said. Don't just touch them. It's too dangerous. They're part of Solovyei. When he figures out that you wanted to take it, he'll be angry, and you'll be stuck with him for a thousand years.

—Really, a thousand years? Kronauer said sadly.

—One thousand eight hundred and twenty-six years or more, Myriam Umarik specified.

He made a slight gesture impatiently. Solovyei's omnipresence annoyed him, with these constant mentions of magical threats, every one of them numbered on a massive scale. He stood up immediately; he wanted to curse the president of the kolkhoz in front of his daughter. He let go of the monkey wrench he had been holding. The sudden change in position made him feel dizzy. Starbursts circled around him. He staggered, caught his balance on the fire hydrant. The red paint on the hood flaked away under his hand. He turned toward Myriam Umarik and looked directly at her, longer this time than a minute earlier when she had approached him, but he no longer saw her clearly. He tried to fight against his shakiness, his nausea. Now, the sun lit up Myriam Umarik's face. In the middle of a few stars he saw that she was smiling at him, he saw her large white teeth, her thick mouth, her slightly too-big incisors, and at the same moment the colors weakened and he felt the world give way under his legs.

—Hey, Kronauer, what's wrong? Myriam Umarik asked.

He waved his hand in response. He had opened his mouth but couldn't speak.

—You're not going to do the same thing Barguzin did, are you? Myriam Umarik said.

—What thing? Kronauer stammered.

Barguzin, he thought quickly. Myriam Umarik's husband. She's not a widow. The Gramma Udgul warned me. Especially not to hang around her. Especially not to anger Solovyei. Especially not to hurt any of his daughters at all.

A thousand years, he thought. One thousand eight hundred and twenty-six years, or more.

Then the shadows came and, from his point of view, he disappeared.

− 8 −

• Kronauer's loss of consciousness persisted for several hours or a day or two or a little more and, essentially, it kept him from being present when Solovyei and Morgovian came back to Radiant Terminus.

When he woke up again on his spartan bed, Kronauer had a feeling of déjà vu. He no longer gave off a filthy vagrant's smell, but once again the daughters had carried his comatose, heavy, inert body to set him down in his more or less prison cell, and this thought made him ashamed. The door wasn't locked, the building was empty, and he went to take a shower. Then he went out onto the street and that was when his life as a refugee in the kolkhoz began.

It was a regular, boring life that followed a rhythm firmly established by Hannko Vogulian and Myriam Umarik, who helped him to find his footing but also tried to let him do as he wished. He often saw the two women and, less often, Samiya Schmidt. She avoided him and only talked to him in the public library, where she spent several afternoons every week, and even then it was just to make sure that he didn't check out a book without returning the one he'd borrowed last time. Their conversations were curt. Once he had registered as a non-resident reader, she mainly suggested novels or satires written by Maria Kroll and her imitators, Rosa Wolff, Sonia Velasquez, or others lesser known but far more aggressive. Not wishing to contradict her, he always accepted her suggestions. He read these books in the solitude of his room, feeling unhappy to only have these tomes, which he wouldn't have chosen on his own, to devour, whereas his preferences skewed toward socialist-realist, post-apocalyptic, or historical fictions, or toward silly and sentimental stories. However, because the feminist works had been foisted on him, he made the best of the situation and obediently renewed his knowledge of male brutality, the ridiculously animalistic nature of all sexual relations, the systematic practice of rape in the relationships between men and women, the impossibility of envisioning a sexual activity that was enjoyable and shared lovingly without somehow defiling the female body.

During the day, he assisted Abazayev, or Barguzin, or Morgovian, or Solovyei's daughters when they asked for help, which wasn't often. Work in the kolkhoz didn't call for special knowledge and he was limited to basic cleaning or maintenance jobs. There was no agricultural production just then, and there weren't any animals anywhere. When Kronauer mentioned his astonishment at seeing the communist cooperative stocked with flour, yak butter, and ingredients used to make pemmican, or even blocks of prepared pemmican, Morgovian turned gloomy and spouted off nonsensical explanations about merchant caravans coming by, which he claimed were connected to lunar cycles, then he lost all confidence in his words and eventually stopped talking without having said anything comprehensible. When Myriam Umarik was asked the same question, she shrugged her shoulders and jokingly wondered whether he had been sent by the Orbise to verify Radiant Terminus's records and pore through the list of the cooperative's suppliers. A little later, the one-armed Abazayev, whose relationship with Kronauer was crude but trusting, gestured with his working arm to talk about something else. Kronauer didn't ask again how the kolkhoz was provided with food and natural assets. He wasn't trying to figure out anything about the oddities in the way the kolkhoz functioned, partly because he didn't want to look like an oversuspicious snoop, and also because he didn't care. He just wanted to settle in the Levanidovo without any trouble, because going back to the steppes didn't make sense anymore.

Going back to his death, without comrades, without Vassilissa Marachvili, without Ilyushenko.

He had learned that the expedition to the Red Star sovkhoz hadn't produced any results. After having searched high and low through the grasses, Solovyei and Morgovian had come back to the Levanidovo empty-handed. Neither Ilyushenko nor Vassilissa Marachvili had left a message behind, and, in all likelihood, they had gotten on the train with the soldiers, since the convoy had disappeared as well. The news had torn Kronauer apart for several days. He knew he couldn't do anything, but he was tormented by the thought that Vassilissa Marachvili might have been assaulted and that, if she hadn't acceded, she might have been enslaved and forced to fulfill those roughnecks' sexual fantasies. At moments he also imagined a happier adventure, an unhampered departure, and then he wasn't upset that he had been left behind without any explanation, assuming that it had been a way for Vassilissa Marachvili and Ilyushenko to survive somehow. Which didn't keep him from feeling a twinge in his heart when he thought of Vassilissa Marachvili.

It was Hannko Vogulian, not the people who had gone, who had summed up the story of the fruitless Red Star trip for him. When they had come back to the village, Kronauer was still unconscious, and then, as soon as he'd woken up, Hannko Vogulian had rushed to tell him everything, in hopes that he would stop worrying about his lost comrades. He didn't show his grief or his shock, and he indicated without wasting any words that he had come to terms with this act of fate and now wanted to become part of this kolkhoz by fulfilling the tasks entrusted to him. However, in hopes of getting more details, he sometimes asked for a few more particulars. Myriam Umarik was happy to talk with him, but she didn't have anything useful to add. Morgovian, who had gone on the expedition, barely said three sentences on the subject. He repeated that they had, Solovyei and he, combed through the grasses, combed through the environs, that they had seen traces of ashes, the remnants of a bivouac, but nothing else. Kronauer's insistence put him in a bad mood. As for the president of the kolkhoz, Kronauer rarely saw him on his way, and always off in the distance. They passed without waving, and it would have, of course, been out of place to stop him to ask what he had seen at the Red Star. The idea of initiating a conversation with Solovyei didn't even occur to him, since he, even more than the Gramma Udgul, seemed dark and hostile.

• In short, he had passed out, he had woken up, and now he belonged to the small cohort of the Levanidovo's inhabitants, more or less dead or living, with a status he had trouble appreciating, because he never knew what he was in the kolkhoz—a prisoner on parole, an unwanted guest, a refugee begrudgingly accepted more out of duty than compassion, or already a full member of the Levanidovo's community. President Solovyei's watchfulness weighed down on him, the forest surrounding the village dissuaded him from going elsewhere, into the uninhabitable zone where he knew he would only last a few days. Physically, he hadn't regained the energy he'd had as a soldier in the Orbise, he felt like he was in bad health, fragile, much like Barguzin who fainted often and who, without the Gramma Udgul's attentive care, would have long since been carried in his terminal form to the edge of the well, to meet the warm and welcoming heart of the nuclear core two kilometers down. And, on a psychological level, he suffered from confusion, his mind troubled by hazy memories, long-winded dreams, and the constant certainty that he'd already lived what he was now living once or several times. These problems didn't bother him much on a day-to-day basis, but they cast a gloom over him, because he didn't know if the excessive radiation was causing him to suffer a serious degenerative illness, or if Solovyei had possessed him just to mess with him, playing with him like a puppet before sending him back to the steppes, brainless and stupid, or to the bowels of the earth.

• For weeks now, he had gotten dressed with clothes taken from the dead or from the surviving cripples in the kolkhoz, from nonexistent husbands, from disappeared sovkhozniks of similar height. He felt perfectly comfortable in them. The things he had brought upon his arrival had long since been cleaned and dried, brought to his room, put in a box that he had shut and never opened again. His coat, however, had been hard to wash. The lining came away in shreds. He had spent time stitching it back together and clumsily patching the pockets, the right side, the collar. He did the same for the rest of his rags. He mended them and reinforced them as best as he could. He wanted to be able to reuse his original outfit if he was ever asked to return the clothes lent by the kolkhoz. But, deep down, he knew that they would never ask. Radiant Terminus functioned on ideological principles that didn't match up to the collectivist norms of the Orbise, but, as far as the allocation of goods went, the end result was the same. Disdain for property was, as had been the case throughout the Second Soviet Union, commonplace in the Levanidovo. It was a place where the Party had been extinguished, where the Party no longer existed, but where the idea of reestablishing capitalism and the bourgeoisie hadn't occurred to anyone, and besides it had to be asked just what this thing called capitalism would have looked like at Radiant Terminus, and what bourgeoisie could be called upon to oppress the working class. In any case, if by some miracle the enemy had braved the radiation to come implement its barbaric program in the Levanidovo, they would have met opposition so radical that its programmers and hit men would have swiftly been sent to the pit, along with other dangerous trash.

• While the sunlight caressed him, Kronauer thought about the kolkhoz, about his provisional stay in the kolkhoz, about the provisional that threatened to become permanent, and about everything that seemed strange, misunderstood, or incomprehensible. He had just kneeled down once more by the fire hydrant by Myriam Umarik's house. The leak showed ill will and Kronauer's repairs had only held for a few days, after which the seals had loosened and everything needed to be reset. Barguzin hadn't been interested in the problem and, even though the puddle in front of his house had been growing larger, he was counting on Kronauer to put things right again.

Kronauer was now listening to the water hissing under the hydrant's hood and, rather than dealing with the problem, he stayed idle, unmoving, and almost drowsy.

A heavy door banging startled him. Hannko Vogulian, Solovyei's oldest daughter, had just left the Soviet, which was also where her father lived.

She came toward him.

Her princess-like face shone under the sun, more Yakut than ever before and more magical than ever before. Her hairstyle had changed, her hair was now in two long black braids that were no longer tied around her forehead in a crown. Over the weeks, Kronauer had learned to look directly at her. He was no longer bothered by the disparate colors of her two eyes, as he had been at the beginning of his stay, and now he actually tried to immerse himself in those eyes, because he found them both wonderful and touching. Although he was deeply troubled by reading Maria Kwoll, he didn't hold back from imagining Hannko Vogulian stretched out beside him, tilting her body mellowed by the exhaustion of love and displaying one of her precious-stone eyes, sometimes the black onyx one, and sometimes the tiger's-eye one with flaming depths. He imagined it or he remembered it. She whispered magical and perfectly indecipherable syllables, maybe affectionate and maybe spiteful, in the shadows. It was one of those scenes that he wasn't sure had happened in reality, in a dream, or in one of the false memories that he suspected Solovyei of having cleverly implanted beneath his consciousness, while he was sleeping or passed out. He would have liked to know, but he would have never dared to ask Hannko Vogulian just to have a clear conscience. Sometimes he scrutinized her with the idea of finding some hint of complicity, he interrogated her mutely while considering the dampness of her eyes, the movement of her hands, her way of walking toward him. But he did this haltingly and he never got any answer. Whether among her sisters or on the Levanidovo's empty main road, Hannko Vogulian remained aloof and never deviated from her unfriendly stiffness.

She stopped three paces away from him.

—You're going to be transferred, she said.

—But I've just gotten used to my cell, he joked.

—There's no heat where you're sleeping, Hannko Vogulian said. The cold's coming. We're going to put you in another room. There's a radiator that heats properly. It's the same boiler as the one for the showers.

—All right, Kronauer said.

He looked at her tiger's eye. He dove in and lived another life in there.

• He bent down and walked his fingers behind the pipes to see where they came out. From time to time, when he touched something hard, the finger that had been pricked by the phonograph needle came back to mind, and, for half a second, he felt like the needle was sinking into his finger again and burning it. The wound hadn't even left a scar, but at moments like these a quick pain shot through his entire hand, like an electrical shock. His fingers snagged along a metal bas-relief and he shuddered quickly. He caught himself, he didn't want to explain once again in front of Hannko Vogulian what had happened with Solovyei's phonograph. But she noticed the movement of his shoulders.

—What's wrong? she asked.

—Nothing, he said. I thought a bug had bitten me. An ant or a spider.

—There aren't any spiders left, Hannko Vogulian said.

—That's not something I'm very sad about, Kronauer said as he kept following the pipe.

The water beaded between his fingers. I can't do anything about that, he thought. It's not even the seal. It's the clamp that's deformed.

I'd have to take it all apart and take it to a fitter, or find something equivalent in the Gramma Udgul's bric-a-brac. A spare fire hydrant. No idea whether she'd have one. And it's too much work for me.

Hannko Vogulian was wreathed in light and, even though he knew she was still looking him disdainfully, he looked at her with a happy smile. He had long since realized that she was even prettier than Myriam Umarik and, because he now knew how to look at her two eyes, he didn't hesitate to look at her directly.

They talked for a minute about spiders, the steppes, the big steppe spiders called mizguirs or mazguirs which had been completely eradicated by radiation in just a few months, before inexplicably reappearing on the expedition Solovyei and Morgovian had taken the day after Kronauer had come to the Levanidovo.

Once again, Hannko Vogulian recited what sounded like an official version of the events, a coherent whole that Kronauer had already heard from various sources, and which barely varied in its terms. Having arrived by the railroad, Solovyei and Morgovian had surveyed the hill overlooking the Red Star sovkhoz. They had shouted, combed through the grasses, examined the grasses and what they revealed of man's passage. Nobody was there. Aside from the traces of the soldiers having bivouacked several meters away from the rails, there were no clues. They had explored the environs for a long while, in case Kronauer's comrades had been abandoned after being violated or executed. They had searched through the sovkhoz's ruins, including the farthest-away buildings and in the place where the nuclear generator was still buzzing, surrounded by burning blocks that had burst from its core. But nothing. No corpses, not even crumpled ryegrass stalks that would have given them reason to suspect that there had been a crime.

—Maybe the soldiers offered to let them get in the convoy. If they accepted, they'd be far away by now.

—I can't believe that, Kronauer replied.

It was a phrase he usually uttered at this point in the conversation.

—They would have left a message, he continued.

—They didn't leave anything, Hannko Vogulian said.

—A message for me, Kronauer mused. In writing or some other way. They were waiting for me. They knew I was coming back.

They stood there for a minute, thinking. Upright and facing each other in the center of the Levanidovo.

—Vassilissa Marachvili was dying, Kronauer continued. She couldn't be moved. She wouldn't have gone far.

—Solovyei said that was your fate, Hannko Vogulian said.

—What was? Kronauer asked.

—To have dying women nearby.

Kronauer shrugged.

—What does he know, he whispered. What does he know about my life.

—I don't know, Hannko Vogulian said after a short while. Maybe he saw it in the flames.

He tried to find a hint of sympathy in Hannko Vogulian's tawny eye, he admired it once again just then, the nonpareil color, but his search was fruitless and he quickly turned away.

—What flames, he finally grumbled, unconvinced and hardly expecting an answer.

• As he didn't dare to meet her astonishing eyes, presuming that she would see some insolence in his own, he turned toward the countryside that he now knew by heart. The village's main road turned into a path that led to the forest and stopped by the first pines. At that point, it became an impassable forest trail, which Kronauer had taken to get out of the old forest and which he would never cross in the other direction, toward the marshes, the dark silence, the furious trees, and the giant anthills. The Levanidovo was an enclosed area and Kronauer no longer knew exactly which direction he should look to imagine the exact location of the Red Star sovkhoz, the railroad, and the steppes. As for the rest, the other directions, Morgovian had suggested that there was nothing beyond the trees, that the stretches of larches had no limits and if anyone should go there by mistake, they'd go in any direction, and only go deeper, tragically, into the taiga.

Kronauer didn't linger on the dark line encircling the kolkhoz and he briefly contemplated the completely yellow meadows, the distant farms in ruin, and then he noticed Abazayev's apiary and he saw Abazayev himself walking between two rows of beehives toward the valley. The Levanidovo still functioned somewhat normally, despite losing its inhabitants, its dogs, and its cattle.

—This Vassilissa Marachvili, did you know her well? Hannko Vogulian cut in. Were you lovers?

—We fought together, Kronauer said. We fled together.

—And slept? Did you sleep with her? Hannko Vogulian asked.

—Hmm, I don't remember, Kronauer said with a blush. Maybe once or twice. Or maybe not at all.

—If you slept together, then she was your wife, Hannko Vogulian decided. But if you didn't, then who was she?

—I don't know, Kronauer said.

They didn't talk for a few seconds. They thought about themselves, about marriage, about copulations such as the ones Maria Kwoll and her disciplines had described and such as the ones they had experienced in reality, about Vassilissa Marachvili, about Irina Echenguyen, who had indeed been Kronauer's wife, about Schulhoff who had indeed been Hannko Vogulian's spouse, however briefly.

—She was in very bad shape when I left, Kronauer said.

He wanted to call up Vassilissa Marachvili's image again, as she had been when he had abandoned her, which he had carried with him while fighting his hardest against all appearance of emotion and grief, the last image of Vassilissa Marachvili.

—You see, that's exactly what Solovyei's saying. That your specialty is being accompanied by a dying woman, Hannko Vogulian remarked. You've always got a girl in bad shape beside you. Dead or dying.

—No, Kronauer said.

—He says that all your women will die close to you, one after the other. Already there's been Vassilissa Marachvili on the steppe. Samiya Schmidt in the forest, during her bout. Irina Echenguyen in the Orbise. And certainly there have been and will be many others.

—Why are you talking about Samiya Schmidt? Kronauer asked angrily. She was never my wife. And besides, she's not dead.

—What do we know? Hannko Vogulian said.

—What? Kronauer asked. She was unconscious in the middle of the forest. I brought her back to the village on my back. Nothing else happened between us. She came back home sane and safe.

—That's not what Solovyei says, Hannko Vogulian said.

—Instead of listening to Solovyei, you could just ask her.

—We asked her, actually.

—And? What did she say?

—She didn't say anything. She barely talks at all anymore. She barely talks at all ever since she came back from the forest with you.

• —Listen, Kronauer. You came here by accident and not by choice, Hannko Vogulian said. You're our guest. We're not asking your opinion. And if you want mine, my opinion, you'd do best to turn your tongue in your mouth seven times before talking about Solovyei.

—Why? Kronauer asked. Because he's watching me? . . . Is he listening to us? Right now, is he listening to us?

—Maybe, yes. In any case, he hears us.

—I don't believe that. And even if he did hear us, I don't care at all.

—He doesn't like you, Hannko Vogulian said.

—Well? Kronauer said back.

—No, really, he doesn't like you at all, Hannko Vogulian insisted.

part two

ODE TO THE CAMPS

– 9 –

• Vassilissa Marachvili had closed her eyes the minute Kronauer set off. She opened them fifteen minutes later without saying anything, and then, because for her it was the end, she did not open them ever again.

Ilyushenko had to fight against his drowsiness. If he didn't let himself go completely, it was more out of solidarity with Kronauer, who at that moment was walking toward the forest, toward prospective help, and less because he was nervous about losing sight of the soldiers farther down the slope. He went back to Vassilissa Marachvili and watched her breathe. He had to stay on his knees, in a painful position, so as to resist the temptation to lie down next to her and not think about anything until there was nothing left. At that moment, she seemed peaceful, but death's approach clouded her face. A gray dew broke through her grimy skin, amid the hardened flecks dirtying her cheeks. The blood had withdrawn from her dried lips. She had vomited when they had come to the Red Star. Her ragged battle-dress stank.

Half an hour passed.

Half an hour had passed.

The sky was less bright. The gusts of wind diminished. The grasses exhaled their scents of stalks threatened by rot and they remained unmoving in their yellowing green. Kronauer had disappeared toward the forest.

—He's on the way, he'll come back, Ilyushenko murmured, as if he was answering Vassilissa Marachvili.

She didn't react. Ilyushenko sighed. I hope he'll come back, he thought.

This was the end of their vagrancy as a trio. After wandering, after bivouacking in the ghost towns, close to the abandoned cores, hunger, thirst, silent bombardments of gamma rays, Vassilissa Marachvili's shared love. They had ceased to be a small inseparable group. Kronauer had left, he would soon disappear into the taiga, he was at risk of starving to death beneath the trees. As for the two who had stayed back, Vassilissa Marachvili and Ilyushenko, it was clear that they were no longer an active group. Exhaustion had been slowly breaking them apart. They barely communicated anymore. Hidden in the open, forced to wait and stay immobile until the soldiers left, until some kind of help came, they were no longer able to comfort each other.

If Vassilissa Marachvili passed on, the very idea of helping one another would founder, the idea that had kept them together thus far.

• Farther down, the soldiers barely moved, and when they did it was slowly, as if radiation or illness had drained them of all energy. Standing upright without support overwhelmed them. Every moment they stopped moving, they put a hand on a freight car or a comrade so as not to fall, and, for two or three minutes, they looked like they were about to faint, catching their breath hunched over like old men. Some, betrayed by their trembling legs, had fallen down and, scattered in the grasses, they seemed dead. Others, affected by some huge weakness or a no less huge inertia, hadn't gotten out of the cars. Those soldiers simply stayed sitting on the floorboards, their legs hanging and their faces turned toward the sky, their eyes closed in the sunlight. The most valiant ones seemed hyperactive in contrast. They had formed a small detachment that ended up collecting wood splinters and boards to make a bonfire on the ballast. It looked like none of them were talking to each other, either because words were deemed unnecessary for accomplishing basic material tasks, or because each of them preferred to be locked up in harsh or tragic or simply unbreakable solitude within themselves.

Afraid that a reflection off his binoculars would draw a shooter's attention, Ilyushenko watched them with his naked eyes through the grasses' unruly ribs. The uniforms were in tatters, stripped of any distinctive insignia, more worthy of prisoners of war than of soldiers in the field. He couldn't figure out which corps they'd originally come from. And why exactly they were being stationed near the Red Star sovkhoz was a complete mystery. They were barely out of the train and none of them had gone off to explore the ruins. Although they were far from any theater of operations, they had stacked rifles outside the freight cars and, essentially, they followed a certain military logic. Two men had positioned themselves at each end of the train, one between the rails, the other leaning against the locomotive, and, even though they were dozing off pretty quickly, they were there to keep watch. Every so often, one of them woke up and immediately checked something in the countryside, then in his rifle, then went back to sleep.

Several possibilities. Ilyushenko couldn't stop going over them. These people's identities. Their raison d'être. Their origins. A group of partisans doing what they'd done in the Orbise again in empty lands, hunting traitors? . . . Or a Freikorps that had broken away from the Orbise? . . . Or were they deserters who, like us, had abandoned the army in despair? . . . Mutineers who had no other place to go? . . . Or who wanted to join the enemy? . . . Partisans returning to capitalism? Or bandits? . . . A group of irradiated suicides, having decided that they no longer had anything to lose, tempted to commit thefts and crimes to while away their last weeks of life, having tossed aside the Orbise's ideals of honesty and brotherhood? . . . Dangerous? Not dangerous?

They had hesitated the whole time, with all these unanswered questions turning in their heads—to go meet the soldiers? Stay hidden? . . . As he had thought about it, Kronauer certainly must have relived the hell that Irina Echenguyen had crossed, the hospital besieged by a violent troop of thugs with dogs' heads. That nightmare. He had talked about it once, one evening by the fire, furtively and choosing his words so as not to seem tormented by pain. He had managed not to dwell on horrible details, but Vassilissa Marachvili had become increasingly sad. She must have identified with Irina Echenguyen and, when Kronauer stopped talking, she hadn't said anything further. Ilyushenko, though, despite not having experienced such barbarity up close, knew enough about collective behavior to be wary of this zombie brigade setting up camp by the Red Star. They seemed calm, but any horde of males could suddenly lose reason and become aggressive. This also went for these slow-moving soldiers. And now the Orbise's shining beacon no longer cast light on the world or on the little area where its last partisans had been. So all the savagery would come back. All that we hadn't been able to eradicate during our all-too-brief centuries of power. The moralities of killers and rapists would supplant our own. Ancestral cruelties would no longer be taboo and, once again, as in the hideous period preceding the establishment of the Second Soviet Union, humanity would regress to its earlier stage as cavemen. Its ideologists would rally around those who had once advocated inequality and injustice. Its mercenary poets would sing the culture of masters. Ragtag soldiers would no longer be kept on a leash. The old dance of idiocy and blood would play out again.

• The last gleams of the setting sun had dissolved beyond the horizon. The evening began to blue the space. Ilyushenko spent the last minutes of the day repeatedly scrutinizing the soldiers who, at the bottom of the hill, had settled down around the fire. In vain he examined their half-alive half-dead, expressionless and gray faces. Now he used his binoculars. At this hour he was no longer in danger of being betrayed by a reflection of light on their glass. He nervously scanned these heads covered with dirty hair, these bodies clothed in army rags. He didn't try to read the words on their lips because, most of the time, they didn't talk. Then, as his inspection hadn't turned up anything useful, he lay back down behind the curtain of high grasses and let the useless optical instrument dangle from his neck.

• Night fell.

Vassilissa Marachvili groaned quietly, with such weakness that her voice didn't travel more than a meter.

Then, both of them, she and Ilyushenko, slept. Ilyushenko dozed off and woke up suddenly. The sky was dark, with clouds going past and no moon. The all-too-scarce stars sparkled behind a veil and illuminated nothing. Night dampened the steppes. The grasses and the earth let their autumnal scents bloom, full of putrefaction and insects that had died in the early frost. Around him, Ilyushenko heard vague squeaking, here perhaps the final screeching of grasshoppers and there perhaps the deep roots hardening for the winter, rhizomes. He really was concerned about only one thing: hearing Vassilissa Marachvili's breath. At the bottom of the hill, the soldiers weren't moving. The fire by the rails was no longer red. Ilyushenko tried to keep watch for as long as he could, and then, his eyes shut, he did his best to make sense of the night's distant sounds. Then he abandoned the effort and went to sleep.

In this way the night went by. Then came the morning accompanied with a light fog, and then the fog dissipated.

• The sky was gray-blue and sunless. It stayed that way the whole day.

Vassilissa Marachvili was stationary. She didn't ask for anything, she didn't complain, she seemed not to be suffering, she breathed regularly and almost noiselessly. Ilyushenko lay unmoving on his side and let the hours go by. He gently touched her wrist, or his hand lingered on the veins of her neck, to make sure her blood was still pulsing, or on her forehead, to wipe away the moisture. Later, in the early afternoon, he paid attention again to the men camping at the foot of the hill. In the light of the dawn he had confirmed that they were still there, then he had lain back down by Vassilissa Marachvili, as if total indifference had crushed him. Now, his face was hidden, his skin irritated by contact with the spiky plants, the chilly stems, the prickly leaves, and he went back to his job as a watchman.

The sentries had resumed their positions. Other men had replaced them, unarmed, which made Ilyushenko think that maybe the convoy had brought two sorts of travelers, one being military, and the other being civil, the two indistinguishable, clothed in the same interchangeable rags from the lost war. Then this idea floated away. It didn't lead to anything. Either could be hostile. Just like the previous night, he couldn't figure out what these men were waiting for. They were prostrate in the grass, around the extinguished campfire, and, despite the daylight that should have invigorated them, most of them were still lazing around or sleeping. Some had headed toward the area of the sovkhoz and they walked there with extreme indolence. Sometimes they went inside ruined buildings to bring out something that seemed salvageable, or a piece of wood, a splintered plank, and then they sat down, exhausted, and didn't move for an hour or two before getting back up and going at a cautious pace toward a new goal.

• The day went by in this way, in slowness, without any collective initiative, without any describable activity. Late in the afternoon, Ilyushenko became dizzy. He stopped watching what was happening by the tracks or in the sovkhoz and stretched out by Vassilissa Marachvili. Above them the clouds drifted, high up and heavy with dark shadows rather than rain. The hours flowed by, one after the other, in silence, in the grasses' trembling, in a few echoes of the sparse conversations that started up by the cars or the locomotive. Then the sunset came.

Vassilissa Marachvili hadn't regained consciousness. Ilyushenko gently caressed her face, the top of her neck, her hands, but he had stopped wiping away the bits of muddy dust, furrowed by trickles of sweat, which etched the patterns of death into her features. As the sunset deepened, drops of blood beaded around the corners of her eyes, beneath her nostrils, at the edges of her lips. She was no longer breathing calmly. She made no sound aside from irregular and hoarse breaths. Whether unconscious or still able to take in comprehensible fragments of the world, she gripped Ilyushenko's hand, and he didn't let go. For the first part of the night, her misery didn't change measurably. His heart breaking, Ilyushenko stayed right against her, he leaned over her, and in the darkness he watched as she traversed the last moments of her life.

• In the darkness, beneath a handful of stars scattered among the clouds, on the ground that had swiftly lost the day's warmth, in the middle of what might have once been farmed land but now, after the nuclear catastrophe, had merged with the indistinct sea of now-unnamed grasses, in earshot of the soldiers and their strange convoy, at a short distance from the abandoned Red Star sovkhoz, from its ruins and its small uncontrollable reactor, Ilyushenko watched as Vassilissa Marachvili traversed the last minutes of her life. Her dying lingered, as if imposed by a sadistic fate that loved emotion and suffering. Finally, well before dawn, Vassilissa Marachvili let out her last sigh. She tensed, and then relaxed; Ilyushenko let go of the fingers he had intertwined with his own, moved her arms into a natural and tranquil position along her body. Then he stayed flat on the ground for an hour, closed off to grief, open only to elementary sensations, to the dampness of the night and the grasses, to the occasional and miniscule ruptures in the shadows, to the terrible smells that came from his body and that of Vassilissa Marachvili.

• The sky didn't show any indication of brightening soon. The air was getting colder. Cramps settled into Ilyushenko's legs. He got back up and moved his limbs. His joints hurt. He warmed them with movements calling to mind the exercises of octogenarians. On the horizon a half moon had just emerged, bestowing only some pathetic light on the steppes. He said to himself that, despite everything, if the sentries hadn't fallen asleep, they now had a golden opportunity to spot him, because aside from him everything for kilometers around was completely petrified. He waited for the sound of a gun being cocked, a gunshot, but nothing came, and the moon disappeared. Then, without even wondering whether it was a good or bad idea, he hefted Vassilissa Marachvili's body and began to drag her toward the railroad.

After the day's end, the soldiers had lit a fire and some of them had stayed there for the night. The fire was now out, but throughout the last hours Ilyushenko had examined it so many times from the top of the hill that he knew exactly where it was, and now he oriented himself by a small red smudge that still breathed among the embers. He went down the slope without taking the least precaution not to be seen. He was wholly focused on not falling and not handling Vassilissa Marachvili's remains disrespectfully.

Once he was fifteen meters from the embers, one of the soldiers who had been sleeping haphazardly by the fire came out of his lethargy, turned on a flashlight, and pointed the beam at Ilyushenko. He froze in the light, mesmerized, filthy, silent, a strange vagrant from the steppes with his only baggage being a woman's corpse. The soldier turned off the flashlight without asking him what he wanted, what he was, without welcoming him or inviting him to come join the sleepers.

The night had not yet come to its end and it was cold. Ilyushenko stayed for half a minute without taking a step, enough time for his retinas, rendered temporarily useless by the light's beam, to regain their ability to distinguish black from white. None of the soldiers around the fire said a word and, as they didn't snore in their sleep, it occurred to Ilyushenko that they too, like Vassilissa Marachvili, hadn't survived. He set her morose weight on the ground, taking care that the corpse wouldn't bounce disgustingly against the earth, and then he went to the fire pit and sat by the kindling to stir the embers with some splintered wood. A flame crackled on one of the planks, red and gold, but the fire didn't catch and, after several pointless attempts, Ilyushenko gave up. He hadn't even been able to warm his hands.

The soldier with the flashlight was talking now. The last of the flames reflected off his shoulder, in his feverish and exhausted eyes, against his leathery physiognomy, then the light diminished again and only his voice was left.

—We don't eat human flesh, he said.

—Oh, Ilyushenko said.

His throat and tongue were dry. The vowel had been hard to get out, it had grown from a wheezing sound, and then he coughed. The soldier held out a flask. Ilyushenko let the water soak into his mucus before he swallowed. It had a vinegary taste. He gargled carefully so as not to choke or set off spasms that would paralyze his stomach.

—Marxism-Leninism forbids it, the soldier replied as he took back the flask.

—Forbids what? Ilyushenko asked.

—Eating human flesh.

—Yes, I know that, said Ilyushenko.

—So why did you bring us that? asked the soldier.

Ilyushenko finally realized the misunderstanding, but he was too tired to be annoyed.

—You can help me take care of her. I don't want the crows and ravens devouring her on the open steppes.

Another bout of coughing shook him. His listener, who couldn't possibly know how dehydrated he was, didn't offer to quench his thirst again.

—We haven't eaten anything for weeks, but we'd never eat human flesh, he continued.

Ilyushenko's body forced him to lie down by the ashes. His eyelids closed heavily, his heart beat as if he was in a deep sleep. The bodies stretched out around him encouraged him not to fight it. Even the pain of Vassilissa Marachvili's loss had gone hazy. Suddenly, he was no longer thinking of anything, but the smell of carbonized planks and the absence of warmth and light.

• When day broke, the stiffened soldiers sprawled out and yawned. With immense laziness they got up and began to walk. Some went off to take care of their paltry urges, others went back into the cars to stretch properly. A few were still lying on the ground, breathing slowly and waiting for the sun to appear and warm them up.

They offered Ilyushenko water and shared bits of pemmican with him. He had to wait until sunup before hearing the sound of their voices at last. They talked a little about one thing or another, about the end of the Orbise, about egalitarianism, about the officers who had committed suicide or who they'd had to shoot, about their hopes of having finished their interminable travels. They had gone in and out of irradiated zones for a month without finding anything even vaguely resembling an oasis. They felt like they were going around in circles. The destination they dreamed of finding was a work camp that wasn't marked on the railroad maps, but which they had heard about. They had crossed the entire network together searching for what they considered a happy end to their wandering. In a camp, one of them said, they would be taken care of and finally be free. They glanced around and talked like they were insane. They also talked about Vassilissa Marachvili. The one who'd had a flashlight, and who the soldiers had elected captain for a week, suggested keeping her where the nuclear generator was, so that she would be safe from predators. They had been eliminated by radiation, the captain said, and would continue to be eliminated for eternity's entirety. Several soldiers nodded. He's right, one of them said.

Ilyushenko was easily convinced. He had absolutely no desire to bury Vassilissa Marachvili. Leaving her alone near the core was a form of slow incineration, and in any case far preferable to rotting slowly underground, among the beasts, the earthworms, the centipedes, and the larvae.

− 10 −

• Five foot soldiers volunteered to help transport Vassilissa Marach-vili to the defective reactor. They positioned themselves to carry her in an almost brotherly, certainly attentive way, and, having bypassed the locomotive and crossed the tracks, they went shakily through the tall grasses and undergrowth toward the small sovkhoz's nuclear build-ing. They went past collapsed administrative buildings, a former pigsty that still smelled of manure, two collective residences that didn't emit any human odors, and, after taking a road that had once been asphalt, they came to the entrance of the generator. The soldiers set Vassilissa Marachvili on the doorstep and, feeling that they had done their job, they left Ilyushenko with the corpse and went back toward the Red Star's entrance and the railroad.

• The building's door was shut, but not locked. Ilyushenko cleared away the dirt that had built up at the foot of the door, pushed on the latch to pull the panel open, and went in. It was a technical control room, with pipes of different sizes, monitors, knobs, meters. They had all burned and been completely ruined when the concrete surrounding the adjacent tank had burst, and violent streams of fusion wastewater had flowed in its wake. But then the eruption had calmed, and final-ly, after several decades, the space looked like a room full of broken machines that had burned a long time ago and were now waiting for total overhaul. By some miracle, two lamps still worked in the middle of the soot-black ceiling. This miracle was due to the heroic liquidators who had managed, right after the explosion, to reestablish a provisional electric supply in order to carry out emergency operations on the tank, and who had died forgetting to turn off the lights.

Under the lights, there were two stools, and on the stools, two men sitting.

The first one was an impressively sized man, a hairy fiftysomething giant Ilyushenko decided had to have come from a Russian bylina, or maybe one of Tolstoy's short stories describing countrymen whose appearance and style hadn't changed for a thousand years. This man had a sheepskin cloak wrapped around his shoulders, and was dressed in a deep blue muzhik's shirt that was perfect, silky, and unwrinkled, with billowing gray serge pants tucked into waxed boots, and, if he hadn't had a rifle by his shoulder and a robber's ax in his massive black belt, he could have come right out of a tranquil story of an unchanging Russian or Siberian village, living from day to day and having escaped the course of the centuries and their jolts, having ignored the Mongolian invasion, serfdom, collectivization. But there were these weapons, and his magnetic, yellow gaze, which Ilyushenko couldn't hold for more than a second, an outpouring of golden fire that opened out to the hereafter, adding an extremely unnerving dimension to his person. It was Solovyei. He had come to the Red Star sovkhoz as soon as Myriam Umarik and Hannko Vogulian had taken charge of the unconscious Kronauer, and he had arrived at the reactor building early in the morning.

On his left Solovyei had Morgovian, a man who Ilyushenko immediately thought looked sickly, terrified of his companion, and generally insignificant.

Ilyushenko wasn't prepared for this encounter and he blinked rapidly without saying anything, wondering if his brain, exhausted, wasn't somehow playing tricks on him, and if he hadn't begun to hallucinate as a result of the heavy bombardment of rays from the tank.

Maybe I'm dreaming or dying, he thought.

He turned toward the door. Vassilissa Marachvili lay on the door-step. The soldiers who had brought her there had gone back.

Or maybe I'm already dead, he thought.

• —Oh, good, the enormous muzhik said in a deep voice. You came with your daughter.

—She's not my daughter, Ilyushenko said. She's Vassilissa Marachvili.

—Is she your wife? the enormous muzhik said.

Ilyushenko didn't know how to answer. This interrogation seemed uncalled for.

—She's dead, he said.

The enormous muzhik nodded with a tilt of his chin. Unable to meet his gaze, Ilyushenko looked at his mouth, lost amid the black beard. The hair wasn't fake. If he lived in the area, this man must have made some sort of pact with the radiation, which turned everyone completely bald before killing them.

—For me, wife or daughter, it doesn't matter, Solovyei said, oddly proud. Bring her here, so we can see if she's really dead.

Ilyushenko balked. He had never willingly obeyed orders.

—What about you, who are you? he asked.

The other man smiled like a wily muzhik, raised the hands that he'd set on his massive thighs, and gestured vaguely behind him.

—There's a kolkhoz back there. We're self-sufficient. I'm the presi-dent. And your name is Ilyushenko, am I right?

Ilyushenko nodded.

—Did you talk to Kronauer? he asked.

The enormous muzhik frowned. As if he wanted advice on what to say, he turned to the worn-out kolkhoznik watching the conversation, his head slumped, quiet and frightened.

—This bastard Kronauer will get what's coming to him, he grumbled.

—What did he do? Ilyushenko asked.

—He took his sweet time with my daughter, the enormous muzhik said angrily.

Despite his exhaustion, Ilyushenko couldn't bring himself to believe something so unlikely.

—What daughter? he asked.

—Morgovian's wife, said the muzhik, pointing to his companion with barely veiled displeasure.

Now that they'd noticed him, Morgovian sat up and muttered two or three disjointed words. He took off his hat and fiddled with it to look busy. Now his head, bare of all hair and covered with numerous scars, was visible. He had the head of a zek with only fifteen years left before freedom.

—I don't believe that, Ilyushenko said.

—Did you say her name was Vassilissa Marachvili? the enormous muzhik asked, changing the subject.

Ilyushenko nodded with disdain.

—Bring her here, I told you, the enormous muzhik said.

Ilyushenko went out of the building and dragged Vassilissa Marachvili inside. He set her down in front of the two seated men. He felt like he was presenting a game bird to some hunters and this so disgusted and upset him that he couldn't stay upright; instead, he sat by Vassilissa Marachvili, touching her arms, her torso, her face, without any further thought as to the men there, since he was trying to be one with her body. He took in her smells of the steppes and earth, of dirty clothes and dead flesh, and, out of friendship and empathy, and also out of hostility toward the two kolkhozniks ordering him around, he refused to think of her as a corpse.

Vassia, he thought.

• Ilyushenko and Vassilissa Marachvili had met several times at cell group meetings before the fall of the Orbise, and there was already a friendly bond between the two of them when they joined one of the partisan units hoping to defend the Orbise one last time for the sake of honor without any prospect of victory, however small, even in the smallest battles. The group they belonged to had been wiped out in a matter of hours. One evening, with their front broken through and the self-assured enemy sitting quiet until the next day's offensive, they had gone into a bombed-out house, lain down on an undamaged bed, and made love, awkwardly and fearfully, telling themselves that in any case they only had a few hours to live and whatever happened to their bodies didn't matter. The next morning, they both went into a rear-guard formation, an unpromising brigade made up of survivors intent on hampering the enemy before disappearing. That was how they met Kronauer. And Vassilissa Marachvili did fall a bit in love with him, but then the three of them had gotten caught up in the whirlwind of civil war, and they no longer had the time to figure out the state of their sentimental relationship triangle. Their commander wanted to send them on ridiculous kamikaze missions, and ally with communist creatures from other solar systems that he was claiming to talk to telepathically. They had to separate from him by shooting him, as has already been described elsewhere. Then they decided to flee by going along the taiga, through the steppes dotted with cities, small towns, and industrial and agricultural centers, nearly all of which had had their nuclear cores breached at the same time, rendering uninhabitable an immense region the size of a continent and now abandoned. Behind them the enemy was reestablishing capitalism and undertaking massive bloodbaths in order to start afresh, but in these areas unsuitable for human life there was nothing left to fear. Now they just had to go forward, toward death, helping one another. Vassilissa Marachvili hadn't really weakened until the last week of their trek. Kronauer, who was most resistant to the exhaustion from hunger and radiation, had often carried her on his back, but Ilyushenko had often taken turns as well. They kept heading toward their communal end. For both of them, Kronauer and Ilyushenko, Vassilissa Marachvili was not a merely circumstantial companion, but more like a special sister. A small and very special comrade.

And suddenly Ilyushenko realized that he was going to leave her here, this woman he'd loved, respected, and considered special, in this room where a nuclear disaster had occurred and where, over the course of centuries and even more, a silent and devastating and inexorable eruption would continue. He had certainly thought about this before, but suddenly he was completely aware of it. Here, in this ruined technical building, with carbonized walls, Vassilissa Marachvili's immense solitude would begin.

Vassilissa Marachvili's immense solitude.

But the presence of these two unlikely kolkhozniks kept Ilyushenko from communing with her, kept him from saying at her bedside, internally or out loud, his good-byes or words of comfort. He would have liked to talk to her some more, to speak his pain. And now everything was unraveling between them. He needed peace and quiet to make sure that the few washed-out images still connecting them were firmly fixed in his mind and that they wouldn't fade away too quickly. He needed time and absence, emptiness. Solovyei and Morgovian had no reason to be present in this moment of grief. They were totally external to his mourning. He needed to ask them to leave the place. He would ask them to go, to have the decency not to be present here. He would explain that this was a private funeral, that only concerned the dead woman and himself, and that they were of course excluded. Yes, that's it. He would get up and firmly ask them to go and wait outside. And then, if needed, they could resume their conversation.

• Without any concern as to what Ilyushenko was thinking, Solovyei rummaged through a bag that he carried on a strap. He took out a bit of dark brown pemmican, wrapped in oilpaper. Reaching over Vassilissa Marachvili's body, he handed the packet to Ilyushenko.

—You can last weeks in the open steppes with that, he said. Go southwest with the soldiers. Go along the tracks. You'll end up settling down somewhere. The distances are vast, but you'll still get somewhere and make a place for yourself there.

Ilyushenko got up and, without a word, caught off guard, accepted the gift the enormous muzhik had given him. The amount of pemmican was impressive. There were at least three kilos of it.

—What about Vassilissa Marachvili? he asked.

—I'll examine her. I'll take care of her. She's at the end of her rope. She won't go far.

—No, you won't. She's dead.

—She's neither dead nor alive. That's what will save her. At that point, we'll work on her.

Morgovian, who up until that moment had been nervous but hadn't opened his mouth, inexplicably broke in.

—We can fix her, he stuttered.

Ilyushenko had a large empty pocket in his dirty deserter's coat. He was stuffing the block of pemmican in it. He stopped doing so and looked up at the kolkhoznik who had just spoken. He met his furtive, small-statured zek's eyes, somehow able to compromise with watchmen and barracks wardens, seeking out consensus rather than conflict and physical threats. But more than anything he saw in those eyes a vicious tone, a lazy and self-assured lust. Now he had the impression that he had brought Vassilissa Marachvili not to villagers impervious to radiation, but to two necrophiliac degenerates practically proud of it.

—I'm not letting you touch this woman, he said.

Solovyei held his arm in front of Morgovian to keep him from saying other nonsense.

—Morgovian is right, he said. We can fix her. But it's a great deal of work.

—I'm staying right by her, Ilyushenko said. I have no reason to leave her with you. I don't have any faith in you. I have no idea who you are. I don't know what the story is with this kolkhoz.

Solovyei pulled himself off the stool he had been sitting on and stood up straight. Making sure all the while to keep his cloak on his shoulders, he stepped over Vassilissa Marachvili's body and drew close to Ilyushenko, in a stance that wasn't aggressive in and of itself, but which could hardly be seen as neutral. His hands certainly didn't caress the head of his ax and instead dangled along his colossal hips, open and innocent, but his entire body was a dangerous mass. He left no doubt that if there was a fight he'd be on top in less than three seconds. He was gigantic and, as one of the powerful lamps in the room backlit his head, it created a halo that made him seem like a fantastical creature. Ilyushenko looked up at him, not wanting to seem intimidated, and immediately beheld a vision of his hairy face, carnivorous and taunting, a face that persisted in formidable flames, that did not even twist, that was both woolly and blinding. Then Ilyushenko met Solovyei's tiger-yellow eye, his hypnotic iris bereft of warmth, and the two came face to face.

This kolkhoz president doesn't scare me, he thought unconvincingly. He's just a kulak from Tolstoy's time. An uncollectivized country bumpkin turned crazy and depraved by the gamma rays. Maybe there isn't even a kolkhoz where he lives. He's the sort to live in his hallucinations.

Ilyushenko endured Solovyei's gaze for two seconds, then the duel shifted against him. The other man didn't blink and Ilyushenko felt a wave of bad light entering him, invading him to the marrow and depriving him of all willpower. A vertiginous nausea began to overpower him, and he was already wondering if he would faint or vomit, but, more than anything, he was aware that deep down he was losing his mind and that he had lost his mind as well as the struggle. The comparison was worth what it was worth, but it was perhaps the sort of reflection that occurs to a fly when, after having been caught in some slime, it realizes that it's just been whelmed by gastric acid that will turn it into food.

—The story of the kolkhoz is my story, Solovyei finally said in a strong and whistling voice. It's my business. The kolkhoz is my dream, and it will last for all the time I want it to. It will last as long as I exist, and, in it, I'm accountable to nobody. As for your daughter, I'll take her under my wing. You want her to stay here, getting blacker and blacker and deader and deader? Is that what you want? For her to be under the rays, more and more alone and ghastly?

Ilyushenko didn't know how to respond. He struggled mentally to figure out whether the golden liquid paralyzing him was outside him or not. Disorganized under-thoughts babbled in the subterranean corridors of his memory, formulated in a magical language of which he did not understand a syllable. More generally, the world as a whole escaped him. He barely heard Solovyei's question, and Solovyei answered it for him.

—Of course not, you don't want that. You'd rather that she keep on living, but you don't know what it takes for that to happen. Well, instead of entrusting her to this crazy reactor, you're going to entrust her to me. I'll fix her and I'll take her to the kolkhoz. To Radiant Terminus. The name of the kolkhoz. That's what has to be done. Nothing better for her.

At that moment, Ilyushenko slowly moved his right arm over his eyes, as if to protect them against a blinding light, and, without a word, he staggered and lost consciousness. He stayed upright, as if turned to stone, he didn't fall to Solovyei's feet, but he barely had any consciousness left.

—Of course not, Morgovian said. Nothing would be better for her. That's what we'll have to do.

—Of course, Solovyei confirmed. That's what we'll do.

• The space was lined with ruined pipes and meters dangling at the end of cables like carbonized foxtails, the control screens showed more cooled bits of lava than electronics, the ceiling was thick with sooty dust, the walls had undergone a terrible cleaning by fire, the concrete barrier separating the room from the tank was furrowed with several large cracks, and the ground was cluttered with blackish concretions, ashy fragments that didn't crumble under footsteps. It was a repugnant background. Still, the harsh and violent electrical light bathed the scene with a sort of theatrical normalcy, as if it had been painstakingly put together by a stage electrician for an unspecified post-exotic performance, an unspecified little tragic sketch like the ones that had been popular after the end of the First Soviet Union, without special effects, with comedians who stood almost unmoving next to each other, in this

unnerving mental nudity characteristic of the work of Leonor Ostiat-
egui, Maria Sauerbaum, Maria Henkel, or other dramatists of the time.
A theater scene showing what happened after the end.

And here there were four characters: first a woman in rags mimick-
ing cadaverous rigidity at the others' feet; then a seemingly self-effacing
kolkhoznik who hadn't gotten off his stool since the first lines; then a
paralyzed deserter, wearing an extremely dirty soldier's coat, with a bag
on his shoulder and a pair of binoculars taken from a corpse and, on
his neck, a spider web that was intended to mark his affiliation with
the worker's and countryman's camp; and finally a gigantic muzhik in
his Sunday best, with a beard and a wreath of hair sticking out here
and there as if run through by an electrical current, with a magician's
yellow eyes that were wholly unbearable. Four actors who couldn't
have had much to say to one another, so different were they from each
other. And, indeed, the dialogue among them had finished. Now, only
one performer had everyone's attention.

Only Solovyei spoke.

Only Solovyei currently had a non-mute role. He performed a
play comprising a monologue, a talkative block aimed at the listeners who made him stand out all the more. Essentially, he steered and
spoke a dream, as the dead did after their dying, as all the dead tried
to do in the hope that their last conscious jaunt still had a bit of flesh,
still contained some non-solitude and adventure. As most of the dead
tried to do in vain. But Solovyei had succeeded, he had succeeded in
constructing this solidly and, if not for eternity, at least forever. And
now he was managing his dream without worrying about decency or
plausibility. The image had solidified, the scene in progress no longer
required any of the actors to move, and only he spoke. The time for
talking was reserved entirely for him. The light didn't particularly flat-
ter him, although he was in the center of the theatrical space, but all
the sound was his. He towered over Ilyushenko and Vassilissa Marachvili, and without caring about the nightmarish length of his discourse,
he unfurled it.

• —It's not my intention to teach you a lesson, soldier, but it's stupid on your part to talk about faith. Faith has nothing to do with it . . . It's a completely different question . . . I'm going to tell you, Ilyushenko. You can consider yourself already dead. I suppose you already know it, more or less. So, in these conditions, what good does it do you to make trouble for this girl? If you're already dead or something like it, close to toppling or walking through death, what good does it do you to fight so that nothing happens to your daughter? She's here in the radiation chamber, and because of that, but mainly with my help, she can regain a bit of existence. I'm not promising the world, I'm not saying she'll come back entirely, but that she can regain at least a bit of existence, yes . . . Oh, yes . . . that I can do . . . You, however, can't stay busy with her. You've done everything you can, but now it's done. You've done what you could, which is to say nothing . . . Soon, you'll leave with the soldiers, for you there's no other direction, and, if you want my advice, you've got nothing to lose there. They, too, are already dead or something like it. Close to toppling, but far from extinct. Thanks to me, in a certain way, far from extinct . . . You'll all get back on this train and leave. What for, in what direction, you ask. This is my answer . . . We all have dreams. Even in the middle of the black space, we keep on functioning that way, in hope and in dreams . . . It's our fate as conscious creatures . . . Whether we like it or not . . . Before life, and especially after, whether we want to or not, we advance that way, in dreams . . . And moreover, often we're inhabited by dreams of dreams . . . You, along with the others, the prisoners and soldiers in the convoy, you have something inhabiting you. That'll become more and more clear to you, over time . . . You all have the dream of settling into a place where you'll finally be at peace. Whether you're already dead or in the throes of dying or becoming dead, or still soldiers, or already prisoners, or already transformed forever into the living dead, or disguised as alive or as dead puppets without any idea of who you are. These are distinctions that don't matter to you, and even less to the others who don't know about any of you and don't care . . . You dream of finally making a home in a place where you're not forced to be anything other than what you are, you dream of going into a camp and never leaving again. Finally, a reward for your efforts . . . for your persistence . . . finally imprisonment in a camp where you'll be protected from the horrors of the outside . . . This dream we've all had at one point or another. Well, I'm telling you, Ilyushenko, as I stand here speaking to you, I've seen everything, it's no worse to dream it, even if it seems a bit strange to the living, to the dead, and to the dogs. It's no worse. And in any case you'll leave with them and, once you've been carted around in a cattle car for a while, you'll be one hundred percent like them. They're no longer of this world, and neither are you . . . Nor am I, nor your daughter Vassilissa Marachvili . . . but now we're not talking about the same worlds, you wouldn't understand . . . No matter, the two of us will be separated soon and never brought together again . . . well, yes and no . . . when I want to I can see who I want to in the black space or in the flames. Don't try to understand that. We're no longer similar or comparable creatures . . . You're a brave soldier of the Orbise, you're used to generosity and the Orbise's brotherhood, and I . . . I too was once used to that, but I quickly learned to cross black space and the flames, and that . . . those things change everything. When you know how to come and go through the flames and when you know how to sleep and wake up in black nothingness, existence is nothing like in the Orbise . . . you live your life like a thousand plays, a thousand comedies and a thousand tragedies that never end, and not like a crummy short walk in the Second Soviet Union or I don't know what's even worse . . . You can't understand and I don't expect you to understand. So why am I telling you this, and what do I expect of you? . . . I don't expect anything special, soldier, I don't expect anything from you. Just for you to go back to the convoy, for you to leave everything behind you and let me take care of your daughter. This Vassilissa Marachvili, she's already out of your life. Whether you still think of her or not doesn't matter now. She's no longer for you. I don't know her very well yet, but I can tell you she's a pretty girl and a good girl, brave and ideologically healthy. She couldn't handle the exhaustion of the irradiated steppes, that's not something you can hold against her. She has so much radiation in her body that she's already made of something other than real flesh, and that's exactly why we'll be able to bring her back . . . Because of the radiation we can fix her. If you have the expertise and you don't balk at the work . . . It's magic as much as science, but fundamentally it's science more than anything. I don't say art because I don't have that ambition. In any case, I assure you that we can fix her . . . and all right, she won't be like before, she won't have any of her own memories from her existence before, and once she's woken back up she'll be a little soft and stupid, but at least we'll have given her back the minimum for living. She won't know that she's alive and she won't have much of a brain, but it's a hell of a lot more than plain and simple death. She won't be living or dead, nor a dog, and once again she'll be a pretty and good girl, brave and ideologically healthy . . . Good. You wonder what will happen next. I won't hide that once she's revived I'll give her to Morgovian . . . Morgovian, you know, this tractor driver here with me right now . . . Morgovian's a good sort, he'll know how to take care of her. He knows how to take care of tractors, he doesn't talk too much, he's able to be faithful and tender. He made a mistake marrying one of my daughters. That upset me. He married Samiya Schmidt. She's the one who asked, and, in the end, it wasn't his fault, but it was still a mistake, a big mistake. It was done, there's no crying over spilled milk, but it upset me very much . . . Morgovian's a good sort, I just said it and I'm not going to say otherwise. But I don't want him spending his life with what remains of my daughter Samiya Schmidt. She's not for him. I know that he didn't hurt her very much, she's against intercourse . . . and him, he's a bit impotent . . . that's how he is, and the radiation didn't help . . . But in any case this union wasn't meant to last forever . . . We'll sort the whole thing out once Vassilissa Marachvili's back in shape. Samiya Schmidt will be unmarried again and that's the best thing that could happen to her. She's not doing well, and her marriage has only made her shakier. When she gets worse, if she gets worse, I'll be there. I can go into her dreams, she'll never be all alone, there's nothing to worry about for her. I can go in and leave as I wish into her reality and her dreams. Whether it bothers her or not I can go in. It's a safeguard for her. I have my way of taking care of her. It concerns the two of us, her and me, and it's not your problem, Ilyushenko . . . It's nobody's business . . . It's not Morgovian's business, either. As for Vassilissa Marachvili, I'll put her in the Soviet away from everything, to start with. In the basement . . . Your comrade Kronauer won't know anything about her. Morgovian won't visit her at first. Nobody will come to bother me while I work on her . . . How long? Is that what's bothering you? How long will I be working before she comes back? . . . Well, I don't know at all . . . What I know is that once she's come back into existence she won't have needs or much of anything in her head. But we'll take care of her in the Levanidovo then. You won't worry about her, Ilyushenko. Instead of her broiling slowly in this awful reactor, we'll care for her at Radiant Terminus, we'll save her, and we'll extend her as if she was born in immortality . . . She'll last a long while, you can be sure of that. She'll endure. Everybody's a bit like that in the Levanidovo, you know how the song goes . . . Only there's this Kronauer. I hope he won't get in our way. I'm watching him, but he's unpredictable and our goals aren't the same ones. He ended up in the Levanidovo even though he shouldn't have been there. Maybe I should have broken his skull instead of putting him in the prison. I don't like him. He's not really part of any stinking category, politically he's not too dirty, but I don't like him. Samiya Schmidt was in the forest with him and ever since she hasn't said a word. He's got some sort of infectious unhappiness in him. If he ever hurts my daughters it would be hell for him, and that . . . that I would make sure to last a long while . . . Look, can you imagine a thousand six hundred and nineteen years of confusion and fear, two thousand four hundred and one years of suffering, or even more? That's what he can expect if he ever hurts one of my daughters . . . Same thing if he tries to find Vassilissa Marachvili and visit her and hurt her in the Soviet's basement. For me this man will always be accompanied by a woman dying or dead. I saw it in his dreams and his memories. Right there on the surface, barely any digging needed to find that . . . The women he's known have always ended up with him, dying or dead. And that's also why I don't want him to hang around my daughters. First of all because they're my daughters and second because I don't want them to end up dying or dead by him . . . In any case, not right now . . . He's got a filthy fate and that'll last until the black space, it's not worth hoping otherwise for him . . . It'll last forever . . . It's not his fault, have to see how he was before he was born, whom he got his misfortune from, but, right there, I don't like it at all that he's talking to my daughters . . . I'll have to go into him to keep him from going too far. I'd have liked for him not to come to the kolkhoz, but he came and, for me, the damage has been done. It's not the same for you, Ilyushenko . . . you I'm sending back with the soldiers, you'll travel by train and they'll be the ones you set up your new life with . . . if you can call it that . . . something like that . . . You'll go with them toward a camp . . . it'll take however long it takes . . . five hundred years, two thousand years . . . and even if you find one, a camp, no saying that they'll accept you . . . But well, that'll be your life from now on, Ilyushenko . . . Whatever happens, you'll be too far away from the Levanidovo and my daughters for it to bother me . . . And so far away from Vassilissa Marachvili . . . Because I'll tell you, Ilyushenko . . .

Solovyei kept talking and talking, fiercely but droning on, or sometimes with an inappropriate intonation that suggested that behind his words were magical forces he could barely control. He wove a cocoon of words around Ilyushenko, likely to permanently take hold of Ilyushenko's body and spirit, and his fate as well. Every so often, he readjusted his cloak, which tended to slip off his shoulders, over the shining cloth of his countryman's shirt, or he set his hand on the head of the ax resting by his belly. He clearly took pride in playing a terrifying character and, despite his diminished audience, he overdid it a bit.

• Ilyushenko was frozen, facing him only a pace away, a muddled look on his face. He didn't seem irritated or disapproving. He stood sheepishly, his arms at his sides, as if he had given up all free will, and he listened patiently and even deferentially to the explanations he was given. Clearly, he didn't have any kind of answer to provide, and soon enough, like an onlooker who didn't have to say good-bye to anybody, he would leave the technical room to begin his new life as a wanderer searching for a camp.

Morgovian sat and watched indifferently; he had his usual appearance of a farm worker weighed down by the harshness of country work and by the uncontrollable complexity of human relationships. He was the only one of the four sitting down. When he heard his name spoken, he barely looked up, and certainly not at Solovyei, and as he blinked he listened to how Solovyei had decided his life and his domestic future, then he shrank down even further on his stool.

Vassilissa Marachvili herself played an even muter role than Ilyushenko and Morgovian had. She didn't express anything audible, visible, or legible. She remained stretched out in front of the stools, on the hard ground sprinkled with dark crumbs and compact remnants resembling excrement sculpted in ebony. She was evidently not in a state to understand the words of the president of Radiant Terminus, but Solovyei's voice must have magically entered her marrow or what remained of it. She perceived these very, very vague echoes, and she waited for what would happen next.

– 11 –

• Ilyushenko left the reactor without looking back. He stumbled over the steps, nearly falling, and immediately stopped moving for a minute, swaying because he had trouble regaining his balance. He stubbornly turned his back to the building that was momentarily holding Vassilissa Marachvili's body and the two kolkhozniks who had promised to give her some sort of rebirth. Ilyushenko himself would go his own way and abandon them, this body with its unlikely fate, its hypothetical future, and it was heartbreaking, but all the same there was a chance that something good could happen to her, something that, for Vassilissa Marachvili, would ultimately be less dismal than death—assuming such an eventuality existed. The idea of a posthumous life had never really occurred to Ilyushenko. He was not inclined toward mysticism, and like us all he preferred to explain the world's oddities through dialectical materialism, evil plots hatched by enemies of the people, or the unexpected detours of five-year plans. However, oddity or not, for Vassilissa Marachvili there couldn't be a better prospect for the days to come. This president of the kolkhoz really seemed to know what he was saying about reviving those dead from radiation, and in any case he couldn't do anything worse than the worms, bacteria, and scavengers that would have attacked her body if it was put in the earth.

Now he was walking through the ruins of the sovkhoz and, as he got farther away from the nuclear structures, he asked himself several novice questions about the existence that might continue after death.

About the length of this phenomenon, about what would happen during and after. The questions were formulated in such a muddled way that he didn't even dream of an answer. Lurching beneath the gray-blue sky, in the knee-high and waist-high grasses, he had trouble fighting the mental void Solovyei had dug in him. Along with the narcotic torrent of Solovyei's monologue and the effect of his golden gaze was the dizziness due to his half-hour stay by the fuel rods. The images floated disjointedly in his immediate memory and he was barely able to keep Vassilissa Marachvili's memory at the forefront of his thoughts.

He muddled together the arguments for why he was saying goodbye to Vassilissa Marachvili and, more specifically, giving her body to a Tolstoyan kulak and a stupid countryside proletarian. He postponed the possible remorse, and especially sorrow, caused by her death. His knowledge was hazy, his steps were uncertain, and he shifted directions, rhythms, stopped. His face was an impassive but tortured mask, as if he had come out of an electroshock session.

He stayed groggy like that for fifteen minutes walking around in circles, aimlessly and slowly around the ruins of a pigsty, and then his dizzy spell lifted.

And now he went toward the railroad tracks with a steadier gait. He went up the Red Star sovkhoz paths that had once been asphalt. Under his feet, the grasses crackled. A good number of them had already dried out for the fall. He crushed them, leaving in his wake a powder redolent of hay. Sometimes he had to go onto a trail through the bush-covered areas. The convoy was close now. He went past the dark rectangles of homes darkened by time, the windows behind which foliage had burst through furniture, floors, and windowpanes, then he left through the sovkhoz entrance. Above him, the red tin star hadn't completely lost its original colors. Maybe because he wanted to be moved by something that wasn't himself or his grief, he thought intensely about what this decrepit star represented, and he was glad it had stayed in place. It would remain for a long while up there, on this solemn frontispiece, for several decades, protected from vandalism by nuclear silence, indifferent to the vileness and defeats overwhelming the metropolises and continents filthy with capitalism and blood. It will keep shining on us, he hypothesized, it will shine on and on over the places where we are, in the lands and in the dreams forbidden to the living, the dead, and the dogs. This is what he repeated to himself while walking—partly personal thoughts, still weighed down by bits of Solovyei's monologue, part of which had been transmitted directly to his consciousness with its sorcerous components forgotten.

• Unhurriedly the soldiers came and went around the wagons. The engineer had lifted one of the metal panels covering the diesel engine. One of his comrades, who hadn't gone up on the bridge with him, was giving him one-word suggestions every so often. The engineer was busy with an oil pump, rubbing something with a rag, and then he went up to the front of the motor, as if to smell it. The two men were in work uniforms, and looked more like convicts than soldiers. The technical problem didn't seem to be seriously worrying them, or interesting the five or six spectators nearby who were also wearing mixed-up rags, from both the military and the prison. Once the engineer had closed the hood, his technical adviser waited until he had gotten back to ground level and offered him a cigarette. They sat next to each other on the ballast. Other soldiers loaded up bits of wood in one of the cars. The captain, the one who had pointed his lamp at Ilyushenko that night, was going around the groups and giving orders here and there in a conversational tone. Evidently the convoy was getting ready to leave.

Ilyushenko went up to see the captain and asked if he could join their group and set off with their company toward adventures, or at least toward whatever direction they had decided on. They had kept talking about the existence of a camp where they hoped to be welcomed and to end their days, and Ilyushenko said that this goal suited him and that he wasn't even looking for something else from existence. He took out of his pocket the massive piece of pemmican Solovyei had given him.

The commander wasn't a talkative sort, but when he saw the pemmican he couldn't hold back a surprised and slightly greedy face.

—I'm not going to enjoy it all by myself, Ilyushenko said. We're sharing it as comrades in arms. If we leave together, we can last a hell of a long time with this.

The commander asked Ilyushenko his name and interrogated him about his service status, his relationship to egalitarian ideology, his military abilities, but also the camps, general human happiness, the assassination of those responsible for general unhappiness, his connection to animality, to brotherhood, to Bolshevism, and to shamanism in general. The interrogation finished, he told Ilyushenko that he still hesitated to attribute the status of soldier or prisoner to him, but that he didn't see any reason to refuse his presence in the convoy.

—What's that you have on your neck, a spider? he suddenly asked.

—They screwed it up, Ilyushenko explained calmly. It looks like a punk tattoo, but it's a hammer and sickle. It was done by a comrade who didn't have much skill.

—We don't accept anyone anyhow, the captain said hesitantly. Sometimes we come across agent provocateurs of the enemy. Have to execute them before they corrupt everyone.

Ilyushenko knew that there was wavering. He gestured resignedly.

—I trust you to distribute pemmican, the captain concluded. No more than a sliver a day and in strictly equal parts. We'll leave in the afternoon. I'll tell you which car to go in.

• The captain was named Umrug Batyushin. His life had started somewhat chaotically. His father, Choem Mendelssohn, was a bird, and his mother, Bagda Dolomidès, was Ybür.

Choem Mendelssohn and Bagda Dolomidès worked at the Brussovanian Colony, a forestry complex where they slaved away, he as a foreman for the logging area and she as a supervisor for timber shipments by water routes. As a bird, Umrug Batyushin's father wasn't appreciated by his bosses or by the convicts in the brigade under his watch. He repeatedly escaped falling trees that were somewhat suspicious and, twice when he had come back from an executive meeting to his house in the black of night, strangers had carried him away between the shacks and beaten him up, breaking his nose and teeth, shattering his ribs, and, finally, pissing on him. Bagda Dolomidès, Umrug Batyushin's mother, complained to the authorities, objectively presented the facts as well as the medical reports and the X-rays clearly showing the broken cartilage and bones, but, in the absence of witnesses and motives for the crime, the investigation came to the conclusion that there had been a simple drunken brawl like the ones that broke out every day in this place, and the complaint didn't result in anything. When Umrug Batyushin's father was attacked a third time, he didn't get back up.

Having buried her husband, Bagda Dolomidès decided to leave the hellish world of the complex and to seek her fortune elsewhere, even if that meant risking all the dangers of a flight through the taiga. She had more energy and steadfastness than Choem Mendelssohn, she could set aside her womanly weaknesses when she had to confront adversity, and she would have already left without a second thought if she hadn't been caring for little Umrug Batyushin, who wasn't capable of making any efforts or sacrifices himself just then. Umrug Batyushin was going on three years old, but he was rather sickly and wouldn't have trotted more than a kilometer without trouble. He would have held his mother back if she'd dragged him along, holding his hand. Bagda Dolomidès bound him to her bosom, which was large, and she balanced her charge with a backpack in which she had put, aside from dried food, a pistol that she had filched from a guard after getting him drunk.

The taiga didn't scare her; she was used to its contact, its smell, its oppressive darkness, its endlessness. She was an orphan and the people who had found her lived in a small outcrop surrounded by forest, where the inhabitants were, aside from the representatives of the authorities, mostly hunters and workers for sawmills, furniture factories, or logging companies. Then she had gotten transferred to the Broussovonian Colony where her contract specified that she had to stay a good ten years, and once again she lived very close to the trees and very close to the black limits beyond which the world changed, beyond which the world only obeyed the laws of vastness, twilight, and wild animals.

Right after bypassing the complex's gates, she slipped past the first lines of pines, reached a cluster of larches, and immediately put as much distance as possible between herself and the Colony, which stretched out a great distance in every direction, but which had major gaps in its network of roads and pathways. She was counting on this weakness in the infrastructure to keep everyone from giving her trouble after her first day of walking and, for fifteen hours straight, she didn't stop for even a minute to catch her breath. Umrug Batyushin sat quietly against her breast without whining. She hadn't given him anything to drink before leaving so that she wouldn't have to undo the straps to let him pee, and, realizing that in any case he was tightly strapped to his mother's chest for the tedious journey, the little boy was steadfastly silent and slept as best as he could.

Eventually they had to cross several streams, ponds, and even shallow lakes, which Bagda Dolomidès knew the names of, because for years, having been put in charge of delivering wood by floating it down various waterways, she had constantly been studying her maps. The second day, she caught a fish close to Kuduk, another one close to Ulakhan. She didn't meet anyone, she never heard dogs barking. It was the middle of summer and the wolves had gone hunting farther south.

By Charang, after ten days of walking without any surprises, she was attacked by a bear. It reared up ten meters in front of her, showing its teeth with a throaty growl that didn't leave any doubt as to its intentions. Bagda Dolomidès set aside her fear for later, didn't lose her cool, and, while talking at the bear in a shrill voice that surprised it, she slipped her hand into her backpack, pulled out the pistol, and emptied the cartridge clip into the animal. It, more scared than wounded, took flight. Bagda Dolomidès couldn't stand on her two legs anymore. She sat on the ground and breathed frantically for several minutes. Umrug Batyushin whined and sniffed beneath her chin. Bound against her as he was, he hadn't even seen the bear.

The echo of gunshots reverberated deep into the silent forest, and it caught the attention of a small group of bandits. They, five of them, set eyes on her trail. They quickly surrounded her and, after collectively raping her, suggested that she join their group and go with them to a place called Mudugan where they had a base and where, according to them, she could safely leave the little Umrug Batyushin, such as when she went with them on expropriation raids or to assassinate local capitalists. Bagda Dolomidès wasn't taken with the idea of being the shared female in a group of robbers, and besides she knew nothing about this place called Mudugan that they had mentioned and which they bragged was calm and relatively comfortable, so she expressed reluctance and hesitated for several minutes. But since night was coming and Umrug Batyushin was still crying unhappily, and since aside from being criminals and rapists they seemed to be brave; she made the decision and followed them. Deep down she realized that in spite of what had been the best time to escape, the warmest months, she wouldn't have managed to cross the taiga all on her own, and meeting these men seemed providential. She would never have said it out loud, for fear of giving over her allegiance so pitifully, but she suddenly felt that they had saved the two of them, the little Umrug Batyushin and her.

The group was made up of three young hotheads and two older men who had plenty of common sense. The older ones were in charge. They were fifty or sixty years old, and on their arms were tattoos in blue ink, with motifs of intertwined snakes, barbed wire, and faces of angelic girls like those that bandits had dreamed of for centuries. At night by the fire, they took part in gang rapes with the same loutish and morose energy as the younger ones. When they came to Mudugan, Bagda Dolomidès negotiated with them for periods of intimacy and rest, which they gracefully allowed her, since they were so happy to have found their base again, where they could finally wash and sleep without having to be on constant lookout. And besides, over the course of their days traveling in the forest, they had adopted her as one of their own.

Mudugan was a typical village of thieves, built in the middle of the forest in a gap that barely deserved to be called a clearing, so tightly did the trees encircle the log houses. There weren't any paths that had been marked to get there and it was inaccessible to anyone who didn't know exactly where the ravines and undergrowth were. That was where Umrug Batyushin learned to live his life as a self-sufficient child, there where he learned to shoot rifles, to carve up elk, and endure cold and hardship, as well as bear the howling of the wolves that were rare in the Brussovanian Colony's area, but which every winter came right up to the house and prowled on the doorstep or sniffed the edges of the little windows once night had fallen. In the houses, not a lamp was lit after the evening meal, to economize and because the idea of staying awake by the wood-burning stove with a book in hand barely occurred to the bandits. However, there were a handful of books at Bagda Dolomidès's place, souvenirs of fruitless expeditions to unlikely hamlets or encounters with unknown corpses, always inexplicably far away from everything. Aside from collections of official lyrical poetry, there were two manuals for Bordigist agronomy and a thesis on the application of egalitarianism in extreme climactic conditions or even after death, off-putting opuscules that couldn't have intrigued anybody, but which allowed Umrug Batyushin to study his alphabet and learn a few new words. The little Umrug Batyushin heard the wolves clawing and whining on the other side of the wall and it never bothered him in the least. He was often alone, whether because his mother was keeping this person or that person company, or because she had left with the others for a raid. So as not to be found, the band did their work far away from its base, and Umrug Batyushin could easily end up the sole inhabitant of Mudugan for weeks.

Then there was an early summer marked by a long wait for the bandits to return, then a middle summer. The weeks went by. Eight, then nine. Umrug Batyushin had gotten sick twice after eating large and appetizing mushrooms from tree stumps, but, after several days of diarrhea, he got better. He ate hare meat, squirrel soup, crow soup. The days were interminable and he ended up filling them by haltingly reading the books that had taught him how to read. Aside from the swarms of flies and mosquitoes, a tiny audience gathered to listen to him, two or three furry caterpillars, several ants, sometimes a few fox cubs that still had everything to learn. From the doorstep of his cottage, Umrug Batyushin went back over the basics of what he knew. He taught lessons on the necessity of collective discipline in the tundra, he discussed the ways of eradicating the idea of individual profit when there was nothing but lichen to eat and the temperature was below negative forty Celsius. It was during one of these conferences that his existence changed. Uncle Ioura, the oldest of the thieves, broke past the first larches darkened and out of breath, then he said that the raid had gone bad, that self-defense militias had ambushed them, that all the others had been killed, including Bagda Dolomidès. And that, although he had shaken off his pursuers for about ten days, they had to leave Mudugan.

The oldest of the thieves had a sense of responsibility. He liked Umrug Batyushin, but he couldn't hang onto him for the years to come; the boy's training as a bandit hadn't culminated yet, and besides, enough proletarian morality subsisted in Uncle Ioura's heart for him to realize that the existence this child was promised could be something other than a suicidal mixture of taiga, violence, and illegality. Which is why, after having bundled up a rudimentary pack for the boy, he guided him through the trees to a fuel depot close to Yuunkiy-yur, where Uncle Ioura had once lived with his family. Crossing the trees took them six weeks and, when they knocked on the door of the old man's distant cousins, the road had just been turned white by the autumn's first snow. The old man greeted his parents, explained the situation to them in a few sentences, said good-bye to Umrug Batyushin, and went back into the forest.

From that day, Umrug Batyushin's daily life and future changed dramatically. The fiftysomething couple he had been entrusted to comprised two excellent people, communists gifted with generosity and compassion. Although delighted by the prospect of safeguarding the future of a child who had fallen out of the sky like this, the two of them had enough common sense not to let him languish with them, cut off from the world and in the extremely limited environment of the gasoline distribution base at Yuunkiy-yur. Once they had established a proper relationship with Umrug Batyushin, and started to take visible pride that their adoptive son was well-versed in tundra ideology and official versification, they sent him to board at the secondary school in the nearest city, Somodiokh, which was easily accessible in the winter, when anybody could trundle on the river ice to cross the three hundred kilometers separating it from Yuunkiy-yur.

In Somodiokh, Umrug Batyushin, who could have failed school and been a hooligan given the way he had spent his formative years, became a model student. He was doubtlessly somewhat coarse and overly quiet, and his comrades saw him as someone who could slice up squirrels, imitate barking wolves, and describe the copulations between his mother and the bandits, but his teachers talked of him as a healthy and hardworking student, attracted to the natural sciences, certainly clumsy when he was justifying his enthusiasm for the Bordigist principles in agriculture, but able to recite by heart a certain number of paragraphs on basic dialectical materialism. When people teased him, about his assassinated bird-father, about his Ybür mother turned whore in the taiga, about his lawless uncles or his adoptive parents who stank of fuel, he only hit once, but so hard that the teasing stopped. After a test the semester after the fight, he earned the right to wear the Pioneers' Scarf, then the years went by, and as a mustache darkened his upper lip, he began to go to the Komsomol meetings.

Everything went well for him, and, one summer when he went up the river in a boat to embrace the two old Yuunkiy-yur communists, he told them that he had been admitted to a technical school in a department that would prepare him for a career in lumber, and then a professional career that would bring him back to the taiga. They were all overjoyed, his adoptive parents most of all, because now he wouldn't just be useful to the society he was giving the best of himself to, but he could also move closer to Yuunkiy-yur, get hired at one of the various local lumberyards and, when he visited them at the fuel distribution base, receive their affection and moral and material support. The couple was starting to get old and, despite resisting every petit-bourgeois and egotistic tendency, wanted to have Umrug Batyushin nearby and dreamed of family meals, jars of mushrooms offered as they said their good-byes, lazy Sunday walks along the river between the warehouses and the tanks.

For Umrug Batyushin, a peaceful existence as a worker seemed preordained, but the global situation had gotten worse and, in the area as elsewhere, the consequences could be felt. People thought they had been crushed forever, but the enemy summoned up its strength, resurged everywhere, and had already turned into an ever more devastating cyclone. The Second Soviet Union headed full steam toward its collapse. The wars that had been dormant violently broke out again. The omnipresent nuclear power plants everyone had counted on to help do away with the State and give the most distant regions total energy autonomy didn't fulfill their promises. Most of them broke down, creating immense strains on all five continents that nobody could even hope to clean. Unnerved by the prospect of humanity's end, the populations lost all their loyalty to collectivism, and were seduced by all sorts of political monstrosities, if they provided even a slight contrast to their bleak present.

The Orbise called for help. Umrug Batyushin enlisted for its defenses at all costs, and instead of following a carpentry or logging course, he left with a volunteer regiment toward the capital, where he learned to handle weapons he'd never even heard of until then, learned to fight and to obey catastrophic orders without arguing, learned bitterness, learned to survive in the midst of bloody defeats, and, when the Orbise after decades of resistance collapsed miserably and he himself was killed, learned to wander through the irradiated zones and to go farther with the others, whoever the others were, and however far the distance remained for him to go before closing his eyes for good, or at least before finding concentration housing that suited them.

• Ilyushenko got into the wagon and right behind him someone, probably the captain Umrug Batyushin, pulled the sliding door shut and locked it. End of scene, he thought. Beginning of the trip. He sat on the floorboards, which smelled of piss. There were things next to him, bags, rifles, a box of ammunition. The car was filled with half a dozen soldiers already sitting quietly and looking ahead with vacant eyes. There was enough space for everyone. As well as light, which filtered through the air vents up top. The floor was built out of wood beams and, during the stop, the soldiers had cleaned it by scrubbing it with fistfuls of grasses. After a quarter of an hour, the engine started. A whiff of diesel fuel wafted through the car's panels and stayed there. The car shook a little. As far as transportation conditions went, he had seen worse. Ilyushenko let himself be lulled into drowsiness until night, and then, when night fell, he gave himself over completely to the shadows.

– 12 –

• The next Saturday, toward the middle of the morning, the train stopped in the middle of nowhere. They had come to a mountain range. The countryside was split between rocky undulations, scattered clumps of fir trees, and small valleys covered with dead grasses. The sky was pale blue. It wasn't sunny. The doors opened. Everyone was numb and reluctant to move. Even opening their eyelids took effort. After some fifteen minutes readjusting to the world, Umrug Batyushin poked his head into the wagon and announced that a general meeting would be held in the middle of the afternoon, and on the agenda would be allocating responsibilities, selecting a new captain, and preparing an evening of folk songs during which pemmican would be distributed.

Ilyushenko acted as if he wasn't numb and made his way down to the ballast, and then he went away from the rails to empty his intestines and bladder. He carried out this operation out of sheer routine. He didn't feel the urge and, although the idea was disagreeable, he could only explain this absence of desire in one way: he no longer really belonged to the world of the living, with their physiological needs and ritual defecations. He tied his pants back together without having expelled liquid or waste and he angrily told himself several truths that were best to admit to for once and for all. That he was already dead, that Solovyei had bewitched and abused him, that he would never see Vassilissa Marachvili ever again—things like that.

It was beautiful out, but the sunlight was barely warm. Around the train hung a strong stench of diesel fuel. The conductor hadn't turned off the engine yet. He walked up the small steps and, without lifting the protective panels, he listened to the rumble in satisfaction. Then he went back into the cabin and shut it off. Then silence reigned over the countryside, the cloud of diesel fuel dissipated, and everyone took in the scents of wilted foxgloves, icy earth, and gravel.

Ilyushenko helped unload some wood for the evening's campfire. Then he stretched his legs by walking along the rails, behind the train. Now that he fit in the collective, he could understand its functioning more clearly. There were thirty-two people there, who at first had been split up into two distinct groups, the prisoners and the soldiers, and then they had lost their original character and completely set aside their status within the convoy. They all thought about one thing: getting to a camp quickly, harshly regimented or not, to be together forever behind barbed wire.

After an exchange of ideas with his travel companions, Ilyushenko knew a little more about this peregrination he was part of. This search on the rails for a concentration haven had already lasted months, if not some incalculable bardic time. The diesel tractor never broke, fuel supply problems never cropped up, and, as in a nightmare where everything repeated endlessly, the convoy slowly devoured kilometers, week after week, shaking and jolting and roughing up its human cargo day and night. Stops made the journey less horribly monotonous, moments of relaxation, usually Saturday nights. The tradition had been established to halt the train and organize an all-nighter around the fire. It was a chance to close ranks, reestablish discipline when it had slackened, and, if the captain decided it was necessary, to remind everyone of the indestructible ideological foundations undergirding the trip, our terminal trip to the camp. The men listened obediently to the instructions and the discourses, and they expressed their intent to put them into action as best as possible. But above all they waited for the end of the evening, the performance that groups of them in turn improvised after nightfall, when the flames burnished and oiled faces. The time did come when those who had the talent declaimed epic chants, invented poetic or comedic monologues, or recited propaganda texts that had stuck with them in their earlier life, or parts of communist, post-exotic, or feminist romånces. The audience accompanied them by approving or voicing speeches, as we did in the old days during Korean *pansori* performances, when Korea still existed and we still believed in beauty, the future, and the impossibility of death.

• After the meticulously egalitarian distribution of pemmican flakes from his block, Ilyushenko rose in notoriety and also in popularity. Umrug Batyushin had handed over the captainship to a prisoner named Pedron Dardaf, who immediately took on his hierarchal responsibilities, sent out sentries to increase the security perimeter to the cairns behind which prospective attackers could have hidden, and went to see Ilyushenko to say that he would most likely succeed him the next week.

—Eh, Ilyushenko said.

—Everyone knows you'd be a good captain, Pedron Dardaf said.

—Why would they think that? Ilyushenko asked.

—Because you distribute food impartially, and also because you took good care of your daughter, Pedron Dardaf said.

—That wasn't my daughter, Ilyushenko responded. That was Vassilissa Marachvili.

—Was she your wife?

Solovyei, Ilyushenko thought immediately. Physically and socially, Pedron Dardaf didn't resemble the president of the kolkhoz, but he seemed to have the same incestuous confusion between girl-daughter and woman-wife. This sensation of déjà vu, of having both seen and heard it before, rather than fading away like an insubstantial veil, overwhelmed Ilyushenko. The veil of light weighed on him like lead. This Solovyei slipped inside me and he's following me, he thought. He left a trace of himself in me right when I lost consciousness in the little Red Star reactor. He focused on hiding his unease from the other man. He suddenly had the suspicion that he was being observed from within by Solovyei. Then he revolted against such a wholly irrational intuition. What was this situation with Solovyei, he wondered. I shouldn't stray that way. I shouldn't believe that. Marxism-Leninism forbids it. That's just an idiot's nonsense.

He forced himself to answer Pedron Dardaf. He wanted to hear the words come out of his mouth, rather than confide his thoughts to an interior voice.

—Sure, he said, Not my daughter. My wife.

—For me, wife or daughter, it doesn't matter, the new captain said in a glum voice.

Ilyushenko peered into Pedron Dardaf's eyes. He couldn't make out any golden streaks, any yellow leer like a bird of prey or a magician, and yet Pedron Dardaf had repeated, word for word, the strange sentence that Solovyei had pronounced in the nuclear reactor room. It can't be a coincidence, he thought with a twinge in his heart. The captain's reusing those words because they're dictated by Solovyei. Maybe, once people left the Red Star sovkhoz, we all became bodies inhabited by Solovyei. Who knows whether this magic muzhik hasn't taken advantage of us being dead, and if we aren't all puppets within a theater where the manager, the actors, and the audience are all one and the same person.

But no, he thought. Inhabited bodies, a tiny hermetic theater. Someone who had fun with corpses, who manipulated corpses to see what happened with them. Those things that couldn't ever exist.

Ilyushenko rubbed his hand on his neck, over his tattoos. He knew right to the millimeter where exactly the sickle, the hammer, and the unfortunate frieze of submachine guns massacring the image were. He acted like he was wiping away some sweat, but he was actually trying to reassure himself with these simple and solid symbols. He hung onto these familiar lifelines so as not to drown in the mysterious darknesses of the world. Workers, countrymen, and soldiers united so that humanity could escape the abyss. That's concrete, he thought. That's not vague imaginings, Solovyei's dreams, or something else entirely.

Fortunately there was still Marxism-Leninism, he thought. Otherwise we'd be in a filthy, shitty nightmare. Who knew if we'd be able to differentiate between classes, and even between the living, the dead, and even the dogs or that kind of thing.

• When night fell, everybody gathered around the fire, except for the sentries keeping the group safe.

Two detainees and a soldier had decided to perform that evening. The soldier had a harmonica that had suffered considerable damage, but he was able to get three chords out of it, which, according to the other performers, would be enough to keep the orchestral background going until midnight. The soldier was named Idfuk Sobibian. The detainees bore the names of Matthias Boyol and Schliffko Armanadji. Before being brought into the convoy they were in a transit camp for bad elements and rightists. Their camp had been attacked by the enemy and they had escaped the massacre by sheer miracle. Matthias Boyol was a remarkable storyteller, had belonged to a theatrical troupe, had perfect enunciation, and, when he declaimed particular passages while singing, sang perfectly. Schliffko Armanadji willingly ended up singing the bass notes and beginning the harmonics that would accompany the solo.

—We'll perform a tragicomic threnody for you, Matthias Boyol announced.

For a minute, there was just the silence of wood burning, with an old plank's hissing groan, a quick spluttering, some crackling, and then Idfuk Sobibian began to blow out and inhale through his harmonica. The chords were melancholy and the musician kept repeating them in the same order. Schliffko Armanadji waited for Matthias Boyol to begin speaking before accompanying him with a throat song. This went on for the first few minutes.

Then Matthias Boyol, who had stood up, pronounced the beginning of his monologue.

He turned toward the fire and said:

—The ode to the camps unfurls on the tongue, no matter the tongue, no matter the time of day or night, and no matter the moment of crossing or collapse.

We listened to him while breathing as quietly as possible.

The night was thick.

The night was cold and thick.

—No matter the moment of death, of crossing death, or collapse of death, Matthias Boyol concluded. The ode to the camps unfurls.

Schliffko Armanadji had begun to emit a throat song. From time to time he punctuated it with a breath that ended on a deep note, then he went on. The strange sounds coming out of his throat merged with the harmonica's skeletal melody.

—Nothing can replace the camp, Matthias Boyol continued, nothing is as necessary as the camp. Nobody can deny that the camp is the highest grade of dignity and organization that a society of free men and women can aspire to, or, at least, already sufficiently unfettered from their animal condition to endeavor to construct freedom, moral progress, and history. No matter what we say or assay, nothing will ever equal the camp, no collective architecture of the human species or its like will ever achieve the degree of coherence and perfection and tranquility compared to the prospect that the camp offers to those who live there and die there. Everyone knows that the camp doesn't suddenly come out of nowhere. We must understand how it is the result of our long history, how it's a final stage of the history that entire generations have made possible by their sacrifices. The camp doesn't suddenly come out of nowhere, it ultimately comes once the animal darkness somewhere begins to brighten with someone's earliest enthusiasms, and then when this dawn intensifies thanks to the generosity and the self-sacrifice of the majority. Then we are on the way. Touched by this light, the distant descendants of the pioneers finally begin to concretely form the camp, they skin their hands on barbed wire, they willingly deprive themselves of food and sleep to go more quickly and, finally, they build to the last detail the camp. But, even if we don't keep in mind this aspect of capping a thousand years of construction, which gives the reality of the camp all its extraordinary and moving significance, we must recognize that nothing is more justified, whatever the point of view you hold, than for everyone to stay definitively and generally inside or outside the camp. Even the most obtuse philosophers now admit that cloistering oneself in the camp has become the most beautiful gesture of freedom that can be accomplished as a human female or a human male on this planet.

Matthias Boyol fell silent. Schliffko Armanadji did so as well. Only the harmonica continued its monotonous musical setting, which, now that the discourse had broken off, seemed to be a musical setting for nothing.

We thought of the camps.

We all had in our heads images of camps.

Once we are there, we thought, all shall be well.

We had in our heads the vague hope of finally being welcomed forever within the camps.

As long as we came before we were forced to live outside, in this rotten world, we thought.

The fire had died down. Our captain took out a plank lying nearby and used it to poke at the heart of the fire, stirring up several sparks and glimmers. The fire started back up. Everyone pensively watched it blossom.

Once again, Schliffko Armanadji began a throat song. The melody was harrowingly simple. Schliffko Armanadji's voice wasn't audibly feminine or masculine. It escaped all characterization of this sort. It was neither human nor alive. For two or three minutes, maybe more, the harmonica combined with Schliffko Armanadji's strange vocalizations.

The deep black, barely starry night.

The fire, its flames flickering, its tar-tinged scent.

The sparse ground. Beside us, screes. The idea that a mountainous landscape lay beyond.

The echoes of the fire on the nearby outcrops.

Reflections moving over our faces furrowed with exhaustion.

Schliffko Armanadji's metallic modulations.

The harmonica. Three minor chords.

Then Matthias Boyol started speaking again.

—Nothing is more desirable, especially for someone born in the camp, than life in the camp. This isn't a matter of scenery, or of air quality, or of the quality of adventures to experience before death. It's only a question of a respectful contract between fate and oneself. There, everyone has an advantage that none of the preceding attempts at an ideal society had managed to achieve. Once everyone can claim a place in the camp and once nobody is ever refused entry or goes back out, the camp will become the only place in the world where fate deceives nobody, because it conforms concretely to what anyone can expect to await him or her.

Without looking at us, Matthias Boyol sat back down and held his hands toward the flames.

His accompanists were silent.

For several minutes, Matthias Boyol warmed his hands by putting them near the flames, without expressing anything other than the wish to be less cold.

Someone, from the depths of the night, asked him if that was all, if he had finished his discourse.

—Yes, he said.

Then he repeated in a less assured tone, as if asleep:

—The ode to the camps unfurls on the tongue, no matter the tongue, no matter the time of day or night, and no matter the moment of crossing or collapse.

• Matthias Boyol had been a comedian in an agitprop troupe. He had gone to spread the message on the front, in the factories, in the evacuation zones, there where simple newspaper articles or speeches broadcast on radio weren't enough to convince the population that it was on its way to collective happiness, or, at the least, toward the end of its unhappiness. They were called the 343 troupe, and it comprised girls and boys loyal to the Orbise and deeply passionate about their theatrical activity. Unconcerned about the precarious conditions in which they mounted their performances, they always gave their best. They staged playlettes with themes that for the most part had to do partly with defeat, hell on earth, the end of humanity, and partly with the most effective ways to transform defeat into resounding victory. Lines of dialogue and outrageously black situations resulted in a joyous atmosphere that was wonderfully optimistic, and the crowds that watched these farcical performances of the apocalypse were often swept by waves of laughter. They were fleeing from fatal radiation, their homeland had been wiped off the map, their sole prospect was a communal grave, but, in front of Matthias Boyol and his comrades, they burst out laughing.

The troupe had been authorized by the capital's authorities, however the local branches of the party didn't particularly appreciate his humor, and they perceived ulterior and counterrevolutionary motives. After two trimesters of activity in tent cities where the refugees awaited their departure for elsewhere, the authorities had asked the troupe to dissolve itself. Matthias Boyol, who was 343's founder, and invested body and soul in his theatrical work, had taken this request as a demand from uncultured brutes, but also and especially as a personal disaster. And, indeed, from there he had lost control a bit, socially and intellectually speaking. The members of his small group had scattered and were no longer in touch, but he was determined to keep the 343 troupe going against all odds, paying no heed to the hostility he had aroused in the official organs. He wandered on the periphery by dormitories or in the seemingly infinite avenues edged with army tents, and he kept on giving performances, even impromptu ones for just one person. His repertory was limited to madmen's monologues and post-exotic meditations in free verse. He blended in with the street singers and fortune tellers, but every so often he was stopped and reprimand-ed, as always happened with the bad elements. These interrogations exasperated him, the interviews with the corrections officials depressed him. Soon he foundered completely. He made several suicide attempts during his monologues. Then one of them was successful and he was taken to a neighborhood morgue run by Buddhists, pompously called Future for All. Unable to deal with the flood of corpses, the Buddhists were overwhelmed and let the dead take care of things themselves. If the *Bardo Thödol* was read somewhere, it was in a distant room, and Matthias Boyol didn't hear anything. After several days of waiting in a jam-packed corridor, he was transferred. He found himself detained in a transit camp for rightists, self-harmers, suicides, and representatives of the fourth stinking category. There was nothing for him to do but wait for a favorable opportunity. Once the camp was hit by an enemy attack that had razed the next city over with bombs, he didn't wait and got in a convoy on its way to a better world, an ideal camp—for anywhere.

– 13 –

• Clack clack, clack-clack. The convoy moved forward slowly. Clack clack, clack-clack, clack clack, clack-clack. After wending through a mountainous area, the rails rediscovered the hilly monotony of the steppes. On the horizon, strips of birches and distant clumps of pines rose and fell. Sometimes the rails also crossed a terribly unwelcoming and black stretch of forest. For hours, the train advanced in a straight line, clamped between two compact rows of hundred-year-old trees. On the right and on the left for several meters was a grass that was still very green. Despite the autumn chill, it had retained an aggressive greenness. It made up a carpet of unusual thickness, so primeval as to be frightening. Immediately beyond that, the larches rose up. Ilyushenko looked at this image through the gap of the sliding door. The wall of trees was impenetrable. Ilyushenko didn't feel the same repressed disgust for the taiga that his comrade Kronauer did, but, in the long run, this curtain seemed dreary, ill-suited to human life, and he shut his eyes to daydream. He only opened them again when the light had changed, whether night had fallen, or the convoy had finally left behind the botanical thicknesses.

Without regard to the calendar that set the convoy's regular Saturday stops, the conductor occasionally took the initiative to stop near hamlets or little abandoned kolkhozes. Most often they were units too small to have been given reactor cores. Their inhabitants had nonetheless fled for safer regions, or they had died and didn't come forward. They opened the doors wide, a sentry climbed on the roof of the first car, the captain staggered by the rails, leaned on a wheel, and waited for his body to regain a bit of energy. The locomotive driver became invisible, likely plunged into a deep sleep after the strain of driving. Soldiers and detainees took hours to wake up, sometimes more than a night. When they had regained enough strength, they divided up responsibilities without planning, heading out to do their business or what served for such, meandering along the tracks. The ruins weren't always unvisitable, and they began to look for wood to burn, for tobacco, for useful things. They sometimes found books, and those they brought to the captain. He exercised his inborn privilege as arbiter of ideology and decided, after a cursory look, whether they had to serve as kindling for fire or deserved to be added to the itinerant library in the fourth car. The captain sorted them wholly arbitrarily, guided by such considerations as the thickness and the quality of the paper rather than the literary value of the volume. And so burned, illuminating the night, brilliant post-exotic works such as *Grasses and Golems* by Manuela Draeger, *We Are Twenty Years Old* by Ellen Dawkes, *Autopsy of a Korean Woman* by the Petra Kim collective, and others.

• The next Saturday, the train stopped near a group of five shacks. They were positioned near the tracks, in a bare landscape, evidently without agricultural ambitions. And at first their presence seemed somewhat mysterious, then Pedron Dardaf offered an explanation— the countrymen living there used to be responsible for providing bread and water for the prisoners on their way to the camps. This confirmation that they were indeed on a path leading to concentration structures overjoyed the men and also reflected on their mood. Once Ilyushenko had finished distributing pemmican, Pedron Dardaf began the transfer of power that he had promised. The operation took place without the least solemnity and without any difficulty. It wasn't even necessary to call for a show of hands. Ilyushenko waited for several seconds without saying a word, sighed, and ordered that they demolish a shack and transport the pieces in the second car, in order to increase their stockpile of wood to burn in the coming week and later on. The soldiers stacked their rifles or leaned them against the cars, and then mingled with the detainees, and they all began to work with motions from beyond the grave, as usual.

Ultimately, there was nothing new on the trip. Only unimportant details. For example, in one room Umrug Batyushin found a book that he brought to Ilyushenko for him to decree its immediate future— bonfire or library. The cover had been torn off thirty years earlier. It was an anthology of short texts by Maria Kwoll, an author easily iden- tified for explicitly laying out her hatred of sexual relations, at every moment and on every page. Ilyushenko ran through three paragraphs, which brought back every manifestation of desire and as well as loving tenderness to the original brutality of the animal night, to the urgent darknesses born in the Paleozoic era, forcing living creatures to tear each other apart, to rape each other in order to gruesomely perpetuate their species. Maria Kwoll saw in the vertiginous moments of orgasm a portal that led directly back four or five hundred million years. Ilyush- enko said to Umrug Batyushin that he didn't really know what to do with this book and that, for now, he would keep it. Umrug Batyushin waited patiently for his decision in the position that corresponded to standing at attention for dead soldiers. In reality, Ilyushenko felt shame at throwing a book into the fire, which was more often done by the dog-headed enemies, but, at the same time, he couldn't bear and had never borne Maria Kwoll's rants. And, ultimately, when the sun set over the steppe and the fire needed small twigs and paper to take hold, he tore out the pages and put them right on top of the sparks. It was the beginning of the evening, nobody asked any painful questions about our genetic heritage, and for him personally, this attack on post-exotic literature gave him no remorse.

Those present around the fire were less numerous than at the last festive evening. Several were resting in the cars, unable to move or express interest. One of them, according to the news related around noon to the captain, had fled. It was Idfuk Sobibian, the harmonica player. The captain hadn't ordered anybody to search for him. This man was lost, no matter what. He had condemned himself to the most awful solitude. And there was no point spending hours tracking him down just to bring him back to the convoy and shoot him for deserting.

• When the fire had taken on beautiful tints of orange-yellow, golden-yellow, coppery-red, with occasional threads of pure gold that dissolved in the night with a hiss, Ilyushenko got up. Around him, a good twenty bodies were outstretched, mostly listless, and five or six were sitting upright. They all had their eyes turned toward the flames. Their eyes all reflected in the same way the powerful color of the fire, the inhuman yellows, the rapacious and devouring and hypnotic yellows that Ilyushenko had only seen in a gaze one other time, not long before, in the Red Star sovkhoz.

Solovyei, he thought bitterly. Him again. I'd forgotten about him. This necromancer of the steppes. He's come back here. This awful kolkhoz matchmaker, this reviver of cadavers, this horrible shadow, this giant impervious to radiation, this shamanic authority from nowhere, this president of nothing, this vampire in the form of a kulak, this strange man sitting on a stool, this abuser, this dominating man, this sleazy man, this unsettling man, this nuclear-reactor creature, this godless and lordless hypnotizer, this manipulator, this monster belonging to who knows what stinking category. He's there again. He's made himself scarce for days, but he's come back up from the depths. He watches me through the flames. He watches us all and he directs us from the flames.

It was a reflection meant to be fleeting, but Ilyushenko took several seconds to come out of it. Well now, he thought, there's no basis for that, it's the effect of having been rocked and shaken around for days. It's obsessive thought in a stewing brain. Mental flatulence, nothing more.

Several soldiers had turned their heads toward him and, as he had taken up an oratorical pose, they indicated that they were listening. This made it easier for him to escape Solovyei's pull. He was now the captain, he had much more important responsibilities than mentally going over his irrational fears and troubles. He had to talk to his men. He cleared his throat and did so. His voice came out painfully and he had hoped it would ring with more authority, but he didn't stop to reinforce it. Even if his exclamations were pronounced with a hoarse breath that had nothing warlike about it, he went on.

—Comrade soldiers, comrade detainees! . . . We are engaged in an expedition that seems fruitless . . . However, necessarily, we are approaching our goal! . . . Our objectives will be achieved soon . . . we will finally see standing in front of us the fences and barbed wire beyond which we can lie down, beyond which our survival will become meaningful . . . Let us stay united, as we have been until tonight! . . . Let us never break this unity! . . . Together, we form a brotherly corps that nothing can break . . . not our feelings of ultimate defeat . . . not the political aberrations now everywhere on the planet . . . not the radiations silently broiling us . . . not the tricks of the enemies of the people . . . not the terminal nastiness of our fate . . .

He no longer knew quite what to say, and, for half a minute, he struggled for words.

The sparking of a plank catching fire.

The twilit sky turning black.

All around the endless, slightly rolling steppes, exhaling their last scents of not-rotting flowers, its shades of hay also not yet rotting.

Much closer, the mustiness that accompanied the convoy, rusted iron, diesel fuel, dust, grease, excrements, and grime.

The living fire.

The men in a circle not far from the flames, inwardly in a good mood, but outwardly tattered and depressed.

Their eyes often lowered, but open enough to show both sclera and iris reflecting the flames, merging into a single coppery yellow thing.

—Let's stay united in our happy brotherly hardship, Ilyushenko finally said before sitting back down like a heap. Now some music! . . . Start celebrating! . . .

• Matthias Boyol got up and Schliffko Armanadji followed suit. They prepared for the traditional Saturday evening performance. Now that Idfuk Sobibian and his harmonica had defected, their group was musically impoverished, which was why Matthias Boyol had decided to break up his text by alternating medium-ranged recitatives with parts he sang. Schliffko Armanadji would bring in throat songs and harmonics during the recitatives. A detainee named Julius Togböd offered to accompany the singers on the Jew's harp. He had found the little instrument lying among the debris of the second shack and he confessed that he didn't really know how to use it.

—Doesn't matter, Schliffko Armanadji said encouragingly. If you lose the thread of the melody, we'll find a way to help you.

—The important thing is that you don't leave them all alone, Ilyushenko remarked.

—We're going to perform a burlesque glorificact.

For no reason, since it had no importance, the former captain Pedron Dardaf came out of his apparent torpor, raised his hand like a kid questioning his schoolteacher, and asked:

—Tell us, Boyol, is there a difference between a burlesque glorificact and a tragicomic threnody, like the one you recited for us last week?

Matthias Boyol looked disconcerted for several seconds, because he was already absorbed in the performance, which had started silently within himself, but he answered gracefully:

—No, Pedron Dardaf. It's exactly the same thing. It's exactly the same poetic bullshit.

Then the musical declamation began.

• —Every man in love with liberty, Schliffko Armanadji sang as a prologue, and every woman equally in love, he continued, must have in their minds the incomparable ideal of the camp, its absolute splendor, and never stop at what is actually revolting in the camp, the organized squalor, the deplorable sanitary conditions, the terrible promiscuity night and day, the arbitrariness of the camp managers, the guards' primitive savagery, the violence between detainees, the dogs' lessons constantly broadcast on the dogs' loudspeakers.

Julius Togböd's Jew's harp began to produce an arid melody. It was too soon. Matthias Boyol let Julius Togböd do his best, with two notes, for two long minutes. Then, once the uncertain musician lost heart, he waved approvingly.

—In some cases, he said in a storytelling voice, the train stopped in the open country, such as when a switch presented the conductor with a logistical problem, but also due to a global disinterest for the trip, shared equally by the detainees, their escorts in uniform, and the technicians caring for the machine. Everybody ended up outside. If this pause came after sunset, we relived, after getting off the train, particular moods of railroad displacement that refused to degrade in our memory, whether we had had the chance to experience them elsewhere in our own existence or in an earlier existence, much earlier, on the lines to impenetrable prospects, centuries earlier, such as Cusco–Puno, or Irun–Lisboa, or Vladivostok–Khabarovsk, or Irkutsk–Ulaanbaatar, or Kimchaek–Hongwon, whether we had received them and integrated them into our fundamental emotions during movie screenings, had already experienced them upon contact with wonderful black-and-white films that were silent or punctuated by the noise of vapor escaping, often with the image of ourselves or others like us, dressed as wretches or adventurers, an image that overwhelmed us, an overwhelming image that paralyzed us with grief, because it was associated for us with an imminent slide for the characters toward nothingness, it signified failure and ending, it warned us of separation, of terminal decline, and the end, and for us who no longer differentiated between characters and spectators, this was no longer fiction but another disastrous page in our reality, already written, already darkened by the indelible ink of our future to be placed randomly in our past or in our future.

Matthias Boyol paused gently. He was breathless and needed a few seconds before breathing normally. Next to him, Schliffko Armanadji had swelled his lungs and, after a sound that resembled a sigh, he sent up to the sky an ascending lamentation, entirely in unearthly *do*s and *mi*s.

—I'm thinking here, Matthias Boyol concluded, of particular films by Yuri MacMakarov that affected our entire generation, *Before the Defeat, The First She-Wolf,* or *Myriam's Voyage* being the most representative of his oeuvre and these themes.

A moment of silence that was broken only by Schliffko Armanadji's throat whispers.

The fire crackling, sometimes accompanied by a shower of sparks.

The reflection of the flames in the eyes of everyone present, as if detainees and soldiers were dead beggars imagined by Solovyei.

The night with scents of grasses and railroads.

Fleeting memories of images from Yuri MacMakarov's films.

Matthias Boyol had already returned to his declamation. After half a minute, his voice built up toward a song.

—And so we went out into the nocturnal emptiness, orienting our chests and shoulders to avoid the full brunt of the icy wind, we imagined ourselves on a deserted platform, suddenly enveloped in a jet of vapor, as if we had just said good-bye to a female lover and already no longer saw her; a soldier offered us a cigarette, we took a puff before passing it on to someone else, then we moved away to squat and pretend to empty our bowels and intestines which hadn't held anything for weeks. It was a ritual like any other, a way of showing that we hadn't broken with existence and that we still had bodies and elementary bodily functions. Then, having restored order within our underwear or in what served for it, we resumed more vertical activity. We slowly went around the train. We came back up the convoy toward the locomotive. We listened to the earth's noises, the shrieking grasses, the frost crystals beneath our feet.

• —The stop lasted half an hour, Matthias Boyol sang, sometimes much longer, and then it was followed by a long hour of rounding everyone up, warnings on loudspeakers, whistle blasts, and horns. The roll call was done in confusion but not in violence. The soldiers responsible read their lists with difficulty, stumbling over last names and first names and, it has to be said, without caring. We hauled ourselves once more into the cars, in any case, as many of us as we were, hardly willing to stay alone in the open steppes, to have no food and no help forever, a thousand leagues from any inhabited land and cut off from civilization by the insurmountable fences of the horizon. When someone went missing, we notified the soldiers. They first lost themselves going through lists, trying to find the missing person in their papers, then they declared him or her never registered and therefore nonexistent, then, as we insisted, they started the roll call all over again. That gave any latecomers or half-deserters the time to discreetly return to his or her original group and allowed accompanying staff to once again question the veracity of our words. But sometimes the absence was confirmed, and then the soldiers looked to and fro more than usual around the convoy. A soldier climbed up the middle car in order to shine the spotlight. After one or two minutes we called "warming up," the spotlight worked, and a large and blinding brush hollowed out a formidable tunnel through the night, ending very far, on vague natural obstacles that for a second took on monstrous shapes over the hills with their burned grasses burned further by frost. We suddenly made out an oblong portion of the prairie, punctuated or spotted with stains that were geological wounds or patches of rotten peat or patches of ice. The stains were never silvery, never agreeable to look at, they were always gray-black or dark brown. Sometimes the incredibly powerful lamp surprised in its beam a quadruped mammal animal far off, which we tended to describe as a long-haired cow but which the Mongols and Tibetans in our company, having more knowledge than we others, refused to call yaks.

At that moment, Julius Togböd woke up and held the Jew's harp between his lips again, and, as the sounds that he achieved were suddenly completely perfect, the two others fell silent. They stood immobile, surrounded by shadows and moving reflections, their eyes closed, and listened, while rocking gently back and forth, to Julius Togböd's solo.

Julius Togböd's solo.

A little wind carrying the perfume of unknown grasses.

The heat from the fire.

The earth increasingly damp as the night advanced.

The end of Julius Togböd's solo.

• —The spotlight was hard to move or reorient, Matthias Boyol continued, immediately accompanied by Schliffko Armanadji's throat singing. We heard the soldier on the roof cursing some kind of handle system or some kind of rack and pinion that wasn't responding to his entreaties and pushes, his expectations. So the spotlight sometimes stayed locked in a single direction, the one where the long-haired cow had been surprised and continued to tilt its nose toward this bizarre sun that was bothering it during its restorative sleep and ruining its long night. But what usually happened was that the beam managed to reach a neighboring hill, and, halfway up its slope, a second cow or an old demolished shepherd's hut, and it would stop there, unresponsive to insults or kicks from the soldier's clumpy shoes, until an officer ordered the apparatus shut off. There were also times when the spotlight fell and lit up the sky violently, thereby becoming once more what it had been before its fatal agglomeration with the rack and pinion, an element of defense against airplanes. The entire convoy, soldiers and prisoners alike, stayed there with mouths wide open beneath this immense luminous column, dreaming of unlikely enemy bombers who had come from amid the clouds or ether, and then, too, a non-commissioned officer or somebody like him had to come to put an end to the oddity, and, only then, after further imprecations and a string of stinging blasphemies, the light went out.

• Julius Togböd's lips were bleeding. He had been playing the Jew's harp while holding it wrong between his teeth and he had cut himself. Still, after his recent solo, he had become convinced that he was indispensable, that without him this concert would lose all its symphonic appeal, and he had enough sense of duty to play his part despite the pain tormenting his lips. Once again he held the metallic body between his incisors and began to pluck the reed. Now he drew out a fuller range of sounds than at the beginning of the performance. He knew it and felt a certain pride, which was enough to keep ignoring his burning lips.

With Schliffko Armanadji, Julius Togböd improvised a wordless duet because Matthias Boyol, when he realized that the Jew's harp would sound once again, had let his sentence end.

A minute of pure musical happiness passed.

Several detainees or soldiers gently rocked their torsos back and forth, like priors of a prehistoric religion or like contemporary madmen. They kept watching the fire, barely blinking.

A bit of wind forced the flames to twist.

Pedron Dardaf added a plank to the blaze.

Ilyushenko added another.

Sparks swirled toward the deep black sky.

The duo stopped. The music persisted in the listeners' heads as the fire's roar increased.

The fire's irregular rumble.

The fire's gaze on us all.

The wind's cold whisper.

A waft of excrement from the cars.

Then Matthias Boyol reintroduced himself in his tale, in the assured and strong voice of a comedian used to a large audience.

—In reality, he said, we almost never found any of the missing people with this method. Every so often we recaptured a latecomer, in a sad state among the shrubs and unmoving due to a supposed diarrhea which the light never indicated in any way, and who, after several seconds of humiliating illumination, slowly gestured and got dressed, but the fugitives, to my knowledge, the actual fugitives escaped our searches. So we had to wait until daybreak. We others were consigned to our cattle cars, behind the sliding doors that the soldiers took the opportunity to shut with a particular rage, or we had to get into groups at gunpoint, in a humdrum valley near the tracks, which we preferred because that way we might spend the night under the stars. We improvised a bivouac, occasionally finding enough dry grass to pile up and make a fire, with hope that the flames wouldn't be too fleeting, then, once the embers were no longer red, which is to say right away, we curled up into balls to sleep.

For a full minute the musical accompaniment to the text had been growing in power. Julius Togböd seemed to be caught in a frenzy. He turned toward the fire, toward the orator, toward the fire, toward the orator, and he made the iron reed vibrate continuously as it reduced his lips to pulp. Schliffko Armanadji accompanied him, took up some of his rhythmic phrases, harmonizing brilliantly with both the Jew's harp and Matthias Boyol's discourse.

—When dawn came, he said, a non-commissioned officer hauled himself to the top of the central car, next to the projector that the day had rendered even more useless than the previous night, and he looked in the distance through binoculars. We were every one of us hanging onto the narration he would make, and he knew it. I think that he didn't see anything, didn't perceive anything, wasn't able to obtain any image of a man running desperately, but that, for instructional purposes, he tried to instill a healthy fear in our hearts. "There he is," he said in a strong and decisive voice, as if he was taking the floor at an anarcho-syndicalist meeting, as if he was banking on immediate clamor, on applause, cheering. "There are wolves nipping at his heels, he's lost, he doesn't have any chance of escape, the wolves have split up, soon the biggest one will cut off his path." Then he continued lying, describing the attack that would happen or had already happened, describing the wolves' pelts, the nasty looks they gave one another, their curved backs, their dirty teeth, describing the skinning. We listened to this report in silence, while we took care of our morning tasks: summary toilet, intestinal evacuations, preparation of coffee, shift change.

Matthias Boyol cleared his throat discreetly and continued.

—I say shift change, he said, I mention the shift change, because that happened often, not every day, but often, and, when we were all outside for one reason or another, that made things easier. By "shift change" I mean this moment when we replaced the soldiers as escorts, while the soldiers took our place as detainees. There were only a few leather belts and rifles to exchange. It was an agreement that we had made in dreams upon departure, so that none of us could benefit from overwhelming advantages while roving, and which we carried out without fail, in dreams as well as in reality.

"Let this sad example serve as example," the non-commissioned officer was saying all this time. "Every escapee is condemned to ruination. Fleeing our collective means throwing yourself to the wolves. It means facing terrible moments of fear and pain all alone, as if there aren't already enough when we're together. The escapee has no future. We can certainly say and explain, nothing can replace the camp, nothing is as necessary and healthy as the camp."

He always had the same triumphant intonation of a practiced orator, but we still didn't know exactly who was talking, a non-commissioned officer who was lying about a deserter, or a representative for the prisoners who was taking advantage of his position high above us to tell stories, to moralize, or to rattle off a string of nonsense.

• It was past midnight. Matthias Boyol's voice faded, giving way to the last melodies; then Julius Togböd took the blood-stained Jew's harp out of his wounded mouth, then Schliffko Armanadji stopped emitting harmonies, returned with a suddenly deep voice, continued in this way for four or five seconds, and then finished with a final sigh.

Another hour went by. Nobody wanted to leave the fire to lie down on the dirty car floorboards or shiver on the icy ground.

As captain, Ilyushenko felt that he had to say something, and ask the three performers for a complementary speech.

—We have to conclude, he said, turning toward them.

There was a quick approving movement among those who, around the still-flickering fire, hadn't sunken completely into their meditation or into nothingness.

• Matthias Boyol had sat back down in front of the flames, and, when his captain spoke, he got back up without a word. They had given the three performers a good spot. Schliffko Armanadji and Julius Togböd got going, ready to accompany him once again, but he waved them away. He would conclude solo, without embellishment.

He let half a minute go by, mentally preparing for what he would say, then he started to speak. He pronounced his discourse in a weary voice.

—Everyone knows, he said, everyone knows that the camp is the only unimaginary place where life is worth the trouble of being lived, perhaps because our awareness of being alive is enriched by our awareness of being such in the company of others, in an effort of collective survival, an effort that's certainly useless and difficult, but with a nobility unknown on the other side of the barbed wire, and also because our awareness of being alive is fulfilled when we see how, ultimately, classes have been abolished all around us. Elsewhere, outside, everyone has to wait for periods of disaster or wars for an equivalent sentiment to arise. The camp doesn't need successive cataclysms or bombs raining down for its inhabitants to enjoy mutual aid and fatalistic brotherhood. Everyone knows that the camp is more uncomfortable, but more fraternal than the lands that make up the rest of the world. Whether in the center or at the edge of the camp, no thinker would utter calls for collective murder or incite pogroms or political, religious, or ethnic intolerance. The camp is a place where assassins only act when absolutely necessary, or on a whim, or out of passion, or because they have a new knife to test out, but never for useless and revolting reasons like those on the outside. Whether analyzing from a global angle or rather a very detailed one, the camp only presents advantages for the population assembled there, and that's why a large majority of unfortunates still living outside the camp try at all costs to enter, dream constantly of the camp, remain jealous of those who were able to enter before them. Few are the opponents of the camp within the camp, and incoherent are their arguments for ways of existing as those who stagnate or degenerate outside the barbed wire in unequal barbarity. Small in number are the camp theorists who call to leave the camp, who denigrate the camp or dream of abolishing the system of camps, or who recommend a larger opening to beyond the barbed wire and recommend merging the camp with exterior territories. Spoken from the windows of psychiatric institutions, their discourses are heard, but do not take hold. If applause breaks out, it's most often to recognize their humor or their comical faces. They would certainly need minds as deranged as theirs to appreciate their insane ravings. Essentially, in the camp, no person gifted with reason would question the humanist superiority of the society that blossomed within fences, and nobody would dare to deny the centuries of penal knowledge and constant improvements in the organization, in the philosophy, and in the intimate and fundamental logic of the camp. That's how it is.

– 14 –

• In the middle of the following week, the locomotive whistled several times, awakening everyone or at least those who were still of this world, and the train braked, apparently sharply. It was well past noon. The sun shone without heat. Some of us groaned, wondering what was happening, and, realizing that the convoy wasn't moving anymore, we went to the doors. They weren't locked. Upon departure, Ilyushenko had forgotten or pretended to forget that he had to lock the cars harboring detainees. The exhausted heads taking in the daylight were bedazzled for fifteen minutes. Bodies stretched, with the yawns and moans that usually accompanied the operation, but, for a good while, nobody felt well enough to get out.

Crows cawed above the train. The once-jumbled steppes filled again with non-human murmurs. Close to the rails were a half dozen young pines, alone in the middle of a landscape where trees were scarce. They must have served as a gathering point for all local fauna. On the branches, invisible, greenfinches were chirping, and among the trunks jerboas, themselves also invisible, were starting to squeak. A dazed cricket flew just inside the car where the captain was still lying down. He put out his hand to trap it and add it to his pemmican provisions, which were still substantial but diminishing. If Marxism-Leninism forbade eating human meat, it hadn't said anything about eating insects, or if so in apocryphal texts that had never been debated or distributed among the masses. Ilyushenko's movements were slow. Without much difficulty, the cricket escaped its predator.

Then the conductor came out of his cabin and jumped into the ditch grass. His name was Noumak Ashariyev. The second engineer went down the steps, leaned on the ramp, and lit a cigarette. He went by the name of Hadzoböl Münzberg.

Several meters from the locomotive, between two railroad ties, a beggar was sitting cross-legged. He murmured and every so often he slightly anxiously tugged back onto his shoulders a coat made of ribbons and shreds of cloth that he must have taken from the shamanic altars in the mountains. The ribbons had once been multicolored, but years of exposure to the air had faded them, which reduced the coat to two or three armfuls of brownish tongues. When this coat slipped, it uncovered the flabby skin of his torso, along with a beggar's shirt and strips of grimy cotton that seemed to be plugging the holes of his ribcage.

—Hey! Noumak Ashariyev said. Do you want to die, you old slob?

The beggar looked at him hazily.

—I'm not as old as I look, he said.

—Well, you're definitely not deaf, so do you want to die or what? the engineer asked.

—If I want to die, this is what he's asking me, this comrade, the beggar mumbled. Are they really asking me that?

Noumak Ashariyev shrugged. He looked around and exchanged a dumbstruck glance with Hadzoböl Münzberg.

—A train's coming, and you're still sitting in the middle of the tracks. You wanted to get run over?

—Didn't you hear it whistling? Hadzoböl Münzberg cut in from the top of the steps.

—The whistles, I've had enough of them, the beggar answered while pulling his foul coat over his shoulders once again.

Just then, a soldier came and poked the beggar's stomach with the end of his rifle to invite him to stand up. As he observed the man's lack of movement, he didn't try to threaten him any further, and he said:

—Have to refer this one to the captain. Can't shoot him like that without a trial.

—And this one who wants to shoot me, the beggar grumbled to himself, raising his voice to be heard. But where we've ended up, my word! What world we're living in!

• The suicidal beggar was interrogated by Ilyushenko in the middle of the afternoon. Several detainees and a handful of soldiers watched the interrogation, which happened on the rail tracks at the exact spot where the beggar was sitting. In order to increase the audience, because he didn't want to abuse his prerogatives and carry on an investigation discreetly and arbitrarily, Ilyushenko decided to have a special distribution of pemmican. Only those present there could have some, even though it was just a flake per person. This was still enough to attract a small audience. Each one sat somewhat at random while solemnly eating his mouthful, certainly less than three grams. Before stuffing his own mouth with the miniscule portion of food, Ilyushenko offered some to the man he was about to question. The man refused.

—No, I've lost the habit, he said, it makes my stomach hurt. Once the cramps start, I have them for a month.

He had the well-controlled voice of a street actor or singer. A little hoarse, but well controlled. He didn't have any difficulty answering the questions and, as the hours went by, he told his story.

His name was Aldolay Schulhoff.

• Aldolay Schulhoff was born in a region, which, two years after his arrival in the world, had watched a fuel-rod pool go up in fire. The flames had hardly been spectacular, but the teams that had tried to overcome them had seen their numbers and spinal cords melt down in a matter of days, and, as the experts had estimated that the flow of fatal radiation from the vessel would decline on its own over the decades to come, they left things as they were. A huge cortege of refugees began walking toward a mythical west, where the radiation victims thought they'd find the Orbise's capital, and the little Aldolay Schulhoff took his place there, but the hullabaloo and panic were so great that, after the third day of the exodus, his parents lost him. After several hours wandering among thousands of strangers, he had been taken in by a butcher couple that had fattened him up rather than raised him, with the never-explicit but always-understood intent of having him on hand in case of famine. The famine never came to be, they gave up on caring for him, and, a year later, they brought him to a charitable organization, The Eleventh-Hour Brothers, with charitable aims that, like the couple's, were very much cannibalistic instead of altruistic. At six years old, he finally managed to escape the Brothers, who hadn't mistreated him, but still looked at him like an animal to be butchered and were overjoyed to see him growing round. Luck had been in his favor. After the battles south of Bogrovietsk, he ended up alone in a blazing neighborhood, left to his fate by the Brothers, who, seeing their eleventh hour come at last, had preferred to sacrifice a potential feast rather than their own skin. When an Orbise squad had gotten to the heart of the inferno, the soldiers had found the little boy and brought him out. After a short stay at a hospital where he was treated for minor burns, Aldolay Schulhoff was put in a Party orphanage. It offered him security, room and board, and most of all they raised him in accordance with his intellectual capacities, which were considerable. Aside from the natural sciences and the pillars of revolutionary knowledge, they had taken into account his aptitude for languages and music. At fifteen years old, he had mastered Beltir, Koybal, Kyzyl, Kacha, Old American, Camp Russian, Olcha, Khalkha, and he already played the Asiatic zither, the chatkhan, the yatga, and the guzheng perfectly, and sometimes he could also take out an igil and draw out extremely enthusiastic sounds, especially when he used it to accompany traditional or improvised throat songs. His voice went as deep or as high as he needed and, as he articulated well, it was a delight to hear him perform long shamanic ceremonies or lyrical epic poems, which were done in the style of the steppes, the taiga, or the stony desert. Soon he was old enough to leave the school and make his way through existence and, while staying in touch with the school that had shaped him and which invited him every so often to give evening performances, he decided to go out in the streets, travel from city to city and from village to village, and share his talents with the humble, dispersed audiences of proletarians, countrymen, and wretches. Over the years, he split his time in this way between the capital and the paths that led to the ruined regions, stricken by ecological disasters and radioactive silence. Whether the group listening to him was full or merely a group in tatters, he was always warmly applauded. In more than one backwater city he was asked to stay as an official musician, promised basic fees in kind, unlimited access to the collective canteen, and peace and quiet. The women flocked around him and he often ended up breaking his proletarian monasticism to accept their advances. Still, he didn't settle down anywhere. He always preferred moving around, taking his songs elsewhere, and, even when that meant bringing an affair to an end, he endured the sadness of separation and didn't hang back. Then he went deeper and deeper into old irradiated lands, into regions of impenetrable forest, and, even as he continued to give concerts, the number of humans or their like constituting audiences became scarcer and scarcer. And one day he had ended up at the Radiant Terminus kolkhoz, and there his existence had completely changed.

—I've already heard of this kolkhoz, Ilyushenko cut in. I met its president.

—Really, Schulhoff said in shock, you met its president?

—Yes, said Ilyushenko. I didn't like him.

—Solovyei? An enormous muzhik with golden eyes, an ax on his belt?

—Yes, Ilyushenko said. He came during my wife's funeral. He messed with my head in exchange for a block of pemmican. I didn't like him.

Schulhoff scowled and asked for a cigarette. Hadzoböl Münzberg, the second conductor, gave him one and lit it. He had a heavy scout's lighter from the Red Army that he'd found in a dead man's pocket.

The trembling steppes.

The sun's last rays.

The rusty smell of the train wheels.

The diesel engine that, despite being turned off, still stank of diesel fuel.

A raptor's shriek high above.

A blast of almost icy wind, then a lull, then a second gust, then calm on the surrounding steppes.

The smoke escaping from the lips of Schulhoff, Ilyushenko, Hadzoböl Münzberg, Umrug Batyushin, Noumak Ashariyev, and several other detainees and soldiers.

A long moment of silence.

• —We're not leaving right away, Ilyushenko decided. We'll bivouac here.

As the captain responsible for everyone, he gave instructions to position sentries, prepare a fire, and take those who hadn't survived out of the cars and take their bodies a respectable distance away. And so Pedron Dardaf, Babur Malone, and Douglas Flanagan were placed behind the pines, and the necessary incisions were made on their bodies to attract the vultures and hasten their sky burials.

Then the interrogation resumed.

New passengers had come out of their torpor, come down to the ballast, and come over to the spot to watch the performance in which Aldolay Schulhoff was starring. Now there was a little crowd in front of the locomotive. The men were mostly apathetic, but they got ready to hear what he had to say. Some were wallowing in the ditch and had their backs to Schulhoff and Ilyushenko, but most of them waited for the suicidal beggar to unburden himself of his story and conjure up images in their heads.

Aldolay Schulhoff asked for another cigarette. He tasted the first puffs without closing his eyes, but with a dreamy air and without saying anything. Then he continued his story.

• He described his arrival at the Levanidovo. The Radiant Terminus kolkhoz had seemed strange, but welcoming.

—What did it look like? Ilyushenko asked.

—I'd say it looked like a village from the Second Soviet Union, Schulhoff said. Small farmhouses throughout a tiny valley surrounded by a forest, a main road with the faux-classical style soviet building, a horrible hangar at the top of a slope for storing irradiated objects, and the feeling that, aside from a handful of tough nuts, nobody had survived. The feeling that most of the houses were uninhabited. And besides, it was just a feeling. There weren't even a dozen kolkhozniks still alive, as far as I could tell. Maybe there were still intermediary humans, neither dead nor alive, able to get up and take a few steps, without much thinking or talking, but they stayed in their houses. They didn't show themselves. Those, I can't say how many of them there were. Maybe they didn't even exist. Still, among all the kolkhozniks who were also plenty odd themselves, there was an engineer between life and death, peasants who were barely worth more, an ancient woman more than a hundred years old and covered with medals because she had been a heroic liquidator, and the three daughters of the kolkhoz president. The daughters were all evidently crazy and mutant. They were bald but you couldn't tell, unless you spent the night with them. They wore very elaborate, effective wigs that made them look normal and attractive, with long hair that was fine and very black. Well, normal, yes and no. At first glance, maybe, but you could certainly see before long that something wasn't right. Their eyes, their mannerisms. They seemed happy enough, but something was off. There was immediately no question that they were enjoying a supernatural existence, whether they had genetic predispositions that allowed them not to be affected by radiation, or whether they had magic helping them out. At first I thought that the magic came from the old granny living at the top of the village, in the hangar for nuclear junk. She spent her time by a well that the reactor core had dug, when the plant broke down. So, maybe she was adding a bit of magic to the kolkhoz's machinery. But it was actually the kolkhoz president who did it all with his magical powers. The one named Solovyei. He's the one who kept the kolkhoz apart from the rest of the world and he's the one who kept its inhabitants from sinking into nothingness. He had this power. He had to hatch one of his dream visions down there and he grafted it onto a village that existed before him, or maybe the village was created out of nowhere by him. I have no idea. One of his daughters, the youngest one, claimed that he lived inside a nest of flames and that from there he steered the world of the village and its surroundings. She hated him. What's for sure is that he was the complete master of Radiant Terminus. Nobody was permitted to exist in the kolkhoz unless he'd gotten control over them in the heart of their dreams. No one was allowed to struggle in his or her own future unless he was part of it and directing it as he wished. He transformed everyone into something like puppets, and, so as not to be bored, he created puppets that resisted him or who could deceive him or cause problems, but, in the end, he was the one with the final say on everything. Radiant Terminus wasn't really a kolkhoz, it was more a theater to keep him from spending eternity yawning and waiting for the world to break down and, for those who lived in the village, it was a filthy dream they could never escape. But it took me a long time to understand all that. I understood it later. Much later. In there I met one of his daughters. Like I said, they were all crazy and mutant. They were also very beautiful. The one I met had an eye like her father's, glittering yellow, and the other was deep black, wonderfully deep. I was enchanted by her gaze, and she was also a cautious daughter, a bit reserved, a bit cold at first, but she turned out to be sensual, intimately generous, I'm telling you. We fell into each other's arms and got married. But her father didn't grant his blessing. Her father was jealous, possessive, he wanted her all to himself. And that was why everything turned into a nightmare.

—What was her name? Ilyushenko asked.

Schulhoff looked down and groaned.

—I don't know. I don't know anymore. Her father took the name out of my head, right before expelling me from the Levanidovo, right at the beginning of my journey. He soiled my memory so I couldn't take refuge in it during my journey.

—What do you mean, he took the name out of your head? Umrug Batyushin asked.

—I'm going to tell you, Schulhoff said.

Silence fell.

Soldiers and detainees alike watched him, some indifferently, others pitying him.

Schulhoff didn't say anything else.

He stayed there, sitting, filthy and tattered, vaguely inhuman, his face gaunt and dirty, and he breathed heavily, with irregular inhalations, as if he were crying.

• Ilyushenko rubbed his neck, harshly caressing the etching that expressed his loyalty to the Orbise. Making contact with these talismans didn't inspire him. He had listened attentively to Schulhoff, but he had trouble determining his honesty, the amount of fabulation and slyness that could have crept into the story, and he hadn't really rejected the possibility that he might be a creature commissioned by the enemy, a human or almost-human decoy intended to keep the convoy from reaching its goal.

Dusk hung over the steppes.

Three or four crows had settled on the pine branches and, looking sidelong, mistrustfully, they examined the corpses of Pedron Dardaf, Babur Malone, and Douglas Flanagan. They didn't caw. They had to be thinking about what they would do the next day, when the progress of the sky burials would depend entirely on their initiative.

The sky wasn't already gray or black.

Ilyushenko ordered the group to move and set up about twenty meters away from the rails, at the spot chosen for a campfire. He touched Schulhoff on the shoulder to invite him to get up and Schulhoff, who until then had refused to leave the tracks, did so without protesting and followed Ilyushenko toward the grassy indentation in the earth where the interview would continue. He walked unhesitatingly, without really staying in a straight line, like he was sick to his stomach, and every two steps Ilyushenko caught him and helped him regain his balance. He smelled cowpats, rotting hay, irradiated horsemeat, cloth bandages, nights spent waiting for death, stone altars, solitude.

• The smoke from the first burning planks.

For kindling they had several small clumps of wood, but mostly material the detainees had picked from the itinerant library: pages of post-exotic romånces that light up easily, an essay on Altaic languages, propaganda pamphlets on hygiene in extreme Siberian conditions, on modalities of proletarian dictatorship in case the entire working class disappeared, on the persistence of music, art, religious and magical beliefs after death. The bittersweet smell of carbon from all these texts.

Then the uncertain smoke of the first planks.

A bit of varnish caramelizing on a board taken from who knew what ruin.

Gas escaping from blisters hidden beneath the exterior.

Fibers that catch, already burning without flames, but with a visible heat shimmer that dissipates the smoke.

Then the fire crackles and turns red.

Finally it turns magnificently red, and already nobody thinks about its miraculous birth.

• Sitting by the fire pit, we soldiers and detainees focused on the golden yellow of the flames. We barely moved, we allowed the night to gain ground both above the steppes and within our bodies. As if numbed, we admired the ephemeral spirals, the twists toward the sky, streaked for a very brief second with coppery red, and then evaporating, and then reappearing in the same place, not exactly identical, wonderfully different, endlessly lively and beautiful. As always, the dance was as surprising as it was repetitive and, as always, we had the feeling that it was speaking mysteriously to us, or rather to each of us individually, and that with a language that didn't use words it awoke within us old images, images buried in our animality, images of submission, of fear, and of wonder that persuaded us to loyalty to the fire. We didn't blink our eyes enough, and, after a moment, our ocular globes were stinging and feverish. To be honest, even as our personal exchange with the fire rallied us oneirically, we didn't lose a bit of the conversation that was going on between our captain and the suicidal beggar. Every so often we brought our hands closer to the fire to light our cigarettes. Our faces were roasting and our backs were icy. Lethargy overcame our muscles. Our intelligence wasn't far from nodding off, either.

—You were talking about being expelled from the kolkhoz, Ilyushenko said. The father of the daughter removed your memory after the expulsion.

—Not all my memory, Schulhoff corrected. Just a part.

He gave a concert in the former Pioneers' House. The Soviet Assembly Room benefited from good acoustics. Most of the Levanidovo's mobile inhabitants had come to listen to him and seemed moved by his songs and his narration. Even the president of the kolkhoz had shown interest in the performance and clapped loudly. Then, when everyone had left and he was lighting a cigarette, one of the kolkhozniks had invited him to cross the street and enter the Soviet, in order, he claimed, to "receive his reward." He went in without any suspicion. Barely had he crossed the doorstep when he found himself already under Solovyei's power. Behind him the door had shut without a noise, as if instead of wood it was a mattress fitting into a quilted rectangle. He took three steps into the darkness of the entrance hall and already he was walking someplace without walls, already he was moving through a black hallway that led into the infernal realms of Solovyei. Dread gripped him. He tried to retrace his steps, but the path was void of all markers and, no matter which way he went, he went deeper into a shadowy trap. The farther he walked the closer he drew to the president of Radiant Terminus. He was waiting for him at the end of the path. He was calm and gigantic, with an ax. His hair flew around him as if electrified, his beard looked like a ruff of hirsute lava. Incandescent and hirsute. He welcomed Schulhoff unsmilingly, but his terrible, rapacious, yellow gaze sparkled with satisfied malice. They were facing each other, close enough for a duel, in a space lit by a spotlight that blinded Schulhoff even when he shut his eyes or turned to avoid the light. "Whether you have eyelids or not," Solovyei announced in a deep, mocking voice, "you'll never see anything through your eyes independently ever again. You'll see what I want you to see, and only that until the end." They stayed for a long moment without talking. Solovyei took his time and Schulhoff knew he was screwed. The place resembled a lunar crater, or the inside of a gigantic cauldron that was filthy, or a gas station after being bombed with phosphorus. It was filled with disparate objects, charred farming machines and small bowls, basins and buckets in which embers were constantly stirring and sputtering. Drops of black oil fell from above. Schulhoff thought of an oneiric variant on the Gramma Udgul's warehouse, and he also thought that Solovyei had lured him underground, to the bottom of the well that the nuclear core had dug in its stupid fury, after breaking the chains that had imprisoned it. "You're not entirely wrong," Solovyei said in response, although Schulhoff hadn't spoken out loud. "In reality, we're in my house, which is to say everywhere. We're in the old forest, in the dreams of my lovers, and in the heart of the flames. We're before and after, even if there's neither before nor after, just a present with no beginning or end. We're in my nest. You can't understand, you can't even imagine it, you have no idea of ubiquity and paradoxical lengths. But, even though you can't understand, you'll endure. It's a mystery you'll never get used to. And I'm not going to hide that it will make you suffer, Schulhoff. You'll never get used to it. Even in forty-nine times forty-nine years you still won't have gotten used to it. Two thousand four hundred and one years, if I've done it right. You'll find the time long, Schulhoff. Understanding nothing is very, very difficult. For you, this will be painful and endless." While he talked in this frightening way, Solovyei drew back several meters and then came right back up to Schulhoff with a phonograph and some cylinders. He set it all on a wobbly table, its legs warped by fire.

—Go faster, Schulhoff, Ilyushenko cut in. You're annoying us with all these details. We're not at a festive evening, with songs and musical accompaniment. We're in an interrogation. The embellishments don't matter. If we're listening to you, if we're losing our time to sleep by listening to your twaddle, it's just to know whether or not you should be shot.

—I know, said Schulhoff.

—So how did he supposedly take away your memory? Ilyushenko asked.

—Just a part, Schulhoff clarified once again.

—Yes, Ilyushenko said irritatedly. You already said that.

—He did it with the phonograph and the ax, Schulhoff muttered. But first he told me what would happen to me. Wandering through the steppes and the taiga without ever being able to die. "Never being able to die, never being able to console yourself with the idea of a glorious future, never remembering the treasures of the past." That was what he insisted. A muddled walk, monotonous and joyless, for thousands of years. A murky and stupid eternity. He promised me that I would never find his daughter again, neither in dreams nor in my memories. That I would think of her without being able to remember the moments of happiness I'd had with her, not even her name. He also told me that, during the periods of drowsiness or rest, when I was tempted by forgetfulness, he would make me hear his poems or his whistling. It would appear within myself without my understanding, just so I could remember that I had caused him harm. "And what harm did I cause you?" I asked him then. "My daughters belong to me," Solovyei said. "You hurt them. You interposed yourself between them and me. You married one of them. You were free to do so or not. Now you're starting to pay the price. Don't believe that you can own what belongs to me without impunity. You took one of my daughters. You put your filthy cock in her belly and, even if she didn't complain, you hurt her. Today is the first day of your expiation. There will be tens of thousands more like it to start with, and then hundreds of thousands. Days of misery. Nights of fear and weariness. Do you understand, Schulhoff? Today is the beginning of your hell. You will stay there until your death, except you will never die."

• Schulhoff focused on detailing the manipulation Solovyei had made him endure. The president of Radiant Terminus hadn't imposed a particular physical suffering on him, but at the end of his warning speech he had frozen him, or rather petrified his flesh to the marrow of his bones. In a second, Schulhoff had become a block of hardened wax. Solovyei detached the articulated arm of the phonograph to write on him with the needle, poems on his forehead, on his mouth, on his eyes. Every so often, the president of the kolkhoz took his ax and used the flat of the blade to erase what he had engraved. He smoothed the surface that he had just scraped, then he attacked with another poem or another set of magical instructions. The enigmatic phrases carved grooves into Schulhoff one after another, embedded magical signposts that would guide and poison his journey for centuries and centuries after. "It was long," Schulhoff explained. "It took place in a black and timeless space, but it was very long." Sometimes Solovyei wrote, sometimes he whistled in a deafening way, horribly, or sometimes he was quiet and rocked back and forth, always keeping the same rhythm. Or sometimes he went to set the point and membrane of the phonograph back in place on the apparatus, and he inserted a wax roll. While the horn produced one of the strange verbal compositions he had authored, he watched Schulhoff malevolently and beat the measure with his colossal feet. Time was malleable and stretched out terribly, there were no longer any lights or shadows, and all around, in the various receptacles, small flames crackled and sent off sparks, flares bloomed, became orange curtains, went out with a roar, revived. They certainly emitted fumes, radiation, and toxic gas, but Schulhoff was no longer breathing and the aggressive odors no longer concerned him. He was already immunized against all that was fatal. Drops of black oil fell from nobody knew what vault and splattered slimily on the ground. The phonograph continued its soliloquy in a voice that was sometimes charming, sometimes unbearably pedantic and authoritarian. Often Solovyei spoke in the text that the roll reproduced. He embellished it with additional syllables or approving exclamations, or he reinforced it with a buzzing that underscored the fundamental nature of shamanic singing. The spotlight continued to blind Schulhoff, who had long since ceased to blink, even when Solovyei chiseled words and sentences directly on his corneas. It became part of the image bound to his consciousness from the beginning of the operation, and which nothing would change. However, within this image, and chiefly at its forefront, Solovyei moved, came and went, and frequently changed his appearance. Sometimes he was a hairy and sooty shadow, sometimes a silhouette sculpted in the fire, sometimes a festively dressed peasant.

—Good, said Ilyushenko. And then?

—Then he left me alone and I began to walk, Schulhoff said. I was no longer an inert statue. It was morning in a deserted region, a grassy plain with mountains far off, and, in the middle, the gray-blue reflection of a little lake. I went toward the lake at random. I'd regained the use of my body, of my eyes. I didn't suffer from these inscriptions that he'd engraved in my skin. They had left no trace. I tried to remember what had happened, and what I had lived through during the preceding days. My head was empty. Nothing came back to me. For six or eight months, I was wholly amnesic, then I regained a little memory. Then a little more. I reconstructed it, bit by bit, over the course of years. And finally everything came back to me, except for the name of the woman I married in the Levanidovo. Without her name, I can't revive my memories. I no longer have a precise image of her. The look she had when we were close to one another, her gaze both yellow and black, I don't even know if I'm confusing it with her father's horrible gaze. Without her name, without her image, it's impossible for me to really remember her.

Schulhoff sighed deeply.

—I've lost her, he said. I'll wander like this for twenty-four and a half centuries and more without her name, without her image, and always looking for it.

—Uh-uh, philosophized one of the detainees with his hands held up to the fire, it'll pass. When you lose someone, it passes.

—No, Schulhoff said, shaking his head sadly. Solovyei has made sure it will never pass. He makes me walk from forest to forest, from lake to lake, and when the absence of the woman I love seems a little less unbearable, when the loss makes me suffer a little less, he reintroduces himself in my head and he revives my urge to remember. He whistles in my head until I collapse. He keeps whistling, he sings his sorts of poems. It lasts for days and nights. I can't escape it. I can't die. I'm stuck within his clutches. Within his dreams. No death is available to me. I also wonder if maybe I'm actually inside one of his dreams. It won't pass and I can't escape.

—And after the twenty-four and a half centuries and more? Hadzoböl Münzberg asked.

—After, the same thing, Schulhoff said.

—The urge to be done, Matthias Boyol commented. It's true that it's something that doesn't diminish.

—Yes, a detainee said. Whether you're living or dead, it doesn't diminish.

• When the night was over, Ilyushenko gave the order to the engineer to start the engine again. They tamped down the last embers of the campfire and went to settle back in the cars. The sentries made one last round around the convoy and reported to the captain that there was nothing to report, except that the sky burials had begun at dawn when the crows pecked at a few of the cadavers' hands, then had stopped, doubtless because the birds preferred to do their work without any witnesses. The crows had flown off to the north and had momentarily made way for rats and necrophagous insects. Ilyushenko went past the pines to say good-bye to Pedron Dardaf, Babour Malone, and Douglas Flanagan. The three men were lying on the grass. In spite of their shut eyes and several pallid abrasions on the backs of their hands and their foreheads, they didn't seem to be any more dead or alive than most of their convoy comrades, which is to say we others.

Ilyushenko stayed and didn't move for a minute in their company, then he turned back, aware that he wasn't alone. Seven or eight steps off, Schulhoff was stationed, waiting, on a molehill. When he saw that Ilyushenko was watching him, he shifted his shoulders within his stinking rags.

—Now you can order me shot, he said.

—I have no reason to have you shot, Ilyushenko said.

—I was on the tracks, Schulhoff pleaded. I forced the train to stop. That's like a sabotage or an act of war. People have been slaughtered for less than that.

—Forget it, Ilyushenko said.

—On the other hand, Schulhoff said, I told you bullshit instead of responding honestly to your questions. I took advantage of the good-will of the investigators. I just tricked everyone with my inventions.

—So those were lies? Ilyushenko asked.

—Yes, lied Schulhoff.

Over there, on the tracks, the diesel engine whined.

We never fill it up with fuel, Ilyushenko suddenly thought. We never stock up. We go on as if we were outside reality. The locomotive could keep going like this for years. Why not twenty-four and a half centuries and then some. We, too, we're part of one of Solovyei's dreams.

—And besides, Schulhoff continued accusing himself, I have in my possession, engraved on myself, entire collections of counterrevolutionary poems. It's ideological deviation. That's punishable by death.

—Forget it, Ilyushenko said again, hesitating over the right decision to make.

—You know, Schulhoff insisted. You just have to give the order. And besides, it would help me. It would cut short my suffering.

—You're not a dog, Ilyushenko remarked. If you were a beast, we'd take pity on you. But no, you're not a dog. We can't end you like that.

—No, Schulhoff lamented.

$-15-$

• He or I, doesn't matter. Him or me, same thing. He's there, by the pines, nothing special at first glance. He looks like all the male crows in this area of the world. A little plump, with a gaze perhaps unusually deep, but he resembles every one of them. He's approached the corpses and examines them, taking his time. He hops around and bounces between the bodies, he thinks. He pecks the cold hand of Pedron Dardaf, as if to test out his reaction. And suddenly, as if disturbed by a noise or by a hunch of a hostile presence, he extends his wings and shakes them powerfully and abandons the support of the plants and the earth. For two seconds he rises up at an angle; he seems to be floating effortlessly just a short distance from the ground, then he strikes the air and pushes upward and presses onward again, he beats the transparent space, the fluid space, and he hears his wings flapping and that gives him inexpressible satisfaction, I listen happily to my wings flapping, which tell me unambiguously that I'm there, solid and black, as if fully alive, and he crows twice, a cry of pure contentment, not joy but contentment, the first time out of nothing but instinct, and the second time with some awareness of its cause. It's a self-affirmation, but it's also a call. It's not directed at anyone in particular, not at the fellow creatures that in any case only admit his existence passively. It's more a call aimed at the forces surrounding and carrying him, not a prayer and even less a supplication, more a salute, more a display of affection, which he sends toward the gray First Heaven, and toward the gray Third Heaven, toward Madame Crude Death, toward Our Lady of Very-Hot Vibrations, toward the First Lady of Very-Cold Vibrations, a sonic caress for the Seven Strange Floods, for the Five Snouts, for the Flames of Strange Silence and for the Flames of Nuclear Silence, for the Immense Labyrinths, for the Gramma Udgul, who has always been and will stay alive in his heart, and I'm not forgetting in the list the Second Soviet Union and the Immortal Poets of the Orbise. Still rising up he lands on the peak of a pine, the highest one in the little group of pines at the foot of which these poor morons have set out three of their own for their sky burials.

• From the top of the tree, everything can be seen, and just by making a little effort, almost everything can be seen.

• He tilts his deep-black crow's head, once to the left and once to the right. He cracks open the slightly rough and gray eyelids, behind which was his glassy nictitating membrane, and, beyond that, the indescribably amber-yellow gaze that explains the ostracism of his fellow creatures. His golden gaze, his fiery gaze that isn't warm. Whether his eyelids are closed or not, he sees everything; whether he sleeps or doesn't sleep or doesn't dream, he sees everything. His head pulled back, he runs the bottom of his beak over one of his most important flight feathers. He inhales the smell of his plumage, the nauseating scent of clouds at the end of the night, the scent of trees moored in darkness, the scent of grasses in which steppe mice have urinated, in which dampness has hastened rot, the smell of the icy earth on which these idiots have decided to lay down their dead. He stretches out his left wing and folds it back in, he makes as if to move his right wing, then shifts his head into its most usual position, facing the wind when there's wind. All his joints are in order, nothing hurts in spite of the unfortunate encounters while crossing the long tunnels of black space, the furtive but aggressive birds, with wings that cut like sabers, and horrible, odorless

winds loaded with atomic plague and radiation. He lets a minute go
by, and, as so often happens when he is wearing feathers, he repeats
"He or I, doesn't matter." And indeed I'm not very sensitive to the use
of one pronoun rather than another, because it's all still me, and he
opens his eyes, and with this yellow brightness added to the world's,
the landscape is altered imperceptibly, the landscape becomes an image
in which the idiots come as if they were in a net, unable to escape even
in dreams, and his eyes follow the double line of the railroad tracks
across the gloomy steppes, here barely rising and falling, farther off
the convoy trying to disappear on the horizon as if disappearance were
possible, he didn't fail to notice the convoy of these idiots still wandering in infinite repetition. And I crow.

• The train lurches slowly on its path. The passengers are slumped in
the half-dark cars. They aren't all dead, but claiming that they're alive
would be a bit much. The conductor and the second conductor are
the only ones to still have some semblance of consciousness, however
often they disappear into tortuous periods of sleepiness. They, too, like
the captain, are working this job in rotation and, even if they have the
basic principles of mechanics, even if they do their best, they don't
have much prowess aside from staying more or less awake while the
others sleep. In any case, they don't have much to trouble themselves
over if they want everything to keep working. The locomotive keeps
purring as it goes along, as if its engine obeyed something other than
a miracle I'm bringing about, although the oil and diesel fuel tanks
have been empty for years. The convoy advances. Clack clack, clack-
clack, clack clack. Night falls, darkness spreads over everything. One
of the conductors, say Hadzoböl Münzberg, turns on the headlights
but sometimes forgets to and the train crosses the night without the
tracks in front lit up, in any case, there aren't any traps and it's empty.
No other convoy over thousands of kilometers. Dawn breaks, followed
by a sunny but chilly day, then night falls, the sky becomes starry. In
the morning, a shower. The clouds really move in, then the evening

thickens, becomes inky black. The night is punctuated by volleys of unending rain. In the morning, the rain grows heavy with melted snow. For several hours, the day brightens. Then comes a night of frost. Noumak Ashariyev, who is the second conductor here, does his best to trigger the cabin's heater, but the wiring has been ruined since the previous winter. It keeps the ice from accumulating on the controls, but that's it, there isn't any more that it can do. Hadzoböl Münzberg and Noumak Ashariyev go numb. Every so often they think that the Saturday stop is coming, and the idea of pemmican distribution and a night around the fire revives them for a few seconds, but the rest of the time they jostle around and doze. After night comes day. The steppes have taken on their winter colors. Clack clack, clack-clack, clack clack. At the end of half a week the snow sputters against the locomotive's windows. It wakes up the two men. And as the morning is, despite everything, underway and bright enough, through the moving curtains of the snowflakes I know they will suddenly see a camp, the camp, and I anticipate their surprise, and I let out a caw that they don't hear.

• Hadzoböl Münzberg woke up first and, with a nudge, put an end to Noumak Ashariyev's protracted drowsiness. Now the two conductors were hunched over the dashboard, worried, trying to interpret the forms that loomed in view, or those that grayed beyond the snowflakes. The snow seemed dirty and ocher. It fell flat on the window in irregular spots. The windshield wipers scrubbed them away, but sometimes the mechanism struggled and got stuck, only moving again after two difficult seconds and with a grinding noise. The conductors got so close to the window that their foreheads were nearly touching it. They didn't say anything, but whispered curses and promises of ill will toward the elements, to the windshield wiper blades and their screwiness and recklessness. Chilly whistles snaked through the cabin. It shuddered under the engine's purring. The strip right in front of the locomotive kept cutting through the snowdrifts that had accumulated between the rails.

The notches in the snow set off roars and sprays. In these conditions, it was much harder to make out the clack-clack of the wheels.

Noumak Ashariyev had his face very close to the windshield. He seemed to dislike this transparent protection and, by the looks of him, he wanted to face head-on the masses of snow hurtling against the window. He stayed like that for several minutes, and suddenly he uttered an excited sentence. He claimed to be able to make out a watchtower to starboard and a barbed-wire fence three meters high, and almost immediately two other watchtowers and a long barrier rose up through the swarms of snow.

—A camp! he roared, without hiding his hoarse enthusiasm.

I crowed at the same moment he did.

Hadzoböl Münzberg immediately lowered the brake lever and, when the train had come to a stop, he opened a side window and poked his head out. Noumak Ashariyev was hunched over the control panel. The windshield wipers continued going back and forth and everything could be seen more clearly than when they had been moving. The snow fell in dense and peaceful cascades. It flattened the entire landscape, which was flat and devoid of trees up to a distant and dark line of larches, the border of the taiga. To the right of the tracks, the emptiness came up against another obstacle, this one less natural, made up of high, barbed fences behind which were wooden abutments, watchtowers, and a second wall. It was a sentry walk. Behind that, deep within, were rows of barracks, houses of wood.

—All that time, Noumak Ashariyev said.

Hadzoböl Münzberg pulled his head back into the cabin. His cap was powdered with snowflakes, the snow had accumulated in his wrinkles, on his nearly nonexistent eyebrows.

—It's worth all the effort we made, he said.

—Yes, said Noumak Ashariyev. There were moments when I had my doubts.

—Me, too. I wondered what use there was in going on.

—Of course, but we kept on going. We went to the end.

—It really was worth the effort, Hadzoböl Münzberg repeated.

• The camp was a hundred and fifty meters from the rails. A second-ary track went from the main track to the entrance. It was covered in fresh snow, but its outlines were clearly visible. The junction began several meters past the place where the locomotive had stopped.

—I'm going to clear off the switch, Hadzoböl Münzberg announced.

He was already in the back of the cabin taking down a long sheep-skin jacket. It was torn and greasy. A long while ago, during a stop in a radioactive small town, it had been pulled off a lifeless body. He put it on and got ready to go out.

—Have to wait for the captain's orders, Noumak Ashariyev objected.

—Why? It'll be forever before he wakes up . . .

—All right, the conductor said. When you've made sure that the ice isn't covering the mechanism, raise your hand. I'll go slowly.

Hadzoböl Münzberg opened the door and went down the steps.

—I can hardly believe it, he said.

—Well, we're here, Noumak Ashariyev said. It's unbelievable.

The morning was barely bright. Hadzoböl Münzberg was immedi-ately surprised by the cold and, when he set his foot on the ground, he pulled the fur collar of his jacket around his neck.

Behind him the snow-smudged train now seemed to only contain goods and nothing living. Nobody had reacted yet to the convoy stop-ping. The captain hadn't summoned up enough strength yet to stick his nose out and learn the reason for this abrupt and unplanned stop. The sliding doors stayed shut. Hadzoböl Münzberg walked past the locomotive, which was still puffing a bit, as if dreaming, as if contem-plating after the effort of the journey. The snow fell.

Hadzoböl Münzberg followed the rails to the fork without look-ing back at his comrade, who was observing him from the top of the machine. The ground creaked. With the toes of his shoes, he clumsily cleared the rails to the spot where the wheels would shift onto the auxiliary track. The boards were in good shape, and even if the pulling cable was completely coated in ice, no piles of compacted snow posed a threat to the mechanism. As if to test the path the convoy would soon take, he now went slowly down the start of the curve. The switch stand was fifteen meters from the actual switch. He walked that distance looking up ahead rather than immediately in front of him. He looked at the camp. The auxiliary rails past the curve turned through a right angle toward the entrance of the exterior wall. An unloading platform could be seen through the snow beyond the door of the inner wall; the rails disappeared between the buildings and the view, at that point already indistinct, could no longer be deciphered.

The camp didn't seem to indicate any activity, in any case this part of the camp, perhaps because it was already an hour of the day when detainees, administrators, and soldiers had left for a mission somewhere else, or everyone was confined to barracks because of the poor atmospheric conditions, or this area of buildings was shut down, or all the personnel had suffered devastating atomic blasts to the marrow of their bones and hadn't found ways or reason to defy and survive them. Muffled and silenced by the continual snowfall, the camp didn't leave any doubt as to its status as a camp. The doors were reinforced with metal plates, the barbed fences and the watchtowers had not been worn down by time.

Above the camp, the low sky ceaselessly spat out its gray fluff.

Hadzoböl Münzberg felt his heart swell in joy. The wandering had ended. A few more hours of maneuvers, of administrative formalities, and it would be over.

• He wiped away the snow icing his face and he walked around the switch stand to examine it before pushing down on it.

At that moment, he had a feeling in his stomach that something was wrong.

He looked up into the snow, saw a handful of snowflakes that fell directly into his eyes, then he turned back to the convoy stopped behind him, fifty meters back. Noumak Ashariyev was still pressed up against the locomotive's window and, inside the cabin, he was waiting for the signal to start again and go down the side rails. Everything was frozen in the ground's whiteness and the air's yellowish grayness. Nothing seemed odd, or maybe yes, something did in the sudden immobility everywhere. The windshield wipers no longer moved in front of the conductor's face. The snowflakes kept falling, but with such slowness that they seemed to hang as they fell. Hadzoböl Münzberg turned toward the switch stand with its bulging counterweight, painted yellow and black, as if it was meant to reproduce the basic colors of a steppe hornet. He still hadn't touched anything, and yet the counterweight was moving and drifting toward the sky, massive and floating. And then, no, the counterweight wasn't changing, it was he, Hadzoböl Münzberg, who had begun to turn toward the sky and lose his balance. And only at that moment did he hear the explosion. It took him a second to realize that a gunshot had been fired from the nearest watchtower and that he had been hit with a projectile in the stomach. He had taken a bullet. Doubtlessly to the liver or the heart.

He spun, his arms outstretched, and collapsed at the foot of the switch stand. And didn't move.

The echoes of gunfire hit the line of larches. They came back weakly and died against the old cars with their doors still stubbornly shut. Then the scene was quiet.

• The silence of a wintry scene.

The white ground shining. Aside from the ground, everything is dark.

Gray ridges, innumerable gray piles.

The invisible sky.

The diesel locomotive breathing softly, its steps covered in snow.

The unmoving train, its four cars closed, so nobody could tell immediately whether they held goods, deportees, or worse still.

Far on its left, all around the landscape, the impenetrable black boundary of the taiga.

On the right, not as far away from the rails as the forest, the sentry walk, the wooden towers, the metal brambles.

Then the rails encased in snow, those that went toward the unknown and those that turned toward the door of the camp. White swells on the earth. Inverted furrows.

The watchtowers framing the door.

No solemn inscription over the door, no pompous, welcoming slogan, no name, no number.

If there are soldiers in the watchtowers, they do their best not to be seen.

Hadzoböl Münzberg lying by the switch stand, already dusted, as if in rigor mortis although there hasn't been time yet, no longer breathing, no longer responding to anything.

A misplaced crow perches near his head then lets out a caw before flying off immediately, disappearing over the camp.

Then nothing.

Nothingness lasting several minutes.

The snow falling.

The immobility.

The white silence. Nobody even knows if the locomotive engine keeps grunting back there or not.

• A little later Noumak Ashariyev came out of the torpor that had overwhelmed him and stopped contemplating Hadzoböl Münzberg's outstretched form, now becoming white, more and more white with every minute. He took a felt hat from the nook, put on wool gloves, and went down the steps on the side opposite the camp. He hadn't seen any smoke, any soldier, but he was sure that the shot had come from one of the watchtowers standing by the door. The forest was

much too far away and the idea of a sniper hidden among the trees
made no sense.

He went down the ladder and jumped onto the snow. He slipped,
caught the side of the locomotive. He hadn't shut off the engine and
the wall was warm enough to keep the snow from sticking. The odor
of diesel fuel permeated the air. For no reason, it gave him courage,
which he needed after having watched his comrade die.

He went past the locomotive and bent down and sped up when he
crossed the open space between the tractor and the first car. It was better not to expose himself to gunfire, even if the distance, the shortness
of the oath, and the veil of snow made for reliable protection.

The first car's door slid open half a meter and, breathless and eyes
shut, on his knees because he hadn't come up with another way to
get off the straw he had been lying on, Ilyushenko appeared in the
doorway. He looked every bit like he was deathly ill. He asked what
was happening. Noumak Ashariyev explained it all.

Incredulity was evident on the captain's face.

—They've mistaken us for others, he ventured.

His voice lacked all conviction.

—Have to clear up this misunderstanding, he finished.

• Little transpired that morning. Because of the low temperatures,
the train passengers took time to gain enough energy and a mental
state sufficient for understanding language. The conductor and the
captain took turns delivering the same message to them all: We finally
came to a camp, but there's still a problem to solve before we're welcomed behind the barbed wire, we may have to force our entry so
that the misunderstandings are resolved, sometimes things go well and
everything happens without a hitch and sometimes they go wrong,
Hadzoböl Münzberg was shot dead by a guard, everybody get in position, guns will be distributed once everyone is on their feet, if you
want to sleep tonight or tomorrow in warm barracks we have to replace
the administrative admissions formalities with military formalities.

Detainees and soldiers nodded their heads and blinked. The other parts of their bodies were still numb and it was useless to rush them.

At the beginning of the afternoon, Ilyushenko collected the men within the second car. Three of them were still lying in the shadow, stiff and peaceful, still not out of the Bardo where the regular ups and downs and the cold had plunged them. Schliffko Armanadji, Tristram Bokanowski, Olfan Nunes. The commander wanted everybody in the troupe to hear his instructions, the living as well as the dead, and he wouldn't sideline these three. He had no intention of letting these courageous men feel that they had been excluded from the collective for superficial, bodily reasons. Once the instructions had been given in detail, the men went back to their cars and carried the dead to the caboose, which had always been the storehouse and eventually the morgue from the beginning of the trip, and where Aldolay Schulhoff would watch over them. Considering his state of confusion, he couldn't really be equipped with a rifle. However, it wasn't a problem for him to give moral support to the departed, to grumble stories over them, and be present for them since the rest of the troupe were unable to do so.

Ilyushenko had assigned each member of the troupe to battle positions, reminding them to open heavy fire only if dialogue with the camp authorities had deteriorated irrevocably. Such a shootout was not to be followed by an attack, since our poor knowledge of the place would guarantee a catastrophe. The fire would signify our desire to be heard, it would be a testament to our determination, a cry. They would have to wait a moment after the salvos, a reasonable moment, at least a day, and if by bad luck this despairing fire wasn't understood, we would go back on our way to find a more welcoming camp.

Right before leaving to negotiate with Matthias Boyol in his company, Ilyushenko settled his affairs as if he was certainly going to be shot in front of the camp. To run the operation in his absence, he encouraged the men to approve Shamno Driff's nomination. He would stay in the convoy during the negotiations, and he would take over his responsibilities and his title if things went wrong.

• Matthias Boyol had been chosen for his ease in manipulating words.

He and Ilyushenko went along the train up to the front of the machine, then, after taking a breath, they began to walk on the open ground.

They knew that at any moment they could be the target of a sniper and they went slowly and silently, each of them appraising his existence up to his death and revisiting what had followed, the gloomy trip, the bumps over the weeks, months, and years, the drowsy camaraderie around the campfires, the interminable wait. They had a feeling of tightness in their chests, shortness of breath. At the same time they were calling up their pasts, they focused on living every second as intensely as possible. The sharp air. The whir of snowflakes hurtling against one another as they fell or hit the thick layer, this quiet, continual, and invariable crystalline clinking. The snow grinding beneath their treads. The half-darkness bathing the landscape. The somewhat hazy but very tidy silhouette of the barbed fences, the wooden towers. The impression that they had come to the end of the world.

They went to the switch and turned onto the auxiliary tracks. Without stopping at Hadzoböl Münzberg's body, which had become a mass that was now imprecise in all its contours, they went toward the camp's door. They didn't set foot on the rails so as not to slip. The ballast was tidy, with cinders making up most of it. As the crossties were at regular, predictable intervals, they didn't stumble, and instead stepped over them. Ilyushenko, looking sullen, clenched his jaw. Matthias Boyol couldn't keep his head straight. He didn't look at either the white plain or the increasingly close barrier. He panted and seemed to be closely examining the fifty centimeters of snow in front of them, the long tubes of snow indicating the presence of the rails, the toes of his shoes.

Ten meters from the door, they stopped. The rails went on ahead and slipped under the metal panels painted in camouflage green. There was nobody in the space separating the two walls, no guard at the entrance, no shadow behind the second barbed-wire enclosure, or on the unloading platform that could be made out between the protective screens and the barbs, and, if soldiers kept guard in the watchtowers, they had managed to remain unseen. Everything was abandoned and closed.

Ilyushenko raised his arms over his head, in a pose of humble and total surrender. Matthias Boyol imitated him.

—Captain Ilyushenko has come to the door, Ilyushenko suddenly bellowed, he asks to be received by the authorities!

In his coat pocket, he had only found one glove. His uncovered hand was suffering from the small pricks of the icy snowflakes. The fingers of the other throbbed painfully due to his extreme nervousness.

Matthias Boyol decided to bellow something in turn.

—The detainee Matthias Boyol accompanies his captain and awaits with him the orders of the camp's management! he cried.

• He or I, doesn't matter. Snow or absence of snow, wholly equivalent. Tunnels of flames, taiga, kolkhoz, or steppe landscape, all the same. Here or elsewhere, a same oneiric texture. Thick or fluid, doesn't matter. Same for immobility and agitation, the near present or the distant present. Same of course for life after death or death lived in dreams, or life full stop and death full stop. A single and identical blaze. Either it devours quickly or doesn't, doesn't matter. Either the flames burn or cause shivers, doesn't matter. In all cases one and the same narrative ember. There are only words to set down to brighten or diminish the landscape. The living or the dead equal actors in a theater. Theater or poorly directed dream, doesn't matter. Theater of survivors or strange agitprop session, doesn't matter. Either I go or come, the spots where I tread or perch don't change. Either the speaker is quiet or declaiming, the audience doesn't exist or is the same. Either it's about evil mysteries or silly charades, nobody will hear but himself or herself. Sometimes he put on a blackened mask to better speak the impossible present. Sometimes he screams fire into the nuclear core to better revive those who are alive, those who are dead, and those who are dreaming. Men or women. Despite holding all the power, he doesn't always come to his end and despairs. Either he despairs or rejoices, doesn't matter. For a moment, only his daughters count, then he goes. Sometimes he groans in an uproar at the depths of the fire to try to revive those who are alive, those who are dead, and those who are dreaming. Then he goes. His daughters are countless, he visits them within and often over the centuries, he forgets their names. Girls or women have a same oneiric consistency that satisfies his body or his masks. Either his body is covered with feathers or scales or human skin, doesn't matter. Either he resembles a demonic wind, a bird, or a frightening muzhik, doesn't matter. Either the flames destroy or build me, doesn't matter.

• The detainee Matthias Boyol waits in front of the door, his hands in the air and a lump in his throat at the idea of imminent death. My daughters go about their business in the Levanidovo, stupidly turning around this fool Kronauer. He'll get what's coming to him. I have the feeling his death will last one thousand seven hundred forty-seven years or even twice that if I'm patient enough. The Levanidovo is ready for snow, like here, but the first flakes are still taking their time. The wind smells of larches covered in frost. This idiot soldier Kronauer doesn't even know that he's already dead and his body has been rotting for weeks in a clump of grasses in the steppe, bloated with radiation and ants. He struts around Radiant Terminus like that moron before him, Aldolay Schulhoff, as if he had been adopted forever by the kolkhozniks. I see it as if everything happened at the same moment, from the top of the pine where I'm perched to better see the things in the world and even see you, you too. To see them or imagine them or imagine you, doesn't matter, and to speak them. A minute hasn't gone by since the train disappeared over the horizon and there are already several corpses.

Pedron Dardaf, Babour Malone, and Douglas Flanagan, several meters from the group of pines, already the object of attention for several vultures circling beneath the clouds, and also eight or nine crows hopping in the grass and shouting noisily next to me, as if they too were waiting for instructions to begin skinning.

Schliffko Armanadji, Tristram Bokanowski, Olfan Nunes, lying in the second car, and on top of them mute, tense, watchful soldiers, trying to make out through the car's planks and through the snow what the two silhouettes stopped in front of the door are doing, the silhouettes of their comrades, of our comrades, our silhouettes or theirs, doesn't matter.

Hadzoböl Münzberg, near the switch, already disappearing beneath the white thicknesses.

All those or all the others, detainees, soldiers, doesn't matter. I know that I can revive them when I have any need to. Either they're alive or dead or something else, doesn't matter. These are empty bodies in my theater. At my request they can come to life if I wish it, or fall silent or crawl for two thousand six hundred and three years and then some, beneath the trees until their crawling bores me.

I caw, and he does as well at the same time, down to the thousandth of a second. He caws among the crows. He joins them for a minute, pecks several times at Pedron Dardaf's head, near the eyes. That one, he'll need later. He'll revive him. No matter whether the birds have or haven't nibbled at what for now serves as his flesh. Then he goes back to his perch, cawing. He prefers to stay high to see almost everything. The camp, the old forest, or the Levanidovo, doesn't matter. And indeed, everything's the same. Everything is in the same place, as in some kind of book, if you want to go to the trouble of thinking about it. That's the ambiguity of ubiquity and achronia.

• Let's take Kronauer, for example. Once again he tried to fix the fire hydrant leak and he was in a bad mood, because the seal continued to drip. When the frost had come, the puddle in the street had iced over more and more often and lost its muddy nature, but its size didn't decrease. As he was now the only one in charge of this malfunction, his clumsiness and lack of plumbing prowess turned into a running joke for the villagers, and, despite being humiliated, he laughed with Solovyei's daughters. He gathered up the tools, wrapped them in a rag, and set them on the doorstep of Barguzin and Myriam Umarik's house; then he crossed the street, went into the prison, and returned to his room.

When he opened the door, he caught Myriam Umarik by surprise as she was shaking and flipping through one of the books that Samiya Schmidt had selected for him in the Pioneers' House library. She was clearly looking through the pages for a letter, a photograph, or some paper with notes.

—What now, Kronauer exclaimed, are you spying on me for the intelligence agencies?

Caught in the act, Myriam Umarik turned with a cajoling smile. She didn't seem embarrassed. She delicately set the book on the table, smoothing out the cover with the back of her hand, as if she and the object had had an intimate conversation that Kronauer had interrupted, and which had nothing to do with espionage.

—Wait, she said, it's true, there was a time when we, Barguzin and I, were thinking about submitting our application. We wanted to leave the Levanidovo. But we ended up staying.

—Your application to join the Organs?

—Yes. To join the Organs and get out of here.

Kronauer nodded. No response came to mind. He himself had worked for the Organs, once. Nobody had known, not even Irina Echenguyen, from whom he'd barely kept any secrets. He'd sworn to his officers that he would never speak of it, even after his death, and he wasn't the sort to fall into the trap of a harmless conversation to betray himself so stupidly, especially not on this topic. The memory of his collaboration with the Organs was buried and unexcavable.

Myriam Umarik went back to the small pile of books and opened a second one, as if she was fundamentally interested in Kronauer's reading more than in the documents he might have slipped inside. It was one of Maria Kwoll's romånces, *The Pokrovsk Beggar*, every bit as radical and anti-male as her other writings, where, of sexuality, or at least sexuality between humans, only obscene ashes persisted.

—You're reading that? Myriam Umarik asked.

—Yes, Kronauer replied. I borrowed it yesterday from the Pioneers' House. Samiya Schmidt recommended it.

—It's not for men. Myriam Umarik simpered.

Kronauer pouted and shrugged.

—It's not for girls either, he grumbled.

They faced each other for several seconds without saying anything. Myriam Umarik saw that Kronauer was in a bad mood and she changed the subject.

—You're to be transferred, she said.

—I know, Kronauer said. A heating problem.

• He obediently transported his things into the new room that Myriam Umarik had shown him. She had bragged about the room's qualities, and then left him alone. The room was closer to the showers and much warmer than the first, but, as it didn't look out onto the main road, it didn't have as much light. The window was double-hung, too, which guaranteed good protection against winter's soon-to-be-icy temperatures, and covered with a grille that wouldn't necessarily have prevented an escape, but certainly would have hampered it. Outside, a half-dozen meters away over a murky, bushy terrain covered with dried plants—cramoisines, ditchcroaks, solfeboutes, gaviants—was a wall. It was the house where Hannko Vogulian lived. There were practically no openings on it, except for a dormer window close to the roof and a service entrance that seemed to be blocked off.

The room was clean, smaller than the previous one, furnished with a desk and a narrow bed, as well as a radiator working too hard given the weather. Everything was painted gray. The metal box spring and the rolled-up, rather thin mattress didn't look comfortable. The sheets, however, were linen and smelled good. My new cell, Kronauer thought as he unfolded them and tucked one of them beneath the quilt. Maybe they used it at some point to interrogate kolkhozniks suspected of deviationism, agronomists who had trouble understanding the orders for proletarian morality, beekeepers tempted by anarchy, cowherds applying the fundamental principles of free union too assiduously, sympathizers of the Organs working suspiciously, those who hadn't worked with them, those who had worked overzealously.

He walked away from the window and, as dusk was coming, he turned on the lamp. He pressed the switch, the bulb clicked, reddened for two or three breaths, and then did its job. For no reason, maybe to compensate for the frustration he'd just felt about his inadequacies as a plumber, he meditated for several minutes on the village's electrical current. During the first liquidation, almost immediately after the catastrophe, the engineers had cobbled together a small alternative power plant in the Soviet, underground, using the fuel rods recovered from the Red Star sovkhoz's vessel. This makeshift contraption had radioactive leaks as well, but, according to Barguzin, it could power the Levanidovo for at least a hundred years, after which it would become uncontrollable and turn the village to ashes, and then sink into the earth. Which left enough time to find some kind of alternative, Barguzin remarked. Find some alternative and grow old. Or something else. Something else like what, Kronauer had asked. Ahh, the engineer had said evasively. You know. Then he turned curmudgeonly and put an end to the conversation.

Just as Kronauer was remembering Barguzin's annoyed look, Myriam Umarik knocked on the door and opened it without waiting for his reply. Under the lamp, she was radiant once again, tanned orange, with her perpetually open smile that was easy, mocking, generous, and her slanting eyes, deep black, her eyebrows drawn out, her movements unctuous.

—I forgot to bring you this, she said.

They both stood by the window and began chatting without paying attention to the day slipping over the walls of Hannko Vogulian's house.

Myriam Umarik had brought a basket with clean clothes, Barguz-in's shirts, underclothes picked up from the Gramma Udgul's reserves. Clearly, she was trying to make him forget that just half an hour earlier she'd been caught rummaging through his room without permission. Actually, the reason for her hunt hadn't been to find evidence of Kronauer's connection to a spy network, but rather to make sure that he hadn't exchanged love letters with one of her sisters. That afternoon, once she reflected on Kronauer's relative indifference to her, she'd suddenly had the heartrending realization that a love affair might have secretly started up between him and Hannko Vogulian or even Samiya Schmidt. She had carefully explored every possible hiding place in Kronauer's room, and it was just bad luck that he had come in right when she was inspecting the books, which she had saved for last.

For a minute, they talked about the Levanidovo's radioactivity. The levels had hit their peak during the core meltdown disaster, and then, contrary to scientific studies, they hadn't gone down. All the inhabitants had died at first, as had the heroic rescue workers and liquidators a little later. The local clinic had turned into a morgue, the sick people admitted there had gone and lain right in the refrigerated lockers, and, when there were sheets, they had covered themselves up completely, including the head, and they began to go quiet. The weakest kolkhozniks didn't last for more than a week. Pretty quickly, by the time they had finished building the warehouse that would serve as a symbolic cover for the well the core had dug, there wasn't a single living being left in the Radiant Terminus kolkhoz.

• —Well, what about you, living your whole life here? Kronauer responds. And the other kolkhoz inhabitants, your sisters, your husband?

—No, we're hardened. It's not the same.

—And me? Logically, I'd be liquefying right now.

—You're hardened, too, Myriam Umarik confirms.

Then she bursts out laughing. Her teeth show between her fleshy lips. A lecherous man might, at that moment, imagine sliding his tongue over that white enamel, that he might pull this shining mouth up to him. If one believes Maria Kwoll, no man can resist the constant impulse toward lechery. According to Maria Kwoll, men's thoughts are entirely dominated by and steeped in what she calls the cock's language. No matter what they say or even believe, whether they are conscious of it or not, men can never even momentarily escape the cock's language.

Kronauer doesn't linger over this sight of the seductive mouth. He looks away.

Ten or twelve seconds go by in silence. They think about radiation, about dead kolkhozniks, about liquidators, about lecherous men. Maybe, yes, they both think at least a little about lecherous men. In any case, the idea, and its attendant images, occurs to Myriam Umarik.

—You know, she says, suddenly very serious. If you hurt any of us in the slightest, if you come up to any of us to kiss or penetrate us, Solovyei will know and he will punish you horribly.

—And your husband? he ends up asking.

—What, my husband? Myriam Umarik asks.

—Barguzin.

—What about Barguzin?

—He doesn't have any say in this, if you're affected?

—Affected by what?

—If I hurt you.

—Are you joking, Kronauer? Myriam Umarik asks.

—No, I'm asking you a question.

—Hurt how? Myriam Umarik squirms.

—Well, for example, if I came up to kiss or penetrate you.

—That's none of Barguzin's business, what you're planning to do to me, Myriam Umarik says. It's only my father's business and mine.

—Remember, I never said that it was my intention to do that to you, Kronauer says defensively. It was just a hypothesis put out there, just for the sake of talking.

But he swallows, his gaze shakes, his eyebrows quiver, and Myriam Umarik notices. She smiles teasingly. She doesn't say anything, but her hips sway unexpectedly, and, indeed, her whole body opens up with that teasing smile.

Outside, crows are cawing. They're perched on the prison roof and they comment on the advancing dusk.

• Or, to take another example, at almost exactly the same time, Ilyushenko in front of the camp's door.

—Captain Ilyushenko asks for the admission of a convoy of deportees he captains! Ilyushenko bellowed once again.

The absence of any response weighed on the silence, on the downy decor, on the barbed and glacial decor. Ilyushenko and Matthias Boyol sank in the snow halfway up their calves. They stamped their boots every so often to keep their feet from freezing. They keep their hands in the air as if they had been ordered to do so.

—We came thousands of kilometers, Matthias Boyol suddenly said quietly, as if to himself, but loudly enough to be heard on the other side of the door. In our heads we had a happy image of our arrival to the camp, our enrollment among the ranks of the camp, our allocation to a warehouse or cleaning team, the recognition of our status as political and social rejects, our inscription in the register of those worth shooting. We wandered in hopes of this moment that would crown our existence. We staked everything on our entrance to this camp, we are at the doors of the camp, at the doors of death, at the doors of hell. We ask to be admitted.

Then he began to scream with an actor's ease:

—The detainee Matthias Boyol is at the doors of the camp, at the doors of death, at the doors of hell! He asks for his admission and that of his comrades!

Then there was an invisible commotion behind the watchtower from which the recent, fatal shot had come. An amplifier had just been plugged in. A crude noncommissioned officer's voice moved through the electrical circuits and burst loudly, like vomit, over the camp's threshold, the door, and the fresh snow in which our captain and Matthias Boyol waited.

—Go back where you came from! . . . We're full! . . . Get out of here before we kill you all! . . .

—The captain Ilyushenko cannot believe that! Ilyushenko immediately bellowed.

As he looked for words to argue, Matthias Boyol broke in. They had agreed to act in this way. Matthias Boyol had been selected among the others for his glibness and Ilyushenko had encouraged him to speak, independently of all hierarchical rank, whenever he saw a pause in the authorities' dialogue.

—The captain Ilyushenko will insist, he yelled with more elegance than Ilyushenko. He proposes the integration of detainees and soldiers in good health, workers resolved to pursue with abnegation behind this fence the construction of an egalitarian and fraternal society!

The loudspeaker let several seconds pass. Matthias Boyol, who assumed that they had heard him, took the opportunity to repeat word for word a paragraph of one of his burlesque glorificacts, or a brief excerpt of one of his tragicomic threnodies.

—Nobody can deny, he declaimed, that the camp is the highest grade of dignity and organization that a society of free men and women can aspire to, or, at least, already sufficiently unfettered from their animal condition to endeavor to construct freedom, moral progress, and history. No matter what we say or assay, nothing will ever equal the camp, no collective architecture of the human species or its like will ever achieve the degree of coherence and perfection and tranquility compared to the prospect that the camp offers to those who live there and die there.

The snow fell. From the other side of the door, the noncommissioned officer crackled through the loudspeaker with the stupefied silence of a drunk man. Matthias Boyol's discourse went several meters before being swiftly absorbed by the continuous cascade of snowflakes.

—That's why, he continued, we ask the camp's authorities to respond favorably to our request.

—We've got enough hobos here! . . . the loudspeaker spat out. Go die somewhere else! . . . This isn't a charity! . . . Last warning before we open fire! . . .

• Once the conversation had reached that point, looking bad but still undecided, an incident ruined everything.

Aldolay Schulhoff, who was more or less part of the convoy, but who—more or less because of this—hadn't been given a rifle, left the fourth car. He had been moping around in the presence of the dead being transported as well as the military bric-a-brac, the reserves of covers, munitions, and winter coats that everyone was saving for later, when they were absolutely needed. He had been put in a corner without any thought given to his movements, or the stench of grease and animal piss that his tattered rags, his flesh, and even his insane thoughts exuded. The soldiers hadn't received any instructions concerning him and they mostly kept busy watching the snowy plain, and behind the uninterrupted fall of gray flakes, the heroic silhouettes of their two comrades negotiating with the camp authorities. They cocked their ears, but couldn't make out anything, and had positioned the ends of their rifles in the cracks in the wood that served as arrow slits. When the situation no longer seemed critical, they withdrew their weapons and set them back on the ground, apparently becoming apathetic once more even though they weren't.

Without any awareness of the tactical requirements of patience and immobility imposed upon the train's occupants, Aldolay Schulhoff decided to jump out of his car. He fell in the snow and immediately got up, then he went along the convoy toward the locomotive. The interim captain, Shamno Driff, saw him go by, but he had bigger fish to fry than to worry about a ragged madman. It was only when he approached the switch that he regretted not having knocked him down when he was still benign, because now he realized that Aldolay

Schulhoff's appearance in the middle of these discussions could compromise them.

Aldolay Schulhoff walked past Hadzoböl Münzberg's corpse and, instead of following the auxiliary track to end up by Matthias Boyol and Ilyushenko, who right then didn't see him coming, he began to meander in the field of snow without any particular direction. He sank considerably in the snow, he walked with difficulty, and his revolting shamanic rags gave him the appearance of an imaginary beast, characterized by a hesitant walk and long dirty scales. For a minute he went on like this in silence, watched in consternation by Shamno Driff, who aimed at him but did not dare shoot—then he began to moan incomprehensible rebukes and the two envoys noticed his presence, turned, saw him thirty meters away, and didn't know what to do.

Aldolay Schulhoff was up to his knees in snow. It wasn't really clear whether he wanted to get rid of the snow keeping him from moving forward, or if he was happy there, immobilized by a white manifestation of nature, and if he was ready or not to add his two cents to the conversation that his appearance had interrupted.

—The tortured Aldolay Schulhoff recognized you! he suddenly screamed. The tortured Aldolay Schulhoff begs for you to put an end to his torture!

There was a silence. The interloper gesticulated, churning up snow around him and throwing it childishly toward the far-off barbed wires that he hadn't been able to reach. The strips that clothed him fluttered for a few seconds, giving the impression that he was massive and took up a great deal of space. When the cloth settled back down he once more became what he had been at first, an exhausted and sickly creature whose destiny was to brush past death for one thousand years or more without ever being able to lie down.

—The captain Ilyushenko informs the camp authorities that the tormented Aldolay Schulhoff does not have the status of either soldier or detainee! Ilyushenko declared, suspecting that the upper hand in negotiations had been lost.

Behind the door, at the top of the watchtowers, the answer was still yet to come. The loudspeaker crackled, then it no longer emitted anything, not even the nerve-wracking static that replaced the lack of words.

—I recognized you! Aldolay Schulhoff yelled again.

• The snow falling in big flakes, in vertical lines, without a breath of wind.

Not silence, but an astounding crustiness that can sometimes be heard, sometimes not, depending on the importance accorded to it.

The light subdued by millions of plumed lines.

Three men at the camp's entrance, immobile after having yelled at the watchtowers, the barbed wire, and the door, and time flows.

Seventeen seconds, maybe eighteen.

The loudspeaker falls silent, as if on the other side, at the source of the noise and electric fury, the noncommissioned officer or his representative on earth or elsewhere is too dazed in the face of Aldolay Schulhoff's audacity to envision an immediate reply. Then contact is reestablished. The amplifier reawakens. The loudspeaker belches and begins to whistle hideously. The sound is so piercing that Ilyushenko lowers his arms and puts the palms of his icy hands over his icy ears. Matthias Boyol does the same.

The whistle increases in intensity. The watchtowers on both sides of the door bend like trees shaken by the wind. The barriers tremble. Everything trembles, except for the snow, which falls calmly, implacably, as if belonging to another level of reality. Far off, from such places as the arrow slits in the train's sides, it is hard to see what is happening. Everybody covers their ears, but cannot see anything special, anything new. The interim captain has the impression that the camp authorities have set off a sort of siren alert and he doesn't know how to interpret this, whether it signifies a happy conclusion to the negotiations or a point-blank refusal.

Nineteen seconds. Twenty.

Two things then happen at the same time.

On the one hand, several rounds of gunfire are loosed from the watchtowers, although none of the shooters can be seen. The two negotiators, Ilyushenko and Matthias Boyol, each take three bullets and stagger, then sink into the snow without a struggle. Ilyushenko falls back, Matthias Boyol falls onto his stomach, headfirst. They are no longer covering their ears. They are no longer moving. As for Aldolay Schulhoff, who only participated in the negotiations in a very secondary and unorthodox way, he puffs up many shreds of tissue that seem to belong to his clothes as much as to his body. The projectiles seem to have given him a surplus of energy and, in the time needed for several breaths, he doesn't fall and turns around slowly, as if hoping, by way of life, to realize the figures of a dreamy dance. He has been shot through and he suffers from his wounds, but he doesn't attain immediate unconsciousness. He screams something in the direction of the camp, but it's in a language that nobody on the train speaks, perhaps Old American or Ölöt, and in any case his voice is softened by anger and blood. He screams loudly enough, his voice carries past the barbed wire and past the tracks, but in his sentence there are more bubbles than consonants.

And on the other hand.

• On the other hand, I am happy to see that someone is busy bringing some strange relief to this banal scene. A little bit of supplementary oneiric panache. Someone or me, doesn't matter. I keep from crowing and I let things happen. The loudspeaker provisionally stops its whistling and a needle can be heard settling onto the wax of a cylinder, the squeaking and crackling before the word can be heard. The scraping before the poem.

Suddenly Aldolay Schulhoff pulls himself together and screams several Russian camp phrases—finally in an intelligible idiom.

—We're in one of your dreams! he bellows. The tortured Aldolay Schulhoff speaks on behalf of everyone! . . . We cannot die! . . . The bullets kill us but we cannot die! . . .

A new salvo silences him.

The loudspeaker now projects words over the snowy plain. Whether ears are cupped or not, the word dominates the landscape. Nobody can remove themselves from it. Even the corpses already covered in a white layer distinctly hear it. In a particular way, they too feel the torment of ubiquity. They find themselves both in front of the camp, in the floating world that follows death, and in one of Solovyei's dreams, and, whether they focus or not on what the loudspeaker broadcasts, they have no way of escaping the acoustic layer that envelops them. Farther off, in the train, the nervous or terrorized men are in the same situation. They don't exactly have the same status as the corpses fallen in front of the door, but slim is the edge separating the ones from the others, and, to put it crassly, they can just be lumped together. The poem, as incomprehensible as it seems to them, imposes itself upon them. It burrows deep into them, and very soon it no longer comes from outside, it no longer passes through their eardrums; on the contrary, it gushes in them and invades their marrow and hidden, secret sub-marrow that has been waiting for this magic moment to reveal itself, that has been waiting for this moment since their birth. Soldiers and detainees wobble, suddenly unsure whether they're exhausted, enchanted, or ill, or already passed away. They examine the field of snow, waiting for the order to shoot and terrified by this voice that comes from outside and arises or rearises deep within them. They clench their icy hands around the silent rifles. Their necks stiffen. Their lips tremble, their eyelids twitch. Despite their hardened faces, they all look as if they're about to cry. Some shiver, out of disgust and despondency more than cold. A voice summons up within them images so dark and fundamentally foreign that they hear nothing sensible and see no image.

The images. They are about to cry. They don't see any of them.

• So, thinking that his henchmen and his daughters were about to escape him, to betray him, and even to bruise him, he immerses himself to the bones in the vibrating heart of the flames and he invents others, other accomplices, other girls, other wives, other flames, and first he counted to twenty-seven, and, when the blackness became total, he walked off, there counting to twenty-seven or maybe twenty-seven thousand seven hundred eighty-three, then, wearing out the legs he still had left, he went from marrow to marrow without sparing any trouble, adding rooms and tunnels here and there, adding crackling to crackling, humid bursts to humid bursts, heavens to the Seven Heavens, then he curled up, on pretext of a sudden fit of fever, and whistled some of his odes, repeating several times "Hadeff, derek! Hadeff, dzwek! Hadeff Kakayin!" and, without waiting for the echoes of his screams, without waiting for the impossible soots and the impossible curtains to send back these echoes, he quickly mated with the spouses and the female creatures that rolled next to him toward the pit, and, as some of them complained and resisted his oneiric ramming, he rejected the prospect of descent and went with great footsteps and great noise toward a dream where the protests of his fleeting partners weren't audible anymore, saying, with great wizardly vigor, "This is a forest, this is a village, this is a work camp abandoned eleven hundred thirteen years ago or so, this is an irradiated land where the last beggars perish, this is a travel bag where I put my head so that eternity still has surprises for me," then he made a wrong turn and ended up between six brick walls with no opening, within an oven that had neither a door nor a chimney and, once inside, he yelled out various calls for his henchmen and, convinced that they would not delay, he made himself a chair with the naphthalene oil that he hardened by licking it, then he sat calmly for a minute. The bricks that imprisoned him were sometimes burning at melting temperatures, sometimes icy, close to the temperatures of deep space, of black space and empty space separating galaxies. Neither living nor dead, his henchmen surrounded him; they swayed like puppets hung from nails and even bumped against one another, shaken by nuclear disintegration and silence; time had stopped. He used it to think again about his daughters and their mothers, about his mistresses, about his spouses and offspring, which he easily confused in his memories and fantasies. Then, after a long stretch of lechery and crime, he came back to himself. The henchmen waited in the shadows, in beggar-worker or beggar-soldier clothes. He ordered them to take their names, to deepen the darkness around him and to dance in accordance to the outlines of stories and sketches that he imagined and told them. And so a blind theater was born of which he was the sole listener. He beat the rhythm for different characters' entrances and exits, and in that way he entertained himself, pushing away his immense pain and the immense worries that came with his fate of living and not dying. The darkness was thick as tar and for a long while he chose to stay there, reducing all flow of time to the drumbeats of his hands against his legs. In solitude he spoke the beginnings and endings of novels, saying with a voice that was sometimes whistling, sometimes gravelly, sometimes velvety, and occasionally interspersed with sniggers, "This is snow, this is death, this is a day and a night, this one is my daughter, this one will be sent into his own hell for two thousand thirty-three years and then some." Then he crowed for a long while in the tar, enumerating the decades by twenty-sevens or hundred-and-twelves and some, then, weariness coming, he went quiet.

• When the incomprehensible deluge of words ended, the interim captain, Shamno Driff, gave the order to open fire on the watchtowers in order to bring down the tension that had built up a notch in the men's souls, then, after a minute of shooting at will, he told them to stop. The fusillade made no sense. The camp didn't return fire and didn't suffer any losses. From a strictly military point of view, there had been no situation and certainly no developments. In the cars, among the gas, smoke, and smell of powder, the fighters began to collect the cartridges without saying anything. The captain went to consult

Noumak Ashariyev. He asked him whether the switch had been moved all the way.

—Did Hadzoböl Münzberg have time to push it or not?

—I don't know, Noumak Ashariyev said. I saw him fall under the sniper's fire. I don't remember anything else.

—You're going to go back into the locomotive and you're going to take us at a snail's pace to the junction, Shamno Driff said. If we veer toward the camp, put on the gas and accelerate. We'll break through the door at full speed. I'd be amazed if it held firm. As we go through, we'll shoot in all directions. Once the barriers have been breached, don't slow down. Go until there are no more rails. Maybe that way we'll get into the heart of the camp. They'll be forced to accept us. So what if they punish us for causing damage on our way in.

—And if we don't turn toward the camp? Noumak Ashariyev countered. What if the switch doesn't do anything and we head down the main tracks?

—Then we'll go on, the captain said with a gesture of helplessness. We'll just go farther, until we find a camp with authorities less stubborn than these ones.

There was a silence.

—What about our dead? someone cut in.

There was a new silence.

—Do you have a suggestion? the captain finally asked.

• The car was plunged into the twilight. Outside, the evening deepened. The smell of hot metal, of grease and powder continued to snake past the men. The sliding door was half open, but the smells of combat hadn't dispersed. It was the end of the afternoon, the gray snow falling and the white snow papering the world to the black wall of larches. As there wasn't a breath of wind, the cold was bearable, and in any case the excitement of war had diminished that chill to one of the many impressions to which they simply attached no importance.

In the neighboring cars, detainees and soldiers argued quietly about cigarettes, about eliminating social parasites, and the best tactics for taking the camp by attack and evading gunshots from the watchtowers. We had set our rifles by our feet and we were awaiting orders.

—And our dead? someone asked. Are we going to leave them down there?

—Do you have a suggestion to propose? the captain asked.

—If we leave, who will take care of them? I asked.

—After a while, the camp authorities will collect them, someone speculated.

—If the train disappears, they won't stay like that in the snow, someone babbled. They'll get back up and they'll follow the rails by foot. They can count on Aldolay Schulhoff. That one knows the place like the back of his hand. They won't get lost. You'll see, we'll end up meeting them again on our way.

—I doubt it, said Noumak Ashariyev.

—It's winter, said a detainee. They won't stay here for long. The wolves will come out of the forest. They'll take care of them here or they'll drag them to the shelter of the trees.

—What do you know about what's going to happen? the captain asked philosophically.

—Eh, someone else said. That doesn't depend on them or us.

—Not at all, someone concluded.

part three

AMOK

– 16 –

• Meanwhile, in the Levanidovo, night had fallen. The main road was empty and, although not a flake was fluttering in the air yet, it smelled of black ice and winter. Myriam Umarik had forecast snowfall for the next day, and Samiya Schmidt, in the library, had drily noted to Kronauer that neither her sister's prophecies nor her swaying hips were needed to verify the meteorological evidence. She had abruptly turned her back to Kronauer when he told her that he would rather borrow an adventure book than a new lesson on the repugnant sexuality of males. "By James Oliver Curwood or Jack London," he suggested while looking at Samiya Schmidt's black braids, and her back shook with indignation at the idea of his trying to escape Maria Kwoll and the wholesome theories of her disciples. Small, serious, with this strict hairstyle, she had never lost her unusual resemblance to a Chinese woman from the cultural revolution. "Stories about trappers in the forest," Kronauer insisted. "We don't have those," Samiya Schmidt finally declared without looking at her index cards. "We don't have them anymore. They were too contaminated with particles, they ended up in the well."

The night was like all the others.

At mealtime, Kronauer left his new room and went to the canteen. He only had to walk thirty meters from the prison.

At the canteen he roasted four spoonfuls of flour diluted in water and butter—still astonished as always that the butter hadn't run out, and noticing that the stock of flour seemed inexhaustible—then he poured himself a bowl of the broth gently simmering on the stove. He was alone. The meals rarely varied but the ingredients never disappeared, which he knew because it was regularly his turn to cook. One day, when he asked one-armed Abazayev for an explanation as to this relative abundance of edible foodstuffs in the Levanidovo since the kolkhoz hadn't been in production for decades, Abazayev had looked behind him to make sure that nobody was listening, and whispered that it was stolen goods. "Stolen from who?" Kronauer asked, whispering as well. "From merchants," Abazayev claimed, "from merchant caravans lost in the old forest." Kronauer retorted that no merchant caravan had crossed the taiga for several centuries, and Abazayev was irritated. He considered Kronauer's incredulity rude, but he was especially afraid of having said far too much, and from then on he was wholly incommunicative on the topic. "Is the president organizing the looting?" Kronauer asked, to keep the conversation going. "Is it Solovyei? Is he acting alone?" But Abazayev didn't say anything else and seemed to be mentally incapacitated. "What about the merchants?" Kronauer kept interrogating in vain. "What becomes of them? What happens to them when they are robbed? Does Solovyei kill them?"

• Kronauer finished his meal, washed the dish, and left. The street was lit, he saw Hannko Vogulian going back into her house like a shadow come from nowhere; then he noticed Morgovian, Barguzin, and Myriam Umarik coming out of the Soviet and talking amiably. They stopped in front of the building to finish what must have been a funny conversation because they all burst out laughing at the same time. Then they started walking again. Behind them, the streetlamps shone for three hundred meters all the way to where the houses were spaced farther apart, and then to the black road leading to the even blacker forest. Aside from the echoes of these joyous voices, the village was silent. Kronauer shivered. The daughter and Solovyei's two sons-in-law were now headed toward the canteen. They had stopped laughing. Kronauer waved to them, far off, and without waiting for them to get nearer he opened the door to the prison and went back to his cell.

He read several pages from *The Pokrovsk Beggar*, and became riveted by the intricate plot, but as soon as Maria Kwoll began to hold forth with acidic eloquence on men and their cock's language, their cock's thoughts and their cock's world, he set the book back on the floor next to the creaking bed, turned out the light, and went to sleep.

• A little after midnight, he awoke with a start. He had been dreaming of Vassilissa Marachvili. She was coming out of a hospital, a building that had been spared by the dog-headed men, while all the rest had been vandalized and burned. She was safe. She was very weak, but she was better. He hugged her with an immense feeling of happiness. They clung to each other at the bus stop that would take them back home. Right before waking up, he realized that he had confused her with Irina Echenguyen.

The room had a slight smell of smoke. He propped himself up on an elbow and sniffed the dark air around him. Maybe it came from the radiator burning dust, he thought. There's no reason why someone in the village would be lighting a wood fire. Nobody does that here.

Now that he had been transferred, his view outside had changed. The road could no longer be seen. In the frame of the double window he couldn't see anything except for the wall of Hannko Vogulian's house. On this dull, poorly lit screen, he projected once more what remained of his dream—mainly the dual face of Vassilissa Marachvili and Irina Echenguyen, but he especially tried to keep in his body the emotion of having found his companion once again after a long ordeal, the silent complicity that united them, this drunken embrace in the street, in front of the hospital's ruins. Images and impressions both faded away quickly, but the affectionate languor remained. He didn't move for one or two minutes, trying not to let this warm languor disperse, but it, too, simply became the trace of a memory, something unattainable and sad, practically drained of flavor.

Then he heard a murmur growing somewhere in or above the village, distant cries. As he got up to go to the window, the main road's loudspeakers came into view, squealing several times with feedback, and suddenly they began to broadcast horrible strident clamors, so unbearable that Kronauer froze, then fell back moaning. He began to pace like a panicked animal back and forth in his room. Clenched over his ears, his hands did nothing against the acoustic aggression. He tried to find a place where the sound might be dampened. At every spot, by the window or far away, the whistling pierced and devastated his eardrums just as powerfully. It came from several places at once, seemingly relayed within his own skull. He went out into the shadowy corridor, got to the toilets, opened the iron door to the communal showers. It was worse. The whistling had invaded the night and managed to amplify in empty space, creating sound boxes within the prison, vibrating tubes, and pipes of all sorts. Kronauer went back into the room and sat on the bed, then, once again, he dashed left and right across the room. Then he got dressed. He thought something serious was happening in the Levanidovo, a fire, a new nuclear alert, an attack from who knew what natural or supernatural enemy, and maybe he had to leave the building right away. The air still smelled of logs blazing, the darkness hummed, the stridency persisted, with variations and increases in rhythm that suggested, behind the earsplitting pain that was being inflicted on the listener, a language: warnings, maybe, or calls.

Suddenly, the whistling stopped. For a minute, there was electrical silence and crackling on the loudspeakers. Then Solovyei's recorded voice enveloped the village, thunderous and emphatic, transformed, deformed by the membranes and the needle's jumps, by the Bakelite's imperfections, by the copper, by the stricken silence of the kolkhoz, by the night.

• At first they didn't recognize his silhouette, because the fire was strong and it was hard to see beyond the flames, and also he was crouching in a brick recess, adopting an extremely animalistic and unearthly pose, a pose that barely corresponded to the original structure of his skeleton and that violated all the rules of vertebral aesthetics and underscored just how loose the ties between his skin and his bones had become, and, when they recognized him, a murmur spread, doubtless because they didn't like to witness miracles, whatever they might be, and also because they felt a deep revulsion to the idea that this one who now publicly resorted to magical trances would be one of their own, dead or alive as they described themselves when allowed to speak, an individual they had heretofore considered rather ordinary and even inferior to them and who they had disregarded indulgently, as they disregarded their kind or their own waste, and who ultimately turned out to be deeply unnatural and deeply strange, and, in this growing murmur, frustration, fear, and disgust could be heard, and he, aware of this wave that would crash against him from outside the oven and from a time and space outside the fire, curled up even more against the wall, and, hardly willing to offer those present the spectacle of his combustion, he bent his head further inward, darkening his mouth and his tongue and focusing on intimate whispers more than thundering admonitions, and, now only speaking to his own increasingly black and indecipherable self, he began to give himself instructions for the trip into the heart of the fire and to give advice for the journey among the embers, and he decided not to listen to anything but his own breaths, and, for a minute, he only puffed and panted the orders intended for his least submissive organs, which often disobeyed him despite the emergency, because he had allowed the anarchist principles, that his mouth had never ceased to proclaim all through his existence to prosper in his own depths, then he contracted again and let cryptic images whistle from his lips, and then the audience, annoyed to only receive foul echoes and smoke from him, began to grumble and disperse, and, as he continued to murmur in a cryptic language, refusing to proclaim harangues that they could have appreciated and even fervently repeated, they intensified his withdrawal and left the place, and that's why nobody witnessed the slow dance that he then performed for several hours and at least several centuries, a magnificent dance in silence in the middle of crackles and red clouds.

• There were three cylinders that night. They were broadcast one after the other, but, when the third one ended, after a brief sizzling transition, the first one started again, and once again Solovyei's inscrutable sentences boomed in the night, at full strength through the internal broadcasting circuit of the village, along the streets, the main road as well as the side streets, once again Solovyei's three opaque poems unfurled over the entire valley, from the edge of the trees to the opposing edge of the forest, from the road leading to the old forest to the warehouse run by the Gramma Udgul; once again they had to hear it in its entirety. Kronauer was now sitting on the ground, on the parquet exuding its smell of pine, dust, and liquid soap, he was leaning against the metallic carcass of his bed and he shook his head, as if hypnotized, as if he was a man or a corpse stripped of all desire to go further in existence.

• And, having walked a hundred and sixty-three steps over the orange path, he walked another thirty-nine thousand two hundred and twenty-four, then once again a hundred and sixty-three, then he went back twenty-two steps and took a break to get his bearings, because everything around him was undulating and howling, and nothing seemed stable beyond the flames, and, drawing back a haze of burning hail pounding on his face and the front of his stomach, he began to call, pronouncing at first inarticulate words, as if to clear his voice, then chanting his daughters' names and chanting his own name, affirming in this way his presence in the middle of the fire and wind, then, as the flames didn't stop and, on the contrary, redoubled, he resumed his heavy walking, from that point without putting any stop to his mouth's murmurs and his tongue's noise and his lungs' ironworks, going straight even when he had to sink into the embers up to his knees, going straight no matter the often terrible temperatures of the obstacles, refusing to cough when his throat stung and refusing to stumble more than once every fourteen steps and refusing to believe in the sizzling of his eyes or even less attaching any significance to it and refusing to waste any breath and refusing to lie down or curl up on the ground when he fell and refusing to construct out of his saliva words of distress or disarray, always going steadfastly in the direction that he knew deep within his heart to be the only one and therefore the best, a direction that was neither night nor day nor twilight, then he went thirty-eight steps without moving his feet or legs, then he went thirteen hundred and seven additional steps awkwardly, leaning forward as if a thunderstorm was bending him low, then he expressed an intent to sing odes, then he loudly declared that he was very comfortable in the fire and so well integrated into the fire's texture that soon he would fly great distances while staying rooted to the same spot, and that soon the paradoxes within his mouth would cancel themselves out, and suddenly, as the space around him shrieked and whirled in yellow plumes, he put on a mask of soot and he enveloped himself completely in soot, and he said to nobody in particular that he was coming, that he would come, but the words sounded more like a threat than a declaration.

• From time to time Kronauer looked out the window. The wall of Hannko Vogulian's house was covered with gleams as if, somewhere in the village, far from the center, far from the Soviet, a farm was burning. What are you doing in this kolkhoz, Kronauer repeated to himself, what's keeping you here, Kronauer? You don't get anything about these people, you don't understand what's happening, if you stay stuck here you'll end up in a bad way, this Solovyei is imprisoning you and enchanting you with his magic whistling, there's only one thing to do, Kronauer, leave with one of the daughters, save one of the daughters and flee with her, and then let the pieces fall where they may! Save Samiya Schmidt or Hannko Vogulian or even Myriam Umarik, one or the other, doesn't matter, take flight, cross the forest with her, hide yourselves, put tens or hundreds of kilometers between Radiant Terminus and yourself, don't look back ever again, run as fast as you can while there's still time!

However, his resolutions didn't result in anything. He stayed prone on the floor, almost like a corpse, shaken every so often by a rumble or shudder, and he kept listening to the three cylinders playing on loop, without ever recognizing anything familiar even as he received the words for the fifth, the seventh, the eleventh time. He kept listening to them, and, like a dying person given advice for which he has no use, he shuddered and grumbled.

• He cleared his throat and, because of the absolute black obscuring their perception of things, the rare spectators who had watched him had the impression that he had performed this throat-clearing by using a poker, like a sword-swallower, and several, who considered this sleight of hand insulting, inappropriate, and hideous, were upset. However, he went down the burning debris and the powder, indifferent to the violence of the lightless flames cruelly licking what remained of his skin, and he heard neither the recriminations that arose behind him nor the sharp words from the observers. He suddenly warned them that the worst was yet to come and he told them that they could, if they wished, turn back and rejoin or at least try to rejoin the outside world. That was untrue. One of his followers, named Kronauer—in reality an idiotic soldier—discovered it almost immediately at his expense. Hardly had he begun to retrace his steps when he felt encumbered by a heavy feebleness; barely had he counted four steps backward when a bitterness surged within him, and his skin crackled all over his body, over his legs as much as over the dream of his hands and face that he had been dreaming since the beginning of the fire. His bones whistled, his cartilage was already just ash and smoke. He was a paltry soldier, a good communist but without any magical value, like those picked up by the shovel load in the camps' mass graves. He would have liked to call his comrades for help, but his voice didn't carry and his thoughts, which he tried to express, didn't succeed in crystallizing in words. Then he sat, somehow, in the embers, sobbing, his lungs wracked with awful sobs, trying again to shed the weight of asphalt darkness covering him. A few meters away, but still permanently separated from him, the others took a break and ignored him. "The worst has spared us thus far," our helmsman, who had let the iron rod fall to his feet, said in a low voice. "But now it's different. Those who turn back will endanger the whole group." His vowels were squeaky, his consonants cracked at the least contact with reality or with fumes. "Those," he continued, "we'll have to kill before they do us harm." At that moment, his discourse fell apart, his words collapsed. However, Kronauer's name was pronounced, and they heard it. But he was already beyond reach, burning alone, and nobody tried to go bring him back from the darkness to slay him before the worst.

• It was a nightmarish night. But not just for Kronauer.

– 17 –

• Around ten in the evening, close to the time when, in the prison, Kronauer set his book on the ground, turned off the light, and got ready to sleep, Samiya Schmidt heard Morgovian getting ready and putting on clothes. That didn't match up to his hours or habits. She was intrigued and decided to go see what was happening.

She had gone to sleep early, in this room where she had lived practically as a recluse for several weeks, as she always did after one of her bouts. The last bout had coincided with her encounter with Kronauer in the forest and his arrival in the Radiant Terminus kolkhoz, and she had barely gone out into the village since, avoided talking to her sisters, the kolkhozniks, and her father, and only met Kronauer at the Pioneers' House library, where she only spoke to him in monosyllables.

The hot, peaceful light of the bedside lamp left most of the room in shadow and lit up the corner of the bed where Samiya Schmidt was snugly settled, occasionally turning the pages of *Baree, Son of Kazan*, the only book by James Oliver Curwood within the cabinets of books in Pioneers' House to escape the liquidators. Kronauer had mentioned this novel about the Great North earlier in the day and she wanted to read it before telling him that she had finally found a forgotten copy in a box of damaged books. She enjoyed delving into it. This generous prose, filled with the breath of nature, was a change from the imprecations of Maria Kwoll, Rosa Wolff, and Tatiana Damianopoulos, who replaced the phrase "make love" with "do sex" or "do rut" and who always, no matter the subject of their story, managed to express uncompromising opinions about bodies, their unacceptable physiological mechanisms, sexual impulses, and the cock's language prowling throughout men's thoughts. It had been years since Samiya Schmidt had read anything other than romances and incantexts inspired by these considerations. *Baree, Son of Kazan*, was a breath of fresh air for her.

Although she was sorry to have to stop reading, she pushed aside the sheets and got up. The mirror sent back an image of her rumpled pajamas and her completely bald head. She reflexively passed her right hand over the smooth skin, trying in vain to find traces of regrowth. Then she set her wig in place, thick and shiny black hair with adolescent braids knotted at the ends with red cloth. She hid her breasts, which she considered too large, under a thick, white unisex shirt, put on khaki pants and a quilted vest she could wear on the street in any temperature, especially chilly autumn nights. Once again she looked like a young, well-read girl sent to be reeducated in the country after inciting anarchy in the cities. She accentuated the resemblance by putting on a military cap with a star-shaped badge.

Then she opened the door of her room.

• Since her marriage to Morgovian, Samiya Schmidt had lived in a house with a large portion reserved exclusively for her. Morgovian feared her as a wife and even more as a daughter of Solovyei. Nothing in the world could have convinced him to cross the invisible threshold beyond which she remained shut away. For him she remained a theoretical spouse, a false spouse for whom he felt neither tenderness nor absence of tenderness, in contrast to Samiya Schmidt's unembarrassed ease in visibly snubbing or disdaining him. She didn't share anything with him and stayed obstinately in her world, daydreaming over feminist rantings or losing herself in ideological or agricultural brochures, or listening intently to the abstract noise of radios that no longer emitted music or discourses, but which sometimes sent mysterious crackling into the ether, at the heart of which she always hoped, like a little girl, to distinctly hear her name. Nobody, really, ever came into her private space, except, to her great regret, Solovyei, who did not respect any boundaries and who, whenever he wanted to and without ever asking her what she thought, broke through all her defenses, crept into her no matter how hard she resisted, and came and went within her like it was his own terrain, observing her internal dreams and possessing her completely, towering over everything, showing no difference between the physical and the mental, taking hold of everything. Then, without warning or discussion, having gotten what he wanted, he left.

• The house smelled of paint heating on the cast-iron radiators; she smelled the dust from before winter, she smelled the liquid soap on the newly scrubbed floors and the heather bath-soap that Morgovian had just used in his shower. Samiya Schmidt went past the bathroom and the bedroom where Morgovian lived in his disastrous conjugal solitude. She peeked in but didn't enter. Pinned on the walls were Model Tractor Driver diplomas and posters recovered from the irradiated farms, advocating foot-and-mouth vaccinations for sheep and enlisting in the Volunteer Red Army. The furniture was rustic but not really spartan. It comprised a chest of drawers where Samiya Schmidt knew Morgovian kept a collection of pornographic images that had been commandeered from a salesman's corpse during an expedition in the forest. Because these expeditions weren't mythical. They gave Kronauer, who hadn't been integrated into Radiant Terminus, the least specific answers they could about them, but those accursed expeditions certainly did happen. They regularly took place, perhaps once or twice a year, in the springtime. The merchants dated back to the Middle Ages with their cargo of supplies, they searched for a shortcut through the metaphysical traps that Solovyei set on their path, and, unfortunately for them, they got lost in the old forest where the president of the kolkhoz and several kolkhozniks armed with grapple hooks, ropes, and axes were waiting. The obscene photographs, thus, which properly speaking weren't part of the spoils, had been entrusted by Solovyei to Morgovian, with the order not to distribute them in the population. They had agreed that they would be used for illustrating a conference on immorality in merchant societies, but the conference didn't happen and the illustrations, which were indeed immoral, and certainly very lewd, ended up locked in a drawer where, lost beneath an innocent pile of bolts, spikes, and threaded rods, they waited for nights of animalistic misery to resurface.

The kitchen and the living room were empty. The hallway lightbulb illuminated the steps that went down to the basement. Morgovian had already left the house. He'd gone out that way and not through the front door.

Long ago, a network of tunnels had been dug to allow people to move through the kolkhoz even when the snow, the wind filled with driving needles, and wintery temperatures prevented anyone from going out into the open. The network followed the path of the hot-water pipes and, in specific parts of the route, the underground passages weren't sinister at all, benefiting from satisfactory light and not having been invaded by vermin or dampness. The work dated back to the beginning of the Second Soviet Union and had been carried out by engineers, firefighters, and soldiers who simply wanted to leave behind a perfectly constructed work that would garner a medal or a reduced sentence, and which would resist time, the eventual atomic wars, and the predictable slackness of future generations.

• Samiya Schmidt went down the stairs and reached the tunnel that led to the Soviet. At most, she had to walk seventy meters underground. She walked them all and ended up at the immense former municipal wash-house, in which, as has already been said, the technicians who survived the first weeks of liquidation had time to dream up an alternative nuclear installation, furnish it with fuel rods taken from the pool bubbling in the Red Star sovkhoz, and put them to use before their skeletons scattered inside and outside their carbonized bodies.

Thus for several decades the former wash-house had been the source of energy feeding the Levanidovo: its water heaters, its boilers, its lights, and its various communal and individual buildings, its robust washing machines, its meat coolers, its electric churners, its flour roasters, its stoves, its radio antennas that had been mute in the absence of transmitters, and its chattering loudspeakers.

It was also a vast confusion of unruly pipes, copper, lead, firebricks, and electrical panels. At first glance, someone would think that they had infiltrated a dump for industrial materials or the basement of a factory post-cataclysm. But soon enough they had to acknowledge that the elements, despite their incongruity, were interconnected and followed an overarching plan, which lent an overall unity to at least some portions of this whole. They could imagine that they were in an art gallery, unintentional visitors to a retrospective of particularly aggressive or complex sculptures aligned with destructionist art or other avant-garde aberrations. The depths, their chaos, and the stacks multiplied, but in reality no artist had popped up here intending to construct something beautiful or conceptually torturous. This metal mess was due to extreme emergency, the carnage among the engineers, and also the hallucinations of workers unceasingly deluged by neutrons. The technicians succeeded without any time to evacuate their colleagues' corpses or to organize and streamline their assemblages. Some, despite their death, continued to carry out their duties around the vessels, the pumps, and the turbines, no longer complaining about terrible burns, but disrupting the efforts of the living. The construction continued without a preliminary plan, by improvisation and groaning, and, while several intrepid liquidators piled up in a corner the fuel rods they had carried on their backs and manipulated with their bare hands, the valorous handymen tried to remember why the preceding team of workers had laid pipes and cables there, welded a cast-iron plate here, built a room without any opening there. Their questions went unanswered. While fighting against fear, horrible headaches, the liquefaction of their livers, and a rapid loss of sight and sense of balance, they put together new bypasses, new junctions. Which is why many essential components had been doubled, multiplied, or oddly hung in places that made them superfluous, even monstrous.

When Barguzin was assigned to the construction, the auxiliary station had started to function and promised to do so for several more centuries, even with its leaks and serious security breaches. In the presence of this chaos of cables, tubes, and compressors, he had given up on establishing any semblance of order. He had simply undone those circuits that could only cause damage, and, with the help of several deceased who were still somewhat able-bodied, he tried to seal the central compartment of the reactor. Morgovian, Abazayev, and the daughters of the kolkhoz president all helped out; nobody balked despite the danger and the scope of the task, but, for lack of specific information about what happened in the boiler, construction couldn't be completed, and, all around, it stayed that way. Solovyei regularly went into the boiler, but he claimed to go in for personal and not technical reasons, and he'd come back out without a word, sizzling and blackened, weighed down with radiation and opaque poems. When Solovyei's routine had ended up taking hold of Radiant Terminus, the kolkhozniks put an end to their visits to the former wash-house, and the only two who still went were Barguzin, who dealt with the maintenance, and Solovyei, who engaged in his thaumaturgic activities.

• The kolkhoz president liked this place enough to develop most of his sorceries there, as well as stay there for short periods of drowsiness that, for him, replaced sleep. He left the Soviet's upper floors, he stepped over the pipes and the pumps that murmured on the warm ground, and he snuck into the compartment that held the reactor core. He had set down a mattress in one corner. He brushed the excess plumes running along the wall with an iron rod or his own hands, or he chased them down by huffing and puffing. Then he lay down in the middle of the regular, soothing rumbling. The mattress was fireproof, but had to be replaced often because despite being treated against fire it eventually turned hard and stank of bister and cadmium. When Solovyei wasn't able to relax and had nothing special to do, he leaned against the cement and hummed in tune with the quivering he felt on his spine from the vessel and fuel rods' excitement. It was one of his favorite dens in the Levanidovo, and, even when he was going to a great deal of trouble and working hard, whether in the forest, in the steppes, or within the souls of those he possessed or haunted, he used his powers of ubiquity to stay there again and again. Often it was from there that he launched himself into parallel universes, into strange flames, into empty spaces and dreams where he was sometimes a horribly resentful and invincible shaman, sometimes a magnificent lover, sometimes a traveler to dark worlds, sometimes a necromancer specializing in punishment and camps, sometimes an unforgettable, cryptic poet whose words were nonpareil, forbidden to the dead, to the living, and to the dogs.

• That night Morgovian had put on a peasant's funeral or wedding clothes, and, with his city shoes and his jacket with too-long sleeves, he was simultaneously ridiculous, sweet, and humble. He went around an electronic monitoring block where no light had been turned on, stepped over a large water pipe, and went toward what he knew was both the entrance to the reactor and the threshold of one of Solovyei's sacred domains.

The man in the shadows fidgeted.

—I told you to wait until I called you, he said.

—I wanted to at least see her, Morgovian said humbly. Just a quick peek.

—Today won't be when you marry her, Solovyei said. She's only regressed since she came. I haven't been able to fix her.

—But is it on its way? Morgovian asked stupidly.

—Oh, on its way, Solovyei ground his teeth. I haven't been able to fix her, that's where we are.

—So it's not going well, then? Morgovian sighed.

—That's right, Solovyei confirmed.

Morgovian said something under his breath. He tugged at the bottom of his jacket.

—Well? Solovyei asked.

—Maybe I could see her? Morgovian stammered.

—That's not a good idea, said the kolkhoz president. She hasn't progressed in the right way.

At that moment, Samiya Schmidt came in.

—What are you talking about? she asked.

• For Solovyei, the Vassilissa Marachvili operation wasn't terribly tricky and simply had to happen in several stages. The first stage was transporting Vassilissa Marachvili to the Levanidovo and placing her discreetly in the Soviet's basement, close to the emergency reactor. As Solovyei and Morgovian had come back from their expedition to the Red Star sovkhoz at three in the morning, this first phase had been a resounding success. Nobody had seen the young woman's nocturnal arrival. The second stage consisted of leaning magically over Vassilissa Marachvili, with the sole goal of bringing her back to existence in the form of a creature neither alive nor dead. The third, after Vassilissa Marachvili's awakening, had to lead to her union with Morgovian, to shepherding the new couple toward their honeymoon on one of the abandoned village farms, and to the immediate divorce proceedings between Morgovian and Samiya Schmidt. In that way, which he considered relatively gentle and implacable, Solovyei intended to liberate his daughter from a failed marriage and make her independent once again, and more available to him. He hadn't foreseen Samiya Schmidt's sudden entrance right in the middle of the second phase, at a moment when his attempts to reanimate Vassilissa Marachvili weren't producing the desired result.

• For several seconds, the only noise came from the surroundings. Occasional murmurs in the confused mass of cables. Bubbles of oil bursting in the oil chambers. Flames crackling along the walls, along the mains and pipes with illogical branches. Machines constantly humming. Fuel rods regularly sizzling as they tried to get several degrees hotter. Burning vapors and water whispering as they flowed inside the channels and pumps. Several drops falling and echoing in several puddles in the shadow or in full light. The radioactivity at its peak puffing almost silently.

Solovyei stood in the darkness of his nook, at the entrance to the reactor, with the corpse of Vassilissa Marachvili at his feet. The young girl was lying on the somewhat tarry mattress and, dressed in disgusting rags, she waited in vain for the results of the treatment that had been recommended for her. She wasn't in a worse state than at the time when the kolkhoz president had begun to expose her to radiation and his magical tricks. But all the same, at first glance, her state was catastrophic. The penumbra was occasionally interspersed with layers of dwarf flames. They slowly grew over Vassilissa Marachvili and then disappeared.

In his absurd outfit as a kolkhoznik dressed in his best, Morgovian knew he had been caught red-handed. He shivered despondently without looking up at Samiya Schmidt. He focused on the ground and his already-dissipating soapy smell. The room smelled of plutonium, bubbling water, overheated metal, but around the tractor driver were the noticeable and acrid smells of total dismay and fear.

Samiya Schmidt began to metamorphose in a fury. She drew herself together, her muscles taut, her eyes wide open. A stupefied red guard facing two enemies of the people. A small creature of the cultural revolution, confronted by the dark doings of the people's enemies, contemplating incredulously the victim of their crime, contemplating this disgrace she did not completely understand, but which she knew they could not deny in its disgusting horror. Very small, already very angry, and on the brink of crisis.

Suddenly out of control.

Suddenly truly out of control.

• The president of the kolkhoz raised his arms and then let them fall back along his flanks as if to say that the situation was difficult, but at the same time there was nothing to do but accept it. He rummaged through his thoughts for an immediate truth or lie. His beard was electrified and, as his hair was as well, his head was encircled by bristles and black tendrils that looked like they wanted to fly in all directions, a face haloed in dark rays. His golden eyes sparkled over the mattress that a new wave of plumes had just lit up, as well as its unfortunate occupant.

—Who is that? What is she doing here? Samiya Schmidt yelled, pointing at Vassilissa Marachvili's body covered with caramelized rags, at the face that death had rendered indifferent to everything, in contrast to the sooty ends of her shoulders, of the flesh that seemed twisted by the effects of sorcery and radiation.

Although he usually held back, most reluctant to speak in front of Solovyei, whom he sensed was contemptuous, Morgovian, who had just had a terrible idea, decided to answer right back.

—We're trying to fix her, he said.

—But why? Samiya Schmidt exclaimed.

She moved forward. She shoved Morgovian and stood a meter away from Solovyei.

—What are you doing with this girl? she asked.

Once again, Solovyei raised his arms and let them drop again heavily.

—She was Kronauer's wife, he sighed. Vassilissa Marachvili. She's gone into a dark tunnel. She's neither dead nor alive. We can still bring her out of the darkness, but it's still difficult.

Samiya Schmidt was deformed by a spasm. She felt rising within herself the first swell of an impending bout, and she knew that delirium and agitation would soon swallow her up. She began to hear her skin physically changing and scales screeching as they breached her surface.

She hit her hand against one of the compressors. The noise echoed far more than if it had just been a slap. Already her skin had hardened.

She hit a pipe angled toward Solovyei, then she turned toward Morgovian and violently pushed him backward.

—You want to hurt this girl, she screamed.

—Of course not, Solovyei tried to explain.

He went toward her, arms outstretched and hands open to grab her by the shoulder. He wanted to keep her from attacking the building.

—You're just monsters, she yelled, banging the pipe again. You want to do rut with her!

• The night is long. Very turbulent, very strange, and very long. In several minutes, Samiya Schmidt takes on her furious form. Then she escapes all standards. Neither Solovyei with his very considerable powers nor, obviously, Morgovian is able to calm her down.

She is covered in very hard scales.

She lands terrible blows.

She moves at an incredible speed.

She transforms her scream into energy.

She no longer has blood, or rather she no longer has either blood or the absence of blood.

She is neither dead nor alive, nor in dreams nor in reality, nor in space nor in the absence of space. She makes theater.

She allies with the fuel.

She starts fires of cold flames.

She allies with the void, with the controlled fuel, with the suspect fuel, with the demented and uncontrollable fuel.

She comes and goes at full speed between the two cores, between the well the Gramma Udgul watches and the emergency reactor cobbled together beneath the Soviet.

She pronounces curses, prayers to forces, to the forces she knows, to the forces she has heard of, and to the forces that don't exist.

She runs in the darkness faster than a bullet. She runs in the night forest. She goes beneath the larches to the old forest and then she comes back. Several times she goes around the Levanidovo, running along the border of black trees.

She comes back to the nuclear crackles, she draws circles around the nuclear cores until the oil in the pumps catches fire, she traces circles until the icy flames thunder and twirl around the fuel rods.

She enumerates the crimes of her father and she orders the supernatural forces to bring her father back to the region of the camps, to force him to stay within a nest of barbed wires, in a harsh regime's confines.

She doesn't meet anyone, or rather she refuses to look at those in her way, whether they do or don't belong to the horde of the living, to the cohort of dogs, or to the infinite herd of the dead.

She covers herself in hard and rustling scales.

She covers herself in black droplets.

She covers herself in sparks.

Her hair briefly grows back and grows down to her ankles, then once again her scalp is bald.

She makes wind, she makes theater, she makes black sky, she makes four black heavens.

She calls the forces when she is against the forest, she calls the forces when she sees around her the earth of the tunnels, she calls the forces once she is close to the fuel rods.

She goes to the beginning of time and she blows with a yell, then she reaches the end of time and she blows.

She appeals to the former leaders of the world revolution, she appeals to the great figures, the anonymous masses, the disappeared peoples.

In reciting compact lists, reduced to a short piercing babble, she appeals to the heroes of the First and the Second Soviet Union, those she knows and those she just invented, the major and minor scholars, the inflexible proletarians, the engineers, the veterinarians, the archivists who have already left their contribution to the spinning worlds, the sacrificial liquidators who gave their lives to the molten-down nuclear sites, the heroic detainees and soldiers, the heroic musicians, the cosmonauts.

When she comes back to the boiler room, facing Solovyei, she knocks him over and pummels him, she asks him why he isn't dead, and, when he defends himself, she slaps him with her hands harder than iron and she asks him to stop going into her like an object without thoughts, and she pummels him furiously.

She also asks him to stop going into her sisters like lands of inert flesh, without thoughts or sensitivity to heat and cold.

She makes the cold flames and warm flames burst from Solovyei's body when she touches him.

She beats him, she asks him to stop his worthless immortality and to no longer inflict such worthless immortality on those surrounding him.

In order to humiliate her father she prevents him from replying to the hailstorm of blows she lands.

She crosses the Levanidovo in every direction, she goes through walls unharmed, like neutrinos passing through the earth without destroying the earth or themselves.

She forces Solovyei to run behind her to keep her from setting fire to the village and to put out the blazes she lights, she hears him panting behind her and sometimes she makes a sudden volte-face to bang into him, knock him over, and curse him.

She covers herself in a soot that neither fades away nor crackles, and suddenly she is radiantly beautiful, then again she looks like a free-running and dark creature.

She goes from the Soviet boiler room to the Gramma Udgul's workshop, she slips down the well to the core's heart in the shadowy depths, she goes back up after having touched the heart, she runs again at high speed to the center of the village, she goes past her house, past her room, she doesn't look at herself in the mirror, she goes down the stairs, she comes back to the boiler room, she hits the pipes, the pumps, the doors illogically distributed throughout the jumble of burning pipes, she goes to Solovyei's nest and, when he's in her way, she pummels him.

She goes and flies under the ground as well as above it and sometimes she speeds so quickly she is neither here nor there.

She never touches Vassilissa Marachvili's remains.

She never contemplates or examines Vassilissa Marachvili's body.

She crosses the curtains of flames shuddering on the wall of the reactor, she moves over Vassilissa Marachvili's cadaver, but she doesn't contemplate her or examine her in passing.

She doesn't consider any of the Gramma Udgul's complaints as she exhorts her to calm down and accept her fate, accept the mutations that have seized hold of her, but guarantee her endless existence within the Levanidovo, which encourage her again and again to accept the deathless life granted by her father, to accept her father's monstrosities, to accept her father as he is.

She covers herself with specks of cutting ice.

She covers herself with night.

She makes blinding night, she makes immobile tempests, she makes theater, she makes breaths, she makes sky, she makes twelve black heavens.

She summons exceptional tribunals to judge Solovyei.

She covers herself in a dull plumage.

She covers herself in a black, urticant down.

She makes ink black, she makes theater, she makes blizzard, she makes tar-black, she makes the thousandth stinking category.

When Solovyei transmits through the loudspeakers his dreadful digressionary poems in order to cover the clamors coming out of his daughter's mouth, she traces spirals around the loudspeakers while reciting extracts from epic literature that she knows by heart, or fundamental accusations against her father.

She assembles a popular tribunal, she forms a jury of incorruptible Chekists, Red Army soldiers, Second Soviet Union avengers, exemplary zeks, model detainees.

She accuses her father of the manipulation and sorcery of deceased humans and being proud of it.

She accuses him of vileness and incestuous relations with imaginary daughters, with real, dead, or imaginary spouses, she accuses him of debauchery committed against willing victims, of fornicating with the Gramma Udgul, she also accuses him of having done rut with his own daughters, with a list of girls whose names she says one by one, all without any end to her coming and going down the village's streets and tunnels, with the girls whose names she says at random into the darkness, with unknown women whose names she invents, with girls like Solayane Mercurin, Imiriya Good, Nadiyane Beck, Keti Birobidjan, Maria Djibil, Maria Dongfang, Lulli Grünewald, Barbara Rock, with kolkhozniks lost to memory, with poetesses whose names and faces and poems weren't left to posterity, with the female communist prisoners locked up with him in camps, with counterrevolutionary women and representatives of the first, the second, and the third stinking category, and, to end the list, she accuses him once more of having had ignominious relations with his own daughters.

She accuses him of genetic crimes.

She crosses the Levanidovo while spreading insane rumors and painful childhood memories.

She claims that she isn't even born to an unknown mother, she says that she wasn't born, she covers herself in a tarry mist.

She covers herself in shining dust, she covers herself in shimmering points.

She covers herself in animal-hide straps, she covers herself in frost, she keeps crossing the roads and the tunnels of the Levanidovo with such a speed that nobody witnesses her passage.

She makes poison, she makes hurricane, she makes theater.

Suddenly she is vertiginously radiant, suddenly she sparkles, and almost immediately she is a handful of magical flesh that runs and runs in the countryside and slams into tree trunks, walls of farms where all the animals are dead, Morgovian when he stupidly appears in her path.

She tears Morgovian, she tears his old peasant-husband's clothes, she slashes Morgovian, she destroys his backward body, kept deceptively alive by Solovyei's powers, she takes those spells out of his body, she tries to kill Morgovian when he comes between her and the soviet reactor, every time she tries to kill him.

She bangs the pipes until the metal sings.

She covers herself in the fur of a white she-wolf, and at that moment once again she looks like a lost young girl from the cultural revolution, fragile in her unisex military uniform, her only vanity a red ribbon at the end of her braids and a red badge on her shapeless green cap, and then she resumes her frantic race through the night's flames.

She hits the fuel rods, she wields them, she shakes the vessel water, she can't keep going out of despair, she hurls herself against the silent walls, and on them she leaves traces of soot and despair, she beats the vessel water, she bounces back and forth from channel to conduit, she bounces with fleshy noises against the walls, with clanking noises, with avalanching noises.

She makes revenge, she makes depth, she makes darkness, she makes theater.

She reads a long-winded accusation, she accuses Solovyei of counterrevolutionary immortality, she reproaches him for his habit of illegally penetrating the dreams of his daughters and penetrating his daughters in order to transmit an excess of immortality that they don't care about.

She beats her father, she hits his memory, she dirties his memory as he dirtied the memory of all those he penetrated in order to keep them in a false state, between life and death, she accuses her father of orchestrating the Levanidovo like a revolting dream, of orchestrating the forest, of orchestrating the steppes, and of the concentrational hereafter of the camps, she accuses him for imprisoning within himself all the living and the dead of the Levanidovo and his hereafter.

In front of the popular tribunal, she denounces Solovyei's suspected ubiquity, his affiliations with several stinking categories at the same time, his poor management of the Radiant Terminus kolkhoz, his criminal ways of sourcing provisions, she accuses him of assassinating merchants in the forest, she accuses him of pillaging the caravans, she denounces Solovyei's terrifying stature, his appearance of a triumphant kulak, his magic axes, his lust.

She makes theater, she makes opera, she makes cantopera.

She causes serious damage in the places she passes through and over the bodies she pummels.

Compacting the flood of words as much as possible, she recites in their entirety the Marxist-Leninist brochures talking about the world revolution, the end of history and the joys awaiting the generations to come, the user's guides for fuel cells, hygiene manuals for kolkhozniks, the post-exotic romånces of her childhood, the feminist manifestos for women neither living nor dead, the treatises on practical oncology, the booklets for pig breeders, yak farmers, beekeepers, teachers put in extreme pedagogical conditions, adventure novels set in the Great North.

She hangs from the pipes in which pressurized vapor hisses, she breaks doors, she throws planks behind her, wood shavings, she throws iron plates over her shoulder, locks still surrounded within the meat of doors, she speeds through the night and through walls, vessels, boiling circuits, then she comes back toward Morgovian and she beats him, she heads toward Solovyei once again and she pummels him.

She feeds her impotent rage only images and speed.

She covers herself in strips of flesh, metallic excrescences, organic vapors, and a second later she's already dressed anew in armor of unbelievably hard and rustling scales.

She keeps racing back and forth across the Levanidovo, along its surface and underground.

She makes lightning, she makes bolts, she runs, she imagines that she is dressed entirely in fire and blood.

Then suddenly nobody knows where she is.

She makes silence.

She makes theater in the sudden silence.
She makes absence.
She has disappeared and she is silent.

– 18 –

• At almost the same moment, give or take a few hours, the night declined, declined and transformed into an ugly day. It began to snow over the Levanidovo from the first glimmers of dawn. For Kronauer, the morning followed a night of fiery reflections, hypnotic whistling, curses broadcast over the loudspeaker, fiery sparks within his brain tissue, blackouts, sideration, catatonia. He was lying on the floor of his new room and had the greatest difficulty believing that he had come out of his nightmare. Passively he saw through the double window the drab wall of Hannko Vogulian's house, and, above, a piece of sky transformed into a flat gray anthill. From this discouraging backdrop fell and flew snowflakes that seemed gray as well; dirty and gray. No noise came from outside. After having broadcast Solovyei's verbal diarrhea in a loop, the loudspeakers hadn't made the slightest peep. Quietness was now, in the entire village, absolute. Nobody walked in the main street. The prison was silent. Kronauer felt dazed, as cottony as the snow. Solovyei's discourse continued to turn within him. His spirit was streaked with thick mud and nausea and, from the night's events, he remembered more than anything his own contortions, his despair when, after a minute's respite, the loudspeakers began once more to broadcast shrill signals within his skull, sentences that mutilated reality and poisoned it. He spent hours close to the window, and when he couldn't bear Solovyei's whistling and poetic chasms any longer, he tried to take refuge in the bed, but he doubled over beside it without ever managing to reach it, without being able to plug his ears or hide under the quilt, and then he lost all sensation of time and even space.

He shifted position and then there was Myriam Umarik lying next to him and watching him. She watched him with an attention that could have been as predatory as it was affectionate. Up close, Kronauer could distinguish in her sensual black eyes small shining specks of silver and gold. She was lying on the floor at such a close distance that he suddenly felt her breath: hot, slightly charged, perhaps with hints of roasted flour that he had cooked the previous evening in the communal kitchen. And first he thought that he was dreaming, that he was attempting to heal from the night by consoling himself with an erotic dream. But this wasn't the case. Everything was real. Reality distressed him for a second, then his distress turned to terror. How long has she been here? he wondered. What does she want? What did we do together tonight? . . . Kronauer, you animal with the cock's language, I hope at least you didn't hurt her, otherwise you're done! . . . Kronauer, I hope you didn't kiss or penetrate her! . . . If you've done rut, you'll never escape Solovyei ever again! . . . He'll put you through a thousand years of hell! . . . Your count is good, a thousand years or three thousand, at some point it doesn't matter anymore! . . .

He remembered absolutely nothing that might have happened with this woman. As an animal with the cock's language as well as the cock's thoughts, but not just that, as an animal pure and simple, he realized that Myriam Umarik's proximity had an effect. Between his legs his unfortunate cock swelled and moved and be began to intensely desire this body almost curled up against his, but at the same time he had the impression that he hadn't satisfied this desire either at dawn or before. There was no odor of copulation in the room and besides, he and Myriam Umarik were dressed in a way that didn't indicate recent sexual disarray.

As he hesitated over what he would ask her, she spoke first.

—Don't move, Kronauer, she said. Don't say anything.

This double prohibition only bothered him even more. Of Solovyei's three daughters, Myriam Umarik was the only one who had ever seemed interested in men and who had hardly cared about Maria Kwoll's theories on the ignominy of men—the only of the three he considered capable of slipping into his bed one day without asking him first, at the risk of accusing him of taking advantage or even simply raping. She constantly played the seductress, but she was also the one he'd most distrusted from the very beginning, keeping up a chilly exterior he hoped was discouraging. He had always had the impression that she wanted to lure him into a trap and that, behind her appearance as a vamp, sometimes a heavily exaggerated one, was a vicious desire to see Solovyei cut in and put down his foot. He had even wondered if she wasn't plotting with her father, devising at his expense a cruel snare that they had secretly planned down to the last detail, for the pleasure of watching his downfall and his punishment, at the beginning of his thousand-year-long punishment, to break up the boredom of everyday village life, to honor a five-year repression quota for Radiant Terminus, or simply and stupidly because his presence as a defeated soldier had immediately displeased the kolkhoz's director.

—Nobody has to know I'm here, she finished. Things happened last night. Nobody has to know I hid at your place.

—What things? Kronauer asked worriedly.

—Don't talk, Myriam Umarik said. Play dead.

• In a few hushed sentences, Myriam Umarik clarified the results of the previous night. Samiya Schmidt had experienced a bout, the strongest one to ever hit her. She had run thousands of kilometers at full speed all over the Levanidovo. She had destroyed several buildings and started fires here and there throughout the kolkhoz, in the Soviet's basements, at the edge of the forest. She had opened the well in the Gramma Udgul's warehouse, she had leaned over the pit and she had yelled such insanities and extraordinarily violent accusations against Solovyei that, two thousand meters farther down, the nuclear core had come out of its lethargy, become outraged, and vomited lava. The Gramma Udgul had to go and hunch in turn over the edge and talk to the core to calm it down. Samiya Schmidt had shoved her aside, shut the cover of the well, and, once she was back in the municipal boiler room, she had attacked Morgovian and reduced him to a nauseating pulp that was hard to contemplate without gagging. She had attacked Solovyei and she had jammed an iron pipe into his right eye, which came out of his left ear. She had lost control, and now she had disappeared.

—I have trouble believing all that, Kronauer remarked.

—It's because you're new to the kolkhoz, Myriam Umarik whispered. It looks like a normal place, but it's not.

—I never thought it was a normal place, Kronauer replied.

• Myriam Umarik told Kronauer to be quiet again. She who usually exuded a sort of carnal radiance, she who smiled so easily, who wheedled and cajoled, was now reserved, frightened, and contagious. Her prone position next to Kronauer implied no lascivious abandon whatsoever, no amorous complicity, or any expectation of a caress. All that could be read into it was embarrassment, distress, and anxiety increasing by the second. Her face was frozen in a sharp grimace, her eyes darted. Her forehead was higher than usual, and Kronauer suddenly realized that her beautiful hair was a wig, and that, in the night's confusion, it had slipped back. Her scalp was as smooth as an eggshell. He immediately felt repulsed, as if she had suddenly transformed into a hag, and right then he caught himself. What's happened to you, Kronauer, you're reacting like a livestock salesman who's just found a hidden defect in the cow he's inspecting, did you want to buy her? . . . You thought you could have her but she'd fooled you? . . . This woman isn't something to be bought at a fair, what makes you think you can pass judgment on her, on her body, as if you were one of the male-chauvinist shits Maria Kwoll described? . . .

But he had been deceived, and, a bit rudely, he disobeyed her instructions to be silent.

—Why did you come into my room? he asked. What are you doing here?

Myriam Umarik looked at him, lost, and suddenly she curled up against him and rubbed against him, and then, immediately, perhaps realizing his feelings for her or their feelings for each other, having realized in either case that he had a tremendous erection, she pulled back and pushed him away, as if the initiative had been his and had shocked her. They hadn't kissed.

—Don't think in the cock's language, she shot back.

Kronauer shrugged. He would have had trouble arguing that, after this furtive embrace, he wasn't thinking in the cock's language. He was wary of Myriam Umarik and of the desire he felt for her, he dreaded becoming a pawn in her father's diabolic machinations, and, more broadly, Maria Kwoll or not, feminism or not, he had been schooled to scorn sensuality. But there was no denying that he had started to think in the cock's language.

—I'm not made of stone, he said.

Myriam Umarik's stomach seemed to rise with a wavelet, then stayed calm.

—Of course not. She suddenly smiled, which she hadn't done until then. You're hard as iron.

Her smile was an open one, not even flirtatious. Friendly, in a certain way. Then this moment of gentleness disappeared. Myriam Umarik's mouth became serious again.

Kronauer got up on his buttocks, leaned against the box spring, and turned toward the window.

Behind the windows, the snow was flying. The sky couldn't be seen.

• They stayed like that for a minute, him absorbed in contemplating snow, her oddly lying right by him, unmoving and mute. In a photograph, they could have been the perfect illustration of a quarrel between lovers.

—You have to help us, she finally said.

—Who's us?

—Barguzin and me. You have to help us. We've had enough of living in the Levanidovo. We want to flee. This isn't a life, or a death. We want to say good-bye to all that.

—Ah, Kronauer said.

—We want to start over, Myriam Umarik said.

—But why are you rubbing against me? Kronauer asked, without looking at her, still starting out the window. Aren't you ashamed for Barguzin?

—Yes, I'm ashamed. But I don't know what to do to convince you.

—Convince me to do what?

—To help us.

Kronauer got up and went to the window. The snow blurred everything; even in good weather the panorama was an empty dead-end, immediately limited by the wall of Hannko Vogulian's house. A dark surface, two steps, a black door that evidently had never been opened. There was no view and he would have had to look down to see the entrance on the main road. The snow stuck to the ground. It was already almost half a dozen centimeters thick. No prints of any kind marred the perfection of this mantle. For a second, Kronauer was sorry not to see the trace Hannko Vogulian would have left between the two buildings if she had headed toward the prison at night. He preferred the always slightly hostile sobriety of the older sister to Myriam Umarik's seemingly insincere exuberance. Hannko Vogulian, Hannko Vogulian, he thought furtively in the cock's language. He would have been more comfortable finding himself lying next to her rather than the voluptuous Myriam Umarik. He would have been more certain of understanding what she wanted.

—I don't understand what you want, he said.

He kept his back turned to his visitor.

She got up. He heard her sit on the bed, then readjust her hair on her bald skull, smooth out her skirt.

—Don't talk so loudly, she whispered. He doesn't need to know I'm here and he doesn't need to hear us.

—Who are you talking about? Barguzin?

—Of course not, Kronauer, are you stupid, or what? I'm talking about Solovyei.

—You just told me that Samiya Schmidt stabbed his eye and ear with a pipe. When you get your brain run through by a piece of iron, you're not usually busy listening in on other people's conversations. He may already be dead.

—Don't talk so loud, Myriam Umarik begged.

She really did seem afraid. He went up to her and talked more quietly.

—He's had his brain wrecked, he said. He won't recover.

Now they were sitting on the edge of the bed, side by side. He could sense her shuddering anguish. He wanted to put his arms around her shoulders and wait for her head to rest on his cheek, but he held back. He couldn't be brotherly with this girl. Desire had overtaken him, all the cock's associations and thoughts of rutting. The image of consolatory gestures was overlaid with wanton images and sensations of skin, of flesh, of pawing, of masculine gropes, of possibly shared breaths, of tumbles on the bed, and urgent penetrations. The physical nostalgia of coupling, handed down over two hundred million animal years. He suppressed all this as best as he could, this surge of salacious filth. But, in his consciousness and beyond it, the filth overflowed.

—He'll recover just fine, she mumbled. It's not the first time something like this has happened. He always recovers. He hasn't been dead or alive since he was born. The radiation doesn't do anything to him. Iron through his skull won't do anything either.

—Still, his head skewered by a pipe, Kronauer objected in a low voice.

—It's just theatrics, Myriam Umarik said. It's just a dream. His head skewered or not, doesn't matter. We're all neither dead nor living in Radiant Terminus. We're all bits of Solovyei's dreams. We're all ends and pieces of dreams or poems in his head. What we do to him doesn't matter to him. What Samiya Schmidt did to him that night is like a scene from a book. It doesn't count for anything. It's nothing. It'll pass. Then everything will start over again like before. He likes to go around in circles here, in the Levanidovo, even if he seems to have adventures in other worlds. He enters the flames and he goes elsewhere, on an adventure. But here, in the Levanidovo, he has his ways of amusing himself, and we're his toys. Sometimes he gets rid of us, sometimes he brings us back. He just plays the same scenarios over and over again. He plays us the same cylinders on his phonographs and his loudspeakers. He's the one who decides everything. Sometimes he introduces inventions into his theater, junk that's dangerous for him or unexpected, like you. But at the end of the day, he's always the one who wins.

She was out of breath and stopped mumbling. Her eyes looked up at the drab gray rectangle of the window. The snow fell, thicker and thicker.

—We can't do it anymore, she said.

—I'm not junk, Kronauer clarified. I don't feel like I was an invention of that sort.

—Who knows what you are, Myriam Umarik whispered.

They didn't talk for a handful of seconds. Outside, the silence was total.

—I don't see what I can do to help you, Kronauer said.

—Because you do want to help us, right? she asked.

—Of course, but I don't see how.

—You want to help us without me having to do rut with you?

Kronauer mumbled reflectively. After all this effort he had made to prevent the cock's thoughts and language, he found Myriam Umarik's question particularly inappropriate and stupid.

• Contrary to what might have been assumed at a first glance, Myriam Umarik liked the engineer Barguzin and she had never had the slightest inclination to be unfaithful to him and to do rut with someone else. Certainly, for several weeks she had wriggled provocatively in Kronauer's presence, and every so often she had sent him winks and ambiguous remarks, but this soldier from the capital left her indifferent. The idea of doing sex with him, doing rut or moist hanky-panky didn't appeal to her at all, and, even if she didn't shy away from joking about it, she would have been horrified if it really was a matter of something real and suddenly having to accept that he might pull her against him, knead her, penetrate her, and overwhelm her with his grease and sticky ejaculate.

Kronauer was nothing to her. What she had understood was that, after having crossed the old forest in Samiya Schmidt's company, he ended up in Solovyei's control, but with an intermediary organic status, different from this state of neither life nor death that had reigned over the Levanidovo for decades. Like every other person to travel more than a few days in forbidden lands, in the steppes rustling with mutant grasshoppers and plutonium, Kronauer had certainly reached the hereafter of death, a point of no return in the Bardo of death. Solovyei had seen him approach the Levanidovo in Samiya Schmidt's company, he had put him through a bout of whistling in the old forest, and, instead of annihilating him like an intruder or a wild dog, he had preferred to welcome him to the village without taking away his death, without stripping him of his life as a dead person walking in the Bardo, without completely subjecting him any further to his worlds of dream and flames. Out of idleness or out of negligence, he hadn't made a puppet out of his completely disarticulated intelligence. Contrary to the Levanidovo's other current inhabitants, contrary to Solovyei's three daughters, Kronauer still had independent means within himself. So he could very easily, Myriam Umarik thought, go behind Solovyei's back, which in the eyes of the kolkhozniks and herself was a practically invincible power.

—Did you tell Barguzin you were coming to my place? Kronauer asked.

—I took advantage of the confusion in the night, Myriam Umarik whispered without directly answering. When my father had his eye and brain stabbed by Samiya Schmidt, he lost his means. It was temporary, but he certainly lost them. He came to our place and asked Barguzin to take him to the Gramma Udgul's warehouse. If there's someone who can care for him at moments like this, it's the Gramma Udgul. Barguzin helped him up the slope to the warehouse. And I got dressed and came to your room. It was still deep in the night. You were lying on the ground. I shook you, shook you. I knew that you weren't dead for good, but you weren't moving anymore.

—Well, Kronauer said. At some point last night I went dizzy. I had the impression I was living in a nightmare where I didn't understand anything.

—It's as if you stopped surviving for good, Myriam Umarik said. I lay down next to you. I thought I'd have to wait. I didn't see what else I could do.

—Well, you see, Kronauer replied.

They didn't talk for half a minute, then Myriam Umarik spoke.

—You're the only one who can kill Solovyei, she said.

• Kronauer conceded that, of those in the village, he might be in a better position than the others to murder Solovyei, and he admitted that, as a soldier, inflicting death upon an enemy of the people was his line of work, adding that he personally hated this shamanic brute who kept the Radiant Terminus kolkhoz under his magical thumb, but pointing out that he didn't have an objective reason to carry out the act. He preferred that the sanction be decided by an extraordinary commission rather than imposed by an isolated individual, who could later be reproached for having acted upon private motives unworthy of a proletarian revolutionary. Which was why he recommended putting together a popular tribunal in which the daughters and the sons-in-law of Solovyei would sit as judges, with the Gramma Udgul playing the role of lawyer or accomplice to the accused, and, for example, with one-armed Abazayev in the role of the poor and indignant masses. Moreover, he noted that Solovyei wasn't a being with a fragile constitution, that he certainly had hidden physical resources, not to mention his sorcerous powers, and that his execution risked deteriorating into horrible conditions and even failing.

—It'll be more a battle than a killing, he said. I won't have a lot of luck, even if I catch him off guard.

A shadow passed over Myriam Umarik's physiognomy.

—You have to know what you want, she said with an atypical sharpness. Nothing is ever played in advance.

• Myriam Umarik was now in front of the room's window, half a pace away from Kronauer, and watched the snow falling. Without turning toward her, Kronauer made out in the grayness her attractive curves, frequently shaken by barely perceptible waves. She had set her wig back in place and, dark and full, shining, silky, her hair flowed once again to her waist with delightful naturalness. Kronauer's hands imagined touching them, the movements they would make in this gently rustling mass, its playful scattering, while they rubbed just past the hair, this rubbing that would result in possessing the skin, the flesh, the body of this woman, the male achievement of what the cock's language dictated, what the cock's language had ordered since time immemorial. He meandered on this subject for seven or eight seconds, and then he put an end to his reverie, at least he forced himself to block, to suppress, and to repress the animalistic suggestions that invaded his head and, beyond his head, the muscle fibers and nerve endings that anticipated his touching, his squeezing, his rubbing.

—I'm going to leave, Myriam Umarik said without turning around. I'm going to cross the street. If someone sees me or sees my footprints, too bad. I'll say that I came to the prison to give you clean towels.

—Ah, nobody's going to ask you questions, Kronauer said reassuringly.

Myriam Umarik wavered.

—Maybe not ask me, but rummage within me, she said.

She lingered in front of the window, as if she expected a burning impetus, mischievous or lewd gestures that never happened. Outside silence reigned. The cottony whiteness thickened. It seemed like there was no activity in the kolkhoz.

—Nobody's really going around in the village, Kronauer said, forcing himself to think out loud about something other than copulating with Myriam Umarik.

—Oh, I assure you, people will go around, Myriam Umarik promised. And not just a little. Today is one of the days when the Gramma Udgul opens the well and throws the trash she's picked down to the core. It's been scheduled for weeks. There's no reason that'll be canceled. We're all helping her to do it. And you too, you'll go to the Gramma Udgul's warehouse.

—Nobody told me anything about that, Kronauer protested. I haven't been kept in the loop. I haven't been asked.

—Well, now you have, said Myriam Umarik.

– 19 –

• Once Myriam Umarik left his room, Kronauer nibbled on a biscuit with pemmican, lying fully dressed on his bed and trying to find good reasons to keep living in Radiant Terminus, and, unable to find them, he reconstructed all the moments of his morning conversation with Solovyei's daughter. There were too many parts that had escaped him. He would do better, doubtless, to act as if the dialogue hadn't happened. They had separated without making promises of any sort, and for example Kronauer hadn't committed to attempting to assassinate the president of the kolkhoz. The idea was there, but it hadn't been fully fleshed out into a plan of action. Kronauer momentarily imagined his fight against Solovyei, his almost immediate and wholly inevitable defeat, and he shrugged his shoulders. Fundamentally, he had no reason to throw himself into such a clearly half-baked undertaking. If there was something he had to do in the next day or so, it was to leave the Levanidovo, leave them all in the dirty and crazy hands of their president and progenitor, and look elsewhere for a refuge to die, pretend to die, pretend to live, or practice a humdrum variation on survival, sousvival, or surmorial. The time for reflection having passed, he slept a little to recover from the exhaustion of that night. At the morning's end, he left the prison.

The sky was black, the chill smelled of wolves. Right then, the snow was only falling in occasional crystals that the wind had transformed into spinning, resplendent stars. The traces of the road were barely distinguishable beneath the twenty- or thirty-centimeter snowdrifts that covered it and, once past the Veterans' Hall, which hadn't welcomed anyone for half a century and which was the last building looking out onto the main road, the path leading to the Gramma Udgul's warehouse was indistinguishable from the ditches. Kronauer oriented himself by the footprints of the villagers who had converged toward the hill and he followed them. Equipped with fur-lined boots, a fox-fur shapka, and a winter coat, he enjoyed the moment. It was the philosophy he had chosen to adopt as a way to avoid thinking about what had accumulated within himself over the past few weeks, his heavy thoughts of dissatisfaction, incomprehension, and unease, all the arguments that pushed him to leave the Levanidovo's camp and go back to wandering through the steppes. He took pleasure in hearing his soles crush the fresh snow. In just a little time I will be in the warm walls of the warehouse, he thought, in the middle of that irradiated pigsty. He had never watched the well being opened and he wondered what kind of impression he would have, once the opening was pulled back, as he received the warm breath wafting from the core. The idea didn't frighten him and on the contrary gently added to the sensations of walking, of the squeaking music, of the taste of snowflakes as they fluttered around his lips and he caught them with a flick of his tongue. One or two hours of sleep had gotten him back on his feet. He went into the snow like a gruff bear, but he was in a good mood.

• Once he came into the warehouse, he saw that those inside had been waiting for him and were annoyed at his lateness. Everybody watched in silence as he came down the way to the well. The unhooping and unscrewing of the cover hadn't started in his absence. He headed to the center of the warehouse and took off his coat and his shapka to set them on a pile of metal scraps adjoining the Gramma Udgul's private space. The air was warm in contrast to the atmosphere outside. The noise of his steps accompanied the small buzzing in the mass of trash, and one or two quick hisses from flies being brutally freeze-dried after incautiously venturing between the electric teeth of a harrow or a pitchfork. It's winter, and there are still flies, Kronauer thought. He wiped that thought from his mind, the image of instantaneously carbonized flies, the mutant appearance of the insects right before their transition into full flames.

Three or four meters from the edge, sitting on a milking machine engine doubtless condemned to an impending fall in the pit, the Gramma Udgul smoked her pipe disagreeably. She took it out of her mouth and pointed its stem at Kronauer.

—Well, tell me, soldier, she said without moving her lips or what few teeth she still had in her mouth.

—What? Kronauer asked.

—I wasn't of the understanding that you were in the kolkhoz to coast along, she grumbled. We've been waiting an hour for you.

—I wasn't given a specific time, Kronauer retorted.

The Gramma Udgul spluttered two disappointed syllables and slipped the pipe between her lips again. She reclined on the central part of the milking machine. The suction hoses surrounding it looked rather like tentacles sprouting from her haunches.

—Get to work with the others, she murmured. We're not at your disposal.

—This isn't worth yelling at me over, Kronauer said irritatedly. I don't see why you're talking down to me like I'm a slacker.

Around the well were the tractor driver Morgovian, the engineer Barguzin, Myriam Umarik, Hannko Vogulian, one-armed Abazayev, and three kolkhozniks Kronauer had never seen before. They had empty gazes, slow movements, and an evident lack of energy, and, despite wearing liquidator uniforms, they looked more like detainees sent on a suicide mission than agricultural workers. Kronauer immediately suspected them of not being full members of Radiant Terminus, and, although he wasn't able to tell who they were exactly, he thought that they certainly had to have belonged to a reserve of former workers, zombified by Solovyei decades earlier—corpses that he took back out and reactivated according to his needs, after having put them away somewhere in the oneiric universes only he had access to, or in vaults.

Abazayev was smoking. Kronauer went up to him and asked who these men were. The question was direct and the other man couldn't dodge it, but clearly he had no interest in responding.

—You want to know their names? he whispered.

—Sure, yes.

—Pedron Dardaf, Idfuk Sobibian, Hadzoböl Münzberg. Abazayev rattled them off.

—Never heard of them, Kronauer remarked. I didn't know they lived here.

—You don't know much, my poor Kronauer, cut in Hannko Vogulian, who was standing next to Abazayev.

Kronauer barely had time to meet her double and troubling eyes, the one tiger's-eye, the other black onyx, when the Gramma Udgul broke in.

—Are you chitchatting or are you going to go and open the cover? she yelled in the tone of a site foreman.

There was no immediate groveling, but the conversation immediately stopped and everybody went to a work station. Abazayev crushed his cigarette beneath his heel and began pushing slightly, with one hand, on one of the wheels keeping the well hermetically sealed. Kronauer also hunched over a wheel and turned it. The cover's seal wasn't very thick and gusts of radiation passed over everyone's faces, hot and caressing despite their noxiousness. Every so often, Barguzin coughed. He had caught a cold somewhere, maybe that night accompanying Solovyei to the hangar.

• If a post-exotic writer had been present at the scene, he would have certainly described it according to the techniques of magical socialist realism, with flights of lyricism, drops of sweat, and the proletarian exaltation that were part of the genre. It would have been a propagandist epic with reflections on the individual's endurance in service to the collective. As background noise, perhaps a march by Georgy Sviridov or Kaanto Djylas, rhythmic and full of an infectious and ideologically irreproachable euphoria. But nobody beneath the Gramma Udgul's hangar had the least literary pretensions, not to mention a musical pretension that could be considered radically bizarre. The president of Radiant Terminus, who prided himself on being a poet, was not present that morning himself and, in any case, he had a horror of magical socialist realism, as did many sorcerers who had spent a good part of their existence behind bars. So the scene happened without positive heroes and without the cinematic participation of the smiling faces of miners or anonymous detachments of steelworkers in helmets, without the flag of the working classes waving proudly above the kolkhozniks, without calls for supplementary sacrifices, and without the inevitable final discourses of Party cadets come back from the front with a medal and one less leg. We apologize in advance.

The first thing was to open the well. The metal lid was screwed to an iron base that had been cemented to the rim. Just being able to move the cover meant removing the lead tiles covering it, and, so as not to be hemmed in when bringing the junk to the pit, the tiles had to be set aside and put in a pile. Everything was heavy. The place where the tiles were supposed to be stacked was just past the private corner where the Gramma Udgul lived; for a quarter of an hour everybody came and went, without saying a word, their arms filled with heavy and colorless rectangles, which at the moment they touched or took their place in the pile made no sound at all. A sort of greasy soot covered the surface of these plaques. On his third trip, Kronauer rubbed his hand on his face and immediately his skin was streaked with black smears. Others had done something similar, had inadvertently wiped a drop of sweat from their cheeks, foreheads, and now found themselves with the features of miners. Hannko Vogulian, who took care of her braided wig, had taken it off and set it in a corner, on the winter fur coat she had worn on her way over. She unashamedly displayed her skull, totally bare of down. Myriam Umarik hadn't taken off her wig, but her shirt and her dress were already dirty and, unusually for her, she suddenly looked like a clumsy and strange slob. Nobody talked, there weren't any discussions or reflections or glances. Once the lead was set aside, four men including Kronauer finished by unblocking the cover and sliding it over the earth, which everybody then bent over to move to a place among the bric-a-brac that Pedron Dardaf, Idfuk Sobibian, and Hadzoböl Münzberg, the only three dressed like liquidators, had spent the beginning of the morning clearing.

The team took a short break. Barguzin tottered. He went to lean on a container that had once been a garbage dumpster and which now held clothes, household objects, books, and shoes. Abazayev joined him and they shared a cigarette. The Gramma Udgul came down from the milking machine; she had gone back to her private area and had put together a kettle and mismatched glasses to serve tea to those who wanted some. Hannko Vogulian had lit a little camp stove to heat the water. Myriam Umarik had just taken off her own hair. The two sisters, although their bare heads gave them an extraordinary appearance, were still beautiful, perhaps because their eyebrows hadn't been effaced and continued to underline the marvel of their looks. There wasn't any difference between the color of the skin on their faces and that on their scalps. Myriam Umarik had an orange-bronze tint, while Hannko Vogulian seemed to be sculpted out of bright ivory. Both had smeared their cheeks while working, but they didn't clean their faces. They didn't put any value on their appearance.

Pedron Dardaf and Hadzoböl Münzberg were sitting in the walkway, arms around their knees, eyes expressionless, breath short. Kronauer walked past them and went to lean by Idfuk Sobibian, who was leaning over the edge of the well to look down into its bottom.

They both stayed incommunicative in this position conducive to conversation. The wind purred in the shadowy depths. At the level of the rim, the wind was very light. Near the ledge and even by Kronauer's elbows, a sort of lichen gently glittered; when he put his hand down on it, it was crushed and disappeared with a ripping noise, and took a good twelve seconds to grow back.

—Two thousand meters, and then it's hell, Kronauer said to break the silence.

—Not really, said Idfuk Sobibian.

Kronauer looked at him curiously.

—Hell is on the surface, it's here, said Idfuk Sobibian. No need to dive into the core.

• Before enlisting in the Third Army and leaving to defend the Orbise as a simple soldier, Idfuk Sobibian had lived a rather unstable existence. He was born into a family of dog breeders and, as he was separated from them at eighteen months old, he had never really known what sorts of dogs they were, fighting dogs, sled dogs, or dogs whose hair were sold at markets to the Koreans and the Chinese, despite their prohibitions—nor had he ever known if his parents were affectionate to him or if out of sheer malice they had fed and kept him with the animals. He dreamed every so often that he was lying in darkness and that he was gnawing at a bitch's teat, but he preferred to imagine that this wasn't a childhood memory, and when he woke up with the acrid taste of husky milk in his mouth, he sighed exasperatedly and tried to go back to sleep without dwelling on the subject.

Constant twists and turns of fate marked his first years. The breeders had given or sold him to nomads who had almost immediately given him to one of their old women. The old woman, named Malka Mohonne, didn't travel with her tribe and lived in a tent city erected in the suburb of Buirkott, which at the time was an agglomeration of promising developments. She spent her time smoking fish and talking with Idfuk Sobibian in an idiolect chiefly composed of obscenities and groans that could be equally anti-leftist or counterrevolutionary. She liked Idfuk Sobibian and she protected him from happenchance, hunger, and illness by wrapping him in grigris and jinglebells. The little boy, whose linguistic baggage included at the most twelve Chekist

imprecations, had barely learned to stand when the old lady died in
a tent fire. A neighbor, older but not as foulmouthed, took in Idfuk
Sobibian and, for two years, devotedly and compassionately took care
of him. She was named Mona Heifetz and unflaggingly assumed her
role as grandmother, fed the child as best as she could with whatever
edible foodstuffs were available in the suburb, and taught him the
rudiments of language, hygiene in extreme conditions, and, in the evenings, read him the *faits divers* and the communiqués from the People's
Commissariat for Public Health, which alerted populations close to
the power plants to the measures that had to be taken in case of a
major incident. And appropriately so, because she was in the middle
of describing to Idfuk Sobibian the order and calm that should char-
acterize a massive evacuation when the sirens of the Buirkott atomic
complex tore through the darkness and the exodus began, but in such
confusion that Idfuk Sobibian quickly found himself alone on the
road, surrounded by distraught beggars, some of whom, having come
too close to the reactor in fusion, claimed to already smell the odor of
carbon coming out of their entrails as they grew over with tumors. The
tension and aggressions increased over the hours. Nobody paid attention to him. People reeking of smoke and blood went past him shouting
programmes of reprisal against those politically responsible and against
several ethnic minorities the little boy had never heard mentioned,
although he was part of them. The only adults who noticed his presence looked at him insistently and strangely, as if he were a dog ready
to be skinned and roasted. Dawn broke and Idfuk Sobibian became
scared. He strayed away from the moving crowd and, although he was
terrified, he went alone through a forest path and walked beneath the
trees for a long and frightening half-day. It had been a good idea. The
path led to a practically deserted road on which Red Aid buses were
circulating. Invited to get into one of them, Idfuk Sobibian went about
one thousand eight hundred kilometers without eating or drinking,
over roads full of potholes made dangerous by the occasional remnants
of ice. Then they sent him out, asked him for his identity, wrapped

him in a blanket, and asked him to wait. He was standing in the dark courtyard of an orphanage in Urduriya. He was five years old. Now in the care of a governmental institution, he had every chance of living a normal life, or at least of staying clean and safe until his death. And it's true that he benefited for half a dozen years from all the advantages his foster home provided: a lack of material problems, supervision by fortysomethings, collective education, brotherhood exercises, elementary knowledge training, particularly in the careers of furniture carpentry and guidance for the blind or the heavily irradiated, which were very popular careers at that time when visions of the future began to be tinged with reality. Unfortunately, the orphanage was situated in a risk area, perennially hit by imperialist military incursions and sabotages, and the successive explosions of the reactors, which had provided the region's electricity, put a sudden end to the tranquility the orphans had enjoyed, as well, of course, as to their apprenticeship. Instructed by his memories of the hysterical first evacuation that he had lived through near Buirkott, Idfuk Sobibian didn't follow the tormented flood and, when the educators raced through the hallways to confirm that they weren't leaving behind any stragglers, he hid.

Idfuk Sobibian's independent existence began at Urduriya. It was April, the springtime was early and agreeable. The little boy was part of a band of kids living in autarky, thriving on the inexhaustible reserves left behind by the evacuees, and who fought together against other bands, against the militiamen responsible for preventing theft, against the groups of authentic thieves, and against the horror that was often inspired by the funereal silence in the city. Out of laziness, in the first months they had given a helping hand to the liquidators who worked near the center, but then the liquidators had given up and disappeared, preceded in their disappearance by the militiamen and the final medical-branch doctors and nurses. Despite avoiding incursions close to the reactors, most of the inhabitants who stayed at Urduriya, young and old, suffered a pathetic, swift end. Idfuk Sobibian was one of those rare individuals whom nature had given a body resistant to radiation. Soon he was alone, coming and going in the streets aimlessly and talking out loud without anybody listening, like a madman. Wild dogs, which he had planned on feeding in case he was ever tormented by a desire for meat, were no longer visible anywhere. The stench of a charnel-house reigned in most of the neighborhoods. Every night, the power plant sirens went off. The young boy was smart enough to realize that he wouldn't have the strength to grow up in this morose place, to resist loneliness, to confront winter. He would fade if he didn't leave. It was summer. He put food, soap, thick clothes, shoes, and spare tires in a bicycle basket, and he left Urduriya pedaling with excessive speed, like a hiker.

The roads were empty. They were straight, impractical for biking and meandering. The countryside and the forest were empty. They say that in irradiated zones the animals freed of human presences regain possession of their natural territories and appear at every moment: birds, reindeer, bears and wolves, but he didn't see, anywhere and everywhere, any animal except a single dying fox. She was lying in an indentation in the ground and he stopped to examine her. Without turning her head, she bit into a fox-cub corpse right in front of her snout, then shut her glassy eyes, then bit her dead offspring once more. This was the only evidence of fauna during his entire trip. It took him four days before he passed a truck, and five days to end up in a refugee camp.

Until he enlisted in the Third Army, he lived in several camps: Gargang, Bürlük, Chamoldjin, Badarambaza, and Thochodor, where he spent his adolescence. He was made completely literate and, when it was suggested that he join the Komsomol, he accepted. In the camps he participated in political meetings, progressed in his knowledge of the international situation, listened to conferences of poets of the Party, trained for middle-distance races, and, every week, he went to the barracks to complete his basic instruction for handling arms. At eighteen years old he presented himself at a recruitment office and, after his classes, he was sent to the capital, where he stayed for five months in a self-defense company. Then, as the noose tightened around the Orbise, he asked to leave for the Third Army. He was sent to the southeast front, close to Goldanovka. He was assigned to a decontamination unit. With about forty comrades, he spent a month undressing and showering soldiers who had gone into dangerous zones. The enemy didn't appear. It was a wonderful time, the nights were short, the sun shone. A new summer had started. Once they got away from the decontamination ponds and buildings, once they had left the camps, the air filled with fragrances, sent from the taiga by a warm wind. During a vesperal walk beyond Goldanovka's suburbs, Idfuk Sobibian was caught under machine-gun fire that was both unforeseeable and unerring. Against his cheek the earth, despite the ambient warmth, was icy. He had time to notice this, then he sighed a final breath and curled around his death. As the attacks around Goldanovka resumed, nobody came to recover his remains.

Over the forty-nine days that followed, he went by himself down the path between Goldanovka and Djindo, a morose and abandoned small town. He stayed there for a while to think and to pull himself together. He felt numb, in a state much like hibernation. His memories were difficult to gather together. After several weeks, he wondered if he wasn't floating in an oneiric or Bardic variant of his solitary stay in the city of Urduriya. Then something inscrutably pushed him to get going and so he headed northward, then eastward. He walked with a heavy step without taking into account obstacles. The region was covered with forest, rocky outcrops, valleys after mountains. There were no urban agglomerations and, if he had found one along his path, he would have gone out of his way to avoid it, because he knew that he would be tempted to stop there—and he wanted to get as far away as possible. He felt a violent need for solitude, as well as a deep mistrust toward the living, humans, beasts, and dead alike. Before the first cold weather he came to Kunaley and, deciding that he had walked long enough anyway, or at least that he couldn't go any farther, he went in. It was a small-sized city. He looked for shelter to spend the winter. He first found the house of a widow who welcomed him effusively, as if she was reuniting with an old lost lover—then she began to insult him, after several days, to insult him and beat him. The old woman stank of eau de cologne, which she thought would hide her scent of plutonium and rotting bones. Idfuk Sobibian only stayed with her for two weeks, but when he left, snow was falling. So, seeking his fortune, he crossed the train station that had been bombed or burned five years earlier, saw a convoy that was composed of cars for merchandise and horses or soldiers, and got in, without thinking that the train might start and take him elsewhere. But that's what happened. Barely twenty-four hours had gone by when the detainees got on board, slumped next to him, and fell asleep in exhaustion. A little while after, the locomotive whistled, and the convoy set off, quickly leaving Kunaley for an unknown destination.

The train began to move slowly. Every so often the constantly wheezing diesel motor gave a sharp whistle, like those from steam locomotives, or a two-tone warning with a funereal key that brought to mind for each of them memories of night and distress. The doors were shut, they didn't see what was outside. Several planks near Idfuk Sobibian had come apart and he could put his eye to a crack to examine the landscape, but he didn't have any desire to. Neither he nor his travel companions went to this effort. There were eight of them in the car and they sprawled on the boards or sat somehow, leaning against the walls and protecting themselves against air currents with covers or straw. Nobody talked, or rather the conversations were limited to interjections, but also sometimes plaintive monologues, filled with self-mockery and fatalism. When someone finished his story, silence prevailed again for several days, the time needed to collectively digest the information and the tarry humor. The train never stopped. Someone remarked that between two jolts it was sometimes three seconds, sometimes three hours, sometimes three weeks. And why not three seasons? asked one of the detainees, named Matthias Boyol. In this way small conversations developed and, little by little, the car's inhabitants learned to get to know each other. Detainees and soldiers shared, by and large, the same fate, the same loyalty to the egalitarian ideologies of the Second Soviet Union and the Orbise. They hadn't always made the same choices, and some of them belonged to the stinking categories, but, in short, they were all comrades in arms and, once they got into the train, the differences between them had only diminished.

The train finally braked and stopped, and the exhausted carcass of passengers took some time to forget the swaying that had continually shaken them for days or months, or perhaps even more. A man who acted as captain unlocked the doors and Idfuk Sobibian stepped out onto the ballast. The convoy had stopped at the top of a ruined sovkhoz, the Red Star. It wasn't snowing. On the contrary, he had the impression of having reached a peaceful, summery place, in the middle of a green, silvery, golden steppe, barely rolling, stretching from one side of the sovkhoz endlessly and, from the other, seemingly closed off by the dark line of the forest.

The captain spent the afternoon taking roll call, preparing for what he called the shift change, which meant electing a soldier or a detainee who in turn would be responsible for giving order and ensuring the convoy's safety. He had promised them all a pemmican distribution that evening around the fire. Several cigarettes were lit. Idfuk Sobibian had found several packets in a bag that had hung over his head during the trip and which he hadn't touched, out of superstition and out of lack of initiative. He didn't have any desire to inhale smoke or crumbs of food, but he joined the others and, when they were all assembled around a campfire, he didn't miss the opportunity to eat what had been put in the hollow of his hand, several grams of this energetic mixture that the nomads and the dead consumed when they hoped to last to the end of their personal adventure. And during the evening, listening to chitchat, he learned more about the function and goals of this strange group. He was one of the new guys, those who had been recruited along the way. Most of his companions were old-timers, and had already stopped in front of the Red Star sovkhoz more than once.

—We're turning around, explained Julius Togböd, the captain who had been co-opted at the end of the afternoon. It takes forever, but we're turning around. We're not going to get to where we want.

—It's just unbearable repetition, remarked Noumak Ashariyev, one of the members of the team that took turns day and night driving and maintaining the diesel engine. It's unending and it's endless.

—Oh, it's not that unbearable, said Hadzoböl Münzberg, another engineer.

—It's just repetition, Noumak Ashariyev insisted. It's hell.

—It's not just hell, Matthias Boyol corrected. It's more that we're within a dream that we can't understand the mechanisms of. We're inside, and we don't have any way of getting out.

—Nobody's keeping you from escaping during one of the stops, a detainee suggested.

—Man, you know anybody who's escaped? someone asked.

—I'll have no pity for those who try to escape, Julius Togböd said. We'll catch them and we'll shoot them for deserting. We've always done that and it's not because we've changed captains that laxity is poking its nose here. We have firing squads and bullets. For fighting enemies and also for carrying out justice.

—Well, Matthias Boyol said. We shoot them or we let them disappear without ever grabbing them by their collars. And then, at one point or another, we see that they've reappeared in the convoy.

—Same thing for those who have died in the cars and those who we've left on the tracks, said a soldier.

—Yes, we're always more or less at the same number, said Matthias Boyol.

—It's just unbearable repetition, Noumak Ashariyev repeated.

—We're in a dream, Matthias Boyol concluded. He does to us whatever he wants.

—Who's he? Idfuk Sobibian asked.

—We don't know, said Noumak Ashariyev. But we do know that he does with us whatever he wants. We're in his hell. We were put in there and we have no way of getting out.

• Idfuk Sobibian was just about to ask Kronauer if he had a cigarette when the Gramma Udgul's stern voice ended the break. Solovyei's daughters had finished their tea. They were already headed back to the well, Hannko Vogulian with an assured, almost military step, and Myriam Umarik swaying her hips in a way that Kronauer felt was forced, even pitiful. Abazayev and Barguzin, who were leaning against the container of junk that the Gramma Udgul had selected for immediate liquidation, pulled away and began unlocking the movable wall. They banged on the lever. Pedron Dardaf and Hadzoböl Münzberg, as coolies, had just gotten out of their hunched poses. They got up and they waited, panting, for their orders.

When Abazayev and Barguzin opened the container, some of what had been stored there flowed out with the short roar of an avalanche.

Kronauer and Idfuk Sobibian were still leaning on the edge. The Gramma Udgul ran toward them and sent them off while grumbling some vague reproach, then she leaned toward the pit and talked to the core. As he saw a nearly religious stillness overcome the scene, Kronauer imagined this was a preliminary ritual, necessary for the liquidation to go well, and he, too, froze, his eyes on the old woman. Of all the participants, she was the only one with any hair on her head. Disheveled and sparse, but natural. The others, women and men, were completely shaven or balding, if not completely bareheaded.

The Gramma Udgul told the core that it would soon get the food it had been waiting for, that it had waited weeks for, and she asked it to receive the food not as an offering, but as proof that the Second Soviet Union still faced up to its responsibilities and continued to rally heroes, new generations of enthusiastic and disinterested liquidators.

She beseeched the pile to play its role in this spectacular process of cleaning and to continue collaborating with those who stayed at ground level. Thanks to this unflagging alliance, the Gramma Udgul explained, one day the ground would be again clean, again ready to resume building a more just society and collectively reindustrializing the city and the country. This time they would do their best not to let nuclear rubble accumulate, the Gramma Udgul promised, and especially to restrain the scientists who had disfigured civilization, doubtless because they'd been too indulgent in their margins of error and with their tendency to enjoy the enemy's propagandistic twaddle, the enemy's non-Marxist theories, and the enemy's dollars. Then she emphatically and even shamelessly praised the core. She thanked it for having withdrawn deeply enough for the Levanidovo's existence to continue in tranquility, so that its deadly plumes and its unforeseeable mood swings were not too near. She assured it of the love and respect of every person in the kolkhoz, including those who had already fallen in the line of duty. The Gramma Udgul's voice, which she intended to be energetic, quavered a little, and Kronauer wondered if it really would reach whatever remained down there, formless and liquefied, and maybe hard of hearing, because, although the discourse was amplified by the echoes the uppermost meters of the abyss sent back, it was pushed back to the ceiling of the warehouse by the wind blowing from the burning entrails of the well.

Once her short speech was concluded by a call to the working masses of the Levanidovo and its adjacent regions, the Gramma Udgul got back up. Through her sparse, gray locks of hair she passed an equally gray mummy's hand and looked proudly, one by one, at all those present. Then she ordered Kronauer and Idfuk Sobibian to carry out the first actual act of liquidation of that day: throwing into the void the milking machine she had been sitting on a bit earlier. Kronauer grabbed hold of the machine's body and rolled it to the edge, then over it. Idfuk Sobibian had in the meantime more or less collected the tubes and teat cups. The machine was indescribable, but it seemed a bit like a giant squid and, when it slipped into the void, the tubes dropped by Idfuk Sobibian whipped the air. For three or four tenths of a second, the image of a giant mollusk became increasingly indisputable, then the undersea beast disappeared. It bounced noisily against the well's walls for the first hundred meters of its fall, and then it was quiet. Its descent must have continued, but the echo of its bumps no longer came to the surface.

Immediately everybody went to work. The main task consisted of emptying the container. The liquidators took armfuls of things, which they carried about twenty meters and threw mechanically, but sometimes violently and with pleasure, into the darkness of the well. They went past each other on the paths, occasionally trading thoughts on the work schedule and the lack of a break. The comings and goings were endless, but there weren't enough people to warrant comparison to indefatigable ants, in terms of incoming and outgoing lines. The trash was varied but generally of a small size. Chairs, pickaxes, straw bales, pitchforks and cutlery, household linens, microwaves, computers, fur coats, hardened blocks of meat, sticky masses of unknown provenance, mattresses, detainee pajamas, freezer motors, cupboard doors, hutch sections, encyclopedias republished on paper after the end of the Internet, children's books, tin cans, tools, remnants of bats, anti-radiation suits taken off the corpses of firefighters, remnants of dogs, party dishes, portraits of leaders. When something was too large to be carried without assistance, Kronauer called to the closest liquidator. He avoided Abazayev whose lone arm resulted in his having poor balance and wavering. Often he teamed up with Hannko Vogulian. They both panted, their hips down, backs bent, and they looked at each other without saying a word, or while uttering brief instructions to get their charge to the right place, meaning the abyss. Kronauer admired Hannko Vogulian's eyes and, on pretext of the job currently under way, which required synchronizing their movements and efforts, he plunged into them.

• The Gramma Udgul set on the edge a box full of cylinders that belonged to Solovyei and she wavered, then she brought them back beside her armchair. She was out of breath.

—I can't throw these away, she murmured. I can't really throw these away.

As the liquidators' ballet went on monotonously, and several of them showed signs of exhaustion, the Gramma Udgul leaned over the phonograph and put a cylinder between the grips, then she cranked the handle and set the needle on the black surface. A stimulating melody spread beneath the vaulted hangar, and the atmosphere, which had been morose, changed. It was a First Soviet Union march, from the times of civil war. It called the red soldiers to crush the people's executioners and to put an end to the old world's curses. There was a minimum programme within which everyone could still hear each other. All who were present took in the music with a shiver of optimism, and the pace picked up. The Gramma Udgul kept the rhythm with her feet and hands and, when the cylinder ended, she put the needle back at the beginning.

For an hour, nothing notable happened. The core's food flew into the depths. The radioactive dust burnished everyone's skin. The march played on loop within the warehouse. The container gradually grew empty. Pedron Dardaf and Hadzoböl Münzberg struggled, less and less able to carry things, even light ones. Idfuk Sobibian dawdled in the pathways like a machine winding down. Although they hadn't completely lost their sparkle, the two daughters resembled dirty and bald wanderers. Abazayev hurt his arm on a piece of metal and, when he carried something to the edge, drops of blood fell from his one hand and fluttered everywhere, then down to the core. Barguzin sleepwalked between the container and the well, sometimes overshooting his target without realizing it and then taking half a minute to retrace his path. Kronauer tried to choose cumbersome things, in order to team up sometimes with Hannko Vogulian, whose strange gaze he took in greedily, and sometimes with Idfuk Sobibian, whose calm moroseness he appreciated. By carefully moving around in a seemingly haphazard way, he managed not to ever work directly with Myriam Umarik.

• Around three in the afternoon, the container was finally empty. Everybody, the Gramma Udgul included, had tired of the call for the red soldiers to flush out czars and exploitative vermin, and now silence prevailed, filled with heavy breaths, groans of exhaustion, and also the light atomic roar from the entrails of the earth. The light had dimmed, because the snow had started falling again outside. Several of us were sitting on the piles of debris and slowly massaged our calves or shut our eyes, as if feigning sleep helped the body to regain a bit of strength.

The Gramma Udgul suggested some tea. Kronauer was the only one to get up to drink some.

—It's not over yet, said the Gramma Udgul. There are still carcasses and bodies.

—Where? Kronauer asked.

The Gramma Udgul pointed at a corner of the warehouse.

—Not much, she said. It'll be done in five minutes. Then we'll shut the lid.

—All right, said Kronauer.

He drank his tea and rinsed the cup in a bucket. The cold water just waiting for this beside the table. It splashed and then calmed down.

Kronauer went back to Hannko Vogulian. She was leaning against one of the pillars supporting the warehouse roof. She wasn't slumped down and, on the contrary, she gave the impression of having stretched her spinal column to be more upright and serious than usual.

—There are still carcasses and bodies to throw into the well, Kronauer said.

Hannko Vogulian lowered her left eyelid, completely and without any effect on the other eyelid, as nocturnal birds could. She was now looking at Kronauer, showing him only the obsidian that replaced her right eye. Kronauer was breathtaken. The shining beauty of this gaze gave him vertigo.

Solovyei's daughter tilted her head slightly.

—Are you helping me? Kronauer asked.

—Eh, said Hannko Vogulian. You won't be happy.

—It's not a question of being happy or unhappy, Kronauer said. That's left to do, and then we'll be done.

—All right, said Hannko Vogulian in a weary voice, and she followed him.

• A space had been cleared behind a heap that was essentially a dismantled combine harvester. During the night, someone had lined up two corpses covered with felt rectangles, as well as two lupine cadavers. The wild animals must have wandered into the Levanidovo's territories and immediately felt the effects of radiation in the marrow of their bones. The animals lay on the ground without a shroud. Kronauer took one by the paws and dragged it to the well. Hannko did the same thing with the second. They both pushed their burdens at the same time into the vertical darknesses and then they returned to the combine. The other liquidators watched them from where they were sitting as passive onlookers, unable to get up to give them a helping hand. Barguzin was slumped on a pile of newspapers, his head angled upward. He was no longer moving. He seemed to have once again crossed the boundary separating his sort of life and his sort of death, and for him to come back to existence, before night fell the Gramma Udgul would have to apply her three-water treatment—scouring with heavy-heavy water and deathly-deathly water, completed by an anointment of lively-lively water.

Now Kronauer and Hannko Vogulian spent some time in contemplation. They towered over the wrapped bodies. The corpses beneath the covers.

—We could carry them together, Hannko Vogulian suggested.

—Who's this one? Kronauer asked.

Hannko Vogulian didn't reply. Kronauer bent down to pull away the cover hiding the first cadaver.

—If I were you, I wouldn't do that, Hannko Vogulian said.

—Why? Kronauer asked, pausing mid-action.

—I'd rather not know, Hannko Vogulian said. It's always better when you don't know.

Kronauer hesitated, then he decided to ignore Hannko Vogulian's advice. His arm was outstretched and, carefully, he uncovered the face of the one lying at his feet. Half the head was damaged and, from the bottom of the neck, it was clear that the body had been horribly ruined. It exuded a smell of bad meat, a filthy odor.

—Morgovian, Kronauer whispered.

He put the cover back in place. For seven or eight seconds, he thought about Morgovian. He remembered their laborious discussions, his embarrassed responses about the merchant caravans that allowed the kolkhoz to be supplied with edible foodstuffs and the like. He glanced once again at his hung-up tractor-driver appearance, darkened by intimate secrets, by the knowledge of his overt submission to Solovyei, by his powerlessness, by his failed marriage with Samiya Schmidt. And then he considered the other corpse. Beneath the cloth he could make out an unimposing body. Despite everything, as if he needed to hear something from Hannko Vogulian before proceeding to identify it, he waited another moment indecisively.

—And is that Solovyei? he asked.

—Solovyei? Hannko Vogulian asked in shock. What's wrong with you, soldier?

Kronauer crouched and grabbed a corner of the shroud. Barely had he lifted it when his hand went weak and he let go. Then he grabbed it more firmly and did it again. He couldn't believe what he saw. It was shocking, but more than anything absurd. In pulling away the cloth he had cast light on the face of Vassilissa Marachvili. The decrepit and damaged, but recognizable, face of Vassilissa Marachvili.

At first, he was gripped. Eight, nine seconds. He felt an immense exhaustion. He didn't examine the dead body's face. He looked at it without understanding. Without trying to think that maybe it was another woman, a woman who looked like Vassilissa Marachvili, or maybe that he was in a waking dream and soon the hallucination would dissipate. He stood over her without reacting. He couldn't get out of his stupor. This cadaver wasn't talking to him, refused to talk to him, its features, after so many weeks of separation, no longer aroused the memories that could have harked to a living physiognomy. He couldn't yet associate that which was lying at his feet with the brave woman he had left, in very bad shape, dying, on the hill that overlooked the railroad tracks and the Red Star sovkhoz. He hadn't forgotten Vassilissa Marachvili, their flight after the defeat, the ordeals, the endless walk through the irradiated steppes, he remembered the light touches that had united them, the weight of her weakened body when, those last days, he and Ilyushenko had taken turns carrying her on their backs. But he was unable to make a connection between the living woman in his memory and the dead woman lying in the Gramma Udgul's warehouse.

Then something else clicked inside him and the link was formed.

And, immediately, a torrent carried him away.

He reattached the felt to Vassilissa Marachvili's shoulders, leaving her head exposed. She hadn't lost her hair. Her mouth showed some exhaustion, the shadow of what might have once been a smile, but it was a vague, fatigued smile, and as for the rest of her body, nothing remained of the joyful, touching beauty that had been an integral part of her and which she had tried to sustain for as long as possible. For her two comrades in disaster, all the way to the very end of their pilgrimage.

Hannko Vogulian decided to break the silence.

—Solovyei brought her from the Red Star, she said. He tried to bring her back to life. He really wanted to bring her back, but he couldn't.

Kronauer turned toward her. He couldn't take it anymore: the Levanidovo, its inhabitants, the horrors and oneiric aberrations that had come to pass. He'd had enough of Solovyei's doings, of this permanent presence in the background of space and of the mind. A monumental fury grew at full speed beneath his consciousness. The accumulation of frustrations, unsaid thoughts, and lies from when he'd arrived at the Levanidovo, from when he'd grazed a finger against a phonograph needle, everything that was part of this waking nightmare swelled and roiled beneath his thoughts, threatening to surge outright and destroy everything outside. He didn't look specifically at Hannko Vogulian, or her body, or even her shape, or her gaze. But he shuddered and he didn't even think of hiding that he was about to explode in rage. Almost nothing kept him from falling on her and killing her, and besides, he was only vaguely putting a name to her and this name meant nothing to him, or very little, really very little, not a known woman, in any case. His memory and his eyes only saw an unlit night, his conscious thoughts were stuck on the image of Vassilissa Marachvili's mangled cadaver. As for his hands, they only moved for one thing. To strangle the first person to get in their way, and if that wasn't enough to calm them, to strangle anyone, strangle one by one each of Solovyei's creations living in the Levanidovo, whether they were accomplices, willing victims, or strange living dead. To strangle them, hurt them, undo them, and then, in one way or another, do away with Solovyei and with Radiant Terminus. This was what Kronauer had become in a few seconds: a man gripped, filled completely with loathing, with the hope of criminal retaliation, with night.

• With that, the Gramma Udgul inserted a cylinder between the claws of the phonograph she had just set up. For reasons known only to her, but which didn't have the effect of clearing the air, she didn't ask the liquidators to listen once again to a red soldiers' march. She had just rummaged in the box that she had decided not to throw into the abyss, and she had pulled out a cylinder at random. She shut the hooks of the machine and set the needle on the wax. Solovyei's voice rose in the warehouse. Aside from these incomprehensible divagations, nothing else buzzed around Kronauer and Hannko Vogulian.

• Suddenly he summoned up his strength to express words, and, having set his back on the mirror, he lit eleven candles in a row by bringing them to his mouth. Barely moving, he acted as if someone was standing right behind him and listening between two dreams. The reflection indeed obeyed him and conformed in every way to his desires, and supported his idea that everything was going well as far as his audience, which persisted in turning its back on him without, however, pouring out vile remarks. He coughed, testing this presence—the reflection's pulmonary sacs shook, but it didn't express any discomfort. Then he was already thinking strictly about his next words, he was preparing a speech and some music. The memory that put ideas behind his tongue was wounded and painful; the source of the pain was a knowledge that he had acquired some time ago, when, having consulted fowl entrails and having cross-checked the information obtained therein against the forms of the flames howling around him in the room, he had suspected that his daughter was in danger somewhere in the universe, one of his numerous unique daughters and unique wives, born from unknown mothers and submitting to him. He set himself thus in front of the dark silvering and he waited, and, although the wounds beneath his skull didn't close and he felt almost like he was in his terminal stage, he increased the flux of forces within himself and he projected himself into an image where he appeared under the auspices of a demiurge whose every word disrupted the evil labyrinths of the world. Far off, his daughter Hannko was dying or already lay dead, or was in the process of being born or reborn, and he said: "I just have to shuck the bad minutes, I will shuck the time backward, the wrong way, minute by minute I'll destroy the image of your death until we've undone your death and until your enemies have one by one been brought down, I'll bruise them backward and they'll go quiet, brought down and mute." This he said as he actually was feeling his way: the candles illuminated nothing, they shone in their molten suet sludge and went out and, even when he lit them again close to his mouth, they spread his smell rather than their own, a strong stench of grilled pork rind and darkness. In the room, only one person blazed and entarred himself, and it was him. He asked the mirror its advice on things, on the immediate future of worldly things and on their inverse. The reflection was silent as well, like a hostile, felled, and mute monster. He wiped it away angrily. He wanted to share the image with someone, but the image didn't materialize and nobody responded. Among the thousands of possible daughters, Hannko didn't come forward. The others wandered beside her, like her, destroyed, themselves also hostile, felled, and mute. He saw snow, camps, a frightening solitude, centuries in the forest that succeeded in an undisentanglable mass, but Hannko didn't come directly to him or back on the path he had drawn for her. He saw her from far off, but in the middle of others he didn't even know if that was his little sister or his mistress or an animal, or an ancestral mother of his blood, but harboring an avid resentment at his gaze. He would have been unable to affirm the sort of relationship that each of them had. Squinting in front of the mirror that at every moment became enshadowed, he examined Hannko in the distance, like an enigmatic stranger whom dizziness forced him to seduce or massacre unhesitatingly. At times she lay unconscious in the taiga, surrounded by she-wolves that protected or ate her; at times she spun around a core in fusion, refusing to admit that her father existed and that he could bring her back, if only she gave herself to him; sometimes she was silent and impenetrable, surrounded by hundred-year-old trees and books that, with time, she had learned to read and write. And he suddenly grew angry and yelled: "Hannko, little sister, daughter Hannko, come here! Wife Hannko, forget your hates, forget everything! I'm shucking the bad minutes! Come! Today or in one thousand six hundred ninety-nine years or more, it doesn't matter!"

– 20 –

• Solovyei's voice reverberated in the warehouse, along the metal framework and between the mountains of trash. Things vibrated at the tops of the piles every so often, as if sensitive to the stridency of certain vowels. Rolls of iron wire, sheet pans, bits of grills, harnesses.

Kronauer didn't make a sound. The psychic tension had flowed into his muscles. His body weighed hundreds of kilograms, his brain had gone on hold. Fugs of thought moved in slow motion behind his forehead. It can't be her. But it is her. No, impossible. They couldn't have hidden her all this time without my seeing. Solovyei couldn't have been working on her body all this time. Somebody would have found out. Weeks. Solovyei's daughters couldn't have kept this secret. Myriam Umarik is too talkative. Samiya Schmidt couldn't have that kind of cynicism. Hannko Vogulian has moral uprightness. Or maybe they didn't know, either. Vassilissa Marachvili in the village for all this time, weeks, without anybody knowing. Vassia. No.

I can't believe that, he thought.

He shuddered. He didn't even realize it. He repeated bits of elementary thoughts. From a long way off, the name of Irina Echenguyen sometimes was added to that of Vassilissa Marachvili. Two loved women he had lost, each time in abominable circumstances. Women he hadn't loved in the same way, but whom he hadn't known how to defend. Their falling into the hands of murderers. Irina Echenguyen. The dog-headed enemies. Vassilissa Marachvili. This Solovyei with his peasant magician's head. The phonograph still put out its insanity. In front of Hannko Vogulian, Kronauer's shoulders shook. He cried without any tears. His eyes rested on the corpse of Vassilissa Marachvili and he didn't make an effort not to see her. His ears heard nothing. Of Solovyei's vicious speech he heard and retained nothing.

Then the roll ended. The needle screeched a dirty silence for five seconds, then the Gramma Udgul stopped the mechanism and everything went quiet. Nothing vibrated in the warehouse anymore.

Kronauer moved. He came out of his numbness. He had stopped shuddering.

He got down, lifted the felt cloth, then he carefully covered Vassilissa Marachvili's face once more. Vassia, little sister, he thought. It's over for you. It's finally over. The rest depends on me.

Once again the young corpse became alien to its onlookers. Beneath its dark gray envelope, it had already merged into the infinite mass of the dead, already closer to the tractor driver Morgovian, lying next to her, than to Kronauer, who was the only person present to still have any memories of her. Then Kronauer didn't wait to say good-bye to the outstretched bodies and was already walking away. Hannko Vogulian stood before him, in the middle of the path. He sidestepped her. She tried in vain to look him in the eye, maybe to silently tell him that she hadn't been involved at all in her father's vileness. He pushed past her without turning his head toward her, went past her without slowing down in the least, and began walking between two embankments of debris, through a hallway lined with truck wheels, hurriedly folded canvas sheets, crates, pipes thrown haphazardly, saucepans and frying pans that still exuded the scent of meat, of mushrooms.

He took a detour through smaller alleys, which were rarely used. He wanted to get to the exit without having to go past the kolkozniks who were waiting by the container, as well as the Gramma Udgul. He couldn't bear any contact with these people anymore and he wondered how he had been able to stand alongside them day after day and give in to their needs, and, as shamefully as them, as passively, borne the magical, dark, and incestuous practices that were commonplace in the Levanidovo.

He glanced at the junk while walking. He looked for a weapon. Something he could bury or drive into Solovyei's flesh, something evil, pointed and cutting. Close to the entrance he saw a construction stake and he took it out of the pile of scrap iron surrounding it. It was a solid shaft with a sharp point, and the object was nicely balanced in his hand, slightly rusted, as dangerous as a javelin. He hefted it for about ten seconds. Then he sent it flying into the bric-a-brac.

No, that doesn't work, he thought. In a pinch, it's good for fending off a wolf or a bear. But I can't see myself using that against Solovyei.

And besides, he thought, I wonder if there's any weapon for that.

• Now he was on the threshold of the hangar, at the boundary between the warmth inside and the icy air outside. The warehouse kept producing heat, and as the Gramma Udgul wasn't complaining today about the air flow, nobody had worried about closing the door. The snow had resumed, it fell violently in huge, gray, very fluffy flakes. The low light announced the proximity of the darkness. With this twilight and the curtains of snow it was hard to make out the first houses of the kolkhoz at the bottom of the slope. There wasn't any smoke or movement. The main road was lost in the white. What could be seen was blank of every trace.

Kronauer hesitated as he looked at this dead village. Without warm clothes, he couldn't leave the warehouse. His coat was hanging close to the well and he especially did not want to retrace his steps and come close once again to the Gramma Udgul's lair, with her little kitchen, her armchair, her piles of newspapers, her phonograph, and her old woman's organized mess. Nor did he want to see one of the others again, the kolkhozniks, Solovyei's zombies, Solovyei's daughters.

As if his leave-taking hadn't aroused any feeling, hustle and bustle had resumed in the warehouse. He heard soles squeaking on the ground, some banging against the sides of the well. Those who still had strength had stopped resting. They're liquidating the remnants the Gramma Udgul's picked out, Kronauer thought. Some forgotten things, and, of course, the bodies of Morgovian and Vassilissa Marachvili. They're throwing all that into the core without asking any questions. He raged at them all. He wouldn't go so far as to accuse them of direct complicity in Vassilissa Marachvili's death, but he suspected them of having been aware that her cadaver was there, fully aware, unaware only of Solovyei's working on her day and night with all his revolting habits. They had plotted it all out together. And him, during these autumn months, just an idiot. Drunk on the nearness of Solovyei's daughters, all his morals gone. Waiting stupidly for his cock's dreams to come true. Having no dignity or future. While Vassia. While they'd used magic to grope Vassia.

He stood there, momentarily protected from the cold by the radio-active waves, half a meter from the tracks on which the door slid. He saw the snow thickening two meters in front of him, and in the quiet moments amid the various noises the liquidators were making by the well, he could make out the monotonous twinkling of the icy stars crashing against or landing on their sisters already on the earth. He felt overwhelmed, unable to take any initiative. Despite being confused, almost dazed, he knew that in light clothes he couldn't confront the atmospheric conditions outside.

After a moment, and while he rocked back and forth by the door rails like he was mentally ill, he sensed a presence behind him.

A presence. He sensed it without any idea of how to react.

A few seconds. Then, gently, someone set a fur coat on his shoulders. He turned. It was Hannko Vogulian.

• He looked into the beautiful and strange double gaze of Hannko Vogulian and, immediately, the unexpected occurred. A reversal, a radical inversion of his feelings. Just a short while before, in front of Vassilissa Marachvili's cadaver, he had almost leaped onto this woman to strike her to death. The two of them had been alone and, at the moment he'd wanted to kill, there had been no other representative from Radiant Terminus there. He had almost done it. But in a fraction of a second this urge to murder had disappeared, giving way to tenderness. The effect of this beautiful and strange gaze. Once again, as through the entire autumn, Hannko Vogulian attracted him. Over the last weeks, he had often wanted to lose himself in her eyes, and, hoping that she wasn't aware of the trouble she gave him, he swam magnetically toward her. Sometimes he even had the impression that she expected that of him, that he would gently draw near to her. And here, although the circumstances hadn't conspired in this way, everything came back to this physical need for meeting and fusion, for this urge. So what if I fell into her arms, he thought. What if I cried on her shoulder?

His lips trembled, but he didn't know how to express what had arisen in him. It was a luminous second, but it faded away and everything, once again, became muddled. The idea of crossing the short distance separating them, opening his arms, and giving in to her seemed less and less obvious. Less obvious, less defensible was this amorous urge, assuming that was what this was. Hannko Vogulian, however, showed no emotion. She stood very close to him, she bestowed her extraordinary gaze on him, but she didn't invite anything of him.

He caught the coat before it slipped and he put it on, taking his time, without continuing to contemplate this daughter's eyes. You idiot, Kronauer, he scolded himself, you just said good-bye to Vassilissa Marachvili, and all it takes is for this daughter of Solovyei to appear for you to dream of pressing up against her? As if you didn't know that these impulses have nothing to do with feelings . . . It's just an urge to rut!

Hannko Vogulian handed him a big, brown fur shapka that she had taken, like the coat, from a pile of irradiated clothes, and he accepted it slowly, almost regretting the peaceful normalcy of his gesture. She took half a step backward. She stood upright, rigidly, in her work uniform filthy with filings, soot, and dust, with grease stains on her face and on her scalp as smooth as an egg, because she hadn't put on her Chukchi or Yakut princess's wig. Her eyes didn't blink. Kronauer met them for a fraction of a second and immediately looked away. Her monstrously different, beautiful, and strange eyes. They didn't blink.

—Are you going to Solovyei's house? she asked.

He nodded furtively, then he put on the shapka, finished buttoning his coat, and went back to the doorway. A downy layer several centimeters deep was freezing in the door's track. He looked up at the twilit wall coverings that covered a good part of the countryside. Now he could confront the cold. Now he would go down to the village and fight the president of the kolkhoz. He had a moment of weakness when he'd put Vassilissa Marachvili in second place to fantasize about Hannko Vogulian, but this moment was passing. He was already filled with the idea of the action to come.

Still, at the moment he went into the snow, he hesitated briefly. One second, two seconds. He considered the overcast landscape and he didn't take the decisive step. He waited.

Three seconds.

Hannko Vogulian had just whispered something behind him.

The fur earflaps were folded over his cheeks, they kept him from understanding what she had said. He concentrated, he tried to reconstruct the syllables that the obstacle had deformed or erased.

—Do you hear me, Kronauer? Hannko Vogulian asked, this time a little louder. I'm with you.

She reached out and touched his shoulder. He felt it but didn't react, didn't turn toward her.

—Remember that later, that I'm with you, she said as he stepped over the threshold. Later and always.

– 21 –

• He took one step into the snow, then a second, then he went down the hill, leaving behind the Gramma Udgul's awful warehouse, her awful junk, and her various awful creatures. The snowflakes stuck to his face. He frequently had to bat his eyelashes or blow to keep them off his lips. They were delicate. They didn't melt. Under his soles, the snow groaned. During the daytime lull, the wind had crystallized a crust that now hid several centimeters deep, and every so often something fragile gave way under the weight of his body. When the slope increased, the ice resisted, and then he slipped. As he didn't have gloves, he kept his hands in his pockets, and instead of using his arms to balance, he slowed down so as not to fall over. The light became increasingly gray. A lone crow came out of nowhere several meters from him, cawed, and swiftly disappeared off to his left, doubtless to take shelter in the forest that was already invisible, drowned in the falling night and the snow.

The afternoon was at its end. He was in a rush to get to the village. The main road stretched out, covered in a uniform layer, very white and perfectly blank. Nobody had trampled it for hours. To the left and the right, the first structures of the Radiant Terminus kolkhoz were slowly taking on rounded and softened shapes, lacking all angles. The rest of the Levanidovo was phantasmagorical. The forest encircling the village was no longer discernible.

What's your plan, Kronauer, you sham soldier? he suddenly wondered. What were you planning to do, you crummy fighter, actually kill Solovyei? And how would you do it, and why? And what are you going to do if you don't succeed? . . . And who will you leave with, if you don't fail? . . . For where? With Myriam Umarik and Barguzin, the model couple, a nymphomaniac and a dying man? With Samiya Schmidt and her anti-male books, if she's still alive? With that ice princess Hannko Vogulian? . . . Where would you go? What would you do? . . . Did you think about that? . . .

• Just when he came to the Pioneers' House, a gust of wind lifted the snow off the road and blinded him. He covered his face with the crook of his arm. Without any gloves, his hands were covered in frost. He stopped walking. Until that moment, the snow had fallen mostly vertically and silently. Well, that's the final straw, when the wind's mixed in, he thought. The snow beat against his coat, crackled against his elbow, on top of his head. An icy crust grew between the brim of his shapka and his eyebrows. Several crystals melted on his tongue, unleashing the flavors of winter.

The snow whistled.

The day ended, the road was already dark.

He hunched forward and kept walking. He had put his hands back in his coat pockets and squinted against the pins and needles that the aggressive snowflakes, the half-snowflakes, the miniscule needles inflicted upon his face. His eyelids were nearly shut and he went about fifty meters without seeing anything, then, just as he was about to bump into the fire hydrant in front of Myriam Umarik's house, he swerved and turned toward the Soviet. Forty paces still separated him from the columns and front steps. He crossed the distance thinking about nothing except the cold against his cheeks and the gusts of wind attacking him treacherously, sometimes head-on, sometimes sidelong, trying to knock him off balance or make him change direction. Forty paces, then twelve or fifteen. Without stopping, he went up the steps that disappeared beneath an immaculate layer and pushed open the front door.

The hall was lit only by the poor light coming from the street. Kronauer didn't give any thought to the illumination and right away he stamped and scrubbed his boots against the wall so as not to keep the slippery mass stuck beneath his soles. He couldn't let himself slip on the tiles if the battle against Solovyei took place here and now. Once he was sure he couldn't slip and fall easily, he shut the door behind him. The door banged, the whistling stopped. After the noise of the wind, the sudden silence enveloped him.

He had only been inside once, to inscribe his name in the kolkhoz registers as a temporary resident. Although he knew nothing about the rest of Solovyei's actual residence—the part of the building where he of course had never set foot—he was familiar, more or less, with what seemed to be the administrative section. Outside a side hallway that led to Solovyei's place, there were two padded doors opening onto offices, and the entrance to a storeroom where the liquidators had once set aside smaller irradiated materials, and where even now they kept sensitive objects that had to be categorized before being added to the Gramma Udgul's disgusting piles. Kronauer crossed the hall and, just on the off chance, he tried opening the storeroom door. It wasn't locked.

He went in.

His fingers reached the switch and turned on the ceiling light.

• As if fate had decided to make everything very simple for him right now, at the end of the room stood a gun rack that was missing its lock; it contained two hunting guns and three weapons of war. He took out a Simonov rifle from the First Soviet Union, and an SKS with a scratched handle, but which didn't look too outdated. The cartridges and clips lay in a jumbled pile next to the rack. Without wasting any time he took out a clip and loaded it into the rifle, and then a second one that he put in a pocket. Then he told himself that perhaps he could take a third one and he was about to rummage again in the box of munitions when he heard a noise in the hall. Someone was coming, quite slowly. Trained in the military, Kronauer loaded a preliminary cartridge into the chamber and aimed the rifle barrel at the door. At that moment, an imposing form planted itself on the threshold of the room. The form had a head covered with a travel bag. It didn't seem perturbed by the threat aimed at it and its first act was to turn off the ceiling light, as if following a memo about conserving energy, or as if it preferred the dialogue or confrontation to take place in a thick darkness.

Something twisted in Kronauer's gut. Dread, uncertainty. The darkness had come too quickly. He hadn't had the time to convince himself that this apparition was indeed Solovyei. His adversary's head was hidden beneath some sort of semi-rigid cover, large and invertebrate enough to suggest more a suitcase than a grotesque carnival mask. Two eye-holes had been punched in this vaguely rectangular, tanned-leather case, but in the weak light from the street Kronauer wasn't able to make out its eyes, and certainly not the wild-animal blaze characteristic of Solovyei. Maybe the kolkhoz president had chosen this absurd get-up to hide the wound that Samiya Schmidt had inflicted upon him the previous night? A metal bar had passed through his skull from the right eye to the left ear. Maybe the mask served to protect a massive bandage or a hideous wound? What if, behind the leather, was a face that bore no relationship to Solovyei's, an unknown face? The one standing on the storeroom threshold didn't have a definite height, because the shapeless bag made him taller. As for his size, it couldn't really be assessed, because he was wrapped in a heavy dog-fur coat, a mantle Kronauer hadn't ever noticed on anybody in the Levanidovo. Beneath this mass of pelt, practically anybody in the village could have appeared as imposing as Solovyei.

A heavy silence remained after the noise of the switch being flipped. The two protagonists didn't challenge each other; they seemed to be waiting. The dog-fur coat filled a sizable part of the doorframe and

didn't shrink beneath Kronauer's threat. Kronauer had pointed his rifle
at it and didn't lower his weapon.

In the street there were audible gusts of wind sprinkling snow on
the windows of the hall.

The empty hall.

The shadows of the evening and the storm had annulled all color,
reducing the confrontation to a black-and-white image.

A form frozen in front of the door, half-human, half-animal, topped
with a travel bag that gave him a wild and unnerving look as if it had
come out of a collection of surrealist collages.

The Simonov rifle in Kronauer's hands. A China-made SKS, maybe
specifically the model the Chinese also called Type 56, or maybe not.

The silence between the gusts of wind.

The mild scent of industrial grease coming off the rifle.

The scents of staleness, of cardboard, and radioactive Bakelite floating in the storeroom.

At that point, the mysterious form sighed, a powerful beast's breath.
Then, under cover of the leather, a mouth began to produce a whispered hum that had something religious in its basic musicality. The
hall's emptiness amplified it enough for the words to be distinct. For
two seconds, maybe three, Kronauer thought it was a curse from a
deranged spirit, and then . . .

Kronauer no longer had any hair, but, if he still had any, it would
have stood up on end. Beneath the cotton lining of his shapka, the
skin of his scalp contracted.

—What's your plan, Kronauer, you sham soldier? the masked form
whispered.

Word for word what he had thought at the start of the main road,
right when he had hesitated beneath the gusting wind.

—What were you planning to do, you crummy fighter, actually
kill Solovyei? And how would you do it, and why? And what are you
going to do if you don't succeed? . . . And who will you leave with, if
you don't fail? . . . For where? With Myriam Umarik and Barguzin,

the model couple, a nymphomaniac and a dying man? With Samiya Schmidt and her anti-male books, if she's still alive? With that ice princess Hannko Vogulian? . . . Where would you go? What would you do? . . . Did you think about that? . . .

The voice was deformed by the thick leather membrane it had to pass through, and it reproduced perfectly the questions Kronauer had formulated on the street. It sounds like my voice, he thought despondently. Not completely, but it sounds like it. But no, he thought, I'm not the one talking.

The masked creature modulated and interrupted his speech, as if it was remembering the rough outlines of a song rather than anxious reflections, and certainly as if it didn't attach any importance to the text it was speaking. When it had finished its recitation, it repeated it completely, but this time raising its tone and scattering whining or mocking notes throughout the sentences. The result was atrocious. Then it was quiet.

This could only have been a sleight of hand by this dirty magician, Kronauer thought. It's his way of doing things. A recording through a membrane and, when it ends, he goes over it again. And even if it's not him hiding beneath this disguise, it's clearly one of his creatures.

He held his rifle steadily and his index finger was ready to pull the trigger, but, as he still had his doubts about the target, he waited a little longer.

He knew that, if the gun went off, the bullet would go right into the other's torso.

There's no point in holding off, he thought.

Do it, he thought. Either way I'm screwed.

And he fired.

• The other form took the shot and slumped forward as if he had just been hit in the stomach with a sandbag rather than a bullet, then he stepped back and crept to the left and only then did he begin to emit squeaks that didn't resemble screams of pain, but rather grotesque groans like angry clowns in circus performances. The moans echoed in the hall and Kronauer, galvanized by an adrenaline rush, sped toward the door, intent on seeing the wounded thing's status and, if needed, to finish it off. The floor of the storeroom was covered, it was dark, and he lost time stumbling over boxes containing television or computer screens. His heart beat a fast rhythm, his temples were swollen and pulsating. When he came out into the hall, the wounded thing was making its way outside. It had swiftly crossed the hall, opened the door, and was already disappearing outside.

There wasn't any trace of blood on the tile floor.

I got him, Kronauer thought. But the bleeding hasn't gone on long enough to soak his clothes. Soon it'll make its way down his stomach and his legs.

He was a little annoyed to see that his victim was stable enough to escape the building.

But that was a deadly blow, he thought. It went right through his stomach. He'll die in the street.

He crossed the hall as well, almost running as the murderous excitement of the hunt caught hold of him, and he wanted more than anything to be sure that he hadn't missed his mark. He wanted to see his prey lying in the snow, its coat open on a gaping wound, he wanted to walk up to it, lean over it, hear its death-rattles, and pull off its filthy head cover.

• In the main road, day was nothing more than a memory. The last gleams of light reflected off the ground. Kronauer's gaze swept the area and saw nothing. The snow kept falling with the same intensity as before. The wind blew intermittently, without any fixed direction, in violent gusts followed by unforeseen calm.

Where'd it go? Kronauer wondered.

On the steps, he only saw the footprints he had left right before going into the Soviet building. Nobody had gone down the steps recently. If the wounded thing wasn't a ghost, it still had to be on the threshold.

Tense, ready to fire a second time, Kronauer inspected the esplanade, looked behind the columns decorating the façade. There was no possible hiding place and the snow was unbroken.

Once again, Kronauer felt the skin on his scalp contracting in fear beneath his shapka. He crouched down and carefully scrutinized the traces on the ground. Nobody, aside from himself, had trod on the steps. The adrenaline that had propelled him outside, which had driven him forward like a predator sure of his deed, was already so diluted that it no longer had any effect. He felt his legs shaking nervously.

Solovyei, he thought. Don't think I'm impressed by your wizardry. Your appearances, your disappearances—don't imagine for one second that it has an effect on me. It's just smoke and mirrors. I'm not fooled.

But the backs of his legs and his calves showed clear signs of weakness and he leaned against one of the columns. He had goose bumps.

The wind, which had relented, now increased and whirled around him. The snowflakes hurtled onto his eyelids, agglomerations of stars. He also felt them pounding on his hands. He didn't have icy fingers yet, but he knew that in a few moments he would no longer be able to count on them to pull the trigger at the right moment. He hoisted his rifle over his shoulder and dug his hands into his pockets.

It was night. The Levanidovo's streetlamps didn't light up, whether because Samiya Schmidt had destroyed the public lighting the previous night, or because Solovyei had deliberately turned them off in order to have an advantage in the darkness. The village seemed dead. Nobody had come down the hill after the work day at the warehouse. The kolkhozniks, the back-up workers recruited from the hereafter, and Solovyei's daughters stayed up there, in the warmth, with ionizing rays and the Gramma Udgul. Maybe they had considered it wise not to venture just then into the snowstorm, or rather, predicting the bouts of violence in the village, they had decided to wait until calm was restored. They must be up there, getting ready to spend a night by the well, Kronauer thought.

He had the impression of being all alone in the heart of the Levanidovo, for a duel with Solovyei and its first round finished just now in an unintelligible way. Unintelligible and unnerving.

He scanned the street, which the natural brightness of the snow allowed him to see. Shades in the shadows. Dark masses. Incessantly moving ridges, whirling or vertical. Clear spaces that sheer habit forced him to say were white.

Not a window was lit.

The village disappeared.

The snow whistled in gusts that whipped across his face.

When the wind increased, the flakes hit the Soviet's columns with a flurry of sharp, almost metallic noises.

Nothing living appeared.

I'm going to wait here one moment, he thought. Watch what happens and think about what I should do.

The snow beat against his eyelids, his mouth. He shook the cotton strip that covered his ears and wiped the belt holding his rifle on his shoulder. He quickly put his icy hand back in his coat.

Not worth it if I end up with joints frozen solid, he thought.

• He pulled away from the column he'd been leaning against, and he went down the stairs, then began to walk against the wind for about twenty meters. The street was dark, but there were enough landmarks for him to walk straight. The snow and the wind kept pushing him around. He went to Hannko Vogulian's house and he tried to open the door. Contrary to what had practically been a rule in the village, it was locked. He leaned against it and aimed his weapon at the Soviet. If someone had come out at that moment, he would have shot regardless of the target or its resemblance or lack thereof to the president of the kolkhoz. He stayed there for a minute, plagued by freezing gusts, with the ice crystals clinking on his fur coat, his shapka, his shapka's earflaps. He held his rifle for a steady, intuitive shot, enough to hit any creature that might appear on the steps of the Soviet. But nobody came out. Without hoisting his rifle back over his shoulder, he dusted its upper side, wiped his hands of the layer of snow covering them, and slipped them once more into his pockets to warm them back up.

The snow that had gotten into his pockets melted reluctantly.

He hadn't been able to focus on a specific plan of action.

What if I left for good right now? he thought. What if I went to the forest? There's a hut near the first rows of trees, I can spend the night there, and then . . . Then, good-bye, Radiant Terminus . . .

Of course not, he corrected himself. I have to avenge Vassilissa Marachvili first. I have to finish off this monster. And besides, I'd have trouble finding that old hut, in the darkness and the wind.

Then he thought of Vassilissa Marachvili again. He forced himself to dredge up images of his short time with her. The images were poor, repetitive, and lifeless. A smiling, timeless face, always turned toward him at the same angle. Her body outstretched in the grasses at the moment he'd left her. A kiss at twilight, behind Ilyushenko's back, her lips pressed against his, hands wrapped around his back, but, ultimately, they were anonymous sensations, as those he'd experienced with other girls. He had to admit that the attachment he felt for her was now more abstract than actual. Really, only Irina Echenguyen was permanently etched in his memory, and behind the shock he'd felt when he'd discovered Vassilissa Marachvili's body, a body that had been soiled magically, worked over magically by Solovyei to restore life or quasi-life, beyond the disgust and rage this discovery had provoked in him, he realized that his desire to kill the president of the kolkhoz had murkier roots.

Not worth nitpicking, Kronauer, he said soundlessly, half-opening his lips to blow on the flakes that had settled there, you also want to gun down Solovyei the alpha male, because it's the elder who's dominating the Radiant Terminus pack. That's a reason from the Mesozoic or Cenozoic eras. That's from the night of time and for you it's not honorable.

His mouth barely moved. He chewed as many flakes as words and, at the end of each clause, he sighed.

There's some cock's language behind all this, he kept thinking silently. You can't bear that the kolkhozniks circle around their president like planets around their sun, you really blame those three girls for having been accomplices to their father while you came and went in the Levanidovo like an idiot. You want to punish Solovyei for the abominations that Vassilissa Marachvili had to suffer. You have a gun and you want to shoot anything that moves. But, beneath all that, beneath the awful sludge of murder and vengeance, there's your spasms of a frustrated male machine, there are hundreds of millions of years of the animal cock that order your actions and cock's gestures and your cock's thoughts. And more than anything, that's what there is.

• At that moment in his speech it seemed that someone was coming down the main street, down the middle, up by the Pioneers' House.

It was a quiet spot between the gusts, and the snow fell straight down. It was dense and black, in less and less airy snowflakes, covering every sight in a thick and very, very dark gray curtain.

The form Kronauer had imagined seeing walking from the Pioneers' House disappeared in the darkness and then reappeared, still moving, but without having truly progressed. In reality, despite shaking its arms and wriggling its waist, it was buried in the snow to its knees and was at a standstill. It appeared to be moving. It appeared to be theatrically and grotesquely moving. The massive black coat that protected it prevented any clear determination of whether it was male or female. Its face was hidden beneath a scarf and on its head was a gigantic hat, a sort of incredibly thick Turkmen astrakhan hat with unreasonably long fur, almost as voluminous as the travel bag used as a mask for Solovyei's first creature. It called to mind a blazing sphere that didn't blaze, a burned-out sun flinging in every direction not rays, but its long frozen tentacles.

Kronauer took aim. The black coat was fifty or sixty meters away. He didn't know his rifle well and it wasn't a sniper weapon, but he felt that the bullet would fly toward its goal and hit hard, right in the torso. What if it was one of Solovyei's daughters? he suddenly thought. What if it was Myriam Umarik?

The other's wriggling certainly did remind him of the voluptuous undulations that often shook Myriam Umarik's belly and rear. But the coat erased all bodily shape, the snow blurred the image, the night prevented all certainty. At this distance and in the darkness, Kronauer was ready to shoot at someone whose identity and intentions he couldn't be sure of.

I can't do that, he told himself. That doesn't make any sense.

The black coat in his line of sight had stopped moving. It was now a black stack topped with a sort of black, burned-out star. It was stuck in the snow, between the Pioneers' House and the communist cooperative. Its immobility made a shot aimed at it even more absurd.

On Petrification Considered as a System of Defense, he remembered. A post-exotic work that had been republished at the time he'd met Irina Echenguyen, and which had provoked controversy and several arrests. On pretext of being humorous, the book flirted with several counterrevolutionary positions. Irina Echenguyen hadn't finished it and had criticized it harshly.

He thought furtively of Irina Echenguyen, trying not to remember her unhappy end, then, his finger curled around the trigger, he went back to scrutinizing the petrified form. He stayed there for half a minute, still certain that the tiny movement of his finger on the trigger could send a warhead toward his target and it would land dead-center. The wind hadn't picked up. The snow hailed down on the collar of his coat, on his arms, on the Simonov's breech. At the other end of the bullet's possible trajectory, the black coat was in the middle of the road and, powdered bit by bit with ice, it began to whiten in the darkness.

Kronauer lowered his weapon. He had the idea of shooting at several meters in front of the immobile form, in order to see its reaction and make a decision on the fate that awaited it, but when he started moving and shifting his line of sight, his index finger pressed impatiently on the trigger and the shot went off. The explosion deafened him, he shut his eyes. He opened them immediately, but at that exact moment he saw a light at the edge of his field of vision. A burst of light on his left. Without having taken the time to see if the black fur coat had been hit or not, he turned his head toward the Soviet.

Someone had just appeared on the doorstep, aiming the weak beam of a flashlight at the steps as if to examine Kronauer's footsteps engraved in the snow. Thousands of snowflakes could be seen speeding by in the faint yellow cone that the light projected. The person holding the flashlight was dressed in a dog-fur or wolf-fur coat, and on its shoulders, enveloping and hiding its head, it bore a sort of extravagantly proportioned leather handbag.

Kronauer quickly shifted the direction of his rifle, aimed at the half-suitcase occupying the top of his adversary, and shot. The other gave a sharp squeak, turned off its flashlight, and disappeared back into the Soviet. For eight or ten seconds, there came a string of groans that seemed insincere and strange. The screams echoed powerfully in the hall. Then everything went quiet.

At that moment, the wind picked up.

The snow slapped Kronauer; he suddenly realized that he had started to breathe as if after a violent effort.

The street whirled.

The wind began to whoop around the Levanidovo. Masses of ice burst around Kronauer, on all the vertical surfaces beside him and on his coat.

He was able to see less and less. By the Pioneers' House, if the black coat was still in the same place, it couldn't be seen any longer.

The night promised to be a long one.

• His rifle pointed straight ahead, Kronauer crossed the road and went to the Soviet. The light was meager. The wind threw screaming bursts of snow on him and pushed him violently to the side, without really knocking him over, but forcing him to weave. The chill bit into the tops of his hands. His right finger, which wavered between the trigger guard and the trigger itself, was about to lose its ability to feel. He moved it and pressed it against the wood carcass so as not to risk an accidental shot. The wood was as icy as the metal. Before going up the steps, he looked all around. The snow beat on his eyelids and, past the first few meters, he couldn't make out anything but gray whistling. In the darkness he, too, had become an uninterpretable, half-animal, dangerous form.

He went up the steps carefully, more out of fear of slipping than out of any worry of an assault from the shadows. All sorts of attacks were possible—a gunshot, a knife stab, an ax blow, hand-to-hand combat with an adversary weighing twice as much as he did, who would immediately rip away his rifle as well as half his hand. All sorts of attacks. However, in the current confrontation, he still saw himself more as hunter than hunted. He paid attention to the ground, but he was certain that things were going well. The ice under the thin layer of snow was threatening. It was of a good thickness and wouldn't shatter when he set his foot on it.

Without skidding and without incident, he entered the shadowy space of the hall and shut the door behind him. The blizzard's infrequent groans could still be heard, but so much more weakly that instead of counteracting they underlined the silence that reigned on the ground floor and throughout the entire building.

On the lookout, Kronauer stayed immobile for a long while by the door. At least a full minute. His index finger was in place again to pull the trigger. He tried to catch a movement or breath nearby or far off in the building, but he couldn't catch anything. After this bout of vigilance, he brushed the bulk of the snow he'd carried off his body and his weapon and, as he'd already done earlier, he shook his boots and kicked them against the wall. The noise reverberated in the hall's emptiness. He didn't take any care to be discreet. He knew that his entrance couldn't have gone unnoticed and that his adversary, if he was still in the area and watching him from the shadows, knew his position down to the centimeter.

In order to hear what was around him better, he had untied the string that kept his shapka's earflaps folded over his cheeks. Wherever he was hidden, his adversary didn't make himself shown. Paradoxically, the light in the hall was better than on the street. The natural brightness of the snow, here, wasn't thwarted by whirlwinds. It filtered weakly through the windows, but it was enough for Kronauer to get his bearings and distinguish the whitewashed walls from the black openings that faced him: the hallway leading to Solovyei's apartments, the padded doors that opened onto offices, the entrance to the storeroom. He waited another few minutes for his fingers to warm up, for the snow on his weapon to melt, and for his eyes to acclimatize completely to the darkness. Then, although he hadn't noticed any suspicious noise in front of him, he moved. As he walked with his rifle sometimes pointed toward the hallway, sometimes toward the various ground-floor doors, he went toward the storeroom. He hadn't had the time, earlier, to take a third clip, and he wanted to have a good ammunition reserve. It was also a place he now knew and which, for this reason, seemed safer than elsewhere. He decided to go in, find new clips, wait a little, and think.

•   When he stepped on the threshold of the storeroom, a brutal sensation of déjà vu paralyzed him. I've already experienced this, he thought, as anxiety mounted. He stood in the doorway, firmly planted, massive as a bear and threatening the shadow in front of him. I've already stood like this on this threshold, he was thinking. He paused for a second, and then he regained the use of his muscles. He got a grip on himself. Without letting go of his rifle, he reached with his left hand toward the light switch. The switch produced a familiar noise of mechanical tumbling, but the ceiling light reacted with a dry click along with a flash that blinded Kronauer and didn't illuminate anything. The bulb had burned out. For a second, the white and then red imprint of the incandescent filament stayed on Kronauer's retinas, and, in front of him, he only had an image of total, undifferentiated blackness. It would be difficult to find the box with the cartridges, he groused, half to himself, half whispering. It's too messy in there to find good cartridges just by feeling, he continued. His mouth moved, a weak moaning sound escaped. Then, out of some inexplicable desire to be heard or to hear himself, he began whispering distinctly, like a drunk person or a shaman warming up before a prayer.

—What are you imagining, Kronauer? he whispered. You want cartridges? . . . And who are you thinking of fighting against, you poor idiot? . . . You want to resist a siege? . . . Have you planned a massacre? . . . Do you have a plan, Kronauer, you sham soldier? . . .

As he formulated this last question, something heavy slammed into his torso, stealing his breath and forcing him to stagger forward. An indefinite mass, come out of the depths, had fallen upon him and hit him between the sternum and the waist. The fur and leather of his coat had partially absorbed the shock. He bent down and stepped back beneath the blow. Whatever had jostled him was sizable, contorted, and soft. He immediately rejected the possibility of a bullet shot from a weapon he hadn't heard go off. The silence in the storeroom was resounding. It was more like a sand bag or a dead animal that had flown at him at full speed. A magical projectile or a dirty trick invented by Solovyei, he thought, then, as he was losing his balance, he took a second step backward.

He went back another meter, slipping on the tiles. He had groaned in surprise and pain and, now he was quiet. The sand bag or the corpse that had been thrown at him had bounced somewhere within the shadows and was now heavy and unmoving, doubtless across the threshold. A big dog or human corpse, he thought.

In the storeroom, nobody had given any sign of life. But it came from there, he thought. He stood up slowly. He still had in his stomach a feeling of a brutal weight. A dead animal, a big dog or a wolf, he thought. That's what was thrown at me. Or someone's body.

But that doesn't make sense, he thought. He tried not to picture what had happened. Fear grew in his gut and he wanted to deny it completely.

Now he was in an upright position. Under his right sole, a small lump of ice had gotten stuck and caused his boot to slip to the side when he put his weight on it. His torso and his hips were aching. What I know is that I was attacked, he thought. He aimed the SKS at the depths of the storeroom and he shot twice. The bullets flew into the scrap metal, ricocheted. Something fell, a metal box, its contents scattered quickly, maybe coins or medals, then nothing. In the hall, the echoes of the detonation bounced from angle to angle with evident joy and diminished his bad feeling. The racket was considerable. Then the gunfire unquestionably belonged to the past and now Kronauer felt his heart beating between his sides and his throat.

He was currently standing within the black doorframe of the storeroom, in the center of a swirl of hot grease and powder. And, as no sign of life or death came from the darkness, he didn't know what to do in the face of the shadows, in the face of consecutive magic spells, and in the face of the fear he kept pushing away but which came back again and again.

The fear. It grew, it disappeared, he drove it away. But it was there.

• He ruled out entering the storeroom. No way to know if the two randomly released bullets had hit whoever was hiding in the room— the one who was lurking there, completely immobile and silent, doubtless neither wounded nor dead, holding his breath and waiting for the best moment to counter-attack. The president of the kolkhoz, or one of the servile creatures surrounding him in his hideous poems. In any case, someone who had enough magical powers to send flying a human or semi-human or animal corpse or maybe just a bag filled with organs and meat. Maybe, Kronauer thought, he's planning for me to die of fear. He was ready to fire again and he focused on detecting any distant sound or movement. But he only detected absence.

He crossed the hall backward, constantly watching the black entrance of the storeroom. The light was meager but, once he felt a wall he could lean on against his back, he considered it enough to survey the theater of operations and he positioned himself in a corner. He was away from the windows. If traces of light beams came from outside, none would land directly on him. He felt like he had found a spot hard for a menacing gaze to apprehend. It was an absurd feeling, especially considering the adversary he was up against. But he had that feeling. The SKS in firing position, he moved his line of sight onto the storeroom entrance at moments, or onto the hallway entrance leading to Solovyei's rooms, or the door leading to the street.

As he kept moving his rifle, he wasn't discreet at all, and, having acknowledged that in any case he would be detected by the enemy, he allowed himself to move a little to warm up. He was no longer exposed to the glacial wind, and the coat Hannko Vogulian had selected for him was warm, his fur-lined boots protected him from the cold seeping out of the floor, but anxiety had weakened his body and he was still shivering. His hands didn't warm up. He breathed on them and he shook himself a bit to get his blood flowing again. His stomach still had the sensation of having made contact with this sizable mass that had been thrown at him from the darkness and the more he thought about it, the more he was certain that something vile had hit his stomach. A corpse or a huge bundle filled with grease and meat, he repeated as he tapped his feet on the tiles, as much to increase the circulation through his legs as to make noise and distract his body from the disgust and fear infecting it.

When he pointed his rifle at the storeroom, he forced himself to scrutinize the thick shadows and glimpse this mass that, after having jostled him violently, had fallen on the threshold. It should have been just beyond the entrance or on the tiles, close to the door. But the tiles seemed bare of all presence. But I'm sure I haven't been dreaming, he thought. It hit me sideways up here, it was heavy, it flew toward me at full speed and then I heard it fall on the ground. It has to be slumped over the threshold. Or it crawled back without my noticing. It crawled back, it moved without making any noise, it went back where it came from.

I should have shot at it right then, he scolded himself.

Who knows if it'll throw itself at me again before I can do something to it, he thought. As fast or even faster than the first time. As fast as a bullet.

He stayed calm for several minutes. He aimed at the storeroom entrance, a black-on-black rectangle. A fatal shot could also come from there and, if it was well-aimed, he would be unable to respond. The idea of taking a bullet didn't bother him. Death wasn't one of his wishes, but he accepted the prospect, partly because he was a soldier and partly because it would be a quick way of leaving the Levanidovo and its deleterious atmosphere, its interregnums and its oneiric traps. And at least that would put an end to this hunting amok, this anger amok, and this fear amok, and all that went with it—total regression to primitive hunting, intelligence sidelined for instincts, and, especially, deep down, an irrepressible desire to kill, to slaughter, and to hurt, even if he couldn't remember anymore what had brought about this nightmare.

I don't even know anymore whether or not I've swerved away from Marxist principles, he thought. Then he didn't think anymore.

Half an hour went by. Kronauer started shifting around again. Sometimes he stood, sometimes he squatted. Most of the time, he pointed his SKS at the storeroom's opening, but nothing moved and he had no reason to fire.

• A preternatural peace reigned in the Soviet. Aside from a few gestures Kronauer made, there was no longer any movement. Only the noises from outside filled the space. The noises came from outside and from darkness.

The blizzard's assaults in the street.

The sheets of snow scattering violently against the windows.

The gusts of wind successively filling the street.

And, within the walls, nothing to report.

Waiting. Interminable watching. Sometimes a heavy breath, a worried hiccup Kronauer couldn't hold back.

Darkness. A dark wait. The minutes went by, each one more oppressive than the last. Am I fighting or sleeping? Kronauer thought. A dark uncertainty.

Another half an hour passed.

Unable to bear it any longer, Kronauer energetically crossed the hall, stood at the entrance to the storeroom, and shot three bullets in a row, aiming at the directions where he thought someone could be lying or standing. The bullets hit hard obstacles, walls. He heard metal things flying off and falling with a racket to the floor. Clearly no living or dead adversary made of meat and grease had received a projectile. The empty cartridge cases bounced on the tiles by Kronauer's feet. He let the detonation's echoes, the gunpowder smell fade away. The short seconds of the fusillade stretched out a bit and then dissipated. They hadn't come to anything. Kronauer had hoped for a scream, a sigh, or at least the sound of steel piercing an enemy body. But nothing of the sort came. He didn't move his rifle, he stood unmoving in front of the door, as if puzzled by the absence of any result of his offensive, or maybe also meditating before a hail of bullets came, because he knew he was overwhelmingly exposed to any return fire. He wanted to rock like a bear confronted by some danger, or like a madman confronted by himself, but he held back. In a flash, he wondered if he shouldn't say something, as much to speak to the threats surrounding him, which were becoming less and less human, as to hear some sign of life from himself. Then the idea faded away. The rest of his thoughts were confused. He stayed there for a minute, perhaps two, frozen and indecisive. Then, since nothing had happened, he left.

• He went past the padded doors that opened onto the administrative rooms and, after a last look around the empty hall, he went into the hallway leading to Solovyei's private domain. Now he had gone into a part of the building he didn't know, and he went slowly. For some unknown and unclear reason, he felt that he wouldn't encounter any traps on this floor, which didn't prevent him from being ready to shoot at the slightest shift in the thick darkness, at the least impression of a suspicious presence. He went a meter and a half into the hallway, then two meters. The floor was parquet, the boards groaned. The noise announced his position at every moment. He suddenly hunched down and froze. What good is curling up going to do you, Kronauer? he thought. You're making too much noise, even your coat is whispering when it rubs against the floor. You're drawing attention to yourself. Is that what you want? . . . You want a bastard to gun you down before you've had time to clean out Radiant Terminus?

After several moments of thinking, he decided that the darkness put him at a disadvantage and that he had nothing to lose by trying to turn on the lights. He got back up and went back to the beginning of the hallway. The parquet creaked violently beneath him. All while aiming his weapon at the darkness, he now walked with his left hand along the wall. It didn't take him long to feel the protruding shape of a light switch. He immediately flicked it. The president of the kolkhoz hadn't thought to cut off the power, or he hadn't considered it necessary. Right away, Kronauer found himself beneath three ceiling lights that illuminated the full length of the corridor. The corridor was empty. There wasn't anybody to shoot at.

The décor didn't seem particularly special, and after the action of the previous hours, and beneath this strong light, it was astonishingly banal. Everything was painted in bright colors, light yellow, administrative green. The air smelled of warm radiators and varnish. On Kronauer's right, a set of stairs led up. Kronauer aimed his SKS at the steps and then lined it up with the hallway. He was certain that it was useless to go up higher. A certainty without any basis, but a firm one. At the far end was a set of stairs that led down. It's that way, he thought. He had practically no reason, these scrawny and meager phrases had simply occurred to him.

Two rooms opened onto the hallway. These were soulless spots, with office furniture, mismatched or damaged chairs. Waiting rooms rather than living rooms or bedrooms. In the first one there was a couch and a low table on which a shattered carafe and glasses black with dust waited pitifully. His rifle pointed forward, Kronauer kicked the door, turned on the light, swept his eyes over the space, then he went back into the hallway. In this way he respected the theater of commando intervention in confined environments. Somehow he was still convinced that Solovyei wasn't hiding there, that Solovyei was waiting for him somewhere, in the basement, and he was only delaying the moment when he would have to go underground to find his target. Once he had come out of the second room, he knew that he couldn't postpone the next scene any longer. He would have to go down the stairs at the end of the hallway.

• He didn't count the steps. There were perhaps twenty or twenty-five. When he reached the last one, he was warned by a noise from above. In the doorframe appeared a silhouette, whose head was hidden by a plastic barrel in which two holes had been punched to see. This receptacle had been cut out to be carried on its shoulders, and so it more or less resembled a monstrously proportioned cosmonaut's helmet. In contrast, and despite being enlarged and inflated by a foxtail coat, the intruder's body seemed to be modestly sized.

Maybe it's a woman, Kronauer thought.

Sure, maybe a woman, but, whoever this is, it's one of Solovyei's creations, he finished.

He aimed the rifle toward the hallway and fired. A first bullet doubtless too high and, immediately, a second bullet that hit home.

Man or woman or something else, the silhouette jumped back and, once out of sight, it began to let out glum and inarticulate, sharp screams of pain, despair, or fury.

Kronauer was glad not to have missed his mark. The screams astonished him and tore his heart, but the stupid delight of a hunter prevailed, this physical satisfaction that predators felt when killing. There it is, he thought without elaborating.

He looked up for several more seconds. His hands were shaking.

His amok killer's hands, insane hands inflicting death upon every person he met. They shook.

The screams suddenly stopped. He was standing on the last step of the stairs and he felt himself deep inside the frenetic shudder of having killed.

The light up above went out.

Of course it went out, he thought, without any further explanation.

• He went down the last step and he was in the boiler room and, immediately, some of his energy came back. Now he was very close to Solovyei's nest. Now he was making his way into a territory he knew nothing about and where any attack against him might be fatal. It would be hard to protect himself, he thought. The place was illuminated and, despite the maze of tubes, cables, pipes, and machines, it seemed to provide few hiding places. Kronauer gritted his teeth, took several steps, and stood behind a cistern set on cinder blocks. At least this way he would avoid a shot to his face, and it was also a good vantage point for familiarizing himself with the space where the battle might now take place.

Beyond the installations that stretched out exuberantly over every surface of the basement, there were entrances to tunnels. Kronauer saw them and didn't have any intention of venturing into them. You have no idea at all what's in these tunnels, he thought. Don't get in there, it'll be the end of you at the first curve. He had never been warned of such a subterranean network which, as was known, allowed the villagers to circulate when too-low temperatures and walls of snow otherwise prevented it. They never told me about anything like this, he thought. Just like with Vassilissa Marachvili, they kept me out of the loop. They didn't share any details about anything. Rage filled him again. He swore under his breath against the Levanidovo's inhabitants, against Solovyei, curses in Russian and in camp Mongolian, in mass-grave German. They pricked me with their dirty phonograph needles, he moaned, they numbed my intelligence to the bone, they always set things up so I wouldn't think hard or even very much, wouldn't understand their little schemes!

He caught himself. The rifle was shaking again in his hands, this time more out of anxiety than out of murderous excitement. He leaned against the wall. You have to focus, Kronauer, this is war. Don't waste your energy complaining. The enemy may have already aimed their own weapons at you, this isn't the moment to flinch. He whispered several more Mongolian swear words to take heart once again. In a few moments, his trembling had subsided. He had managed to find at least some of the calm needed to attack and to try to kill.

In front of him, for dozens of meters, the complex, disorganized, and absurd conglomeration that the dying engineers had conceived to guarantee the Levanidovo's electrical permanence stretched out. While figuring out the configuration of the place, Kronauer had a thought for these heroes and heroines, these unparalleled technicians sent by the capital to do the impossible and save the population, or at least assure the survivors a minimum of comfort. Our own, he thought. These courageous men and women who didn't hesitate at the moment of sacrifice, who had said good-bye to rest and sleep, with the self-abnegation that had always characterized the partisans, the unrepentant, and the egalitarians pure and simple. In less than three weeks, while their intestines and their cerebellums turned into ashen rags, they had started on the circuits needed for the turbines to turn and the current to improve. Then they had finally separated from their painful bodies, from their nauseating flesh.

Kronauer put an end to this fraternal homage and for the next minute he was completely occupied with military scouting. To get close to the core he would have to breach a complicated lattice of tubes and pipes, go past pumps, cisterns, oil furnaces turned into steam boilers, containers repurposed as maintenance pools, as well as tar-coated doors that opened onto nothing, which were perhaps intended to be confinement spaces but hadn't been finished in time. This compact universe was bogged down with swaths of cables and a multitude of junction boxes that hung and snaked in every direction. The damage Samiya Schmidt had wrought the previous night had added steam leaks or oil and hot-water runoffs along the walls. The cement Kronauer was preparing to walk along was filthy with black streaks. Who knows if this is heavy water, lively water, and deathly water, or tar, he thought. He noticed the surface, which seemed to shine, several bubbles that occasionally increased in size then burst. Who knows, he thought.

• He began to make his way to the core. He didn't know many of the kolkhoz's secrets, but, thanks to the indiscretions of people here and there, he knew that Solovyei had the habit of sleeping or resting in the Soviet's boiler, close to the nuclear core. He had learned that and, a week earlier, he had dreamed that he himself had come into a small nuclear plant, right behind Solovyei and intending to spy on him. Then he had seen Solovyei go into a compartment where tubes filled with rumbling matter reddened, shaking his peasant's lambskin coat and delivering in front of the flames and for the flames an insane, incestuous poem. This dream-image had startled him when he had awoken, but he had forgotten it, and now it came back in full force, blending without much distortion into the real world. Once again he was in a small nuclear plant, on a path that led both to Solovyei and toward a space of radioactive embers, of shadows and magic. If there was a place where the president of the kolkhoz could be hiding, waiting for the wound that Samiya Schmidt had inflicted upon him to heal, it was certainly there.

• The whole basement was bathed in warmth. Behind the mocking shields, the fissile material radiated. The pipes were burning. Some were covered with glints that looked like lines of insects, and, after sizzling for several seconds, disappeared. Glimmers appeared, dimmed by the electrical light, but white, blue, sometimes a shiny jet-black. The concrete walls emitting the oven's vibrations were barely approachable. At the entrance to one of the tunnels, the evacuation tubes aspirated the clouds expelled by turbines and drained them out by the forest, but the gigantic joints just a bit upwind were already exuding steam. The continuous jets of vapor didn't help the temperatures. Beneath his heavy fur coat, Kronauer was now smothered. Sweat rolled down his entire body. On his forehead, he could feel that the levee formed by his shapka's soaked brim was about to break. Drops were already streaming down his temples, oozing toward his eyelids, stinging his eyes. In the spots where he was holding it, his rifle was wet. He wiped his right hand on his coat. Its fur had imprisoned the molten snow. He set his hand back under the trigger guard. It was even damper than before.

• I shot how many times? he asked himself abruptly. How many bullets now?

He tried to count the shots he had taken in the building and on the street, but he lost count and he left the question unanswered. He had come too close to Solovyei's nest to uncock his gun and look at the magazine, or resume his memorization exercises. Nor was this the moment to remove his right hand and rummage in his pocket for the clip he had commandeered from the storeroom. He wasn't very sure that a cartridge was left in his weapon's breech. He hoped there was, but he wasn't completely sure.

Now he went, centimeter by centimeter, along the wall of a concrete cube where the nuclear core the engineers and the heroes had cobbled together was humming. He had reached Solovyei's nest. The wall smelled of carbonized meat, of actinides. Pipes zigzagged over the ground, crossed at every moment with waves of glimmers that went out and then almost immediately came back, like shivers, like a light feather raised by the wind, like a phenomenon connected to life, to living, or some sort of similar death. The glimmers were gray, sometimes orange. When Kronauer set his foot on one of these tubes, the groaning stopped, but he felt like they were going through his body by his bones, and, a second later, the SKS's barrel in turn bristled with small plumes. On the ground were oily puddles, shaken by ripples, unusually shiny. Kronauer avoided them, but when he couldn't do otherwise, he stepped in them with disgust.

Then he made his way toward the entrance to the concrete cube he had just circumvented. He couldn't get to the actual entrance without crossing a partial barricade of tarry cables and burning pipes. So he was facing a hardened mattress, filthy or powdered with soot, which was surrounded with naphtheous water and shadow. An overwhelming smell of Bakelite in fusion meandered through the black space. As Kronauer had both predicted and dreaded, Solovyei was in his nest. He was sitting on the mattress, his legs crossed, his boots thrown thoughtlessly on his bed, making the place just a little dirtier.

For no reason, this insignificant detail shocked Kronauer. Look at that, this brute, he thought suddenly, this animal, he puts his boots where he lies down to sleep.

• The president of the kolkhoz had a horrible head wound. Already on the path to recovery, certainly, thanks to the unguents and lively water that the Gramma Udgul had applied at the end of the previous night, and because Solovyei belonged to a category of creatures who reconstituted themselves quickly no matter the extent of physical damage suffered, but it was still absolutely hideous, this wound. The iron pipe that Samiya Schmidt had buried in his eye was still there. Solovyei had doubtless asked someone to pull it out, or maybe he himself was in charge of doing that, but the pain had hampered the operation and the pipe was sticking more than ever out of his left ear, streaked with lumpy brain matter and bits of bone. On that side, Solovyei's mess of hair was sticky, as if coated in sludge. The space from where the iron pipe had entered to the left ear was nothing more than a pocket of blood-soaked pulp. The kolkhoz president's face had lost its leonine presence and it took effort to see something other than mutilation and suffering. His working eye was shut. He opened it halfway and for a fraction of a second Kronauer felt all the contemptuous malice Solovyei was capable of, all his baleful mocking, and his rage.

On the mattress, there were untied bandages, compresses soaked with brownish liquids, clothes filthy with lumps like cowpats. And a semi-rigid leather bag, which had been reused and cut out to be used as a massive mask.

He took off his mask, Kronauer thought. Then, under the blow of the gaze that Solovyei had shot him just then, he wasn't able to finish whatever it was. I was at war, he thought. Broken faces, I've seen them. It always has an effect.

Yes, he thought sadly. It always has a hell of an effect.

He stood upright in a lake of black liquid.

• Kronauer's rifle pointed right at the upper part of Solovyei's stomach, right where his neck began.

The discreet whirring of turbines.

A disgusting odor of molten Bakelite.

Other odors, of hot metal, of livid plutonium.

Solovyei sitting on a dirty mattress, a homeless person caught in a cave.

Around the mattress, the ground covered with blistering water, thick like ink.

Solovyei's mutilated head.

His right eye suddenly wide open, cruel, golden.

The pipes crossing anarchically in the middle distance of the image, in front, behind, on the sides, forming miniature labyrinths, following the blueprints drawn by schizophrenic plumbers.

A dry sauna heat.

Sometimes short intense glimmers in the boiler room, like magnesium flames.

Flights of sparkles from the soldered joints, from the mattress, from Kronauer's coat and rifle, from Solovyei's wounds.

A door coated in a velvet of small unmoving flames.

Sometimes the lapping of black-black water, getting angry all on its own.

The nuclear hell behind the door.

Kronauer soaked in sweat, blinded by sweat, smelling all around him the scent of his fear.

Every so often, sniffling from Solovyei, then nothing.

Darkness.

Waiting.

• Solovyei didn't move, he just fixed his hypnotic eye on the man threatening him.

Kronauer, positioned to say several words before firing on the other one, thought for several seconds as to what he might say. Nothing came to him, no vengeful declaration, no argument justifying the execution to come. But there has to be something, he thought. No image blazed in front of him, no depiction of the crimes he could have accused the kolkhoz president of. Only with great confusion did he remember the reason he was there, in this basement, with a weapon of war aimed at a silent, wounded man. A woman appeared in his consciousness, but he didn't recognize her, or did, but so poorly that she was merely a conventional shadow. He had forgotten what Vassilissa Marachvili had looked like before, during, and after the manipulations Solovyei had forced her to undergo. He saw Irina Echenguyen in his arms again, happy and young, then dying in the hospital, then dead, massacred. He remembered that someone had recently said to him "I'm with you," certainly a woman, but he wondered if the phrase had been uttered in reality or in a dream. As for remembering the name of this woman who had assured him of her sympathy, and what sort of relationship he'd had with her, he was unable to remember. Maybe it was Irina Echenguyen again, or Vassilissa Marachvili, or one of Solovyei's daughters, the youngest one, who had the guts to pummel Solovyei and bury an iron pipe in his brain. He didn't even try to bring forth the name or the face of this daughter. He was exhausted. The bout of amok violence was reaching its end, and, like a seizure, it began its ebb by replacing his consciousness with a cloudy dough, full of incomplete images and tears. He felt tired, extremely tired. Not worth the trouble to say sentences, he thought. Not worth the trouble to dig through all the mud of your memory, Kronauer, he thought. A horrible fatigue fell upon him. His brain only focused on trifles: his smell of sweat, the dirty mattress, the fate of Marxism-Leninism.

He held onto his weapon. Well, I have nothing to say, he thought. I only have to finish the job.

With that, he pulled the trigger. The firing pin clicked in the void.

—Ah, I thought you were a good soldier, Solovyei remarked in a cheeky voice, distorted by his swollen mouth.

—I used up my clip, Kronauer explained.

He stood sheepishly, dazed, sweaty and hot, his hands numb.

Three seconds went by.

—Look at that, this brute, Solovyei said cruelly. This animal, he puts his boots where he lies down to die.

—What, what are you . . . Kronauer stammered.

He lowered his eyes, and then his head. The soles of his boots were plunged in a lake of black water. Beneath, something burning was trembling. Irradiated cement, or maybe already the indescribable matter one walks on during the forty-nine days after death, when at least one has courage or luck.

—So what, it's just black water, he said.

It was black water, indeed, or oil, and as it had the properties of a mirror, he saw in it his own reflection. He saw, aside from a fur hat, a bestial killer's physiognomy, his lightless gaze, and, almost immediately, a shovel or a spade coming down upon him. Someone had approached him from behind and, without warning, put him where he couldn't hurt anyone.

So there it is, he thought, someone smashed in my skull.

Then he slumped down and lay there where Solovyei had predicted, in the black water.

– 22 –

• While the bullets flew he shifted his powerfully shadowy path and, all the while hopping from ember to ember, he threw lures behind him that resembled him, gave them life and movement thanks to the memories that he drew both from his enemies' memory and from his own black matrices. The lures caught in his stead the arrows and iron projectiles meant for him, and sometimes he gave them a voice to feign pain and anger, sometimes he arranged for them, once hit, to melt or disappear in a great silence that was like an abdication in the face of reality. We watched this from our hiding places, wordlessly we were there like in a bad dream or a bad book. We hadn't been given any sense of subtlety, we were rough-hewn in terms of intelligence. We understood little and our fear didn't diminish. It never ceased to grow, on the contrary, and it spread within us nauseatingly, scraping and mistreating our secret ducts and our oneiric glands. The soldiers, too, were afraid and shot indiscriminately, perhaps aware that they were floundering in foreign spaces they would never leave, or, in a pinch, they would leave, but not alive or dead, without having won. He, on the contrary and as always, took pleasure in this manhunt for himself, which he knew was doomed to fail, and he had fun with it, intervening in the soldiers' souls and constructing episodes of murder where he was the apparent victim, repeating to our disgust, but with delectation, the scenes where he had appreciated the strange sequence of events, driving the soldiers to the edge of the abyss of their stupidity and his nightmare. The heat was intense. He leaned against the burning wall and, suddenly uninterested in the events under way, he sang old prison songs he had learned in his youth and, after a moment, he felt nostalgia for his previous existence, comparing it to the inescapable eternity he had enjoyed ever since his entrance into black space, into our reality, and into many other intermediary spaces he jealously kept the keys to. The fire buzzed alongside him in the form of a basso continuo. He let thirteen more centuries go by, then he began whispering the names of his wives and the countless daughters he had had with them, and who had all helped him not to die of boredom or not to wilt away in his dreams, and then he began to list the names of the numerous camps where he had dragged his rags and his bones, then he went on to chant the identities of the enemies he had decided to punish when the occasion presented itself, in whatever universe they had taken refuge in so as to escape his vengeance. He kept inventing these golem-crows that he sent for observation in the minor worlds of the taiga. Time dripped around him in little drops, making him think of wax or liquid basalt. When the heat was too tremendous, he put on once more his gloves and mask, which was also dripping with lava, then he crouched down as he often did, showing to those who were curious that he wanted more than anything to go back to the ashes. Around him weeks flowed by, then years, then he shook off his muteness, stood back up, and abruptly started, not without sniggering, dictating several long poems. The soldiers were now far away and they were dust. We ourselves had renounced his company and the manna of his speeches, and, dispersed or wandering elsewhere among the dead, we were no longer able to hear him.

part four

TAIGA

narracts

– 23 –

• I woke up later. Much later. I smelled terrible, like waste oil, rotting flesh, urine, world-weariness. Terrible oil, terrible flesh, shooter or shootee's urine, truly terrible weariness. A horrifying smell. I budged a little and the stench intensified. It'll only get worse, I thought. So don't move.

All my joints ached. At the bottom of my rib cage, the pains were fiery. Every heartbeat sent a migrainous wave up my skull. It hit the back of my brain and scattered all over, through my jaw. It broke apart, it dispersed, but, before it had completely gone away, it was replaced by the next one.

I didn't want to open my eyes. Get used to the pain and the smell first, I thought. Accept that banging in your head first. It's flowing past your eye sockets, going from the greasy layer of your eyeballs to the upper half of the vitreous humor, reaching the top of your cheekbones, find a way to bear that. Then you'll open your eyes or vomit or both.

Five minutes had gone by. I hadn't moved a millimeter. I was stretched out by a wall. I could feel unfinished floorboards along my back and beneath me, covered with filth and dried mud. They exuded a smell of earth and wood, which I'd always appreciated even if those were also the smells of coffins. The stench isn't coming from the ground, I thought. It's coming from you.

My eyes were sealed shut by the detritus of tears and blood, and, as I had trouble scrubbing them clean, I gave up. So I must have been crying without realizing it, I thought.

I kept feeling horrible breakers in my skull and I took my time before adding to this backwash the inevitably bewildering images of the place I was in. Of course, I repeated. I must have been crying. Who knows if it was pain or sadness.

Several seconds fell away.

Or shame, I thought.

• So what happened? Before? This night, the days before? Before I slept?

The memories pounded behind my eyes in the same rhythm as the waves of the migraine. Shreds of spumy images. Appeared, disappeared.

I don't remember anything, I thought.

This observation was an exaggeration. But, for the moment, that was where I was.

• The temperature wasn't icy, but I didn't mind that I was wrapped in a coat. Between my body and this mantle there were only indescribable, gray, formless rags like the ones on corpses in mass graves. My body reeked, these cloths gave off whiffs of grime, but the coat was what stank most. The fur had been soaked in grease, despair, and blood, the hairs were stickily clumped together. There were better things to protect against the cold.

I took several deep breaths even if, quite honestly, I had realized that I didn't need or want much air. The mustiness was overwhelming, but the images were gone. Some streaks of memories were replacing them. They flashed haphazardly. A night of hunts, of murders. These facts came in bits and pieces. I had left the Gramma Udgul's warehouse. I went down to the village in the snow. Wind, sharp needles of ice, harsh fall of night. Then and abruptly a sort of funereal dance full of violence and strange opacity. A sort of funereal dance, I thought.

At some point you were carrying a gun, I thought. At some point you were talking with Solovyei. But about what, and what did you do with the rifle, no idea, I thought.

• The cell wasn't anything special in and of itself. A narrow wooden bunk held by two chains, and a hole for pissing that had to lead to a drainpipe outside. Instead of a window, air and light came through a small grille in the door, as well as from the hole for pissing.

So I've been transferred again, I thought.

It would be good if I could open my eyes, I thought. But they're already open, I thought, trying to reason with myself. Otherwise I wouldn't know about the grille, the chains holding these boards, the hole.

Try to open them anyway, I insisted.

For a minute or two, my head had been hurting less. I was still lying on the ground, I was barely moving, I didn't feel like I was breathing, but who knew. New smells were still coming, horrible smells dirtying my nostrils, winding from my coat, from the air outside or from the caves and poorly shut openings of my flesh, including my liver, stomach, spleen, and marrow, the despicable nuances of these inner and outer stenches. It would be better if you opened your eyes now, I thought. Why better? I cut in. Because, lying like this among deleterious gases, you'll end up understanding nothing anymore, fainting again, or depressing yourself. There's nothing special to understand, I objected. I've been transferred. It's already happened to me and it happens to everyone. Well, I thought. It's true that it already happened to you and that it will happen to you one thousand and forty-seven more times, and even ten thousand one hundred and eleven times.

I shrugged. One thousand forty-seven and even ten thousand one hundred and eleven times were numbers that didn't normally come out of my mouth and which more likely belonged to Solovyei's language, to his curses and his threats. All the more reason to open your eyes, I thought, for no reason.

I opened my eyes. I had practically no headache anymore. Around me the darkness was complete. The grille, the hole for pissing, and the boards might have been nearby, but whether my eyelids were raised or I'd let them rest, the darkness was complete. It was complete, heavy, and oily.

So I'm in black oil, I thought. In heavy oil, in heavy-heavy oil, in heavy black oil.

• Shit, I swore in Russian, Tyvan, and camp German, I'm here deep in black oil and it looks like I'll be here for one thousand forty-seven years, or even for ten thousand four hundred and one full years!

− 24 −

• His bloodthirsty frenzy had barely ended when I had one of my henchmen, Münzberg, knock him out, then, once he was already soaked with the black and horrible oils of death, I carried him to the heart of the flames and set him there, making sure he dried out high against the fuel rods and slipping between his bones the magic words necessary for his eternal unhappiness, for the punishment I'd warned him about, and, therefore, to maintain both the mental and physical activity he would have exerted in the real and imaginary worlds where the constant backwash of incantations would push him, would give him some semblance of activity and crush him. After eight hours or so he began to moan again, then thirteen years went by. I had things to do and I barely worried about him, and, although every so often I came to rummage in his soul so as to keep pain and confusion in his memories, I was happier to let him wander endlessly from image to image without his being able to grab onto anything tangible. Most of the time, I left him to Münzberg and my henchmen, as well as of course the cruel spirals of black space. I know that he often complained about little things, neglecting the crux of the matter, unwilling to ponder what the future had in store for him, plunging those he'd known into the same yellowing backwater of idiocy, refusing obstinately to consider the low level of inexistence he'd come to, refusing to see that from now on he would be eternally dead and subject to the whims of nothingness and chance. His lucidity came poorly, in fits and starts. His animalistic stupidity was evident. From a militaristic, ideological, and sexual point of view, he was composed of more or less carbonized scraps and rags that combined haphazardly over his years of sleeplessness and unraveled terribly during his years of sleep. The very mediocre fate of this Kronauer had bothered me from our first meeting, but mostly it was his person I hated. From his appearance in the region he had begun to tiptoe around my wives. Wives or daughters, doesn't matter. Quickly enough, when he was at my mercy, I wrapped him in hides and furs and I increased the stench of the black reactor I had stuck him in. Then, whether I interceded or not, he would have nightmares for at least one thousand forty-seven centuries or lunar half-years. The lights weakened within his skull. Everything in him became muddled. I enjoyed it for a minute, then four hundred and four years went by. The heat didn't diminish, I stayed stuck to the brick all that time, singing and whispering sometimes in one dream, sometimes in another. Münzberg and the others had long since been forgotten beneath the ashes. I stayed for several more decades in complete immobility, then I began whistling so that new henchmen would materialize, and daughters, wives, and marvels would resurge again from the soft pits, the tarry steppes, and the fiery forests. The tunnels around me roared then went quiet. Insects floated between me and the wall like moving embers. I hadn't stopped whistling and fluttering around. Sometimes my feathers caught fire, sometimes not. I stayed by the brick and I was elsewhere, far away. The soldier began to groan again between the fuel rods. Once again I shook him and worked him with a poker. This necessary routine didn't bore me. However, after having watched the hell in his head glow red, I spread my wings and left the place.

– 25 –

• Then, like it or not, a hole of seven centuries.

• The railroad hadn't been in use for seven hundred years and, over the kilometers, the rails had sunk into the earth. Or they had disappeared among the grasses. The wooden crossties had rotted, the ones the workers and the prisoners had made with cement had disintegrated. Occasionally an intact portion of the tracks survived in an unexpected place, at the bottom of a valley or between two ramparts of larches. The metal crumbled once someone stepped on it. The tracks no longer existed and were so fragmented that they could no longer serve as landmarks for potential vagrants, whether in the steppes or in the forest, each of them ever encroaching upon the other. The fact was that nobody was crossing the region or even the continent anymore, and so useful signposts for travelers no longer concerned many people.

   The population had diminished dramatically. The cripples and the dead were barely enlivened by the spirit of adventure or the needs of exile. The conditions of life had changed. Those who were still able to lead a whit of existence generally preferred not to go far from their individual territories, from the refuges they had somehow secured while waiting for extinction—a hut with a vegetable garden and a few hens, a former kolkhoz, the ruins of a work camp, a grain silo, an abandoned nuclear power plant.

• Hannko Vogulian had chosen to reside in a clearing within the taiga, several kilometers from a long ditch where the remains of the railroad could be seen. A logging village had doubtless been built there, in an already-hard-to-imagine era of the Second Soviet Union, but there was no longer any trace of the houses and the roads from that time. The village had been self-sufficient when it came to energy sources and Hannko Vogulian's cottage was built on the residue of the small nuclear core. Nobody knew who had built it, perhaps a team of fickle engineers who planned to stay there until the atoms' rage subsided, or the liquidators intent on making themselves useful one last time before their muscles stank like something was burning. The solid logs defied the passage of time. The building had taken on a slight slant, but for hundreds of years it had continued to perfectly fulfill its function: to protect Hannko Vogulian from bad weather—in the winter from gusts of snow, in the summer from swarms of flies which were themselves indeed on the brink of extinction, and in all seasons from attacks by wandering soldiers, psychotics, and wolves. The structure of this small-windowed izba wasn't particularly special, aside from having been constructed above and around a well, as once had been the Gramma Udgul's hangar. Hannko Vogulian, who wasn't nostalgic for the Levanidovo, nonetheless appreciated settling into a place with familiar characteristics, since it adjoined a pit out of which an invisible mist of radionuclides flowed. The well wasn't as impressively proportioned as the one the Gramma Udgul had presided over, and the bubbling magma hadn't descended to such breathtaking depths. The core had also lost a large degree of its radioactivity rather quickly, which didn't keep it from giving off an agreeable warmth, enough to make the months of blizzards and ice less difficult. Besides this advantage, Hannko Vogulian found a certain sort of companion in the pit, a mute interlocutor, and even if for several decades she had avoided doing so—disgusted at the idea of repeating the Gramma Udgul's witchy actions—now every so often she leaned over the edge and told the core about her day-to-day life, or stories from her past that came to mind, and, when her voice gave out in exhaustion, she stayed for a long while in the same place, sitting still, as if trying to make out precisely which stage the corium's fusion had reached, or as if waiting for a response.

• Hannko Vogulian was old now, very old, and she lived as a recluse. At the beginning, Solovyei had kept on visiting her, using her dreams to enter her and invade her, completely taking over her and her space to walk in her house and snoop around the well, looking for a memory of the Gramma Udgul. He had harassed her that way for something like three centuries or so, but then he had stopped appearing, without any apparent reason and without any farewell.

She lived in total autarky. Once she finished with her housekeeping, once she had walked past her rabbit traps, and once she had buried a vagrant she had killed because he had bothered her, which happened once or twice every twelve or fifteen years, she went back to her place, checked her rifles, and barricaded herself. Then, so as not to spend her evenings moping around gloomily, she wrote.

From the Gramma Udgul's warehouse she had saved unused school supplies and ink. This allowed her to keep a diary that she sometimes forgot for several years, only to take it back up suddenly on a whim and without worrying about explanations. She inscribed the paper with harmless remarks about her days. However, the priority was for her to do what she called "reviving prose." She was determined to reproduce in her little notebooks the memories of her readings long ago, in the Radiant Terminus kolkhoz. She had read far fewer books than her sister Samiya Schmidt, but now that she no longer had access to any library of any size she was sorry not to have any works to break the monotony of her nights, to brave everything's remoteness and the knowledge of being one of the only survivors. So she tried to reproduce, on the yellowing grade-school paper, what remained within her of the literature that was dead and gone.

But she had never been an attentive reader, a model reader, never a good reader, and the contents of the novels she once had sped through had now vanished, not to mention their form, which for her had always been a wholly unimportant element. Outside the titles, which in any case she had difficulty remembering exactly, the texts gave her trouble. Under her pen, the post-exotic fictions or the socialist realist sagas, broad at first, became a welter of a few dark pages, even more disappointing than their ancient originals. Most often she was disgusted by the result and, when she had finished a volume, she filed it in a corner of the izba without reading it again. She was most proud of herself when she tackled what remained of her memories, the collections of lyrical poetry, and the brochures focusing on agricultural techniques, pigpen hygiene, the maintenance of dairy materials (churns, creamers, and sterilizers), bookkeeping for farms, security for power plants. On all these subjects the detailed information came back to her and, little by little, she managed to reconstruct the basics of these pamphlets, with their diagrams for illiterate peasants and even with their most distinctive illustrations.

But it was the anti-male pamphlets by Maria Kwoll, Rosa Wolff, Sonia Velasquez, or Luna Galiani that emerged most powerfully from the point of her pen. They had been engraved even more brilliantly than all the rest in her memory. The substance of these little books had always answered her questions, her anxieties as a young woman, which hadn't been possible with the Marxist classics or the social-skills manuals sent by the Orbise. She lit the lamp, she began to write, and she felt as if Sonia Velazquez or Rosa Wolff were holding her hand and guiding it, generously allowing her to speak and rant against the violence all females had suffered since the middle of the Paleozoic era and, closer to us, during the previous twenty thousand years of human history. She had already reproduced in this way, almost without mistake and without reproach, a good fifteen or so incendiary feminist productions of the Second Soviet Union.

• However, her resuscitation of texts also involved a portion unconnected to general literature, but focused exclusively on the cultural life
of the Radiant Terminus kolkhoz. A section that didn't have its sources
in books, properly speaking, because they came from Solovyei's cylinders as they'd marked moments of crisis, everyday life, nights of crime
and incest in the Levanidovo, days of work among the junk stored
at the Gramma Udgul's. Frozen on the acoustic cylinders, Solovyei's
voice resonated from the loudspeakers along the main road, but it also
echoed in his daughters' dreams, including those of Hannko Vogulian,
where the kolkhoz president entered forcefully to attend to his lustful
or impenetrable affairs.

While Solovyei had carried out these nocturnal visits, Hannko Vogulian hadn't dreamed of setting down these hailstorms of sentences that
she had always considered as repugnant and detestable as the intrusion
they accompanied. But then Solovyei had stopped appearing within
her and, after a century or two, she began to feel nostalgic, not for
her father, whose monstrosity she continued to hate, but for his ranting creations. Solovyei's sad poetries had found a refuge in the inmost
parts of her memory, she had buried them as far as possible beneath
her consciousness, and yet, now that she was calling them up, she was
exhuming them willingly and without any apparent deterioration.
Once again they were well-articulated, imprecatory, and bombastic;
once again barely comprehensible and unnerving. Hannko Vogulian
copied them down quickly, as if being dictated. She omitted practically
no figure of speech and sometimes was sad not to be able to express in
her writing the needle's crackle on the wax and the tonal variations her
father loved, because they hypnotized or frightened their listeners.

• When she was captivated in this way by her task as a copyist, she
sometimes intoned or hummed the strings of words that hung in front
of her, and it occurred to her, confusedly or quickly, that her proximity
to Solovyei hadn't really ended, that no separation had taken place, and

that she was still, or at least she had clearly become once again, a creature imagined, possessed, and brought to life by Solovyei. A daughter of Solovyei, a daughter for Solovyei.

A female annex in Solovyei's life: nothing more than that.

− 26 −

• He got up, pushing against the boards. The chains groaned. He went to the hole for pissing and expelled the few drops he had in his bladder, then he got dressed. Horrid smells came from his body and his clothes at the slightest movement he made. They swirled around him and upset him.

So, Kronauer, he said. The next time you decide to stay in jail, make sure to take a bath first, otherwise I won't come with you!

He walked away from the hole and, as the cell was narrow, after four steps he touched the door. From the grille he could make out the thick shadow of a hallway. He brought his nose to the small mesh. In that spot the air was a little less nauseating than in the cell.

His headache came and went. Behind his forehead, in his eyes, the pain thrummed, sometimes slackened, sometimes swelled in forceful waves.

Well, he thought. It's still better than lying outside, pecked by crows and vultures.

The smell of the metal grille mixed with that of his sniffing and breathing. Others before him had been there, hoping to see in the hallway a slight change in the atmosphere, an indication of the time, the day, the nearness or farness of death.

Other smells.

The smell of muddy snow carried on the detainees' boots.

The smell of muddy snow, penal blood, muscle fatigue, penal cold, and filth.

The smell of holes in other cells, and the smell that he himself left against the grille, of a hairy, famished, muddy, and dead animal. He walked away from the opening and went back to the boards. Now he was sitting on the wood, head hung, his forehead in his hands. He was slowly trying to figure out what had happened before. He could barely reconstruct the passage of days and nights that had preceded his incarceration. The fragments appeared amid chaos and didn't coalesce into a story or a life.

At some point he took off his coat and set it in a pile next to him, feeling as if he had accomplished something difficult.

His mind was full of massive holes.

He stayed that way and for two or three hours didn't move. Without his coat he was just in rags. Occasionally he saw an image of himself in his mind, and he felt that he looked just like an ordinary detainee, chiefly male, in a torn uniform like a convict's, a beggar's, a soldier's, or that of someone buried in a shallow grave.

• Around eleven in the morning, a watchman came to open the door. The lock let out several lazy hiccups, then the iron plate squeaked on its hinges and Kronauer stood by the partition, standing mechanically at attention as if he had learned in the night of time the disciplined behavior of basic egalitarianism in concentration milieus.

The watchman was named Hadzoböl Münzberg. Kronauer recognized him easily. The day of feeding the core, they'd both taken a box with several puppets and video games out of the container. Hadzoböl Münzberg had a glassy stare then, a slow and weary pace, and Kronauer had figured out that he was one of Solovyei's zombies. He had also thought of the children who had once played with these things and who must not have survived the radiation. When he and Hadzoböl Münzberg had tipped the box over the void, the dolls had slipped nonchalantly toward the abyss. Disarticulated puppets, damsels in plastic. "Dust to dust," Hadzoböl Münzberg had remarked with a sigh.

And now Hadzoböl Münzberg was gesturing for Kronauer to leave his cell.

Kronauer showed him his coat and asked if he'd have to put it on.

—I'm taking you to the showers, Münzberg said.

—Good, said Kronauer as he followed his footsteps.

—You don't have a headache, do you, sometimes? Münzberg suddenly asked.

—I do, Kronauer said. Horrible ones.

They went down the corridor. There were several doors with grilles, but, behind them, Kronauer couldn't make out any breaths or signs of life.

—I'm the one who knocked you out, Münzberg clarified as they came to the shower room.

—Why? Kronauer asked.

—Had to, Münzberg explained.

—But, Kronauer protested.

—I did.

—So you knocked me out, just like that?

—Yes, said Hadzoböl Münzberg. With a shovel. I had to. You had become uncontrollable.

- 27 -

• The shower room had an icy draft flowing through it. Kronauer took off his coat and shivered. But I thought I didn't put it on when I left the cell, he suddenly thought. No, I didn't take it, this stinking coat, he thought. I left it by the partition when Münzberg told me we were going to the showers. So why do I have it with me? he wondered. Right before, he had been walking in the hallway. Did I or didn't I have it on me? He thought about this for one or two seconds. He couldn't decide on an answer. Not that it matters, he thought.

Still, Kronauer, he thought. If you can't even remember what happened three minutes ago, I wouldn't count on your head for much. Who knows what's in there, what sort of mush. Maybe you're already dead. Or crazy. Or you're spinning around in a dream without any hope of getting out.

He got undressed. His old clothes were so vile that he set them on the floor, under the bench in the changing room. Maybe the prison administration will give me a clean uniform after I'm cleaned up, he thought.

A naked light bulb lit the changing room. Aside from the air vents and the entrance Hadzoböl Münzberg had slipped through after giving him a bar of soap, there was no opening. The place, despite the bulb, didn't have enough lighting. Everything was wood: the floor, the walls, the ceiling, with logs, boards, grates over the drain holes. It's suffocating, he thought. The mustiness of damp, of wet pine and dirty clothes. Beyond the changing room was the actual shower room. Not very big. About fifteen meters long. Oddly, he had to go all the way to the back to find a water inlet, a single hanging showerhead.

- You want me to say it, Kronauer? he thought as he walked barefoot over the grates on the black, slightly viscous surface. A single shower, in a communal bathroom, that's impossible. That just doesn't happen.
  You're not in reality, there you have it, he thought.

- However, he felt the mossy, slippery slats beneath him, and, beyond his own stench, he could smell around him the violent odors of soaked larch, steeped in bad soap, sordid water, with an aftersmell of excrement, urine, and blood. It was real and didn't belong to a dream world. Unable to more clearly make out the status of the world he was maneuvering through, he turned the knob in front of him and squatted beneath the shower head. After several liters of cold water, the stream became pleasant, very hot, but not burning.
  He surrendered to the water without moving. The rain bombarded his head and he realized that since Hadzoböl Münzberg had left him, he had forgotten his headache. All the more reason not to completely believe what happens, he thought. It's disappeared, I won't complain. But it's not natural. The drops hit his smooth scalp. He shut his eyes. He had quickly come to a minute of calm passivity.
  Dripping liquid at a delightful temperature.
  A nearly fetal position.
  Half-darkness.
  Solitude.
  He hadn't even started to wash himself yet, blissfully unmoving, when he heard someone opening the door to the room. All right, he thought without opening his eyes. Münzberg has come with clean

clothes. A gust of sharp air hit his calves. He huddled even tighter beneath the water.

It couldn't be better, he thought. I couldn't be better.

Then he made the mistake of opening his eyes.

There were several people in the changing room. Hadzoböl Münzberg was there, indeed, holding an enormous mass that didn't look like clean clothes. He was accompanied by the Gramma Udgul, Samiya Schmidt, and Solovyei.

Kronauer immediately shut his eyes.

Well, apparently not, he thought. It couldn't be worse.

- Münzberg came and went. He went into the hallway to find several masses wrapped in waxed canvas, sheets, or various rags. He dragged them and set them between the changing room and the space for showers, for the shower. Sometimes he could see exactly what sort of packet it was. Sometimes an arm hung out, covered in a sleeve of a winter jacket, a foot with shoes to brave the snow. Hadzoböl Münzberg was carrying corpses. He set down his loads without any apparent emotion, as if he was indifferent to his lazy character, then he went back into the hallway to get another one.

When Münzberg was done, Solovyei pushed the bench to sit right behind the barricade of outstretched bodies. The Gramma Udgul sat next to him. They resembled a peasant couple in a rural train station waiting room and both seemed to be in a bad mood. Samiya Schmidt disappeared for a minute then came back with a stool. She sat far off, close to the revolting pile of Kronauer's rags. In what looked like a tribunal, she could have been a third judge, a representative of the masses, or a witness for the prosecution. She hung her head, sullen and stricken.

Then Münzberg shut the door and stood on watch. At the other end of the room, Kronauer had covered his crotch and stayed under the hot water, in a frightened nudist's pose. He waited under the flowing water. He didn't know what to do.

• Solovyei's two yellow eyes glinted. If he had once been wounded, there was no sign on his face. His dead eye had regained its evil power and its gleam. The hole in his head had been soldered shut.

—Let me get dressed, Kronauer begged.

—I'm the one giving orders here, the president of the kolkhoz said.

The wood in the room meant the acoustics would be good and his voice rolled powerfully toward Kronauer.

The Gramma Udgul packed some tobacco into the bowl of her pipe. Solovyei set his massive hands on his massive thighs and seemed to be trying to remember the broad outlines of the affair he would be judging. His long, natural hair haloed around his large, hostile muzhik's head. It shone with oily reflections beneath the lamp. The iron bar that had skewered him from eye to ear now belonged to mere memory.

The kolkhoz president looked up at Kronauer, his golden eyes without any visible white, his wild animal eyes that didn't bring to mind a peasant but an unknown creature, bearing a relationship of pure convenience with peasantry and even with the human species.

—So can I come out of the shower? Kronauer asked.

—Be quiet, the Gramma Udgul said.

• Solovyei jumped from subject to subject in order to discombobulate the accused man and make it impossible for him to defend himself. Every so often, he summed up the main charges, and then he gave equal weight to blood crimes and miserable ordinary details of life in Radiant Terminus. According to him, Kronauer had intentionally half-fixed the fire hydrant in front of Myriam Umarik's house, which had turned a large part of the main road to mud. He had unfairly taken Barguzin's shirts. When his turn had come to work in the kitchens, he had prepared a porridge of toasted barley with flour and rancid butter without paying attention to the amounts, thereby repeatedly creating disgusting meals. He had hurt Samiya Schmidt when he had brought her back from the forest the day of his arrival. Then he had tiptoed around all the women in the kolkhoz, with the clear intention of sleeping with them and hurting them, the only exception being the Gramma Udgul, whom he had evidently spared, but doubtless because she had brought to light his role in assassinating an officer in the Red Army, and because she had unmasked him as a deserter. Among his Casanovan actions, he had persuaded Samiya Schmidt to read and reread unhealthy pamphlets written by Maria Kwoll and her group of Amazonians, to the point that Samiya Schmidt had lost her spirit and had gone crazy against her father. He had spent his time in the kolkhoz without respecting a single ideological principle, breezing through events like he was an enemy of the Orbise or an idiot. In the Gramma Udgul's warehouse, he had tried to break one of the rare phonographs that had survived the Second Soviet Union's disasters, a machine with great historical and sentimental value. Moreover, the night of the blizzard, he had fired shots at innocent kolkhozniks, hitting his targets perfectly nearly every time, and causing a considerable hemorrhage in Radiant Terminus's numbers.

• —I never fired a shot at anyone, Kronauer exclaimed.
—A semiautomatic war rifle, Solovyei said. An SKS Type 56.
—I didn't shoot anyone, Kronauer repeated.
—Is that nobody? Solovyei asked.

At his order, Hadzoböl Münzberg came out of the doorway he had been leaning in and went to start unwrapping the cadavers lying at the judges' feet.

Although the water was blinding him, Kronauer successively recognized the one-armed Abazayev, the tractor driver Morgovian, Hannko Vogulian, and Myriam Umarik. He couldn't see any blood or wounds on their faces, but, lower down, on the torso, the stomach, all were bloodied.

As Hadzoböl Münzberg paused, the president of the kolkhoz gestured for him to take away the cloths covering the last two bodies. With a zombie's gentle and slow movements, Münzberg did so. In this way appeared the partly smashed heads of the Gramma Udgul and

Samiya Schmidt. Sitting nearby, one on the judges' bench, the other on a small stool, those two concerned seemed not to express any emotions. They didn't react. Münzberg withdrew to lean once again in the doorway. There was a brief pause.

The drops spluttering on Kronauer's skin, on the grating around him.

The mist.

The slightly gray water close to his left ankle, in the spot where he had set his bit of soap. The bar continued to dissolve, leaving small shimmering ripples on the drain occasionally interrupted by bubbles that quickly burst.

The shadow around Kronauer.

The harsh light of the bulb in the changing room.

The shame of being naked like an animal in front of the judges, in front of the corpses, in front of Samiya Schmidt on her stool and in front of Samiya Schmidt lying on the floor, her head exploded.

—And why would I be the one to have killed them? Kronauer asked defensively.

—Kill is a big word, Solovyei acknowledged. But you spent a night shooting at them with a war weapon. They weren't in good shape when we collected them. Whenever someone tried to get close and calm you, you shot them down. This went on the whole night until you were knocked out.

—I don't remember any of that, Kronauer said. Are they dead?

—You're one to ask, soldier, Solovyei said angrily. What do you think you are?

— 28 —

• Samiya Schmidt seemed to be drugged or exhausted. She watched
the debate inattentively and, when her name was mentioned during
Solovyei's accusations, when the president of the kolkhoz pronounced
it in a peeved voice, she didn't jump. She had set her hands flat on her
legs and she didn't move, or only when she raised an arm to twist one
of her braids.

In one of his expositions and almost incidentally, almost cruelly
indicating that it wasn't the least bit important to him, Solovyei indicated that Samiya Schmidt, after the trial, would be expelled from the
reassuring world of Radiant Terminus and would have to walk blindly
for one thousand six hundred and eight or two thousand three hundred and two years or more, without help of any kind, a punishment
coupled with the impossibility of any rest, whether in the world of the
living or that of the dead. The facts motivating such a punishment
were chiefly parricidal attacks, incestuous intrigues both oneiric and
concrete, the feminist ramblings contrary to ideals of proletarian egalitarianism, conflagrations and destruction of public buildings, refusing
collective morality, divulging secrets to the enemy, sabotage.

But then Solovyei pontificated again, cruelly, with Kronauer as the
target. Then the interrogation resumed.

—You hurt my daughters, he claimed. There wasn't a single day
you didn't hurt them or try to do so. In the village you were a lecherous

dog. You were obsessed with your cock. You hurt Myriam Umarik, Hannko Vogulian, and Samiya Schmidt.

—I didn't hurt anyone, Kronauer protested.

Every so often he looked past the judges toward Samiya Schmidt, who didn't meet his gaze. He blinked to get rid of the droplets pouring down his cheeks from the shower and he scrutinized Samiya Schmidt. He had heard Solovyei's threats for her and he wondered what would happen to her and whether, during this long and painful path awaiting them both, during those endless centuries, they would be separate or together, or simply crossing paths at random, when one of their watchmen made a mistake. And suddenly he realized that he was thinking of her in the cock's language and he couldn't help imagining, certainly furtively, but still, her sad crotch, as paramilitary as her clothes. But still.

—You went into your own dreams to hurt her, Solovyei said.

—That accusation doesn't hold up, Kronauer said.

—I saw your dreams from start to finish. I went into them. You hurt them every night.

—I don't remember my dreams, Kronauer said, raising his voice to talk above the noise of the cascade around him.

—But I remember them. I was there. You came and went like a lecherous dog. You mixed up the woman you knew with the woman you wanted to know. Your cock trembled like a stone-age monster.

—But, Kronauer protested in despair.

—You were often accompanied by the dying, Solovyei thundered in a triumphant voice, as if hammering home an unshakable argument. Your wife Irina Echenguyen. Your wife Vassilissa Marachvili.

—She was never my wife, Kronauer cried. She was the wife of one of my comrades, Ilyushenko. We were together in the steppes after the fall of the Orbise. We were irradiated together in the forbidden lands. We were all dying and more.

—Of course, and she, Vassilissa Marachvili, was dying, Solovyei said. You have always been accompanied by women neither alive nor dead. You wanted my daughters to be like them. You hurt them in your dreams. And in reality you shot at them with an SKS Type 56.

—I didn't shoot at anyone in the village, Kronauer insisted. Those are absurd accusations.

• He withdrew into natural sensations. The noise of the shower. The flow over his stomach, his legs. His head no longer bothered him. He didn't look at the corpses lying at the judges' feet, or the judges themselves. And he didn't look at Samiya Schmidt either, but, in the background of his thoughts, he couldn't contradict the sludge rising and falling in himself and thoroughly dirtying what little reason he still had. He didn't remember having had a rifle, he didn't remember having assassinated the kolkhoz daughters, but Solovyei's accusations had lodged deep in him and he now wondered if something scandalous hadn't obsessed him, recently or not, connected or not to his stay in the Levanidovo. And what came from the depths had no relationship to reproachable military activities, or to his rejection of Marxist-Leninist morality; in contrast, it had more to do with the images of copulation embedded within himself over millions of years, with immemorial fantasies, urges to rape, animal tremors, and groping or dominating vulvas. With the language of the cock.

Amid these noises of water, these drops and trickles, he unwillingly came back to Samiya Schmidt sitting on her stool, and every so often he undressed her and considered her in a dreamy way, without any particular desire, her soft woolly crotch.

—I didn't shoot anyone, he finally said once again.

—If you're going to just say shit like that, the Gramma Udgul suddenly said angrily, you should shut up, Kronauer.

• The soapy water scattered in grayish glimmers beneath the drain and then gave way to limpid water.

Now Kronauer wasn't thinking of anything, wasn't listening to his judges, and wasn't trying to recall any memories. He stammered a childish argument, more for himself than for his listeners, and, like a mentally handicapped person, he slapped the palm of his hand against the floor next to his left thigh to make squirts and bubbles.

– 29 –

• After years of seclusion in a nauseating darkness, one morning Kronauer noticed that the door of his dungeon was open. He went through it.

As he hadn't walked for a very long time, he crossed the hallway with difficulty. He tottered. He had to stop several times. The cells he went past seemed empty, and besides, he had never heard noises from them, or rather noises that could be attributed to human sources. He had concluded that he was the sole prisoner locked in this building. When he came to the corridor that led outside, he paused. If a watchman saw me, he thought, he wouldn't think twice before shooting me. Then he pushed the heavy door. The lock wasn't bolted.

The abrupt contact with natural light blinded him. It took him several minutes to become accustomed to day again. The sun wasn't even shining; it was overcast, filled entirely with slate-gray clouds. A fall day, Kronauer thought.

A very gloomy fall day, he thought.

He went straight ahead, minimizing his movements, his arms away from his body, as if, having just learned to stand upright, he still had a long way to go. He blinked away his tears. It's because of the cold, he thought. He hadn't taken his coat and, although the air's chill bothered him, he refused to go back. Too bad, he thought. I'll cover myself later. I'll find something along the way. A cover, a soldier's coat, a wolf's hide.

• The camp was extraordinarily vast but empty. No fence delineated any limits. Dilapidated or in ruins, the barracks were arrayed monotonously. They went on for two kilometers, then they became sparser, giving way to paths that were less and less clearly marked out, to black pools of mud, to potholes and clumps of pines massive crows were perched on. The birds watched Kronauer. They shook their wings and beaks every so often and hopped from branch to branch without cawing. They tilted their heads and, even if they pretended not to be interested in him, they examined him.

The buildings had endured the attacks of hundreds of seasons, and most of them were nothing more than squalid piles of boards. As the wind sharpened, Kronauer stepped over the remnants of a doorstep, pushed aside the remnants of a door, and began to rummage through the remnants of a windowless dormitory. He told himself that maybe he'd dig up something to protect him against the cold, or some sort of pittance for the days to come. The dormitory didn't have anything useful. The bed frames had caved in with the vicissitudes of old age. The floor wasn't strong anywhere, it seemed about to collapse, he had to follow the joists so as not to fall through. The floor and the walls had broken in several spots, which let through light but also a stream of sharply whistling air. The building ended with a room that might have been a storage room or a medical annex. An infirmary, he thought.

Inside were an infirmary cot and a rotting, empty armoire. Nonetheless, in a corner was a crate the previous inhabitants had forgotten in the confusion of being evacuated, or for some other inexplicable reason. It was black with dust, but solid. Kronauer spent half an hour prying it open. He had lost his dexterity, his youth, and his fighter's rage, and he also didn't have any tools at hand. It was dark. The crate had been nailed shut and wrapped with a metal strip that hadn't rusted enough to submit to Kronauer's obstinate but powerless twisting.

After resisting for a long time, the crate finally opened. Kronauer took out first a white liquidator's uniform, with gloves, a filter mask, and insulated boots. It was odd material that he knew he would never use, but which had the benefit of protecting everything that was stored inside it—clean clothes, quilted jackets, army boots, and the fur hats worn by prisoners. Kronauer immediately stripped off his rags and put on a brand-new zek's uniform. He didn't really want to admit it, but he knew, deep down, that he looked sharp.

When he left the infirmary, a gray wind was blowing from the forest. He felt warm in his new clothes and he happily inhaled the strong resinous smell sweeping the camp. I don't know if I'm escaping or not, he thought, but in any case I should get to the forest by nightfall. I should leave the camp for good and reach the forest by nightfall.

- Sometimes ditches at the bottom of which black oil stagnated.

Once or twice, crows flying north.

Sometimes heaps of iron that once had been trucks, jeeps, electric generators.

Again, aromatic winds from the taiga, accompanied by sharp gusts hinting at sleet or snow.

Sometimes a slanting watchtower about to fall, sometimes a perfectly upright watchtower missing the ladder that would have let people up to the platform.

No fence. No sentry walk. No barriers. The same world throughout.

Well, maybe the fences had been useless at some point, Kronauer thought. Maybe nobody else saw any difference between the carceral interior and the concentrational exterior.

Gusts of wind, whistles, then silence.

Here and there pines, thickets of birches.

The trees growing everywhere in the remnants of the camp.

The soil hard, as if icy.

Tar patches.

The grass in short clumps, very yellow, sometimes dark brown.

I don't even know the names of these grasses, Kronauer suddenly realized. These are new species. These are new species, but they're dead.

• Crows were perched on high branches. Three, four. They were pecking at lice and nonchalantly surveyed the comings and goings or sem-
blances thereof. Kronauer made his way through the barracks of the
abandoned camp. They watched him.

Them or me, doesn't matter.

Sometimes I cawed as I spread my wings and I acted as if I was only
interested in myself, but I actually wasn't.

• I'll never ever get to the forest at this pace, Kronauer thought.

As he turned around to see how far he had walked, he noticed a
human form walking in the same direction as him. A broken-down
building hid whoever it was, then trees kept Kronauer from following
with his eyes, then the figure reappeared. They were now separated by
about two hundred meters and Kronauer still couldn't make out the
features of his or her face. No rifle on the shoulder, no hint of a pistol
on the belt, a generally gray appearance. A prisoner, Kronauer thought.

The other person was physically diminished and, despite the fluffy
clothes that made him or her look bigger, looked more like a teenager
than an adult.

Kronauer stayed between two pines and waited.

That couldn't possibly be Samiya Schmidt, he thought.

It was.

She drew near and, when she was four steps away from him, she
froze. She was out of breath and, beneath the shapka covering her
head, her face was muddy. Exhaustion had swollen her eyelids. Her
revolutionary-Chinese-doll physiognomy had diminished to the point
that it was hard to connect her now with the juvenile enthusiasm of
struggle against the Four Olds. Only her sulkiness remained, only a
sort of withheld feminist rage that Kronauer, as a male, risked bearing the consequences of. Up close, it was clear that she was dressed in
clothes too large for her and in poor shape. It was also clear that she
had put her full effort into catching up to Kronauer as quickly as possible, and that she was now at the point of exhaustion.

They eyed each other for a long minute without saying anything. In an unexpectedly coquettish movement, Samiya Schmidt brought up her hand, rummaged beneath her shapka, and pulled out the two braids that had been hidden there. The braids now framed her head, ending at vermillion knots that weren't too wrinkled and generally happy, restoring a little joyful youth to her appearance.

—Do you recognize me? Samiya Schmidt finally stammered in a trembling voice.

—Of course, Kronauer said, unsure what else to say. We worked in the same kolkhoz.

• Sometimes I cawed as I spread my wings and I acted as if I was only interested in myself, but I actually wasn't.

The grasses, for example. The dead grasses. If I had been asked, I could have named some of them.

Allwoods, torfelian, curse-grass, solfabouts, garveviandre, twirlvains, ulbe-bayan, grandoiselles, ourphonge, ever-fools, ditchcroaks, white Tatars.

– 30 –

•   Dawn lasted for half an hour, giving way to a persistent grayness that already presaged the darkness of evening. Hannko Vogulian checked that her rifle was loaded and went out. The snow in front of the house was intact. Farther off she saw wolf tracks and, around the carcass of the man she had killed a week earlier, an impressive number of symbols inscribed by birds of prey. They had touched down, pecked, followed, and bickered with each other, hopped away to tear up the bit of flesh they had gotten, and, after digesting they had defecated left and right. The carcass had been moved several dozen meters, as if the animals had wanted to make him disappear in the forest. The wolves had torn off a good part and the birds had attacked the face. Hannko didn't lean over to do a medical or butcher's appraisal. She was unable to identify the person she'd shot. She simply knew, instinctively, that she had never met him. She also knew that there would be nothing left at winter's end because the big and small scavengers could continue cleaning up. And if in the first days of thaw she still found human residue and shreds, she'd scatter them beneath the shrubs, as she had done since time immemorial, for eight hundred eighty-nine years or more. There were already several places like that in the area. Not a huge number, since the visitors were far and few in between, but still several.

• Farther off, Hannko Vogulian came across the remains of an encampment. She had expected this discovery. A week earlier, she had smelled some wood burning, so unexpected in the middle of her winter and her solitude that she had immediately prepared for an enemy attack. The encampment had been set up in a gully about a kilometer from the house, in what had once been a bear's den. The man had draped a cloth on poles to guard against gusts of wind and snow. On a flat spot nearby, he had made a fire out of needles, pinecones, and twigs. He had hung up his pans, a sort of kettle, several indescribable cloths, and a bag where the animals couldn't reach them. So he had intended to come back, doubtless after having explored the area and after having put together a plan of action to capture Hannko's house by eliminating its occupant, moving in, or by unloading his weapons and supplies.

Hannko Vogulian untied the strings and cords and took them with her. She never had enough at hand. The cooking utensils were revolting and she barely glanced at them, left them in the snow where they fell. The bag's contents, however, brought a satisfied smile to her lips. There was reindeer jerky, berries for making tea, scissors, material for carving up game, balls of tarred thread, hinges for traps. Looking through an inner pouch, she laid hands on a trapper's lighter like the ones Red Army scouts used to have, heavy and inexhaustible, and she also took out wads of sheets from a disintegrating book, clearly meant to kindle a fire rather than to instill poetic emotions within their reader. She collected her loot and went through the woods back to her solitary residence.

—That was a close call, she whispered as she skirted the frost-covered bushes. That one seemed like a clever little shit.

She liked hearing people give advice. For centuries she had been talking all alone and she considered this a dialogue.

—If I'd opened the door to him, he'd have given me a hard time, she continued.

—Of course, she said.

When she came to the clearing, she made a detour and at first she avoided looking at what remained of the man's corpse; then she changed her mind, went up and stopped by the scraps of his blood-soaked jacket. Despite the cold, the smell of mangled flesh, excrement, and grime were overpowering. Visible beneath the fabric was a broken ribcage, hardly cleared of the organs it contained. The bustle of the predators wore on for several nights.

Without looking at the man's head too closely, she spoke to him.

—Well, my boy, she said firmly, as if persuaded that this way the sentence would, after traversing the icy air and then the black space of the Bardo, reach him. Well, my boy, what a state you've been left in by these assassins!

• At night, she took out her diary, which she hadn't looked at for a month, and she began to write. The dates were all made up. She wrote them at random, only certain that there were still fifteen or sixteen more weeks before the thaw, and using this estimation as a basis for giving her calendar some degree of credibility.

• *Friday, November 2.* Identified, from the east, a human smell. Barricaded myself in the house and stood ready. Smelled like a wandering soldier and campfire. At night didn't light the lamp. Was in shooting position all night.

Saturday, November 3. At daybreak, saw the prowler hiding behind the trees to examine the house. The wind had covered my footsteps and he had to be wondering if the house was inhabited or not. The wind had changed direction and didn't bring me his smells. This prowler had a hunter's patience. He didn't come into the open and barely moved. Used binoculars to examine his face. A survivor or a dead man. Bearded and dirty. Verified that it wasn't Aldolay Schulhoff. Knew this somewhat, but verified. At the end of the afternoon the prowler decided to leave the thicket and, as I had him in my line of sight, I attacked him. I aimed at the middle of his stomach. He fell down and didn't move anymore. As I didn't want to have any doubts about his state or any further worries, and as night was about to fall, I took aim at him even more carefully than the first time and I shot a second bullet. Right where the neck meets the shoulder. Decided to stay shut up for the next few days. The corpse would attract animals. Decided to stay shut up for the next few days, away from the animals.

Thursday, November 8. Went out. Twilight and cold. The prowler had been torn apart by wolves. Pecked at by crows. Will deal with what's left in the spring. Can barely see it from the window, no need to clear the scene. Went to find the place where the man had set off toward the house. Found his encampment and requisitioned whatever I might need. An army lighter. Baits for traps, cords. Also half a book. No cover, no title. Post-exotic narracts. Read two or three. Total garbage. Good for starting a fire.

- 31 -

•   At the moment the flames stopped roaring, and perhaps a little
later, several years later, because now and for a long while you
haven't been calculating time the way you used to, for a long while
you haven't cared about clocks and calendars, so at this second
you entered a place that had to be a black lake of tar and naphtha,
and for the first while you stayed there without any preconceived
ideas and even any ideas at all, busy leaning and loafing and waiting
lazily for what would come next, the time that outside would see two
or three successive generations go by, satisfying yourself with the
thick silence surrounding you, liking this thickness akin to nothing
else, sometimes attacked by the miniscule din of a bubble slowly
rising from deep down below, and then you heard this noise that
was honestly barely perceptible and you made it the basis of a long
piece of music, with a rather unvarying melody that didn't charm you
but in which you inserted some dancing modulations and overtone
sounds from your glottal cavities and your various diaphragms or
what passed for them, also taking pleasure in the spare time you
had available, which allowed you to watch films of your previous
existences slowly or on loop, to stop as needed on the most powerful images and meditate on the interconnected dreams that had
crystallized in your memory without worrying any longer about any
difference from your memories of reality and, because you were

staying there and barely moving, you took some of the exploits that
had piece by piece comprised your life and its countless variations, you took them to speak them and in so doing relive them, yet
not neglecting these heroic moments or these oneiric evils or the
numerous intersections of difficulty and confusion, because, deep
down, your existence, although nicely organized by an iron ideology
constantly soaked in the wellspring of black magic, which in and of
itself multiplied the realms visited and embellished them with items
incomprehensible to dead human bodies, to living human bodies,
and to dogs or the like, male or female or dead or the like, so your
existence, despite being rich in clear and easily situated events was
also disastrously muddled, to the point that you ended, or rather
you started, by confusing daughters, wives, and mistresses, simple
crimes and massacres, proletarian morals and vile reveries, tyrants
and prisoners, birth and death, and, for some time, you justified this
difficult wayward trend by leaning on the Bardic yet nebulous theory
of canceling out opposites, of dissolving contradictions in an inde-
terminate and, certainly, a sometimes nightmarish, sometimes not,
oneiric mass, and, as you wanted in spite of everything to preserve
in history these never-ending trips of wandering and nothingness,
and not to limit your words to a hagiographic tale in which you
would have been the leader, you refused the method that would
have forced you to separate the narrative grain from the baroque
chaff and you began declaiming, first, as an introductory prayer,
calling forth your secret henchmen, then creating by your mouth
the shadows of those who had crossed your path or wandered by
accident on the same fate you did, then, the prayer spoken and
the shadows formed, you put on the rags of one of your characters who wasn't the most glorious one, you reincarnated yourself in
the unkind figure of Solovyei, and, for several empty and moonless
years, because in the tar and the naphtha you were bathing in there
was no longer any sky or idea of a sky, during these heavy and dark
years you were entirely in your narrative, then the accumulation of

anecdotes exhausted you, you felt full and thought of being quiet. Your secret henchmen didn't respond to your call, or so quiet and small were they that you didn't notice them. The blackness of your solitude tended to make you fall asleep. You bellowed several more names, you summoned other henchmen. Altoufan Dzoyïek, Döröm Börök, Elli Kronauer, Toghtaga Özbeg the Old, Maria Kwoll, and several hundred others who had played a role in some of your most recent adventures, then you listed your daughters, your wives, and your mistresses. The days went by, none appeared, and as the sound of your voice horrified you, you closed your lips. What stood in for your grimace expressed discontent. The length of your sulking barely matters to us. Your sulking or ours, doesn't matter. Then the flames returned.

– 32 –

• No moon for a thousand years. We get used to it. Yes, that's what's best to do, get used to it. No more moonlight, no more romantic walks outside the yurt, no more penal insomnia punctuated by strange nightmares. We don't look up anymore at the velvety firmament, at the blue gaps underscoring the clouds, at their fanciful flight, at the stars, we don't get stirred up as we face the gray immensities of the steppes. All that doesn't exist anymore. Only the deep black darkness and the walk. They call that the amber in their illegible poems. A thousand years in amber, and then *nichevo*. They or I, doesn't matter. They proclaim it in a hoarse or despondent voice, and then they rant on incomprehensible topics. Not amber. Not the least light, it's more black space, an absolute solitude and a black silence that nothing breaks, except sometimes infinitesimal avalanches, infinitesimal squeaks, as if beneath our feet we were crushing something, such as hideous soot or cinders reduced to powder, yes, this might well be black space. Only, the length of the trip doesn't correspond to what we once had in mind, when we were dead or dying or alive, this sort of state, and when we listened to the monks' speeches on that subject. Here the length of the trip stretches out unbearably. Forty-nine days pass, then three hundred forty-three, then we have to count in groups of years, then in centuries. Under our feet the ashes make few sounds, except for when we lose consciousness and when we enter nightmares. We rarely lose consciousness, if you must know, we rarely dream, it's always the walk that keeps you going. Previously, while imprisoned for armed attacks or dissidence, time stretched out similarly, monotonous and exhausting, but at least the prospect of dying at the end of the stay assuaged our anxieties. Deliverance wasn't an empty promise. Besides, we always had a fellow inmate who was Buddhist and who described what happened next, a forty-nine-day-long transition and, almost immediately, entering a new skin. While here, all prospects have been extinguished, like the light and like the moon. We also get used to the absence of prospects, whether with bitter resignation or natural passivity, we get used to it. A thousand years. It's more approximation than any verifiable number. We're counting fairly approximately, of course, we're no longer counting in days or years, and very quickly we're just at the nearest century. A thousand years in amber, meandering in the deep black darkness, walking endlessly and rarely dreaming, and then *nichevo*. Sometimes we end up at an unforeseen fork, we're pummeled by Solovyei or unknown zeks or henchmen and Solovyei's daughters. Sometimes we come out into the open air, into a concentration paradise or a convoy of dying people, but that doesn't last forever, almost immediately the black comes back, and for the next two hundred and three years we no longer hear talk of anything, we no longer hear any voice nearby and we have to curl up mentally so as not to scream in fear. We also get used to these episodes, and, ultimately, we consider them purely delirious or oneiric surges. In all cases, the moon is absent. Sometimes we also come to a cul-de-sac, we bang on walls on all sides that, for lack of imagination or out of exhaustion, we claim are made of bricks like those of ovens, we imagine that we have gone into an oven as the walls are burning. We turn around and grope around, trying to recognize the space, which is full of silent vibrations and heat. Suddenly there's no longer any way out. Everywhere are bars that have reached the maximum temperature of matter, there are hermetic walls that are painful to approach, and we are submerged in the waves of a black inferno, within the devouring and oily black flames. Then we scream in fear, we moan or we crow poems, unlikely biographies, torn bits of lives or memories. Then, when we have gotten used to our umpteenth prison, we act as if nothing existed, we make the best of a bad situation, we do our best not to be dead or alive and, after another few centuries, we fall silent.

− 33 −

•   Having written in her clumsy handwriting "we make the best of a
bad situation, we do our best not to be dead or alive and, after another
few centuries, we fall silent," Hannko Vogulian added a correction in
the margin: "our best not to be dead or alive, even as daughters, wives,
or widows." Then she shut her notebook and set it on a shelf and, at
the same moment, she had the physical, violent feeling that someone
was watching her.

—Don't tell me you're back, she grumbled like an animal, tensing
up to avoid or endure an attack.

She turned. She moved like a wolf.

Aside from the yellow cone of light traced by the lamp, the house
was sunk in a comfortable darkness. The well's cover was ajar, the corium buried farther down gave off a pleasant warmth, gentle radiation
nullified by the walls and the low temperatures outside. All around, a
ranger's furniture, pelts, utensils for the bathroom and for the kitchen,
a sink in which the water from the well was cooling down. And on
the planks that served as shelves, blank notebooks, already-filled notebooks. And two rifles hanging next to a bear skin.

She didn't notice anything unusual.

Her certainty that she was being watched only increased.

Long ago, back when Solovyei went into her world and into parallel worlds as he liked, and when he went into everybody's dreams, this

horrible sensation most often preceded one of her father's intrusions. This was an alarm, an alarm that warned her of a danger she couldn't do anything against. Deep inside, physically and mentally, her dread intensified. This lasted, redoubled, for half a day, half a night. Then Solovyei entered her and walked inside her without any consideration, inside her dreams, inside her private memories, like it was conquered territory, sometimes indeed considering her a companion worthy of attention, even tenderness, but most often paying no attention to her happinesses and unhappinesses, coming and going erratically, building refuges she had no access to within her, soliloquizing opaque poems. Then everything ended, but she woke back up devastated, humiliated, and horribly sad.

And this horrible impression had just arisen again in her, without warning, and with a force intensified by its unexpectedness.

• She went to reinforce the lock on the door with an iron bar, then she took down a rifle and turned off the lamp.

Behind the windows, the snow gleamed weakly.

—Maybe it's not Solovyei coming, she whispered. Maybe it's just a prowler who saw the house and wants to hurt me.

Now she went from one small window to the other to examine the landscape. She sniffed the odors the wind carried, the grease and hints of grease, but she couldn't discern any particular presence. She tried not to expose herself to bullets from a potential shooter. With her dark agate eye, she tried to make out the miniscule changes in temperature where the first arboreal barriers stood, it swept across the heaps of snow and the underbrush between the trunks, with her dark agate eye she looked for traces of life. She resorted to her yellow tiger eye to analyze the cracks in the nothingness and the night, in order to focus on something dead. She couldn't distinguish anything at all. The clearing was illuminated by the residual light imprisoned in the snowdrift, and all the rest was darkness. Stars and moon belonged to another universe.

Then, very distinctly, she saw a shape on its knees in a sniper's position, hidden behind a bush at the foot of a larch. The form had taken aim at her. A tenth of a second later, she saw the spark of the cartridge that had just been hit; then another tenth of a second passed, and, right by her head—which she'd barely had foretime and forethought enough to move—the glass exploded.

She immediately crouched down.

Moving like a crab, treading on the shards of glass that had flown far along the izba's floors, she got into a shooting position that she knew was undetectable from the outside, a murderer perched between logs. She had regained the calm she'd lost after having put her notebook away. Now, as the confrontation neared, she was much more self-assured. Hannko Vogulian was a warrior. She would set her rifle barrel in the small groove dug into the wall. She was sure she could easily aim from there, in complete safety, and fire a fatal shot. After centuries and before the species had deteriorated, she had cocked her gun from this invisible slit at wolves, reindeer, bears, and various vagrants.

She was in position. Her opponent had just moved and, deep in the night, she recognized beyond a doubt the sly and sullen figure of Samiya Schmidt. The girl had grown old, time and weather had articulated her features, but she continued to wear the silly teenage braids that framed her face. Hannko Vogulian saw all the years spent in Radiant Terminus flash before her eyes, and she remembered how Samiya Schmidt had always managed to get out of communal tasks. Between bouts, she consistently found a way to do nothing, or to claim that organizing and maintaining the library in the People's House was exhausting enough. Hannko Vogulian had always hated her and, contrary to Myriam Umarik, for whom she had sometimes had a deep affection, she barely considered Samiya Schmidt a sister.

She aimed carefully. Even though she was hidden behind branches and a thick haze of darkness, Samiya Schmidt didn't stand a chance. For no clear reason, Hannko Vogulian decided to wait a bit before pulling the trigger. The other one wasn't in any more a rush to fire her shot.

• For several long minutes, the two women watched each other silently, unmoving, in the shadows. And suddenly Samiya Schmidt's sharp voice tore the night:

—Hannko Vogulian! she yelled. Queen of the whores! You slept with Solovyei! Every night you slept with your father!

What is this idiocy, Hannko Vogulian thought. What does she want, this little shithead? She's the one who's been letting Solovyei into her bed while that idiot Morgovian was shaking with fear!

—You liked it when he hurt you, Samiya Schmidt continued.

Her voice screeched so loudly that it seemed like a gigantic bird was bellowing.

She isn't human at all anymore, Hannko Vogulian thought. She's never really been, but now she really isn't anymore. Who knows if she's already grown wings on her back!

—You schemed with Solovyei to make Aldolay Schulhoff disappear! Samiya Schmidt declared.

Hannko Vogulian had her line of sight right above Samiya Schmidt's collarbone. She tilted the rifle barrel down imperceptibly and fired.

The commotion in the thicket was frightening. Samiya Schmidt had instantaneously turned into an ear-splitting, furious monstrosity. Her soldier's clothes had transformed into thousands of whistling strips and plumes flying in every direction and filling an immense space, and didn't quite correspond to anything living or dead. It was seamless, it went off in the undergrowth, and, at the same time, it stayed in the same place, like a sort of whirlwind of droplets and heavy, black crumbs. Hannko Vogulian fired a second bullet.

—Go back where you came from, shithead, she whispered. Go back to Solovyei's cowpats. You never should have left.

• Much later, everything had calmed down. There was no longer a single fragment of glass on the ground. The shattered window was intact again. Hannko got back up. She set her rifle on the log wall, lit the lamp, went to find the notebook she'd been using for her diary.

She was tired, but she sat at the table, leaned over the paper, and wrote:

Saturday, December 9. Dreamed about my little sister Samiya Schmidt. Almost unchanged. Like herself, still had her little braids, looking like a reeducated Chinawoman. Didn't have time to talk to her much. Nostalgic for the time when we were all together at the kolkhoz. Centuries have gone by. Seven or eight, maybe more. Nobody left to remember Radiant Terminus or the Second Soviet Union. Nostalgic for all that.

– 34 –

• Having left the last watchtowers behind, Kronauer and Samiya Schmidt disappeared into the forest. They were about a hundred meters apart and sometimes a little more, but they were careful not to lose sight of each other for too long. When Samiya Schmidt lagged too far behind, Kronauer slowed down. They both walked with some effort. After the first kilometer the underbrush thinned out. They had to cross scrubby spots, or shuffle through beds of small prickly bushes, which had grown heavy over the summer with berries but now were reduced to dead, spiky branches. They also often had to avoid spots where their feet would slowly be sucked in by mud. They were afraid to wander into marshy traps that they might not escape. Sometimes, beneath the humus, muddy water or black oil or a disagreeable mix of the two gurgled. The oil came from overgrown former cities or former military bases. The taiga had ultimately prevailed over these ruins, after only a few centuries, but industrial pollution was still omnipresent, no matter how ghostly, and by all indications it would take several millennia to disappear. Samiya Schmidt and Kronauer went more and more slowly, and at the end of the day, when the shadows had grown thick, the distance between the two of them diminished and they finally found themselves side by side, out of breath and trembling.

They hadn't exchanged a single word.

Since they had left the camp. They still hadn't spoken to each other.

• Samiya Schmidt went and leaned against a trunk. Kronauer followed suit. For a little warmth, they hugged each other, and once they were sitting at the foot of the tree they stayed shoulder to shoulder, thigh to thigh. Their legs were pulled close to their chests, their hands were in their pockets. Now the darkness was complete.

The forest rustled, ferns scraped, barks crackled, practically nothing. There weren't any animals nearby. The temperature dropped a little more, then it leveled off just above freezing.

Kronauer inhaled the scents from the earth and the trees. Bears had come by several days earlier, evidently to gorge on berries before hibernating. The strong odor of their urine had soaked the mosses, the dead needles. What are you talking about, Kronauer, he thought. What do you know about bears. Who knows if they've actually disappeared all this time. You don't know anything about them. You only know about camps and black oil.

You're just thinking up bullshit, he thought.

And suddenly he jolted. What about Solovyei? That was a horrible man, he promised you an eternity of suffering. What if you're still one of Solovyei's puppets, neither alive nor dead, within one of Solovyei's dreams?

An unbearable thought. He pushed it away as he wrinkled his nose, he smelled once again what wafted around him. Aside from the traces the bears had left, he could smell Samiya Schmidt's odors rising to his nose, everything that her body and the rags of her quilted clothes exuded, eight hundred and twelve years and some of painful memories, the filth of the prisons, the sludge of nights spent in makeshift shelters along the railroad tracks, or otherwise beneath the larches. Like Kronauer, she hadn't taken a bath for one or two generations, and perhaps even more. She smells just like I do, he thought.

• After several hours of night, a reedy, tinkling sound rose. Drops fell in the distance on a surface already filled with water.

—You hear that? Samiya Schmidt asked.

Kronauer nodded indistinctly. It was the first time Samiya Schmidt had broken her silence. And yes, he heard it.

—So here we are, Samiya Schmidt said. When we first saw each other, it was in the forest by a spring.

She was whispering. After this total absence of communication, two or three sentences that had come in quick succession seemed like logorrhea.

—That was a long time ago, Kronauer broke in. You were dying.

He, too, was talking with strange fluency, as if he was alive or at least had died fairly recently.

—I carried you on my back, he continued.

—Yes, I remember, she said. Thank you.

They listened to the distant noise of the spring for several minutes. Kronauer was surprised not to have noticed it earlier. Maybe the water's influx was weak and intermittent.

—You're barely doing much better today, Kronauer said.

—That's because I've been hit in all the worst spots, Samiya Schmidt said.

Then she pushed her hair back and opened her clothes to show a hole at the base of her throat and another just north-west of her right breast.

—But who shot you there? Kronauer asked.

—Hannko Vogulian, that whore, Samiya Schmidt whispered.

She let Kronauer digest that information. She herself needed some silence. She remembered the confrontation, or tried to.

—She has her father's magical eyes, she finally said.

The disgust in her voice was evident.

—That's all right, Kronauer said consolingly.

He distinctly remembered Hannko Vogulian's strange gaze, that admirable and strange gaze that he had eventually come to appreciate, back in the time of the kolkhoz, in the time of the Levanidovo, centuries ago.

—She hits the spots she wants down to the millimeter, even in the darkness. She's a bitch. A perfect copy of her father. He lives in her.

—Oh, really, Kronauer said to keep the conversation going.

—He visits her. When he's in her, there's no difference between him and her.

With that, Samiya Schmidt's secrets ended. Long minutes went by, then half the night. Neither of them nodded off.

For no particular reason, Kronauer thought it was a good idea, at the darkest, coldest, dreariest point, to continue their conversation.

—And you? he asked awkwardly.

—What, me? Samiya Schmidt immediately replied.

She got up abruptly. Although she had seemed despondent and unable to move at all, Kronauer heard her move away from him, walk through the trees, hit the trunks and bushes, whisper and yelp. She ran and leaped at a manic speed. She had discovered the spring and, every so often, she slapped the calm puddle nearby. She moved around until dawn, then she came back to sit by Kronauer and, in the next days, she didn't speak a word to him.

− 35 −

• Going aimlessly through the taiga was a perpetual ordeal for Kronauer. He didn't necessarily show it, but fear twisted his stomach far more often than hunger did. Getting lost didn't mean anything, now he was always wandering and lost, but, such as when he had been dozing for a minute and regained consciousness, the first feeling he had upon waking was interconnected with a primitive fear of the forest. For hours afterward he would remember this painful awakening, the nauseated feeling of having to confront once again silence and noise, shadows, the smells of plants that were rotting or doomed to do so, the odors beasts had left behind, the lack of sky, solitude, the gaps quickly closed, the confusion between the path already followed and the one he would have to keep following incessantly.

• Of the four seasons, only fall was agreeable. The ground hardened, which made walking easier, the wild grasses and summer scrub diminished, fell back to the ground, the flying insects became rarer and rarer. There was less suffering than in winter, when surviving in the snow meant behaving like a Paleolithic man, or in the spring, when he had to deal with the mud, the racket of the birds, and the annoyance of carnivores intent on getting fat again. The summer months were nice, but they were short and squandered by the nightmarish presence of the last fleas, midges, and mosquitoes.

• There were years when Samiya Schmidt disappeared completely. One morning, she wasn't there anymore, for example, without any clear explanation, and her absence might last a month, but also three or four years, or even fifty-six or more. This defection was fine by Kronauer. He was used to her, but he couldn't help thinking of her as one of Solovyei's creatures, and therefore as someone who played a role in the thousand-year-long punishment Solovyei was meting out. His relations with Samiya Schmidt were somewhat fraternal and underscored, on her end and despite a long coexistence that ought to have allayed all tensions, an irrational distrust, bouts of sulkiness, angry gestures. They barely talked, each one shut up in his or her own lonely meditation, sometimes going for several weeks without exchanging a word. They didn't touch each other, even though physical contact wasn't a problem. They could grab each other without any revulsion in emergencies, when one of them was in a bad situation, a leg stuck in a pool of asphalt, or fainting in exhaustion by an anthill. When she had used up her last strength, he carried her on his back to a shelter and, when they were really too cold, they hugged each other. But, for the most part, they behaved as if they were two people who had no reason to feel each other, to caress each other, to palpate each other, or even to hold each other's hands and stroke each other. The only thing they did together in any way was walk among the trees from dawn to dusk, from autumn to autumn, one decade after another.

Also, during the periods when Samiya Schmidt no longer accompanied him, Kronauer didn't feel any sensation of emptiness. His daily routine wasn't affected and he didn't feel any nostalgia for their silent, halting, useless partnership. After a variable amount of time, often an immoderate amount, Samiya Schmidt would eventually reappear at the foot of a tree, and they would resume, without any particular explanation, without her being willing to talk about her absence, their communal progress.

To summarize: the years without Samiya Schmidt neither unnerved nor unsettled Kronauer.

• When he was all alone in the taiga, Kronauer sometimes stopped, lit a fire of branches, and launched into a monologue both internal and expressed in halting, completely spoken, or moaned words. He spoke of the Second Soviet Union, the Orbise, and his comrades who had died in battle, killed by enemies or radiation from the lands or the poisoned villages. He recited several extracts from Marxist-Leninist education manuals that he still remembered, then, when night fell, he spoke to the one love of his life, Irina Echenguyen, and he told her of his pain when he had pain, his small adventures in the heart of the forest, his dreams when he had dreamed, and, if he had the time before sleepiness overcame him, he tried to put a number to the temporal enormities that now separated him from Irina Echenguyen. Eight hundred and thirty years, he grumbled, as a horrible headache blinded him. Nine hundred and forty years and five months. One thousand nine hundred seventy-seven years or so.

• I am nothing anymore and I miss you.

• In a labyrinth of the taiga I walk in the company of a girl, Samiya Schmidt. I miss you. For the last two hundred years I've been thinking about you more often than before. Samiya Schmidt is unpredictable, she has her father's criminal violence inside herself, she is still haunted by her father even though he hasn't appeared for half a millennium. She's inherited bad dreams of her father. Often she loses all control over herself. She breaks those ties that connected her to a human form. She once resembled a soldier from the cultural revolution, and, when I found her upon leaving the camp, and even if she had grown much older, she still looked a bit odd, but now, during her crises, she doesn't look like anything. She sprawls out, she expands, she inflates, and in a few seconds, where there was an exhausted or nervous girl is now just a moving mass, an indescribable mass made of black feathers, blackish whirlwinds, and harsh whistling. The trees shake, the darkness pulses, time's passage increases violently or slows down. It's a horrible scene.

It's impossible to watch without being deeply unsettled. I can't help but feel petrified, feel like I'm inside a strange image, lost in a hostile mental territory, like I've fallen into the atrocious fears of childhood, been watched by unknown adults, or become dough to be shaped in the hands of a malevolent magician. Samiya Schmidt stretches out, she no longer has any limits, over hundreds of meters she screams and lets her anger, her rage flow, she shakes the trees, night and forest shriek deafeningly over hundreds of meters, the shrieks are interspersed with sobbing or solemn lines and curses. I try to take refuge in memories, I curl up at the foot of a shaking larch, on the snow that rises in oppressive spirals. The darkness thickens, the sky crows, there is the crackling of flames, but no fire anywhere. I take refuge in the distant past, in the traces that remain of our life together and our love. I miss you.

• The dog-headed enemies. After your murder in the clinic, I killed a few. Seven, maybe eight. In ambushes, of course, with the help of our best comrades. We identified them, we fixed our eyes on them. One after another, over fifteen days, we killed them. I won't tell you how, once or twice, it was very dirty. The eighth, we didn't have time to make sure, we had to pull back, others were coming. The guys we killed had dog heads, but, underneath, there was no physical difference between them and us. We had so much difficulty understanding, but they could have believed the enemy's sordid theories to the point of taking up arms against the Orbise and becoming a group of monsters with sadistic, monstrous practices. In any case, they massacred and raped. I don't know if the ones we killed were the ones who attacked the hospital. We didn't interrogate them. We killed them without wasting any time talking. Even among us we didn't say anything. We killed them and we separated. I forgot the names of our best comrades. For a long time, they persisted in a corner of my memory, but I had been instructed never to reveal the list to anyone. Over the years I did everything so that they wouldn't come back. We've acted as on our own and we agreed that our actions would stay secret forever. The civil war flared, the abuses and reprisals followed one another, the Orbise broke apart, but, as for this precise sequence of executions, our lips were sealed. Out of friendship and out of respect, in your memory, I don't know. It wasn't a heroic feat. We were silent as the grave. And now that I try to retrieve these names, they don't come. I'd like to speak them in your direction, so that you know which men were thinking of you when they killed these dog-headed brutes, so that you speak to them affectionately if you meet them, but their names have vanished. I'll make up a few here. Dobronia Izaayel, Rouda Bielougone, Yair Kroms, Solaf Onéguine, Anastasia Vivaldian. They're beautiful names, but they're not the right ones.

• When I came to the clinic, nothing in the wing they destroyed had been washed or cleaned, nothing had been put back in place, but the bodies had been taken away. The guards let me go into the main room where the butchery had happened. The IV bags had been thrown on the ground, some still hung from the stands that hadn't been knocked over. The serums had mixed with pools of blood. The militiamen responsible for carrying the bodies had tried not to set their feet on the spilled liquids, but they hadn't been successful and there were so many footprints and dirty streaks that it was impossible to go into the room. I didn't walk on the dirty tiles. I took four or five steps and I stopped. The room smelled like sickness, pharmaceutical products, and bestial rotting. There were few bullet holes in the wall. The dog-headed men had attacked their victims without finishing them off with their pistols. I didn't have any desire to visualize the horrifying details, the way it played out. I stayed there unwillingly and powerlessly. On a nightstand next to the bed where you usually were when you hadn't been brought into the treatment room, I saw a book that a visitor had recently offered you, a book you had told me you didn't enjoy, but which you told me you still hoped to finish reading before dying, a romance by Maria Kwoll that denounced once again the savage nature, the grotesquely hideous nature of all sexuality. I don't know if you had the time to finish this romance before being martyred. I myself decided never to read it before my death, and then, when I was in the Radiant Terminus kolkhoz, I looked for it in the library, but Samiya Schmidt didn't have it. I stayed there for a minute without moving. I stayed for two, maybe three minutes, but not more. My mind was empty. I hadn't made any promise. I thought of you without seeing you. I barely looked at the crime scene. My eyes were riveted to the cover of this book. For hundreds of years I have been trying to remember its title, but I've forgotten it.

– 36 –

• Curtains of blood, curtains of flames, absolute darkness, absolute oblivion, absolute knowledge, no more place or time, and you
pull back the threads that extend your fingers, you pull back the
feathers that extend your wings, you pull back the wandering souls,
the drum beats in you is not a heart is a drum, is not a drum is the
horrible pestle of the world and of hells, nothing exists anymore,
absolute absence, and you wring your hands while screaming, you
shake your wings while whistling, no more place but you are in the
heart of the walls dripping with plutonium, you are in the middle of
the trees, you are standing among the clouds, above the steppes,
no more place but you are at the center of the kolkhoz ruins and
around you is only a silent rumbling of burning death, the drum beats
and resounds, the hundred-year-old trees are your henchmen, the
drum beats is not a drum is the slow spurt of sap in the arteries and
veins of the larches, the drum beats with notes so low they're inaudible but shaking the earth and grasses, shaking the flames, taking
all stability from the flames and upsetting them, is your voice, is not
a drum is your voice, your growls when you shake while whistling,
your cawing, is not your voice is your magic thoughts in the middle
of nowhere, curtains of blood around you you are neither born nor
to be born, curtains of flames envelop you you are not dead or to be

reborn, you beat your massive wings you are motionless like a dead dog, you whistle horribly, the trees bend wildly and stand back up, nothing dances, nothing dances or moves, no shaking, no waves, you open your wings as if to fly away but you don't fly, you pull back the crows that have flown in your stead, not a single crow disobeys you, you pull and you clutch the threads that link you to the human marionettes that have survived, neither dead nor living they have survived, sometimes you name them while cawing or crowing, you name them in coded languages that nobody has learned or unlearned, sometimes you call them one after the other for hours on end, but most often you only grant them pathetic anonymity and you throw them nowhere, you force them to wander without your help on pretext of respecting their individuality, wandering without your help in the unknown, or maybe you carve them up, or, if these are your daughters or your wives, you marry them, the drum beat is not a drum is the breeze in the depths, is the backwash in the depths, the drum beats the larches run in all directions then lie down then stand back up, lie down then stand back up, there is neither darkness nor light, is not a drum is your iron will and your fiery rage exerted upon what is absent and what has never existed, is your heartless and insane word violently shaping emptiness and nothingness, you send flying to the heavens feathers and needles as if you were a tempest, but heaven is absent and has never existed, only your mentally crippled and mutistic marionettes, only your senseless marionettes are witnesses to the storms that you create, you pull back the strings connecting you to them, only they are hearers of your word, for the rest there is nobody among the dead and nobody among the living, humanity has been swept away, humanity has dissolved into nothingness, excitedly it has wended down the path of abysses and it hasn't left salvageable organic crumbs, total forgetting, total absence, total darkness after the curtains of blood and the curtains of flames and after the black oil, and you sway and you rock while making the remnants of eternity, you dance on the tips of wings while using actors' and actresses' remains for your theater, you are neither here nor elsewhere, you cross the taiga while chirring the remnants of songs and fragments of theater, if you were living you would be an immense black bird, you would fill immense sections of the old forest, you would live hidden in your nest or in a kolkhoz invented for you alone, patiently awaiting crazy beggars or travelers, awaiting for twenty years beneath the trees the arrival of a survivor, one hundred and forty-nine years, eleven centuries awaiting the presence of an exhausted or already-dead survivor, twelve thousand full lunar years, patiently awaiting the resurrection of at least one living or at least one dead, awaiting that in vain, the drum beats an endless death knell, the drum beats it recites total dissolution, the endless flow of the end, if you were dead you would be an endless animal, you would have for yourself alone the forest to the oceans, the forest with all its animals that would obey you, its grouchy, greedy, lusty, and stinking animals, and to relieve your boredom, to leave the forest and this bestial promiscuity you would dig in the nothingness of the tunnels opening onto new universes, but there is no longer place or time, only the drum that does not stop striking and striking, is not your wings that strike the ground is the drum, is not the wing beats of those who survived and obey you, or the footsteps of dancers you animate by pulling back magic and silken ropes, and black feathers that tremble, there is nobody at the end of your strings, when there are male dancers you eliminate them out of jealousy and when there are female dancers you marry them, then you reject them, then you forget them, then you reinvent them with their remains, the drum does not stop striking, absolute and definitive forgetfulness, absolute obscurity, neither hope nor despair, outpouring of forgetfulness and nothingness, and you soar into the middle of nowhere, you do not make a movement in the middle of the flames and the blood, you like the rhythm of the drum, you accompany it while whistling the name of your disaster marionettes, you are at the end of your black theater, even the marionettes are absent, even these miserable marionettes, the drum beats, there are no marionettes, only their misery, only their confusion and their misery.

− 37 −

- Kronauer had started a small campfire. Nearby, less than fifteen paces away, wolves sniffed and, every so often, raised their heads to howl. There were three of them. Kronauer had noticed the smell of their scruffy pelts wafting around him. Dirty fur, scraggly and dirty bodies, the breaths of starving wildlings. They had noticed the fire. Thanks to their animal intuition, to their sixth sense able to detect the supernatural and anomalies in the universe, they knew that a neither-dead-nor-living creature was moving near them, but they couldn't see anything specific. That unnerved them. They asked the snow and darkness in vain, clattered their teeth, and howled.

It had been night for hours. Kronauer continually added pieces of wood to the flames. The ice had melted around the hearth, but the heat didn't reach beyond the first branches and no snow masses had fallen to dust the form sitting right below. Kronauer barely moved. He imagined, rightly, that to the wolves he was just a strange shadow, and that not even his fire was reflected in their retinas. After wondering for a minute how to react, he had finally relaxed. He wasn't in danger. He hated these huge winter carnivores prowling behind the bushes, he hated their breaths, their growls, their urinous mustiness. He didn't like meeting their beautiful murderous gazes. But he had nothing to fear and, deep down, he missed it, because if he had belonged to a normal world the wolves could have shortened his nightmare by attacking him and eating him. Don't think you'll get out of death like that, Kronauer, he thought. Don't think that you'll end up right in their jaws. Whether Solovyei's still interested in you or has forgotten you, you'll keep waiting. One thousand or two thousand years, doesn't matter. It'll go on. Don't count on something else. He felt extremely tired. His mind went blank every so often. Now the wolves were gone. He must have dozed off. He added a log to the fire and began to grumble disorganizedly.

- I miss you, he grumbled.
  Our best comrades, he grumbled.
  Workers, peasants, soldiers, he pondered.
  Prisoners. Singers. Captains, monks.
  He listed several names in a trembling, heavy voice, with pauses that lasted several minutes or several weeks, that sort of gap. His memory and his inventive faculties were getting worse and worse.

- Mikitia Yerushalim, he grumbled with difficulty. Bölögdar Mourmanski, Gansur Yagakorian, Anaïs Apfelstein, Noria Izmayilbekov. Jean Petitjean. Dondör Zek. Sirène Mavrani. Molnia Krahn. Werner Örgöldaï.

- He had dozed off again. His chest too close to the flames. The right arm of his jacket had caught fire. Small silent flames, accompanied with a nauseating black smoke. Then the rags that surrounded the central zipper of his clothes, then one of his shapka's earflaps. The burnt smell hadn't woken him up.

- It'll pass, I say to keep going. He's been through worse before.
  Our best marionettes, I say. Him or me, doesn't matter. When he's stuck I keep going. Zombies, deep shadows, devoted servants. The dead stuck forever in the Bardo. Dead come from the dead. Wives come from unknown mothers. Henchmen. Best puppets and best dolls.

—Samiya Schmidt, I began to recite in a calm but forceful voice. Irina Echenguyen. Elli Kronauer. Vassilissa Marachvili. Barguzin. Hannko Vogulian. Ilyushenko. Myriam Umarik . . . There was a gust of wind. The day had broken, the fire had gone out. The wolves howled. The branches shook violently. The ashes spun around, scattered on the snow mixed with silt and debris. Several crows watched the scene and, every so often, they opened their wings and beaks halfway and cawed. I had no reason to continue reciting my list. The noise was too deafening around me.

Our best marionettes, I said again in a muffled voice.

The list wasn't complete.

Then I was quiet.

− 38 −

• At the same moment, or perhaps a little earlier, let's say for example thirteen hundred forty-two lunar months earlier, Myriam Umarik heard a noise in the distance and woke up. She had been dreaming that her father was visiting her in her house in the Levanidovo, that he had briefly seduced her, then broken all the furniture and all the windows and raped her. She had opened her eyes right at the worst of it, and at first she had trouble leaving behind her fear, overcoming her urge to vomit, and understanding that she was beyond Solovyei's reach, in a reality less painful than that of her nightmare.

She stood up. She had fallen asleep sitting on the little bench that was an extension of the gatekeeper's shed she had made her residence. She had moved there sixty-seven years earlier with her husband, the engineer Barguzin. The night was stifling and she went out to doze in the open air, in light clothes, not caring about the mosquitoes just as plentiful outside the shed as inside.

The sun had risen and sprinkled gold on the peaks of the birches. It was already warm. This was the end of July, in the middle of a heat wave.

She banged on the wooden partition just behind her, so Barguzin would know something was happening outside. Just out of sheer respect for propriety. In reality, over the years, Barguzin had been lying on the bed, inert and mute, and, as the Gramma Udgul wasn't there anymore to rub his face with heavy-heavy water, then with deathly-deathly water, and then to revive him by pouring lively-lively water between his eyes, his state hadn't changed.

—Hey Barguzin! she said in a raspy voice that couldn't be heard by interlopers. I think somebody's coming!

• They had both fled the Levanidovo. Radiant Terminus had become unlivable. Shortly after the massacre, the provisional nuclear power plant had exploded in the Soviet's basement, the accident had ended the energy and hot-water supply in the kolkhoz. A burning wave had set fire to the majority of the kolkhoz's houses through the underground network. Most of the inhabitants no longer showed any signs of life. Solovyei wandered in the main road, inhaling the smoke and silent fumes, walking on the piles of burned debris, whispering or declaiming poems. He walked heavily and proudly as if nothing had happened, and he only calmed down at night, when he went to join the Gramma Udgul in her hangar, which had suffered less than the rest of the village.

Numb with cold and fear, still drawn to the old dream of collaborating with the Organs, Myriam Umarik and Barguzin had left Radiant Terminus a week before the thaw, without saying good-bye to anyone. They had stocked up on several pemmican loaves, enough to last them until spring and through all the winters to come. In a laminated envelope, able to resist decades of rain and snow, they had enclosed a letter addressed to the Regional Commission for Recruitment into the Organs, where they offered their services for all inspections, surveillance missions, or even executions of people's enemies the Organs deemed necessary.

For lack of a post office, the letter hadn't been sent, and even so Myriam Umarik and Barguzin both knew deep down that there was no longer a Regional Commission of the Organs, or any Organs, or even a population to monitor, that there was nothing of the sort for thousands of kilometers, but they felt that they had done something crucial, something that marked their separation from the kolkhoz and its demonic president, and that above all signified their return to general society, which was composed of the living, or at least the dead. And once they had found this gatekeeper's hut after months of wandering, they had settled in with the idea that they would start a new existence there. They would make themselves useful by rigorously recording the passing trains and vagrants headed from the taiga to nowhere. They'd had enough basic Marxist-Leninist training to put themselves completely into policing power.

The line was closed down and no traveler got lost in the area. But they took their work seriously and always stayed on the lookout, certain that their responsibility was to monitor all movements in the region, both military and civil, and, in this spirit, every month they prepared exhaustive reports on the subject—orally because they didn't have any paper to write them on.

• Myriam Umarik got off the bench and looked in the direction of the noise that had woken her up. As there were trees and undergrowth all around, she could barely make out anything specific.

In front of the cottage, the rails had been immersed in grasses and, forty meters off, the tracks joined a grove of birches and disappeared. A thirty-year-old pine had taken root between two crossties and seemed to be positioning itself as the triumphant vanguard of further vegetation. In the other direction, the rails went on for three hundred meters, then sank into a burial mound. There were trees everywhere, with mingled scents, as was often the case on the edge of the taiga. Another time, the steppes had dominated the area, and the forest was now invading it little by little.

Beyond a little curtain of pines, Myriam Umarik saw movement, some colors that weren't those of the forest, then it was hidden by a crease in the terrain, then it reappeared. Branches were audibly cracking and echoing under the mature trees.

Myriam Umarik's heart pounded. She hadn't seen anyone in years and she was afraid she no longer knew how to handle meeting a traveler. Suddenly, she realized she was half naked. She hurried into the hut to put on a skirt and wrap her shoulders in a shawl. She shook Barguzin, who didn't react, and then she quickly went back out to the doorstep. Now she was standing next to the bench and she waited for the visitors to come.

It was a small caravan of peddlers like the ones who had gone from village to village even before the dawn of industrial capitalism. It was composed of three men, one a teenager, and two overburdened animals who seemed to have mutant bovines as their ancestors, and who more than anything looked like obstinate and mute masses, with hair that swept the ground and prevented her from determining the exact number of their feet. All gave off stifling fragrances of grease, which preceded them horribly for a good twenty meters and made Myriam Umarik want to vomit.

The men were wearing lambskin coats, they had colored shirts on, merchants' hats, but their clothes were in such disrepair that the rags had no elegance at all. They had faces darkened by filth, and their beards were thick, which displeased Myriam Umarik, as she had lost all her hair in the Levanidovo while in contact with plutonium, and she had to be satisfied with wigs.

• She let them approach as she stood stock-solid several meters from the hut, then she saluted them in the manner of the Altaic Mongols, which seemed most appropriate, welcomed them, and offered to slake their thirst. All three of them made faces and she went to find a pan filled with water that they would share greedily.

Two were fortysomething men, robust and extremely noisome, and the third was a young adult even dirtier than his elders. Myriam Umarik had trouble hiding her disgust, but she smiled at them and swayed from one foot to the other, which made her look like someone who urgently needed to urinate.

A conversation began. They were salvagers as well as peddlers. They scoured ruins and were looking for a refugee camp or a work camp to unload treasures and products. They asked Myriam Umarik about concentration structures in the area and about any paths that might lead to those.

—There's nothing of the sort here, Myriam Umarik replied.

These individuals didn't please her at all, their activities were clearly associated with those of the people's enemies, and their fetid odors nauseated her.

Then they asked her what she was doing, in the forest, in this hut so far away from everything.

—I'm from the Second Soviet Union, Myriam Umarik declared nervously, while throwing back her head arrogantly. With my husband, here, we watch for trouble. Even in the most distant corners, the supreme law of the proletarian revolution reigns. Here we warn people not to stand on the tracks, to cross them carefully, not to ruin the common good. We alert the authorities to hooligans, suspects, and partisans of capitalism.

The three men laughed through their beards.

Then they tied her up. One of them went inside the hut to see whether the husband she had mentioned could pose a problem, then he came back to say that he was harmless. Then, in turns, they raped her.

– 39 –

• Hannko Vogulian set her pen aside and counted the pages she had
just written. Four. In a week, she had inked twenty-two. She had a
small gleeful smile. Her work was progressing.

Everything was calm in the house and in the environs. There had
been a cold snap and the snow had hardened. The slightest noise in
the forest reverberated for kilometers. Nothing alarming had happened
outside since night's fall. She didn't even need to go to the window to
scan the clearing and its outskirts. It was enough for her to listen. She
could also analyze the air that had entered through the cracks. Smells
of snow, of larches hibernating. She took several deep breaths to find
out more. Outside, a fox had kept watch for a minute before darkness.
It had left its acrid stench in the cranberry patch. Farther off a second
fox, maybe a vixen, had unearthed a magpie carcass and carried it away.
As far as recent traces went, that was all.

Hannko Vogulian adjusted the lamplight, which had fallen a bit,
and picked up her pen. She wrote slowly and without crossing anything out. She was trying to rewrite, sentence by sentence, the original
text of *Dogs in the Taiga*, a little novel by Maria Kwoll she had read
hundreds of years earlier in the kolkhoz library. She transcribed as best
as she could what her memory dictated, but often she was sure she was
inventing and, besides, she was knowingly replacing forgotten sections
with summaries and abridgements of her own, or aphorisms she felt

were appropriate. From a strictly literary point of view, what she was doing was an aberration, but she didn't care. I could say as much, as far as I'm concerned. Her or me, doesn't matter. What did make a difference, ultimately, was that she darkened her notebook with prose.

• Here, a rape scene, Hannko Vogulian wrote in her role as copyist, but she didn't really know if she was speaking on behalf of Maria Kwoll or her own self.

Here a new rape scene. Another one. I've systematically avoided describing them in detail. Alluding to them is enough. For victims, it's unbearable. For witnesses, it's equally unbearable. We're confronted with the filthiness of the cock's language, at one moment or another we have to go along with the exhalations of the cock's language, we have the impression of sharing something with the rapists. Into every description of rape comes an element of complicity. I've always avoided that and it's not because I know Myriam Umarik that I'm going to watch this scene objectively, as a witness, or that I'm going to plunge back into the horror subjectively, incarnating myself within her.

Three merchants wreathed in a fetid aura, men who came from the forest after weeks of traveling without ever cleaning off their excrement or dust, three brutes stinking of sweat from effort and solitude, stinking of emanations from their glands, three harsh males greedy for money, junk sellers and rapists.

I have no desire to make them appear in my writing, Hannko Vogulian wrote, except to kill them, to help Myriam Umarik take revenge, to bleed them messily and kill them.

• Hannko Vogulian sighed. She had changed the name of the unfortunate heroine in *Dogs in the Taiga* and bestowed upon her the name of her sister.

She was reluctant to continue the story where she had left off. In *Dogs in the Taiga*, the heroine's revenge had eventually come about, but the heroine took at least thirty pages to find the right moment, and Hannko Vogulian was torn between her confused, incomplete memories of Maria Kwoll's text and her wish to see Myriam Umarik assassinate her torturers as quickly as possible. She put the rest of the novel off until the next day. As she still had several hours before nodding off, she decided to insert several of Maria Kwoll's aphorisms and reflections instead of rewriting the descriptions of landscapes the author always inserted when she didn't have the courage to continue her narrative. All these images of nature, of trees or grasses that she used to pull out of the hells she had sent her characters to.

• The swamp of their bodies, Hannko Vogulian wrote, the cock's fog of their bodies, the cock's and blood's language, an ideology forged in the Mesozoic era, the pitiful hormonal urges of their sexual organs, their ancestral culture of rape, their sexual education entirely organized around some of them penetrating the others, predatory behaviors that nothing had changed, lewd normalcy, expecting rut, female complacency established by incessant and domineering conditioning, female submission to the cock's language, their permanent apprenticeship to disaster and rape, their ancestral female culture of rape, the feelings of shame, abnormality, or ridicule imposed upon females if they rejected penetration. Expecting moans, trembling, excretions. This deep sexual catastrophe all fell into without a struggle, living and dead alike, comrades and enemies alike, commingled in the same sludge, egalitarian prigs as well as partisans of capitalism and slavery, without a struggle, into this same hideous mire.

• Then she shut her notebook and set it on the shelf.
—Well, I'll come back to that later, she said.
She turned off the lamp. She went to get a white she-wolf pelt and wrapped it around her legs before sitting in an armchair facing the window. Next to the armchair, right by her hand, she had propped up a loaded rifle.

Now—which is to say for several centuries—she was like the Gramma Udgul had once been, never really sleeping. She just dozed in darkness, while murmuring dreams rather than projecting them unconsciously on her inner screens.

And she waited.

– 40 –

• A bird beneath the clouds. Very gray, the clouds, very black, the bird, and when it clicks its wings to regain altitude, it's also noticeable that it's rather large, let's say the size of a human or thereabouts, or a corpse. It clicks its wings forcefully in the wind, at the edge of the haze, but nobody hears it or sees it. It's above the taiga, there aren't many people either on the ground or in the air. The bird stays in the same place, follows a current, glides, comes back. Below, successions of small hills as far as eyes can see, some gullies, millions of trees, no paths, occasional bare patches filled by lakes of dark water or stretches of oil. The sky can't be seen from the earth, the branches get in the way, but it, the bird, notices the smallest detail through the leaves, the needles, as if the earth was naked and deserted. It has this gift. It has this kind of gaze. It clicks its wings to play with the wind, it soars, it drifts, it hides as a floating, unmoving object. It or I, doesn't matter. It doesn't dive, it stays up high, but, no matter the variety of trees it overlooks, no matter how thick and dense the treetops, to its eyes it's as if everything was transparent. It sees everything. But not everything interests it. What it watches is the caravan that advances, with its two overburdened animals, its three heinous merchants, and their captive.

• Myriam Umarik bumps around heavily across one of the beasts of burden, wrists and ankles shackled, she is set like a sack among the bags of clothes and salvaged tools that are the merchants' stock in trade. When they discovered that her beautiful hair was actually a wig, they felt like they had been hoodwinked, and the youngest one had been so overcome with rage that he had unsheathed a knife to cut her throat. The others had restrained him at the last moment. Don't forget that she can, if we bring her with us, spread her legs for us every day, and then, if we've had enough of her, we can cut her up, drain her dry, and turn her into pemmican. And that is how she left her husband Barguzin: as a sex slave and as a future basic ingredient in an energy-giving preparation.

She is sick, her gut is swollen and painful. Her abductors treat her badly, they are full of horrible contemptuous gestures and they insult her when they throw her on the ground to penetrate her. She alternates between nausea, feverish sleep, and prostration. When they rape her, she is now so inert that they no longer need to have two of them holding her down while the third twitches and lets loose in her.

For a week the landscape barely changes. Myriam Umarik doesn't go to the trouble of opening her eyes to make sure. Black pines, larches, sometimes birch trees. The sort-of yak carrying her on its back brushes past mossy trunks, every so often bushes studded with berries, stalks that are flexible and full of sap. It is not fall yet. Myriam Umarik is smacked by the mutant plants and, her face filthy with mud, remnants of sperm, and various juices, she suffocates under the emanations the skin, grease, and wool of her mount produce. She is semiconscious, in a state close to stupor.

But it's a stupor filled with visions and repetitive dreams, and, among these dreams, a bird rises to examine the world in her place, and gives her the impression that she is still alive.

• Left, left, the bird crows silently, commenting on the clicking of its wings. Right. You're lying across the first beast. Right, right. You're going past a birch tree, mutant plants that nobody has named yet are growing under the trees. I'll do so. Redfruit ballerinas, brokenheads, susmanción peppers, birdcatchers' crons, spinelesses. Left, left, right. The silent forest. Only the footsteps of the brigands and their beasts, their breaths. There's nothing useful on your beast. Clothes, bags filled with jewels, kitchen utensils, unloaded weapons. On the beast behind there are pyramids of objects. Left. Left, left. Right, right, left. A computer. Interest: none. Saws. Much more useful. Tools for butchering. A debarker right at your fingertips. You'll use that. At the right moment you'll use it to kill them. I'll tell you. Right, left. When they stop. They're tired. Left, left. They won't fall on you. Not right away and not together. I'll guide you.

• At night they tie the beasts, light a fire in the distance, and share a handful of pemmican. They have put down Myriam Umarik, thrown her on the earth, and for now they're not busy with her. She takes the opportunity to crawl as best as she can toward the beast carrying the butchery tools. Once she's lying close to the beast, she stays calm. A bird talks to her in her head, black and powerful, in the surrounding darkness. The beasts, normally unflappable, seem a bit nervous and pound their hooves against the ground, the rotting leaves. It's a sign. The moment is coming, the bird will guide her to her revenge.

The youngest one leaves the fire and comes to find her. She detests him more than the others because now that the rapes have taken on a less communal nature, sometimes instead of immediately penetrating her vagina he squats over her head, hits her and rubs her face with his vile cock, and inserts this cock between her lips while grunting insane obscenities. But, that evening, after having unfettered her ankles, and doubtless because he obeys a telepathic suggestion from the bird, he begins, while telling her what he wishes, untying the rope binding her wrists. He insults her and, at the same time, he begs her crudely to rut energetically, for a change. Not like an inert mass. More like a girl who likes sex.

To the right, just above, says the bird.

She'd had no reaction at all until then, only breathing as little as possible so as not to inhale the young rapist's appalling breath. She groans a sort of approbation, a half-uttered word that the rapist interprets as thick approbation, and she slowly gets up, giving the impression that she is thinking of some way to satisfy him, and, once she stands in front of him, she waits for the bird to give her orders.

Rise your arm as if to begin an embrace, the bird advises.

Intoxicated by the demand he has made, the rapist doesn't suspect anything. The bird persuades him to relax, and even to close his eyes in anticipation of the surprise in store. In any case, the shadows are thick, and the campfire's flames only barely, barely illuminate the scene.

The handle of the debarker, the bird repeats to Myriam Umarik. A little further to the right.

Myriam Umarik feels around for a second.

Now, the bird says.

Myriam Umarik takes the debarker from its storage spot, immediately at hand and held by nothing, and she drives the blade horizontally between the rapist's shoulders, at the base of the neck. Right beneath the larynx, as she had been told.

•   She does this with a steady, light hand, guided by an image that the bird has projected within her fingers. The man's veins and arteries are spared, but his windpipe doesn't resist, it's cut between two rings of cartilage. And that's all.

The value of a cut of this sort is that the adversary is immediately deprived of a voice. Gurgles don't go more than five meters. Shocked and irremediably wounded, he falls down while thinking of his stupidity and his life now empty of air, rapes, and long-term prospects. First he's on his knees, his hands gripping his throat with the idea of possibly repairing his essential pipe, then crouching on the ground, his legs kicking softly in the darkness. He's not dead. Myriam Umarik doesn't squint in the darkness to see him. The bird takes him by the arms, keeps him from wriggling, and throws him aside. It sets him down behind several trees. An inexplicable wheeze can be heard.

• Then Myriam Umarik is lying on the ground again, two paces away from the beast that provided her with the necessary materials. The beast shakes a little, without ever kicking or breaking its leash out of nervousness. Maybe, in its obtuse animal sleep, it's a victim of disagreeable visions.

Myriam Umarik waits.

The rumble of the ruminants respirating.

An inexplicable gurgle behind a stand of birches.

It is very dark.

• The second merchant comes and doesn't need anything specific from her, he unzips his fly as he mumbles several lewd obscenities. She waits for him to lean over her to slice his throat. Although guided every quarter of a second by the bird, she presses too hard on the neck when she plunges the blade. The bandit collapses, he doesn't scream, but at the same time as the windpipe she has opened several blood vessels that spurt scalding-hot blood on her. The other one rears back. He is straddling her, he noses upward and a fountain of blood escapes from him. She twists to avoid the heavy man's fall, and, when he falls forward, she pulls away quickly. The bird comes out of darkness and drags the merchant next to the first one.

The beast, right next to her, drops a cowpat that will disappear into its disgusting fur.

No more noise.

For a minute, no more noise. Then a log crackling on the fire. Then the third man comes toward Myriam Umarik. He doesn't worry about the other two being absent. He probably should, but the cock's language bawls its desires within him and overpowers his better judgment, defers his better judgment to later. He gets down to see where he'll stick in his penis. But at the moment he begins to undo his belt, which requires both hands, Myriam Umarik receives a new order and she caresses the bottom of his chin with the debarker. The gesture works perfectly again, the third rapist is incapacitated, instantaneously sentenced to silence and the fear of possibly having to breathe for several minutes in unbearable agony, without losing his blood too quickly, among confused thoughts where the cock's language now only plays a secondary and parasitical role.

- Left. Further left. A little bit more.

The bird encourages Myriam Umarik to continue retaliating against the three men lying at the foot of the birches. She obeys it. A little further to the left again. A little more to the left in this hodgepodge.

She rummages through the items the second beast carries on its stinking back. They're packed haphazardly in baskets, boxes, bundles. The debarker was easy to reach. The other butchery tools, not so much. In the darkness she has to follow the bird's directions alone. Now, to the right. More to the left. A little to the left. Below.

Finally her hand lands on an ax and she extricates it from the jumble. Holding it, she thinks of Solovyei, of the hatchet he often carried on his belt. Then she forgets him. Solovyei is far away, lost among the past's abysses, beyond reach for centuries, vanished.

Tottering, she goes back to the men. She goes back with the ax. She threw away the debarker after the third throat-slicing. She feels like she has no more strength left. She walks toward the three men in the darkness, without really knowing what she will do. It depends on her, but mostly on the bird.

When she comes to the foot of the birches, she waits a minute.

The three merchants are lying next to each other, legs splayed. All have their hands around their throats. Two utter a fleshy, almost regular groan, they've managed to find the way to hold their windpipe in the black night, to breathe and survive. A provisional way, but still a way. The third one, in the middle, is dead.

On the other side of the trees, Myriam Umarik hears the fire crackling, the beasts dropping cowpats. The air is warm. It's a pleasant summer night, but the sky is completely black, and, besides, the branches obscure it. It's a pleasant summer night in the taiga and there aren't even flies to ruin it.

Myriam Umarik raises her ax. She obeys the bird.

Left, middle, right, orders the bird.

Between the legs, orders the bird. Left, middle, right.

- 41 -

• —And now? Myriam Umarik whispered. Now what do I do?

—It's best if you keep going, the bird said.

Dawn broke. They were both sitting in front of the campfire's ashes. The embers had stopped reddening, and they stayed there in silence, meditating on things of the world or equivalent subjects. And now a bluish light hung between the trunks and the forest, which until then had been made only of noises and silence, became an image.

Myriam Umarik didn't turn her head toward the beasts. A little farther off, beyond the tufts of redfruit ballerinas whose colors couldn't be seen, was the little esplanade where she had carried out justice. Justice had been rendered without long tragic tirades, or even an attempt at a short speech. Deep in the shadows, she had brought her ax down three times and she had left the place without waiting for anything else. Three ax blows to the pelvis, to her torturers' crotches, to finish off two who were living and one who was dead.

—I could return to Barguzin, Myriam Umarik whispered. I don't know if I'll find the way back, but I can try.

—Sure, the bird said. The forest is a labyrinth. You'll get lost. Better that you go forward.

—Where to? Myriam Umarik asked quietly.

—In any case, Barguzin is deceased, the bird declared pompously, then cawed.

It was hard to determine whether it was a human with wings, or a bird endowed with reason and a voice, or if it was a magical creature, or a corpse. What was clear, though, was that it was cawing.

They were both silent until the day rose. The summer's warmth snaked toward them, with its smells of dry leaves, mushrooms and blueberries, blackberries, susmanción peppers. Thirty meters away, one of the beasts shook its huge, woolly head and dropped a pat. The other did so as well, setting off a clinking of utensils that were now disorganized on his back, then it calmed down. Everything was quiet.

• They didn't talk about what had happened the previous night, or the horrible week that had preceded it. She was covered with stains and blood, but she didn't want that discussed out loud, even with her own voice. When the opportunity arose, she would immerse herself in a stream, a lake, and she would wash herself. For now, she had to forget or pretend to forget the filth, the crimes endured and the crimes committed in revenge.

—Once, back where I was living, there was Solovyei, she said suddenly. Did you know him?

—Never heard of it, the bird lied, then indicated that it would leave.

It waved its wings. They were extraordinarily black.

• —And the beasts? Myriam Umarik asked.

—If I were you, I'd make pemmican out of them, the bird advised.

- 42 -

• Not far from there, if several thousand kilometers aren't taken into consideration and, indeed, if a gap of several hundred years can be overlooked, a new black sea formed in the taiga, along a peat bog already overflowing with slimy water and naphtha.

Aldolay Schulhoff was leaning against a pine trunk and he watched the dinky puddle surging. He watched it appear, well up, grow, and stop increasing. The entirety of the process hadn't required more than eleven months and, when all was done, Aldolay Schulhoff sighed.

—It all came up from the buried villages, he said.

Next to him, leaning against another pine, Kronauer grumbled in agreement. He felt exhausted. He hadn't wanted to talk, but he made an attempt to strike up a conversation with his companion.

—It's like the memories, he stuttered with effort.

His ideas, like his voice, were mushy.

—It's like the memories, he said. It's black oil. It comes up from the buried lives.

—Sure, Aldolay Schulhoff said.

• They had met in an earlier spring. They each, like the other, had been attracted like magnets to the remains of a train car that they had seen through the trees. They had headed toward this unexpected shape and, after walking around it, they had literally bumped into each other.

Their relationship had taken time to settle, because of the difficulty they had communicating in a language they both knew. After decades or centuries of solitary walking, their vocabulary had diminished and was slow to return. But it had come back, at last. A gruff rapport had been established between the two men, and, in any case, neither was aggressive toward the other. In these times when humanity no longer existed, calling this friendship wasn't excessive.

The train car had sunk partway and its roof was broken open. When fall came, Aldolay Schulhoff had spent a long while talking at Kronauer about the possibility of climbing up the wagon's side, up to the hold, and falling into the opening in order to have shelter for the winter, but, after a discussion that had lasted until the first snowfall, they had rejected this bold expedition, feeling, perhaps rightly, that once they were shut away in the car's darkness they would have difficulty extracting themselves. So they had spent the winter as they usually did, shivering as they shifted around the pine trunks according to the direction of the wind, and, sometimes, they managed to light a fire and warm themselves by it while saying a few sentences.

—I don't know why, but I feel like I've already seen this train car, Kronauer said after a tedious silence.

—These rails, though, Aldolay Schulhoff said. The tracks led somewhere.

—There must have been a camp at the end of the line, Kronauer added.

—Sure, Aldolay Schulhoff said weakly. A camp at the end of the line. That would make sense.

—If it wasn't this train car, it was another one like it, Kronauer mused.

They were quiet for a minute. The twilight surrounded them and didn't change. For a long time already there hadn't been day or night. Seasons, sure, but days and nights, no. They stayed that way for a minute, as if they had fallen asleep.

—The locomotive must be down below, Aldolay Schulhoff said.

—Who knows how far down, Kronauer said.

• Aldolay Schulhoff only had the skin on his bones, if you can call it that, but he compensated for his thinness with a uniform of ragged clothes that filled out his figure until he looked like a normal trespasser. For a whole period, in the past, he had worn ribbons and rags left on trees or under rocks by shamans. But in the centuries that had followed the disappearance of the shamans and their devotees, he had made do with what he pulled off carcasses of the dead or their like, from dead birds or animal corpses or soldiers. It was an outfit that evolved at the mercy of his discoveries, which were still extremely rare. It wasn't elegant, this outfit, but in the chill, the wind, and the darkness, it performed the function Aldolay Schulhoff expected of it.

Kronauer, clothes-wise, now barely differed from Aldolay Schulhoff, but all the same he continued to resemble a prisoner who had once been a militiaman, perhaps because he wore a shapka he replaced every so often, whenever he found one on a dead watchman or on officers out of harm's way, regularly and in any case at least once a century, the red star that confirmed its connection to the Second Soviet Union. The rest of his uniform was less stereotypical and more like what the beggars collected perfunctorily in the dumps, back when there were still beggars and dumps.

• Now they were both together around a wood fire. As usual, they were quiet. The night went by, then a day, then another night. The difference between night and day had been imperceptible.

—It may not seem like it, but I was once in love, Aldolay Schulhoff mumbled abruptly.

—Yes, that happened to me too, Kronauer said.

—Oh, Aldolay Schulhoff said. You, too.

The logs crackled. Every so often, a vesicle beneath the bark burst, and for one or two seconds the beauty of a spray of golden sparkles bloomed. They settled into contemplating the fire until it threatened to die. Kronauer added a heavy piece of wood.

—I don't remember the girl's name anymore, Aldolay Schulhoff said. It was in a kolkhoz. He screwed up my memory.

—He? Who was he? Kronauer asked.

—I don't know anymore, Aldolay Schulhoff said. For a long while, I knew, but now I don't know anymore.

When the piece of wood was done, Kronauer added a second one.

—Me too, briefly, I was in a kolkhoz, he said.

They were quiet until dawn. The fire died. The day flowed, twilit, then the evening came, half-dark. They both moved in silence to take off a newly finished log. Fall had come, frost was imminent; it was best to start a good fire or its equivalent. When the wood was sizzling, when the branches were smoking again and blazing, they relaxed and prepared to spend the night by the magical braids, sleeping amiably and chattering. The flames, at their wildest, were reflected against the door of the nearby train car. All around, the forest showed no movement. An ideal background for a conversation about intimacy or lesser things.

—I loved my wife most, Kronauer said. But I met others.

—Other what? Aldolay Schulhoff asked.

—I remember some of their names, Kronauer said.

—Go on, Aldolay Schulhoff said.

Now the fire purred. They enjoyed listening to it. When the music diminished, Aldolay Schulhoff added a branch to the blaze. The branch took its time before agreeing to burn like the others. Then it conceded. It gave off several indecisively-colored flames, and then its lower half discharged overly bright orange flames, overly twisted, before hunching down again, as if sulking. It seemed not to know exactly what it was expected to do. It had plenty more to learn before turning to ashes.

—Say the names of these girls, since you've got them in your head, Aldolay Schulhoff said.

Kronauer collected his memories, his thoughts, his breath.

—Vassilissa Marachvili, Samiya Schmidt, he recited. Myriam Umarik, Hannko Vogulian.

—Never heard of them, Aldolay Schulhoff said.

—Right, why would you have? Kronauer asked.

—Right, why would I have known them, Aldolay Schulhoff said.

• —That was in Solovyei's time, Kronauer said.

—Never heard of that one either, Aldolay Schulhoff said.

—The kolkhoz's president, Kronauer said.

—What kolkhoz? Aldolay Schulhoff asked indistinctly.

They were quiet for one or two days. And as happened from time to time, a solitary crow came and perched on a pine branch, practically on top of them, and settled in as if to listen to their conversation and their silence. It was a powerful animal, of monstrous proportions, with a black beak as hard as steel, with shining feathers like dewy, moist tar. From where they were, the two companions couldn't meet its gaze, but, if they'd had the ability to imagine something of this sort, they would have bet on its yellow eyes, an unbearable golden intensity. The bird appeared comfortable on the branch and barely moved. It barely broke into their dialogue. Sometimes it accompanied it, this meager dialogue, with a ringing caw, or by clicking its wings, and it also sometimes defecated without worrying about which of the two it would hit. But, more than anything, it barely intervened.

• —And your wife's name? Aldolay Schulhoff suddenly asked.

—What, my wife's name? Kronauer was panicked.

—You didn't say it, Schulhoff said.

—No, I didn't, Kronauer said.

In the darkness, he could be heard moving. Suddenly he breathed more loudly. The air whistled in his nostrils or in his mouth, or in what passed for them.

—You told me you loved her, Schulhoff said. Say a name, that'll help you to remember.

—Sure, Kronauer said.

The crow clicked its wings harshly above his head and cawed once, twice. In the suddenly-stolen sylvan silence, this scream seemed to stretch forever. When the echoes had completely faded away, Kronauer pitifully wiped away a dropping that had fallen on one of his cheeks, as if it was a teardrop.

—I don't remember her name anymore, he said. I loved her, yes, that's for sure. But I don't remember her name anymore.

– 43 –

• There were days when Aldolay Schulhoff had nagging memories of having been in love and trying to find his beloved again, and there were gulfs spanning years or decades during which he suffered inwardly without knowing why. His memory was an open wound, a window onto a universe he knew keenly but which was denied him. He couldn't pin any names on the silhouettes he could make out, the images of the past didn't correspond to anything he could actually keep or cherish. His memories were palpably close, but to no avail. Their inaccessibility tortured him.

But sometimes he remembered that he had been a wandering musician and, although in rags, still had several moments of music in his mind. And he wanted to make them resound once more outside, these rags, these moments. It was like the mechanical wish for a last breath. The long tales had lost their coherence, the cycles of byliny had diminished to snatches of disparate fictions. Nothing much had resisted the vast leaching of the centuries. Still, some years bits of songs welled up on the surface of his consciousness, and he was nostalgic for the musical evenings when everybody, himself and his audience, rode on poems and traveled by magic over the immense steppes, through the infinite forests, or into the Second Soviet Union at the peak of its splendor, or toward camps.

And there, at the end of spring, scraps rose to his lips. He told Kronauer about them. He was nearby and half inert, but the idea of another lyrical and poetic evening woke him up and, in the days that followed, he began to move again.

• Scraps of songs. They welled up. Like the black oil leaving the buried villages to form puddles and pools on the earth's surface. Drop by drop, they came back out, and suddenly, once again, they were songs.

• They took up their roles again. Schulhoff was in charge of the main part of the narrative. As he declaimed, Kronauer played a continuous low note, picking up as best as he could several phrases and, when he lost his breath, tapping rhythmically on the train car's door with a stick or a dead branch.

Once the roles had been divided up, they set off to go lean against the train's skeleton. Moving took them some time but they had sworn to give the concert no matter what and the distance didn't frighten them. With this sort of slow frenzy that the heavily burned militiamen have when they climb out of a shell hole, they progressed toward the peak of the ditch. Then they came to the car and leaned against it.

In front of them, several meters of a grassy slope stretched out, past which the first trees stood. At the base of the pines that they had left, there were traces of a campfire, their campfire, and several items they hadn't brought with them, half of a dusty soldier's cover, two sacks that were nearly empty, several logs for later. After some twenty meters of underbrush, the darkness was completely black. In short, only the small space where they were about to give the concert benefited from a little light.

They stopped and faced that. They felt exhausted by the climb, the crawl. For several seasons, they had barely exercised, and they needed to regain their strength at the top of the ditch.

Time went by, as if the performers wanted to see the audience grow before dedicating themselves entirely to epic songs. In reality, the audience was wholly and solely a crow perched on a low branch and which, once or twice a day and two or three times a night, swayed as if alive.

—The bird, Kronauer said.

—What, the bird? Aldolay Schulhoff whispered.

Although they were ready to sing, they were both still very out of breath.

—The same one? Kronauer continued after a minute.

—The same as what? Schulhoff whispered.

—Nothing, Kronauer said.

• They stayed for several more hours, then some weeks prostrate against the train car's door. The twilight in front of them didn't change. Every so often the humidity increased, as if they had come to the end of a night and the dawn was approaching, then the dew evaporated and, in a way, the day surrounded them. But ultimately neither the brightness nor the ambiance changed. Time stagnated and, in any case, it wasn't very robust. That allowed them both to rest, Schulhoff to bring back several supplementary passages of the epic to mind, Kronauer to think lazily about his present and the few things he would lose one day as he met extinction.

Smudges of black oil broke through the grasses and slowly grew. Some merged together.

—What if we sang? Kronauer asked.

—Eh, Schulhoff sighed in a tone that indicated his despondence.

He didn't seem so determined anymore.

—Maybe later, he said.

—It would be better to start before the snow, Kronauer said.

He took the branch he had brought for banging against the car and he struck it awkwardly against the wooden wall behind his head. He was hardly positioned to perform his role as percussionist. Bits of bark and dust darkened his shoulders.

In front of them, perched above their belongings, their empty bags and the logs, the crow shrieked while shaking its wings.

—The audience is waiting, Kronauer said.

He struck the branch against the train car again.

As if affronted in his singer's honor, Aldolay Schulhoff drew up several centimeters and suddenly his low voice could be heard, quickly followed by a sharp overtone song that was inimitable and very beautiful.

—Ah, Kronauer sighed approvingly in comfort.

He hit the car behind him again.

—*The Attack on the Camp*, Aldolay Schulhoff announced once he had finished the introduction.

—Ah, yes, Kronauer said approvingly once again.

Silence settled. The forest was black. If there were still birds and beasts nearby, or corpses in a state to hear poetry, they were unnoticeable, because everything was silent.

Then Kronauer began to play the continuous low note, and Schulhoff sang.

• Schulhoff's tale was confused and spoken poorly, stripped of the vocabulary and style of traditional epics, and on top of that he was singing with a voice that hadn't been used for far too long and was now rusty and unimproved, but in this terminal landscape—half-unearthed train car, larches and pines waning in a twilight without beginning or end, pools of black oil in the depths of the ditch—and in the presence of an equally sparse audience—two vagrants in extinction, if they counted themselves, and a massive and bad-tempered bird that sometimes disappeared, sometimes reincarnated on a low branch—there was something miraculous.

Schulhoff's tale. His song. With a musical accompaniment by Kronauer. In the terminal forest. After such long and confused wandering. After so much time. Outside time. In the silent forest. Something miraculous.

• With several interruptions due to declines in energy, nearly-fatal apneas, or gaps in memory, Aldolay Schulhoff continued in his musical narration and, when he didn't continue, Kronauer took over by delivering the only two things he still somehow had in his head, first a list of wild grasses and grains that a thousand years earlier he had helped Irina Echenguyen to make, and second the list of our best comrades, those who were scrubbed away by fate, shot after a misinterpretation of the Marxist-Leninist classics, reduced to ashes by the enemy, or fallen in unequal battle against the plutonium effluvia that had swept civilization and then the planet.

Aldolay Schulhoff told of the attack on the camp he had been part of. He added spectacular backgrounds and heroic characters, but after several episodes it was clear that he had switched the roles and had set himself in the camp, not outside it. The double fence of barbed wire remained, surrounding the concentration buildings as far as the eye could see, but in the poem, Schulhoff and his companions fought the intruders who wanted to break into the camp to reap its benefits. Guns had been distributed among them all and Schulhoff used them as soon as he had a target in the line of fire. Snow flew in every direction, making the battle doubtful. They had trouble aiming at the convoy two hundred meters from the main doorway, where the shots had been fired from. The arrivals were furious at the welcome their negotiators had been given, and now that they were lying dead in the snow, the camp suffered heavy fire. The delegation had made insane speeches in front of the door, and, when they had been told that there were no more free spots in the barracks, they had grown angry and raised their voices. They'd had to hunt these unwanted spokespeople and, as they seemed intent on staying through the night and maybe even until the spring, the order had been given to slaughter them all. At that point, the situation deteriorated. Hidden in the cars or in the diesel locomotive that had brought them there, the detainees, soldiers, and snipers had peppered the watchtowers and the camp entrance with bullets. Aldolay Schulhoff had heard the bullets' whistling around him. Some had lodged in his torso, inviting him to lie on his back, his mouth open to the sky, as if eager to receive snowflakes on his tongue and as if he was completely indifferent to the sequence of events.

- He stopped.

—Your turn, he whispered to Kronauer.

It seemed like no more words would cross his lips. His head was slumped on his chest. The song had reached a point beyond which nothing was perceptible.

Kronauer tried his best to make a connection. His eyes had been shut for several hours, and he opened them. The note on which Schulhoff had broken off his declamation wasn't too low, which allowed him to take it up without the audience realizing what had happened.

He banged the branch on the wall of the train car.

—Now everybody was lying on their backs, their mouths open to the sky, as if eager to receive snowflakes on their tongues and like me, like Schulhoff, completely indifferent to the sequence of events.

A new strike.

—These are our best comrades, he continued.

He listed about thirty, then he was quiet.

− 44 −

• Like every other morning for the last few thousand seasons, the Gramma Udgul turned the knob on the radio stand next to her armchair. She wanted to know whether civilization had reestablished itself overnight, or at least whether humanity had survived organic degeneration, cancer resulting from generalized radiation, sterility, and the urge to engage in capitalism.

The apparatus emitted a slight crackle and then was silent.

—Maybe there's still a pocket of resistance somewhere, she groused. Our little ones can't just accept total defeat.

She twisted the knob the other way, until the click that marked a break with all possible supply, reception, and hope.

—Doubtless they have something else to worry about than getting the propaganda machines back in order, she mumbled.

No noise rose from the gray ruins around her. Dawn had barely broken.

—Brave little ones, she kept mumbling. Our Komsomols. They're doing what they can.

• She heard herself talking, because she had some hearing left, but she barely understood what her mouth was proclaiming.

Despite being condemned to immortality from her first interactions with nuclear reactor cores, she had finally registered symptoms of aging, and, especially over the last seventy-nine decades, her physical state had degraded. Mentally, she was still alert, but, body-wise, things weren't holding up fantastic, to borrow one of her expressions.

Her mouth, for example. Her teeth had fallen out one by one and none had grown back. Her lips had become deformed and, reduced to two strips of hardened leather, they had partly detached from her cheeks and hung over her chin like sheatfish whiskers. Her tongue, in turn, had lost its elasticity. With such a phonatory apparatus, what vibrated outside barely resembled language. She herself was astonished by the mumbling and clicking she produced and gave up trying to interpret them.

• It was no longer the height of Radiant Terminus's splendor and the Gramma Udgul's hangar had suffered irreparable damage. For a hundred or a hundred and fifty years, it had survived the disintegration that had blighted all the village buildings and the taiga's inexorable advance. But one day the fuel for the small power plant beneath the Soviet had awoken, had suddenly become manic and started working, and from that point on the kolkhoz, although already devastated, already abandoned and left for dead, had gone through another phase of unrest. A series of bizarre nuclear accidents had accelerated the area's decline. The fuel rods had united. They tried to rejoin the core that had taken up residence at the bottom of the well the Gramma Udgul guarded like a dragon over its treasure. The slope's foothills had crumbled, the entire hill had slipped and lost its height, so much that the Gramma Udgul's warehouse building, which was already fragile, had shattered. The warehouse had taken on the look of the iron scrap and girder heaps that had once been shown to schoolchildren in photographs warning them against atomic wars, fires lit by enemies, and apocalypse in general.

Once the racket and dust of the collapse had died down, the Gramma Udgul had looked around her. Her private corner had been destroyed, the pyramids of junk had been scattered, the well's cover had flown off. She had brought her armchair to the well's edge, and, without too much effort, she had reconstructed a lair in the center of the ruins. She had recovered her radio, her kettle for tea, several utensils, the remnants of Solovyei's phonograph, and even seven or eight cylinders that hadn't been crushed during the disaster.

Ultimately, nothing of her existence in the Levanidovo had really changed.

Technical small-scale changes. Ordinary details to go over again. Less cozy comforts. And then this body that obeyed her less and less, these organs abdicating their responsibilities. But, ultimately, nothing of her existence had changed.

• For example, now, when she pined for Solovyei and his abstruse, possibly counterrevolutionary poems, she had to go through much more complex operations than back when it was enough to crank the phonograph handle and insert a cylinder.

Only the horn remained of Solovyei's famous machine. The Gramma Udgul set it on the rim of the well, to take advantage of the vibrations the well's walls provided. She stripped her arms to the shoulders, squeezed her armpit to make a funnel for the horn, pushed down on the lower cap with the shriveled skin covering her ribcage or what remained of it. Her body played the role of the membrane, she turned the cylinder with her left hand, and she scratched the grooves with a nail on her right hand. The result was mediocre.

When Solovyei appeared during these difficult sessions, he became furious with her. He was gently furious, but, still, he reproached her for ravaging his admirable bass-tenor voice, for making his poems inaudible.

—You can't hear a word, he said. It's not music or even speech. It's like someone's shaking gravel in a pig bladder.

He waved his magic hand over the Gramma Udgul's neck, he caressed her back, and while he scolded her, he soothed her. He still felt a tenderness for her that the years hadn't eroded.

—It's a problem with the membrane, the Gramma Udgul said. The needle, that still works, but the membrane's ruined. My skin's too dry.

She tried to talk distinctly, to no avail.

—What? Solovyei asked.

The Gramma Udgul tried to repeat her scientific explanation.

—I just don't understand what you're mumbling, Solovyei said jokingly.

The Gramma Udgul became furious in turn. She knew her speech was difficult to follow, but she accused Solovyei of ill will.

—It's the skin's resonance. And then this phonograph, it wasn't the best quality to begin with.

—I don't understand you at all, Solovyei repeated. You're as clear as a Buddhist rattle being shaken in a bucket of oil.

• —I already told you that you'd do best to throw them into the well, Solovyei says.

—What?

—The cylinders. They're no good for anything. Nobody's listening to them anyway. Throw them to the core.

—I'll do what I like, the Gramma Udgul says.

The president of the kolkhoz resumes.

—They've done their time, he says.

—What are you talking about? the Gramma Udgul asks.

Solovyei shrugs.

The snow has begun to fall again. The twilight has invaded what remains of the former warehouse, several filthy piles of scrap metal, rubble covered with moss, lichens, wild grasses like flying grains, aboufians, döldjinetts, agazilles, torturess violets.

—I'm the one I should throw into the core, the Gramma Udgul suddenly says. I'm the one who's done my time.

—I don't understand you at all, Solovyei says.

– 45 –

• The idea of tumbling into the pit and, after a two-kilometer fall, being swallowed and digested by the core, began to obsess the Gramma Udgul that winter. She had had enough of immortality and felt more and more impotent and socially useless. The liquidation jobs had been successful in the area, there were no longer suspect elements that needed to be alerted to authorities in charge of proletarian morality, and the authorities in turn had dissolved along with the rest of the human species they were supposed to lead into the future, or, at least, toward communism. The Gramma Udgul's existence had consequently lost most of its savor. Moreover, nature had evolved under the effects of constant nuclear radiation. The spectrum of living species had diminished, and, after a short period of mutations when baroque and spectacular apparitions could be seen, sterility had reigned, and the planet had returned to an essentially vegetal state. Contrary to scholars' predictions, which as usual were contradicted by chance, spiders and arachnids in general hadn't filled the spaces opened up by the decline of the animals. For eighty-one decades and then some, flies had looked like they would be a dominant species, and then, in turn, they had been extinguished without leaving any kin. Several survivors in the taiga with feathers or fur eked out a living, but their numbers were negligible, and, in short, the Gramma Udgul was one of the last earthly creatures endowed with a brain and several appendages. If she had been one thousand nine hundred seventy-seven years younger, maybe she would have set out to start, on a small scale, a Third Soviet Union, but now age played its evil stifling role and she no longer had the strength.

• She began to think about suicide and she talked to the core every night, leaning over the edge and grumbling downward. The fact that her fall would end in an apotheosis within fissile material appealed to her more than ever. She had always spoken to the core affectionately, both out of respect for great human inventions, even though everything indicated that the meltdown was complete, and because the atoms' fury had given her exceptional longevity. She had resisted everything and she felt indebted to the wrecked reactors, the flow of corium, the lands sprinkled with plutonium, and, in short, to all that had accelerated the extinction of humanity, of our best comrades as well as our enemies, and of animals in general.

She rambled over the pile about numerous stories concerning her, or she discussed points of Marxism-Leninism barely explored before then, such as reality's persistence within dreams, perpetual wandering within worlds after death, pemmican production, the phonograph's defective functioning, post-exotic poetry. The core didn't respond. The well was filled with poisonous winds and its darkness sometimes seemed permeated with blacker-than-black flames, and sometimes a violent heat escaped as well, but the core remained silent, and no dialogue developed.

• The Gramma Udgul could have easily stepped over the well's edge and fallen as she waited for her future to come to a close. But she hesitated, because she thought of Solovyei and she hoped that he would commit suicide with her. She wanted him to jump with her into the void and they would both sink, hand in hand, in enduring love.

—You have nothing left to do in this world, the Gramma Udgul argued. You only have to go with me. It will be an end like we've dreamed of for a thousand years.

—What? Solovyei asked, taking her in his arms. I don't understand a word of what you're jabbering.

—We're not Romeo and Juliet, the Gramma Udgul protested. But it would still be beautiful to end the way they did. Together. And besides, socialism's construction is over.

—What? Solovyei said while stroking her scalp, her shoulder blades.

—Damn it, the Gramma Udgul said. Let's go. We're too old. Nothing interesting left here.

—Stop talking like that, Solovyei said. You're sputtering nonsense. Like a dead owl jabbering in the tar.

• While the Gramma Udgul was in the doldrums, Solovyei persisted in his comings and goings through the dark or fiery tunnels of dreams, of magical worlds, and of death. But he did also feel less interested now in the events and futures of those he had animated, reanimated, manipulated, or possessed and entered through their memories, through their unconscious, through their after-deaths. There were no longer enough surprises in his theater.

• And so, that evening, they sat down as usual on the edge. From the depths came a slightly nauseating warmth, the core's breath as it was regaining its strength now that the fuel from the plant situated beneath the Soviet had joined it.

Shadows reigned on the Levanidovo. The forest was close, fall warned of winter. A permanent mushy twilight enveloped all the things of the world. Generally, the illumination wasn't the sort to bring joy to the hearts of any survivors.

The Gramma Udgul drank half a kettleful of cold tea and filled a cup for Solovyei.

—It's a white-Tatar decoction, she said when he had begun to drink the liquid she had given him.

—What? Solovyei asked. You're talking worse than ever. I can't understand a single syllable.

—White Tatar, the Gramma Udgul repeated. It'll loosen us up. I couldn't find another poison. It'll relax us before we jump.

Solovyei grimaced in indication that he had given up on trying to understand what his companion was mumbling. Then he reached for the kettle and poured himself some more.

—What is this? He asked. This tastes as good as hell. I hope it's not poison.

—It's white Tatar, the Gramma Udgul said. It's so we'll be drunk before we throw ourselves into the well.

—It's good, Solovyei said. It smells like red currants from long ago, smorodina we used to gather in the old forest. Remember that?

The Gramma Udgul didn't reply and they were quiet for several minutes. Then the Gramma Udgul shifted her position on the edge. Now her legs hung over the void. A small thrust with her butt, what remained of her butt after a century, and she would slip right into the abyss.

—Give me your hand, she said. Jump with me.

—Be careful, Solovyei said.

He took her hand. With the other he rubbed her back. The Gramma Udgul's clothes were nothing more than dusty fibers, and, beneath them, the skin wasn't much more.

—Be careful, Solovyei said again. You could fall.

He leaned toward the shadowy pit. Several meters of earthen walls could be seen, and then nothing. Two thousand meters further down, a magma burned, tarry and terrible, ready to engulf all that reached it from the surface, whether an object, a dead or living animal, or an old immortal creature.

—It would make me happy if we did this together, the Gramma Udgul said.

Then, seeing no reason to drag things out, she pushed with her butt and her left hand, and she tumbled forward.

Solovyei immediately let go. He opened his eyes wide to follow the first twenty meters of her fall. She resembled a small, emaciated animal. Then, without any noise, she disappeared.

• Solovyei was stupefied. He had never believed the Gramma Udgul's jokes about suicide and, in the preceding moments, he had been sincere in his repetitions that he neither understood her words, nor her intentions. He couldn't accept the idea that, right before his eyes, the Gramma Udgul had thrown herself to the mercy of the core. But that was what had happened, and there was no return. All the magic of the dream world was useless to bring a suicide back to the surface. Once the Gramma Udgul came into contact with what rumbled at the bottom of the well, she would be extinguished.

Leaning over the edge, Solovyei considered diving in turn toward the earth's entrails, feeling for one minute the sensation of free fall and, at the bottom, instantaneously dying.

He began to think passionately about the Gramma Udgul. The end of everything, irrevocable extinction, tempted him.

Still, maybe due to the effects of the white-Tatar decoction, he let the minute when his actions could have corresponded to a loving union with the Gramma Udgul pass, and, little by little, he recovered his spirits.

• Night fell over the hangar's ruins, the night or what served for it, a sort of lowering of ambient light, moonless, starless, stripped of anything more or less than the permanent grayness of day.

Solovyei got up and stretched.

—No, he said out loud.

His herculean silhouette could barely be seen. It was hard to determine whether he was a mutant bird, a gigantic sorcerer, or a rich farmer from Soviet or Tolstoyan times.

—No, he repeated. I'm not joining her today.

He cawed over the well, without hunching. His scream crossed the well, the ruins, and disappeared into the silent taiga.

—After all, I'm going to frolic a little more, he said.

And, once again, he cawed.

– 46 –

• He threw into the well the half-dozen cylinders that the Gramma Udgul had spared and, for good measure, he added the kettle and the phonograph horn. If there had been witnesses, they would have reported that his face was soaked in tears but that he didn't seem particularly crestfallen, and on the contrary he seemed full of energy, gesticulating exaggeratedly like a fairground huckster in front of a crowd. In reality, his heart was bleeding. His beloved had flown away forever, nothing interested him anymore, and every part of him was suffering. But he insisted loudly that he could keep on living. Him or me, doesn't matter.

Now he took a breath to recite a poem without any mechanical intermediary.

He leaned over the edge so his voice would be amplified.

This would be the final declamation sung toward the core, because he intended to leave early in the morning, to keep frolicking for an indefinite period—several moments or several centuries—and, whatever happened, never to set foot again in the Levanidovo.

• Then he spread his most painful wing and, when it was completely extended, he spread it even further, and when the largest pinion's tip touched the sky, blackness was complete, and almost immediately he called his dead henchmen to his aid, knowing that nearby there would always be several dead ready to pledge their allegiance, too happy, whatever the often atrocious contractual conditions of slavery that would allow them to regain a little existence, to keep alive darkness and know once again the joys of the tar, and, indeed, several men and women responded to his war cry, and right away they lit as best as they could a candle, a fire, a brush fire, scrub fire, forest fire, so that the world of their master would seem filled with and augmented by lights and, while they were also manifested by songs or animalistic groans, some of whom had forgotten the most rudimentary gestures to be made in front of the flames or some of whom, weakened, could no longer easily adjust the wigs that served as their bodily envelopes, grew fiery and once these who had been clumsy were transformed into torches he listed them, sometimes pronouncing their names hurriedly, like when reading lists during police inspections in front of the barracks, sometimes naming them slowly and respectfully, like when remembering those who lost their lives in battle against the enemy, or in fratricidal war, or fighting against general human stupidity, and, having paid homage to his servants, who left for the ashes, he waited with infinite patience for all that still shone, every ember, to go dark, and once he had become familiar again with darkness, first with the same stentorian voice he had used for the call, then with a wailing and magical voice like the wind, he bemoaned the absence of the world, and the absence of the present, and the absence of his daughters and his wives, all creatures that he had spent his existence confusing for they were so numerous and so similar in what he had done with them, then suddenly, as a chill akin to interstellar ice had slowed his tongue, he went to warm himself in a nearby inn, which he had pulled out of a dream from the previous night, and there, clicking his beak, wrapped in a coat that hid his scarcely respectable shapes, he made a great uproar, claiming to be a prince of thugs traveling between two realities, and to whom every descendant of the great apes, deceased or not, owed fealty, then, as nobody reacted to his palaver, whether nobody had been born or died in the area for millennia, or those present were indifferent to his bragging, or maybe belonged to a dream where he wasn't at his best, he paused in the smoky room, teetered back and forth while pulling down lanterns and lamps, yanking on the chains of several trapdoors that opened onto nothing, and in a terrible mood and, rather than change worlds, he went out into the inn's yard and he made his way to a shack where the engineers had built a small countryside nuclear plant for the needs of the innkeepers and the possible backpackers, truck drivers, or gentlemen whom they welcomed for the night, and probably to rob them and roast them, and, having inhaled the scent of a gust of radioactive materials, he grew delighted at the prospect of once again making contact with the black flames of fuel rods and he didn't take long to discover a way in, and soon he was hunched beyond the concrete, there where he knew began the tunnels that led to unexplored universes, and after having embraced the core for a long while, he turned the page of his aberrant narrative constructions, holding back from setting the torrent of his morganatic, adulterous, or incestuous loves deep within his monologue, and instead of reciting them again in detail to console himself before extinction, he just interminably whispered lists of feminine pronouns, lists of grasses, lists of comrades, and lists of the unspoken, then, already numb, already drowsy, he stopped murmuring.

$-47-$

• Throughout the centuries, Hannko Vogulian's feelings toward written things had wholly changed and, after having long considered her responsibilities limited to reproducing as best as possible the books she had read, from Marxist-Leninist classics to classics of feminist or postexotic prose, she had decided to keep a much more thorough diary, and, little by little, she had come to take pleasure in inventing stories and in depicting ordinary and extraordinary people, which she set as she wished in strange or desperate situations, which she made die if she felt like it and wander eternally through bardic worlds which no death allowed them to really leave, and in any case never forever. She had created her literary world, which at first was influenced by what she had once known in the kolkhoz, in the peaceful albeit incestuous post-nuclear hell of the Levanidovo, but which had then gone in unexpected directions, which she had the greatest trouble justifying logically or empirically. Setting aside the laborious mental copying of novels and brochures that she had ultimately forgotten, constantly trying not to ape her father's abstruse poems, she had begun by listening to the voices guiding her for reality to turn into a dough where the forms obeyed her, and she had ended up magically overpowering her inspiration to write books of her own. Her spelling was now a catastrophe, she wasn't very good with syntax, ink and paper were missing, but she wrote books. In the period of interest to us, and when humanity

had long since ceased to show any sign of life, she was the only survivor
to go to this trouble, which is why we will forgive the mistakes, absur-
dities, and impasses in her narrative flow, as well as the longueurs, and
sometimes, on the contrary, the inexplicable shortcuts or the refusal
to exploit or enrich scenes that could have been, or interruptions in
the recitative. If we try to connect her to a genre, her writing has to
be included in the class of works with strong oneiric content, with,
in terms of politics, a disillusioned relationship to the Second Soviet
Union. Originally, which is to say in her first personal works, traces of
her own background certainly could be detected, but after that these
traces were so diluted that we would have to be sharp critics to find
them, prove them, and make some sort of unreadable or malevolent
commentary.

• She took her time writing, and, as she didn't have anything concrete
on which to engrave her flights of fancy, she pronounced her text in a
firm voice, enunciating her syllables, and she accompanied her diction
with knocks on the wood to indicate the breaks and changes in paragraphs or atmosphere. When she had finished a narract or a chapter,
she stopped for a minute, then she started again from the beginning,
singing in order to inscribe it indelibly in her memory.

• Her works were in principle distinct and she gave them titles after
finishing them, but, although they had their particularities and didn't
reuse the same characters, they could have also been grouped in a single
undifferentiated volume. In effect, they depicted the same twilit suffering of everyone, a magical but hopeless ordinariness, organic and
political deterioration, infinite yet unwished-for resistance to death,
perennial uncertainty about reality, or a penal progression of thought,
penal, wounded, and insane. On the other hand, it's worth noting that
Hannko Vogulian's obsessions as an author reinforced the similarities
of her novelistic plots which had been so different initially.

• Of post-exoticism, which she knew little about, Hannko Vogulian had mainly remembered their formalist constraints, and that's why she persisted in dividing her books into forty-nine chapters or even three hundred forty-three parts, and, every so often, she tallied up what she had produced, with the idea that it might be good to number her works in order to arrive, after several centuries, at a harmonious whole, a multiple of seven or made up of identical numbers, like one hundred and eleven or one thousand one hundred and eleven.

• Certainly difficult to establish calendars after everyone's death, after the death of our best male and female comrades. But let's say that, several thousand seasons after the fall of the Orbise and the end of the Second Soviet Union, the shack Hannko Vogulian had taken refuge in had deteriorated visibly. The logs that made up the walls had rotted, they suddenly broke apart very quickly, the walls and the floor disintegrated, and, in almost no time, the house became uninhabitable. At the center of the ruins, the well persisted for two or three years, then sank into the ground and disappeared. Everything crumbled, turned into humus and magma of humid sawdust. The notebooks Hannko Vogulian had filled didn't last, except for the yellowish agglomerations that the stump mushrooms had shown a predilection for. At that moment, when she no longer had any writing material and was forced to abandon her shelter, Hannko Vogulian threw herself fully into novelistic creation.

• She banged on the remains of her house or on a larch trunk, she spoke prose out loud like she was insane and she repeated what she had just composed by singing and giving her text a new rhythm with her blows. It was easier to understand why her characters occasionally felt attracted to the idea of epic declamations and songs, and why they then hoped for musical accompaniment, or at least a tenor bell or percussions in the background, whether they were improvised or not.

• When she reflected on a story, she examined the world thoroughly with her black eye the color of deep black onyx, the color of a crow's wing, the color of ebonite, the color of black agate, the color of black tourmaline, the color of obsidian, the color of naphthalene death. Then she looked at her novel with her golden eye, the color of tiger's eye, the color of sulfur crystals, the color of yellow amber, the color of coppery lightning. Then she closed her eyes. Then she began to expel air and words and she began to write.

• Although over the centuries Hannko Vogulian had become both an experienced writer and the last living being to have any poetic activity or something of the sort, she wasn't aware of her stylistic mistakes or her poor narrative decisions, she never engaged in a critical evaluation of her work and she never went back over a text once it had been sung and memorized. There was no doubt that if someone had stood in front of her to recite a lesson on the principles of the novelistic tradition, and scolded her for not having respected them, she would have welcomed these principles coldly, and certainly, after having taken aim at him or her, she would have pulled the trigger of the last rifle she had been able to save from corrosion, a China-made SKS, perhaps specifically the model otherwise called Type 56 by the Chinese, or maybe not: a most loyal friend.

• Hannko Vogulian's novels are numerous today and in an excellent state of conservation within Hannko Vogulian's memory, but consulting them requires entering Hannko Vogulian, and that, this abominable breaking and entering, she has not allowed anyone for a long time now.

• She hasn't been able to avoid authorial mannerisms. She or I, doesn't matter. She hasn't been able to avoid coming back, if not regularly, at least with some consistency, to fundamental scenes and situations, to images in which she finds again the heroes and heroines she had lost, often our best comrades male and female alike, images of wandering in black space or in the fire, images of weary conversations at the feet of trees or at the edge of stretches of water or tar, images of eternal lovers never to be reunited, images of waiting in front of the abyss, images of massive steppes and massive skies.

• We were alone with her and none of us ever regretted it, just as none of us men or women ever questioned her attachment to the Orbise and the Second Soviet Union, whatever her position had been vis-à-vis the camps—inside or outside.

• Hannko Vogulian's novels and romånces include pages that could be called normal and others that seem hallucinatory, and, among those, some depict the death of Hannko and her sisters. All were born from unknown mothers and the idea of sisterhood existed in a greater sense, perhaps because most of these feminine figures, whether satisfied or unfortunate, had, over the course of the book, relationships of super-natural violence or companionship with a masculine father-figure or husband who was sometimes a magician come from the Bardo, some-times a bird, sometimes a prince of thieves, sometimes a tyrannical shaman. The sisters find each other again after adventures that had separated them for their entire existence and they die together, or they prepare to die together. Out of this premise comes an oneiric image that clearly belongs to the novel's last breaths. The image is frequently filled with a violent anguish, but despite being terminal it's not always cataclysmic, and, on the contrary, it consists chiefly of shadows and waiting. The sky darkens, it transforms into monstrous organic mat-ter that Hannko Vogulian rarely attempts to describe. This collective death, beneath an inconceivable sky, is also one of Hannko Vogulian's authorial mannerisms.

• Sometimes, like many of us elsewhere, our best male and female comrades, she confused empty space with empty hope.

− 48 −

• Myriam Umarik is the first to reach the clearing. She goes past the thickets that are extensions of the forest and she breathes. It has been a long time since she's put her lungs to work, several years, perhaps. The fresh air whistles along her lungs and it's so unexpected that she feels like she hears rasping and shrillness, but in reality age has made her completely deaf, whether the sounds come from inside or outside her body. Things are usually hazy for her, she goes through silence as if along the bottom of a body of thick water. In any case, whistling or not, this sudden influx of oxygen perks her up. Her blood begins to circulate again, something wakes up in her head, whereas, up until that time, she had kept going numbly and unthinkingly. And then an image comes to the fore.

It's a memory of the Levanidovo. It's like the smudges of irradiated oil that rise from the buried cities, it appears out of nowhere, after an underground progression that lasted centuries. It's a memory that belongs to another existence and, like the puddles of black oil in the underbrush, Myriam Umarik skirts it, but, for a minute, she looks at it.

She sees herself walking on the main road of the kolkhoz, smiling, her flesh radiant, upon meeting the soldier Kronauer, a man who, after seeming to be a red hero, had quickly turned out to be insane and criminal. She goes toward this man, who at the moment is busy loosening lug nuts in a fire hydrant. The pipes leak, the water forms a lake of muddy water in front of her house. Everything sparkles. The kolkhoz's houses, the bits of frost on the water's edge, Myriam Umarik's eyes, her red-copper Kazakh earrings, the gold embroidery on her blouse, her belt. She knows that she is very feminine, sumptuous. She draws near to joke with the soldier Kronauer and instead of laughing with her he shows his bleeding hand, he claims to have been pricked by a needle in the Gramma Udgul's warehouse, he accuses the president of the kolkhoz of having cast spells on him.

Then the image wavers. Then it goes dark.

• Now Myriam Umarik tramples unknown grasses growing in the clearing, amid the roots of red cranberries, Siberian redcurrants, and blueberries. She breaks branches, but, because she is deaf, she doesn't notice and she doesn't care.

The light is very low, as if night was about to fall, but it's lighter than beneath the trees.

The clearing stretches a long way off, its radius several hundred meters. The ground is lumpy, with moss-covered ridges that might well be the last remnants of a city, a camp, or a village. Here and there are stretches of black oil. They're the same color as the sky.

• Careful not to be too conspicuous, my dear, an inner voice advises. She crouches down on the ground.

In the chest pack she's lying on, she takes out two cartridges, the last ones. The first immediately crumbles between her fingers, giving off a smell of mold rather than powder. The second shows fewer signs of deterioration. She inserts it into the barrel of the rifle that has accompanied her faithfully, although it's been a long time since she's had the opportunity to make use of it.

Around her she smells the trembling twigs, the grasses, the powerful scents of the taiga, intensely vegetal now that the mammals and most of the birds have disappeared. She suspects that she will not get back up. She is lying down, the landscape is deserted, she hasn't noticed anything special, but an inner voice has advised her to lie as low as possible. Something terminal will happen. That doesn't bother her too much. But she breathes forcefully, as if it was a matter of bringing together several last lights before total darkness.

One of the bandages surrounding her head is hanging off a prickly branch of white Tatar. The cloth, as mummified as her own flesh, tears. She directs some vague mumbles to her clothes, to her body, to her rifle, to the increasingly black sky. Her head is wrapped in dirty rags and scarves, against the cold, but also because, out of sheer vanity, she wanted to give some volume to what rises up between her shoulders and has shrunk uglily over the centuries, hardly deserving the name of skull.

She speaks in a language she invented in solitude and which resembles half-animalistic babbling. She doesn't hear or listen to herself, but she knows what she's speaking. Reproaches and basic calls. She also talks a little to her scarves, the icy earth, the roots, and the faintly hostile krijovnik stalks. Then she seals her lips and is completely immobile.

• The rifle she carries is a Schultz 73, a weapon made in the Second Soviet Union's armories. For several quarter-centuries she's greased it carefully, without any trouble because black oil abounds in the forest. She found it in an abandoned camp outpost, on the corpse of a watchman who had used it to commit suicide. The outpost was actually the top of a watchtower that hadn't yet sunk completely into the earth. She requisitioned ammunition that hadn't suffered too much from dampness, but, over the years, she used them up, and now she only has one bullet left.

• Samiya Schmidt is the second sister to appear. Like her father Solovyei in the old days, when he walked magically through dark space, she is indescribable. She finds a place at the edge of the forest, she shakes trunks and branches when she whistles. Over several dozen meters the space is disrupted by her presence, the bushes seem to be crushed, the grasses bend, the air grows heavy with opaque comings and goings. She can make out something, but it's not clear what exactly. Sometimes it seems like a broken and gigantic bird. Or a young Chinese red guard. Also sometimes, and now growing, is a feeling of atavistic fear, of all-consuming fear in the face of the unknown, in the face of a magical presence that is there but cannot even be conceived of, and which is impossible to know how to confront or appease, should it ever run riot.

• Samiya Schmidt sees Myriam Umarik's outstretched form at the other end of the clearing, she notices her rifle half hidden by the grasses, and instead of remembering their shared childhood and adolescence in the Levanidovo, or scenes from their calm life in the kolkhoz, she remembers a dream image, a moment so distant that it belongs to the dusty remains of the previous millennium.

She remembers Kronauer's humiliated face, naked under the shower in a strange communal shower room, Kronauer uselessly hiding his crotch from the eyes of the judges and the eyes of the kolkhozniks that he had shot dead, and who have been piled in front of him to make him ashamed. Kronauer is constantly drenched in hot water, he denies, he is powerless when confronted with the fate he does not understand, every so often he looks up at her, Samiya Schmidt, or he looks down at the corpses of her sisters and yet other victims. He tries to answer the Gramma Udgul and Solovyei's questions. He stammers nonsense. He doesn't have his wits, he doesn't have his aptness, he's a lower-ranking soldier, incapable of anything other than shooting his superiors, deserting, and, once he's settled into a welcoming village after his death, massacring the villagers on a useless pretext. She had formerly felt some sexual stirrings during this investigation when he was naked, wet, and ridiculous. She no longer remembers whether what she felt had been rooted in ancestral animality or in the hormones she'd still had at the time. Or whether the emotion was due to the hate she felt for Solovyei, the kolkhoz president who had led the investigation and associated her hideously with Kronauer, as if they had been a pair of murderous fornicators. In his indictment, Solovyei had maliciously and brutally linked her to this obscene and streaming man, to this male she barely knew at the time and who, much later, she had briefly met in the taiga, without feeling any particular attraction or sympathy for him.

She could bring back images where she rubbed shoulders with her sister Myriam Umarik, or even other images of Kronauer, with whom she had still wandered in the Bardo of the forest for one or two centuries, but she only clearly remembers this memory which is a nightmare, Kronauer's interrogation under the shower, in the presence of the kolkhoz's corpses. She ponders it unhappily. She stands just in front of the curtain of trees, she leans her indescribable body against their trunks, she mixes her body with the first branches, the berry bushes, the blueberries, the violet kryjovniks, the thin layer of damp earth, the sunlight's reflections on the puddles of black oil, and she is immobile.

She is immobile, she is thinking, and she is waiting.

• The sky moves over the taiga, the sky keeps darkening, it fills with strange clouds, stranger still than the absence of day and the absence of night.

The sky moves, from the northeast comes a black stain, a crow, then a group, then a substantial flock, several dozen birds, then the number grows, grows, multiplies incessantly, hundreds, thousands, then the quantity of birds goes beyond numbers. Their flights are superimposed, their wings touch, mix, their dark chests press on their dark backs, their feathers rub against their feathers. Outside these screeches, silence reigns. No crowing, no cawing. Although their wings beat in harmony, they look like dead birds, rooks of all sizes, extremely black crows, these various corvines, all dead. The layers are superimposed, mix, soon the thickness of the black is inconceivable, three hundred thirteen meters, five hundred forty-two meters of compacted height. The sky closes off little by little from the northeast. The sky is nothing but a vast sea of crows unfurling from the northeast to extinguish all light. Already the taiga is plunged into darkness. Already only the residual glints allow the clearing to be seen.

• Then a preliminary bird detaches from the mass that now fills the entire heavenly vault. It hovers aimlessly for a minute, then it flies gently toward the ground. It turns around, it slowly takes the path that separates it from the earth. It descends fluffily upon the peak of a pine where it rests, curled up. It's the first one. Others will follow.

• At the same moment, Hannko Vogulian comes into the clearing from the southeast. She is exhausted by the walk and by the decades of unbroken fasting. She comes out from the cover of the trees and she wavers. It has been several years since her movements have had any steadiness. Deep in the taiga she can only move in zigzags, from one larch to the next, with long breaks with her back against the bark to regain her breath before the next step.

She leaves the final tree on her left and she collapses in the grasses, first because she has nothing to lean against nearby, but mainly because she immediately notices something hostile hiding in the landscape. The clearing is five or six hundred meters long, dotted with low bushes and, beneath the inky sky, it is very dark. Nothing unusual, in short. And yet Hannko Vogulian is certain that the calm in this gap is only external. She lowers her head, then she lies down so as not to be noticeable. After several minutes, with minimum movement, she pulls out the weapon she has carried on her shoulder ever since leaving the ruins of her hut, long ago, and which she counts on to survive and keep on surviving forever.

The darkness is thick. Upon carefully examining the nearly perfect circle that the tree's edge sketches, she notices that she is in the line of sight of two rifles. With her black agate eye, the color of naphthalene death, she has identified Myriam Umarik far off, whose grimy and messy turban is undone, baring a shriveled face, more like a mushroom than a face, with vague hints of flesh and the remnants of an expression both idiotic and cruel. Then she turns her copper-yellow eye, the color of amber, to the left and immediately recognizes the deformations of space and shrillnesses indicative of Samiya Schmidt's presence. She examines the image. She finally sees a shadow a little more opaque than the vegetal shadows. She has the impression that an intellect is observing her. At that moment, they both exchange the equivalent of a look, she and Samiya Schmidt. Over there, the branches shake, several bushes twist. The two sisters stand at a distance for a few seconds. A horrible whistle tears the air and then abruptly breaks off.

• Oddly, while Hannko Vogulian is drawing several fragments of information concerning her sisters from the depths of her memory, in order to shoot them down at the right moment, she first dredges up a vision that has nothing to do with what she's looking for. A parasite vision.

She is standing in the Gramma Udgul's warehouse, next to the soldier Kronauer who has just discovered the carbonized carcass of Vassilissa Marachvili and who is sputtering over her, paralyzed by horror and pity. She would like to show him a little sympathy, but he is closed off in his uncommunicative mania. Soon he will go on a rampage in the village.

She remembers this scene, the smell of socks and metal in the Gramma Udgul's warehouse, the smell of Kronauer's sweat, her own smell of perspiration. They have spent the day throwing junk into the well to feed the core. Her wig has slipped and, in front of this man she barely respects, she doesn't care.

Then the image trembles, then it is gone.

Once again, Hannko Vogulian is lying at the entrance to the clearing, in a darkness that doesn't bode well, with her two sisters who have aimed their aggression or their arms at her, and she is exhausted.

• At that exact moment, a small crow lands by her, then another on her right sleeve, then another on her neck. All three of them are extremely black. A fourth settles on the hand rubbing the trigger guard. It is icy. She doesn't brush it away, but waits to see if it will melt. It doesn't melt. Others already dot the grasses all around, the almourol bushes she is hiding behind. She shakes her hand, then sets her bony finger back on the trigger. The crows are descending from the sky, ever more numerous and black. They turn slowly, sometimes carried askew by imperceptible gusts that cannot be heard. They go or come at low heights. Most of them fall straight down, not as quickly, as drops of water but with the same blind determination. A very light chirping can be heard over the entire surface of the clearing.

Aside from this regular chirping, there is no noise.

The last residual lights are dying.

It becomes more and more densely black.

• The crows fall.

They are small, silent, and odorless.

These are the innumerable links of a black sheet unfolding over the clearing.

An impression of black lightness in the air and, on the ground, an increasingly compact layer, which will stay, which will cover everything, and which will not melt.

The three sisters are now frozen, their rifles pointed at each other. They watch each other from afar with hostility and without trying to make any contact. They know that they have reached the end of their path and they refuse to dirty the hours that remain by bringing back the monstrosities they had suffered for a thousand years, by reviving Solovyei, this cursed father who had transmitted the curse of his own immortality to them. Above all, not to remember Solovyei; this is what all three of them are collectively thinking. They would prefer to focus on insignificant images, they mentally find themselves in the company of this unimportant Kronauer, whom none of them had loved and who had come unheeded into their minds.

And, as the layer of feathers thickens, papering shadows over the last dying grasses of this world, they prepare for the immediate future.

Immediate or distant. The future. Where, whatever happens, there would be nothing.

– 49 –

• Aldolay Schulhoff finished singing and, for a time hard to define in the absence of breaths and in the absence of light, Kronauer held the final note, and when he was unable to continue, he continued moving his arms a little, knocking several times on the wall of the train car by banging the back of his head.

Already neither of them remembered what they had said and, in particular, whether they had put themselves in their tales, for lack of any available heroes, or whether they had mixed in their own pasts, or, on the contrary, invented characters and events, or whether they had reused the epic subjects of Siberian or post-exotic or Mongolian traditions, or whether they had included poems and narratives in the gest of the Orbise, and whether they had or hadn't drifted toward disaster humor or camp humor or the fantastic, in order not to overdo their intimate despair, or whether they'd ventured into parallel universes or tunnels or imaginations, which in principle escaped them and forced them to present versions of reality and totally random dreams and where their characters and their voices were nothing. They were now leaning against the raised remains of the convoy, surrounded by the thick shadow of the taiga. The song had exhausted them.

The lack of an audience, in a way, hadn't bothered them, and in this moment when their performance had concluded, it saved them from having to get up to bow, which would have required an effort of them that they weren't able to make anymore. They preferred to stay there, in an exaggeratedly prostrate position, legs splayed and necks bent forward, without having anything else to say or do.

• While they lounged in numbness and in the decline of nearly all their bodily and mental functions, supposedly to collect themselves again after the performance and regain their strength, but in reality because sleeping didn't concern them, the crow that had listened to them up until then clicked its wings and its beak and landed at the top of the ditch, right next to Aldolay Schulhoff, and he had the vague impression that it was scratching at something right under his forehead.

Several hours fell away, then the crow took flight and disappeared.

Now Aldolay Schulhoff and Kronauer waited for evening, or winter. Neither evening nor winter came.

—It pecked out your eye, Kronauer said.

—Who did?

—The crow, Kronauer said.

—Oh, was it him? Schulhoff said. I thought it was you.

—No, Kronauer said.

His voice was uncertain. He didn't know. He mumbled another denial.

—Him or you, doesn't matter, Schulhoff said. As far as it goes.

—It would hurt me if you believed it was me, Kronauer said.

—I don't believe in anything, Schulhoff said. I'm waiting for the end.

Antoine Volodine is the primary pseudonym of a French writer who has published twenty books under this name, several of which are available in English translation, including *Bardo or Not Bardo* (also available from Open Letter) and *Minor Angels*. He also publishes under the names Lutz Bassmann (*We Monks & Soldiers*) and Manuela Draeger (*In the Time of the Blue Ball*). Most of his works take place in a post-apocalyptic world where members of the "post-exoticism" writing movement have all been arrested as subversive elements. Together, these works constitute one of the most inventive, ambitious projects of contemporary writing. In 2014, *Radiant Terminus* was awarded the Prix Médicis.

J effrey Zuckerman is digital editor of *Music & Literature*. His writing and translations have appeared in *Best European Fiction*, *3:AM Magazine*, *Rumpus*, and the *Los Angeles Review of Books*.

B rian Evenson has been a finalist for the Edgar Award, the Shirley Jackson Award, and the World Fantasy Award, and has won the International Horror Guild Award and the American Library Association's award for Best Horror Novel. The recipient of a National Endowment for the Arts fellowship and three O. Henry Prizes, Evenson is a professor at CalArts.

OPEN LETTER

Inga Ābele (Latvia)
High Tide
Naja Marie Aidt (Denmark)
Rock, Paper, Scissors
Esther Allen et al. (ed.) (World)
The Man Between: Michael Henry
Heim & a Life in Translation
Bae Suah (South Korea)
A Greater Music
Svetislav Basara (Serbia)
The Cyclist Conspiracy
Can Xue (China)
Frontier
Vertical Motion
Lúcio Cardoso (Brazil)
Chronicle of the Murdered House
Sergio Chejfec (Argentina)
The Dark
My Two Worlds
The Planets
Eduardo Chirinos (Peru)
The Smoke of Distant Fires
Marguerite Duras (France)
Abahn Sabana David
L'Amour
The Sailor from Gibraltar
Mathias Énard (France)
Street of Thieves
Zone
Macedonio Fernández (Argentina)
The Museum of Eterna's Novel
Rubem Fonseca (Brazil)
The Taker & Other Stories
Juan Gelman (Argentina)
Dark Times Filled with Light
Georgi Gospodinov (Bulgaria)
The Physics of Sorrow
Arnon Grunberg (Netherlands)
Tirza

Hubert Haddad (France)
Rochester Knockings:
A Novel of the Fox Sisters
Gail Hareven (Israel)
Lies, First Person
Angel Igov (Bulgaria)
A Short Tale of Shame
Ilya Ilf & Evgeny Petrov (Russia)
The Golden Calf
Zachary Karabashliev (Bulgaria)
18% Gray
Jan Kjærstad (Norway)
The Conqueror
The Discoverer
Josefine Klougart (Denmark)
One of Us Is Sleeping
Carlos Labbé (Chile)
Loquela
Navidad & Matanza
Jakov Lind (Austria)
Ergo
Landscape in Concrete
Andreas Maier (Germany)
Klausen
Lucio Mariani (Italy)
Traces of Time
Amanda Michalopoulou (Greece)
Why I Killed My Best Friend
Valerie Miles (World)
A Thousand Forests in One Acorn:
An Anthology of Spanish-
Language Fiction
Iben Mondrup (Denmark)
Justine
Quim Monzó (Catalonia)
Gasoline
Guadalajara
A Thousand Morons

WWW.OPENLETTERBOOKS.ORG

**OPEN
LETTER**

WITHDRAWN

WWW.OPENLETTERBOOKS.ORG